Praise for
ABOVE THE LOWER SKY:

"DELIGHTFUL . . .
THE ULTIMATE IN NEW AGE FANTASY"
Locus

"AN ENTHRALLING FUTURIST TALE . . .
DEITZ OFFERS INTRIGUING PREMISES
FOR A 21ST CENTURY CULTURE."
Publishers Weekly

and for TOM DEITZ:

"A MASTER OF MODERN FANTASY"
Brad Strickland, author of *Moondreams*

"DEITZ HAS THE ENVIABLE ABILITY TO
MAKE CLEARLY FANTASTIC INCIDENTS
SEEM REALISTIC AND SUPERIMPOSE THEM
ON A STORY OF GENUINE CHARACTERS
DEALING WITH GENUINE PROBLEMS."
Science Fiction Chronicle

"A COMPELLING CRAFTER OF
CONTEMPORARY NOVELS"
Dragon

"TOM DEITZ IS WRITING
BETTER THAN EVER."
Mercedes Lackey, author of *Magic's Price*

Other AvoNova Books by
Tom Deitz

The **SOULSMITH** *Trilogy*

SOULSMITH
DREAMBUILDER
WORDWRIGHT

WINDMASTER'S BANE
FIRESHAPER'S DOOM
GHOSTCOUNTRY'S WRATH

AvoNova Hardcovers

ABOVE THE LOWER SKY
DREAMSEEKER'S ROAD

THE DEMONS IN THE GREEN

TOM DEITZ

AVON BOOKS • NEW YORK

THE DEMONS IN THE GREEN is an original publication of Avon
Books. This work has never before appeared in book form. This work is
a novel. Any similarity to actual persons or events is purely coincidental.

AVON BOOKS
A division of
The Hearst Corporation
1350 Avenue of the Americas
New York, New York 10019

Copyright © 1996 by Thomas Deitz
Cover art by Daniel Horne
Published by arrangement with the author
Library of Congress Catalog Card Number: 96-96078
ISBN: 0-380-78271-5

First AvoNova Printing: September 1996

AVONOVA TRADEMARK REG. U.S. PAT. OFF. AND IN OTHER COUNTRIES,
MARCA REGISTRADA, HECHO EN U.S.A.

Printed in the U.S.A.

RA 10 9 8 7 6 5 4 3 2 1

For Nancy Knight,
who makes it all look easy

ACKNOWLEDGMENTS

eluki bes shahar
Jennifer Brehl
John Douglas
Amy Goldschlager
Greg Keyes
Adele Leone
Reid Locklin
Buck Marchinton
Martha Valencia Matthews
Michael Matthews
Paul Matthews
Chris Miller
Jeff Smith
Tracy Tate

THE
DEMONS IN THE GREEN

Prelude:
Bytes

1

"At least it doesn't smell like death on TV."

Stormcloud Nez acknowledged 'Bird's comment with a tired grunt, gaze fixed firmly on the big Sony wall-set in his apartment, where an unbelievable scene of carnage was electronically unfolding. He raised that hour's fourth bottle of Dos Equis to his lips and tilted it automatically—nervously. It was empty—like the last three times. His eyes never left the screen.

Lounging on the futon-sofa beside him, Thunderbird O'Connor's expression belied his own observation: mouth drawn into a hard thin line that added years to his youthful face, red-brown flesh along his jaw so taut it trembled, dark eyes bright with incipient tears. A sour taste welled into his mouth. He swallowed hard.

"We were *there*," 'Bird continued finally, "and I still can't believe there were so many. I— Oh shit!" He fell silent, caught off-guard by a particularly graphic close-up rendered even more repugnant by the dispassionate voice-over he only half attended:

". . . While mass beachings of cetaceans—the collective term by which zoologists identify whales, dolphins, and orcas, or killer whales, such as we see here—are not unknown, never before has there been a documented beaching of this species so large. A preliminary count places the number of on-shore carcasses at sixty-three, with at least as many more still floating in the Gulf. Dr. Mary Hasegawa, a marine biologist at the Pan-European Oceanic Research Center, whom CNN contacted by phone, said the toll could easily exceed one-fifty. When we asked Dr. Hasegawa if there was any connection between the beaching and the unpredicted storm that pounded the Aztlan area last night, she told us that it was extremely unlikely that only one species would have been affected by such an occurrence, given that several varieties of dolphins were known to have occupied the same waters at the time. To a follow-up question concerning the so-called dolphin mutilations that have occurred in that locale, Dr. Hasegawa would only state that the matter is under investigation. On a related note, meteorologists have explained the storm—"

"Mute," Stormy told the TV. Silence puddled in the room, broken only by 'Bird's breathing. He'd heard it too many times already: well-intentioned fools trying to contrive rational explanations for that precipitous near-hurricane he, Stormy, and a few others knew had no rational origin. And he'd seen the photos too often as well: masses of black clouds billowing out in the Gulf; sheets of rain slashing Aztlan's shiny new structures like some irate sea-god's flail—that was this morning's hot topic. It had been bad enough, but now it had been replaced by aerial pan-shots of the cliff-ringed coves that scalloped the coast north of PEORCI Point for over five kloms. Five kloms littered with the stinking corpses of whole pods of adolescent orcas, not one of which bore mark of either violence or disease on its elegant black-and-white body.

Five kloms of death.

"Too much death," 'Bird whispered eventually.

"Yeah," Stormy murmured back, wide-eyed. "And far too many ghosts—far too many *chindi*."

2

(Abla Arms Apartments—
Aztlan, Aztlan Free Zone)
(Monday, September 5—afternoon)

". . . Yeah, I *know*, Mom; but it's not exactly *relaxing* to discover when you're thirty years old that you're not entirely human. You—"

The image on the TV—a thin, freckled, worn-faced woman in her early sixties—broke up at that. Network programming promptly reasserted with the premier broadcast of the last *Star Wars* film, which Carolyn Mauney-Griffith had been watching when the call had come in. She bared her teeth like an irate lioness as words paraded politely across the bottom of the screen: *TRANS-MISSION INTERRUPTION. WE ARE SWITCHING TO ANOTHER SATELLITE. WE APOLOGIZE FOR ANY IN-CONVENIENCE.* And again in Spanish.

"Damn!" Carolyn spat, reaching for the cup of Earl Grey on the glass-topped coffee table before her. This was all she needed. First Mom calls out of the Third-World clear-blue, breaking two months of enforced silence during which Carolyn had needed parental advice and/or sympathy more than once. Then, after perfunctory assurances that yes, she was okay and had weathered the storm that had nearly devastated Aztlan just fine; then—*just* as she was finally getting to the heart of a certain major revelation that had turned her world topsy-turvy not three days gone by—*just then* Aztec Telecom flat-lines on her.

SWITCHING, the set supplied obligingly, as though

reacting to her ire. And Mom was back, looking as pissed and frustrated as Carolyn was, for all that her elder's angular features were utterly unlike her own softly rounded ones.

"Not entirely human," Carolyn repeated pointedly, in the unlikely event her mother had forgotten. Nuala Griffith never forgot anything unless it suited her.

The fuzzy image stuffed a lock of gray-shot auburn hair under a yellow hard-hat and sighed meaningfully. "Would you have believed me if I'd told you?" The brogue was growing stronger by the second—which meant Mom's control drive was threatening to crash.

"Probably not," Carolyn gave back. "But all you'd have had to do was produce dear old furry dad and have him do the skin thing, and I'd have believed there were fairies in the garden if you'd wanted."

Nuala's face was grim—and sad, Carolyn decided. "He wouldn't have come, and I didn't know how to contact him—for obvious reasons. Christ, child, I didn't know what he *was* when we met, and by the time I *did* . . . Actually I *never* knew for certain. Only that I met an incredibly beautiful boy one day up near Leenane, that he was wild and mysterious and . . . poetic. And that I made love to him beside the sea, went to sleep in his arms, and woke to find a young seal in his place. I never saw him again—and I waited, believe me: there by the harbor, until your father—your de facto father, if not your biological one—finished the job that had brought us there and I *had* to leave. After that, I blanked it. I'd have gone mad otherwise. See—" She broke off, face awash with tears—the first time Carolyn had ever seen her thus. "This isn't working," Nuala grumbled at last. "We need to do this in person. I need to find out how you really are; whether you're really not—"

"*Human*," Carolyn finished. "Yeah, I'd— Well, I'm not sure I'd like that, but it could only improve things. And"—she cast a distrustful eye at the picture, which was going fuzzier by the second—"it might help things with Kev too. I mean, it'd be nice to be a family again."

"I agree."

"Your place or mine?"

"Actually," Nuala replied, "I was thinking maybe the place where the whole thing started, since I have to do some research at Trinity this week anyhow."

"Leenane?"

"Yes, daughter: Leenane."

"Whew!" Carolyn whistled. "Talk about synchronicity!"

"What?"

"I have to be there too—in a couple o' days, in fact."

The connection staticked ominously.

"Damn!" Nuala growled. "This is *not* working. Tell you what: I'll call back 'round midnight and we can settle the details then."

"And save the big stuff for the one-on-one?"

"A deal," Nuala agreed. "And a promise."

The picture worsened.

"See you in Eireland," Carolyn called to her mother's fading visage. The reply, if any, was lost in electronic fog between Mauritius and the erstwhile coast of Mexico. *Star Wars IX* reclaimed the screen. The sun set. Carolyn sat staring, not watching, whispering every now and then into the darkening room, "I really am *not* human."

3

(Minneapolis, Minnesota)
(Tuesday, September 6—late afternoon)

. . . rain. . . .

Thalo glared out the window at the streaks of soggy silver sliding down the thermal glass doors that let onto his parents' patio. The sky beyond was neutral grey-white: the color of nothing. The downtown towers showed as silhouettes one shade darker: visible, then

gone, like furtive futures glimpsed in a fortuneteller's ball.

"Rain," he grumbled. "*Fucking* rain," he added silently, lest the folks hear and take him to task—again. Twenty-four was too old for that—or to live at home, for that matter; not that it was *his* choice.

"Better enjoy it," his father rumbled behind him: human thunder a counterpoint to that in the sky. Thalo could see him as a ghostly reflection slowly incarnating into color, shape, and clarity as he approached the window-wall. He didn't turn.

"One thing I won't miss in Aztlan," Thalo gave back. "Cold and rain."

His father joined him. Thalo could feel the warmth of that larger, taller body; smell the faint odor of cigar smoke that clung to that corporate livery. *Eau de 3M,* he thought disgustedly.

"Don't be so sure," the older man snorted. "From what I hear about that last big blow, they got five years' ration all at once—in two hours—without warning."

Thalo failed to suppress a smirk, his features shifting from pseudo-Indian to pseudo-elven, even if his new dye-job did not. "Proves what I've been saying about tech. All that science, and still nobody predicted it. Warm and cold fronts just *appeared*, like—like magic—and faded just as fast."

"Magic," another voice echoed behind them: female, shrill and young—and utterly unrestrained by self-consciousness. "Magic! Magic! Magic!"

Thalo couldn't help but wince. It would take more than magic to cure Sara: twelve years old in body, with a mind half as mature, courtesy of a Chinese-made pesticide Mom had inadvertently ingested at a crucial stage of her last pregnancy.

"Magic! Magic! Magic!"

Well, two days hence, he'd be flying down to the world's most magical city to begin an internship at the Kituwah-ne-Cherokee Embassy, and, incidentally, to enroll his sis in a certain famous treatment facility there. If he was lucky, that would be the start of a real future for

both of them. Shoot, they might even find magic. Sara could use all anyone had to spare.

4

(Avis Rent-a-Car # 14—
Aztlan, Aztlan Free Zone)
(Wednesday, September 7—mid-afternoon)

The men *weren't* there—and then, quite simply, they *were*.

Juan Alvarez started awake and cursed himself first in his native Kìché, then in Spanish, and finally in English for good measure. He'd dozed off—again—slumped before the terminal that was dutifully reporting which units should return by the end of his shift, which of them would need servicing, and whether or not he had enough battery packs recharging to take care of anticipated demand for electrics. Dull stuff. Deadly dull, even if this sort of drudgery at Avis # 14 paid a hell of a lot better than picking coffee, which he'd done until the City had got up and running and he'd won this job in the Third Employment Lottery.

Dull, dull, dull. . . .

No wonder he'd dozed off—though the shots of tequila he'd been sneaking all shift hadn't helped either. Still, it wouldn't have taken more than ten seconds downtime for those *hombres* to walk in like that. And if they were quiet . . . well, it really would seem like they'd appeared out of thin air.

No way he wouldn't have noticed them, either; not in those hooded cloak-serape-robe things that had become popular lately, whether worn over other clothes by trendy types, or as sole garments by the increasing streams of pilgrims come from all over the Third World to hear

Green Francis preach the eco-apocalypse up at St. Tek-awitha's. And certainly not with all four of them being big, heavy-featured men as like as four coffee beans. Funny, though, how such big *hombres* could have moved so fast.

Juan shrugged, straightened his corporate serape, and slicked back his hair as he forced an attentive smile. "Yes, *señores?*" he prompted smoothly, as the apparent leader of the group moved up to the other side of the counter, companions crowding alongside, too close for local body taboos. He shrugged again. None of his business. Odd, though, that the parking lot was empty. Not even a taxi lingered out on Olmec lest they be refused. Optimistic sons-of-bitches—for pilgrims.

"We would like a car," the leader announced gruffly, his voice oddly accented, as though parts of certain words fell beneath standard register or rose above it.

Juan nodded. "I will need a license and major credit card."

The man fumbled in the folds of his garment and produced a sheaf of plastic, which he proceeded to sort. Finally he chose one and slid it toward Juan. Their fingers brushed as he accepted it. The touch persisted for the merest moment. Juan felt briefly lightheaded, then started and recoiled, still—apparently—on the edge of sleep. He stared at the requested documentation stupidly, waiting for it to focus. (*Damn!* He really had been hitting the Cuervo.)

"Compact or full-sized?" he asked, while the letters pulsed and twisted and refused to stabilize. He fished in his pocket for something. What . . . ? Oh . . . a pen.

"Compact—and electric."

Juan nodded again, blinked, stifled a yawn—and located the requisite paperwork, then filled in the appropriate blanks, ran the Visa, and snared an ignition card from the rack beneath the desk. "It's the white Dodge Whisper," he told them, pointing through a side window. Somehow they were only three now. He wondered if his mind was still playing games, or if he'd simply miscounted.

"*Gracias, señor*," the leader mumbled, and departed in a flurry of pale tan fabric.

"*De nada*," Juan called back, and returned to his terminal.

Three minutes and another (nerve calming) hit of Cuervo later, he remembered to enter the rental agreement—and was appalled to see his own name and address in the appropriate blanks, with his own signature at the bottom. His hair rose at that, even as his stomach gave a little twitch. No way *that* could've happened. No way he could've been that asleep on his feet. Or that drunk. He'd be fired for sure.

For sure and for real, he determined a moment later, when a further check showed that the credit card that had paid for the car had also been his own—though he no more recalled removing it from his wallet than he did signing that rental form.

But the Whisper was gone.

And then, for no reason he could determine, Juan Alvarez decided that a dip in the nearest canal would be just the thing to clear his head. He didn't remember until the water closed over him that he couldn't swim a stroke.

Prologue:
Hellfire and Damnation

(Episcopal Palace, Aztlan Free Zone)
(Wednesday, September 7—late evening)

His Grace, the Reverend Father Francis Blackmer, first Archbishop of Aztlan, decided he would have to get high.

It was no surprise, really: When the words wouldn't arrive with the proper precision and dispatch; when eloquence danced tantalizingly just beyond his reach; when simple logic seemed as remote an achievement as polling the seraphs on the head of a pin, no choice remained but to seek external aid in attaining those goals. Otherwise, the panoply of brilliances contending in his skull might never fall into line.

Madness, some would say. Or genius—of a peculiarly reckless kind. Blackmer didn't always know the difference. Nor care.

Getting high . . .

Not a course he relished, yet he was willing to suffer it—to serve his calling.

Getting high . . .

The end justified the means.

Getting high . . .

It was a ritual, the same as the Mass and other sacraments. And rituals must be ordered precisely or they lost their force, must be performed in their proper time and season or their efficacy diminished.

He *wondered* at the time, and a gold solar cross in his right earlobe broadcast that information to the appropriate

10

part of his brain: twenty-two forty-three hours. He would begin at twenty-three hundred.

"Save," Blackmer told the computer set into the black basalt block of his desk, then rose, assuming without question that his command was heeded. If not . . . well, the aborted speech had been drivel anyway.

And that was the problem, wasn't it? His speeches had all become drivel. Trouble was, there were only so many ways to express a point before they became empty parroting. No matter how much one *believed* a thing, it was hard to remain fired up while repeating oneself ad nauseam. Never mind that the particular litany he'd been chanting lately had been reiterated to *Newsweek, Le Monde, The Wall Street Journal, The Illustrated London News, The Japan Times,* and a dozen other major newslines and magazines, all in individual audiences. No, what mattered was who heard it this time, namely the OAS General Assembly, plus the odd attending CEO, both gov and mega—the latter increasingly larger, more powerful, and more stable, than governments.

After that, he'd ring up the Vatican and have a little chat with His Holiness and trust his vast popularity in the Third World to ensure that he had a job after.

Sighing, he straightened the loose gauze cassock he wore over bare feet and cut-off Levis, and strode across the thick emerald green carpet toward the window-wall that looked southeast across Aztlan. His reflection resolved as he approached: tall and severe, with an ascetic's slimness that, on the taut-drawn skin of his face, made him look older than thirty-one—until he smiled, when dimples appeared in his cheeks and transformed him into a mischievous boy. And until impatience overruled decorum and segued the stride into a skip.

He wondered if other archbishops ever did that.

Of course, most didn't acquire ThDs in divinity at sixteen, nor archbishoprics at twenty-nine. And most weren't international celebs. Rock 'n' Roll Archie, some called him, for his unrepentant fondness for the loud fast music that had been current nigh onto seventy years. Reverend Green Jeans and Green Francis were other ap-

pellations, born of his equally unrepentant enthusiasm for environmental causes—and casual mode of dress. Francis the Reb was the latest, because he'd decided it was time someone put teeth into Vatican III and took on the Holy Father.

Shoot, the worst good old Michael I could do was excommunicate him, which would be a major mistake with someone whose popularity in the Third World exceeded his own (so CNN reported) by three-to-one. (*"Pride goeth before destruction, and a haughty spirit before a fall,"* a vigilant conscience promptly countered.)

"Dim," he told the lights as he neared the floor-to-ceiling panes that let onto the palace's third level balcony, then "open," to the glass itself. A section slid silently aside. He slipped through as noiselessly. Tropical night beat around him as he drank in the thick moist air of the Caribbean coast. And gazed out across Aztlan.

By day, the sparkling new city—the so-called New World Capital—looked like a couple-dozen chests of pirate plunder flung off the surrounding hills onto a pristine seaside beach, then strewn with blue silk netting and green velvet scarves. Except that the myriad faceted jewels were embassies, ministries, and corporate HQs; the spill of doubloons around them apartments, residences, and shops; while the netting was the web-work of canals that stretched inland five kloms from the Gulf, and the velvet was parks, yards, and grassy plazas.

That was by day. By night it became an amalgam of video game, pinball machine on Dexedrine, and jet fighter instrument panel, with lights glinting and flowing and flashing between larger stationary blocks of color, all centering on the faceted mirror-glass neo-Teotihuacano pyramids of the Big Four embassies.

Yeah, it was beautiful, all right, and Blackmer didn't for a moment deny how fortunate he was to claim pastoral sovereignty over such a splendid flock and fold. Yet his gaze inevitably swept past the city to that which lay beyond the glittering sweep of embassies, and the solar-powered desalinization plant near the point, and the world headquarters of Ford and Honda and Volkswagen

and Exxon Latina and Phillips Electronics and Aztec Aerospace. Beyond even the neo-Gothic spires of St. Tekawitha's, whose nave was half again as long as Canterbury's, and whose vaults, at one-twenty meters, twice that of poor, unfinished Beauvais. Twin holographic towers rose higher still, but, in line with local aesthetic codes, were only activated on feast days and during Mass.

But past them, a border of velvet darkness around the spangled city, lay *El País Verde*: The Green Country— the belt of undeveloped wild that encircled Aztlan like the arms of the archetypal Earth Mother cradling her jaded, urban child.

Trouble was, there was only one—though Caracas, Rio, Ottawa, and Washington had green belts under construction, a dozen more had been approved, and another eighty-six were being considered.

Mostly, they were his doing. Certainly it had been the grassroots movement he had organized while still at Harvard Divinity School that, via the Net, had insisted that Aztlan's planners recall that technozation was not alpha reality, that the Wild had a far more tenured claim. *El País* had resulted.

And now Blackmer had turned his passion to larger causes. Like the rain forests.

Specifically, he was going to address the General Assembly tomorrow and demand they stop the cutting *now*, or he would personally ask the Pope to utilize the vast new temporal powers restored under Vatican III to place the worst offenders—Brazil, Venezuela, Malaysia, and Indonesia—under interdict, *Gaudium et Spes* be damned. And while denying the sacraments might not carry much clout in those parts of the developing world not predominantly Catholic, they certainly would in heavily Roman countries like Brazil and the rest of Latin America. And though the guys manning the 'dozers, chainsaws, and torches might not fear the Pontiff, there was cause indeed to fear over a billion people deprived of the sacraments because of their misdeeds. Employment was fine; being alive to appreciate it was better.

Trouble was, he had to determine the right way to say

all that. This speech could make or break him. It would be his "Gettysburg Address" and "I Have a Dream" and "Who Is Now Our Foe?" all in one—if he could get it right.

But he'd said it all *before*, and all those samenesses were at war in him, drowning a scarce-controlled passion with a flood of verbal ennui. He needed *new* words, *new* sentences, *new* ways to articulate his dreams so perfectly that no right-thinking person could have any option but to agree.

And the only way to achieve that was to get high.

Not on drugs, however—though he'd worked through a fair pharmacopeia before he'd accepted his calling, and done peyote a few times since, with his sometime tennis partner, the High Shaman of the Reformed Native American Church. No, this would be a more subtle form of transcendence. Which he'd best be attending.

He paused in mid-turn, gaze snared by an anomaly beyond the waist-high rampart. A car had eased to a halt at the entrance to Lady Evenstar Park, across the street from the Palace. Anonymous white sedan. Electric. Probably a rental. No big deal, ignoring the hour. Then again, he *was* a celeb of sorts, and was used to having the Palace pointed out by pilgrims and tourists alike. A shrug, and he retreated another step—and paused again. All four car doors had opened, disgorging a like number of figures typically androgynous in their attire: loose tunics and baggy jeans in pale earth tones beneath those hooded pilgrims' overcloaks that had lately come into vogue. All wore their hoods up, however, so he could see no faces; but, he noted absently, they did display a peculiar homogeneity in size and build: taller than the shortish local norm, and bulky. One—the driver—stared up at him, bowed, then brought his hands together in the attitude of prayer. His companions followed suit—clumsily, as though the gesture was not reflexive. Still, save for their awkwardness, such was not uncommon. Sighing, Blackmer returned to the parapet, nodded at the pilgrims, muttered a short prayer that would surely be inaudible that far away, then extended his hands in blessing. Pope Mi-

chael wouldn't have approved—but Mikey wasn't here. If a painless benediction could make even one life better, so be it.

The lead pilgrim looked up, nodded thanks, then waved goodbye and got back in the car. Blackmer didn't stay to watch them depart.

"Close," he told the window behind him, then padded across his office toward the rough sandcrete wall opposite. A round-topped archway there let onto the central stairwell. Starlight glimmered down from a skylight two levels up, and a sharp turn through a plain wooden door to the right put him in his private chapel.

The space enfolded him like a womb: pale, unadorned walls of gold-pink sandstone rising smoothly into a barrel vault thrice his height but spanning no more distance than the outstretched arms of a tall man—which Blackmer was. A single narrow window opposite the door precisely mirrored its shape and proportions, and equally precisely faced Jerusalem—not Rome. A few of the brightest stars glittered there—outshining Aztlan, and more clearly seen because no glass marred that opening. Wind was free to enter—and rain, though it seldom did, last weekend's freak blow being a major exception.

The only intrusions into all that quiet emptiness were the simple raised cube of the altar, a woven mat of Guatemalan wool at the altar's base, and the small cross of reclaimed conquistador gold atop it. (A gift from the Spanish government at the consecration of St. Tekawitha's, that last was an exact, though smaller, duplicate of the one on the Cathedral's high altar.)

Blackmer crossed himself upon entering, closed the door, and paced slowly—reverently—toward the altar, where he knelt upon the mat. A discreet row of stone-veneered keys hid beneath the forward fringe, invisible save at very close range. His fingers danced across them. Concealed speakers awoke and spilled music into the air: a whispery prelude to another piece he'd chosen more carefully and programmed to very specific ends. That one would begin in roughly another minute, but so softly as to be inaudible: infra-sound, like the noise of the tectonic

plates beneath the land. But then the volume would
slowly build until the very walls shook with synthesized
thunder. And Blackmer would ride with it, let it carry
him to a place of higher focus where doubt was unknown
and perfection reigned.

And the piece itself? His latest fav, of course: the Hero
Twins' retrotech version of Handel's *Fireworks*, electronically combined with the same composer's *Water
Music*, with a bit of "The Hallelujah Chorus" thrown in.
The five-minute cut, backed by the Twins' female chorus,
had been a minor hit two years back; this would be a
custom-ordered hourlong variation, with all vocals deliberately deleted.

A pause to appreciate a breeze that had wafted in the
window, and then another button lowered the entire front
of the altar, revealing a spacious shelved compartment.
From it, he removed a single onyx candleholder and a
matching pair of shallow bowls, all of which he set on
the top, the holder centered before the rood. That accomplished, he fixed a new white taper into its receptacle and
filled the bowls with chunks of fragrant resin. Nor could
he help but smile, for both candle and incense had been
gifts from the Hero Twins themselves—which, he reminded himself yet again, was dangerously close to
pride, which was a sin.

Back to the matter at hand.

Homemade matches on the lower shelf ignited a reed
with which he lit the taper and the contents of the bowls.
A final brush of fingers closed the cubby, whereupon he
whispered, very softly, *"Fiat tenebras, et ab tenebris,
lux"*—*Let there be darkness, and in that darkness,
light*—and the ritual began.

Slowly the ambient light faded, replaced with the candle's glare; slowly, too, the old music ebbed and the new
began to swell. Blackmer felt it more than heard it. He
fixed his gaze on the flame at eye level before him, in-
haling deeply to fill his lungs with the sweetly pungent
fumes. It was a new scent—and very nice. He'd have to
ask the Twins where they got it.

Again, he inhaled, a year of yoga having given him

deep control of his breathing. And with fire before him, and music around him, he began to center. To get high. To banish all those clamoring alternatives until all that remained was the One.

"*Pater Noster . . .* " he began in the traditional Latin, thereby forging a deliberate link to the past, to join that he had already wrought to the physical world and the realm of the senses. "*Father, bless this earth, which You have created for us, of which we are all a part . . .* "

The trance fell upon him then, in all its quiet glory.

Peace for a moment—which was normal. And then— for the first time—voices!

They appeared stealthily, riding the sound, the smoke, and the candlelight. Not words, really; more . . . impressions. In spite of himself, Blackmer shivered. This had never happened before. Perhaps he was hearing the tongues of angels—or even God! Another shiver and he slipped deeper into trance, following those half-heard syllables that chimed in time with the Hero Twins' drumming and ebbed and flowed with the flickering of the flame and the inhalation of incense-laden air.

Still no words—though sounds had begun to suggest images . . . to clarify . . .

Heat and light. . . .

Fire! Forests burning. Mountain ranges ablaze with hellborn conflagration. Plains crisped to ash. Rivers evaporating. The sun rising over all: a desert of nuclear fire above poisonous sands stretching endlessly.

A vision! Not what he'd expected when what he needed was words—but perhaps the vision *was* the words. Fire was a principal foe, after all: forests cut, centuries-old trees set alight, slash-and-burn agriculture, entire woods sacrificed for heat. Fire equalled energy—and man's insatiable desire for energy was the principal demon that tortured the earth. Fire. Hell. The devil. A demon, yet still a fallen angel: fallen into hellfire and torment. And man was fallen too—into his own damnation. The fires Satan lit in Hades, those man lit on earth: what was the difference? He had it now: Fire would be the theme of his speech: man denying God as

Satan had done, and forced to consume his world alive
in order to maintain his own hell.

Now if he could only *say* it. . . .

The candle flickered. The music roared past the threshold of conscious hearing. The scent of incense grew
thicker.

Another breeze.

Again the flame flickered.

To speak of a thing with true passion, one must understand that thing utterly, completely, without doubt or
fear. He must therefore (so the Voices seemed to urge)
understand the very essence of fire, to its ultimate heart
and center.

(*No!* another shouted, deeper in his head.)

Fire . . . !

(*"Yes!"*)

(*No!*)

(*"Yes!"*)

(*No!*)

"Yes" won. He would understand fire. He would understand it *now*!

(*"Yes, yes, yes!"*) the Voices snickered—as Archbishop Francis Blackmer stretched his hand toward the
candle flame.

. . . *into* it.

Dark hairs flared and crackled upon his fingers—like
forests incinerating. A pungent protein stench merged
with the resiny sweetness.

(*God help me!*) Blackmer thought distantly, as he
strove to yank his hand away.

Yet he could not! He was trapped—his *self* was—deep
in some awful trance from which he could not revive.

And that self could only watch with sick amazement,
as that hand—which the Voices now seemed to drive in
lieu of his own will—slid deeper into the candle's glare.

Blisters arose on his palm, even as a flimsy cotton cuff
brushed the flame and ignited. And still he did not—
could not—remove it, though his entire garment blazed
up.

His last words were a scream, louder than the Hero

Twin's electronic "*Fireworks.*" And then he lost control of even his tongue, and, until his death half a minute later, heard only strange internal laughter. And, though it should have been impossible, the ghostly receding whir of a white electric rental sedan.

Chapter I:
Homecoming

(Killary Harbour, United Eireland)
(Thursday, September 8—morning)

It was not an image to come home to.

How long had it been? Carolyn wondered. How long since she'd trod the *auld sod* that had provided half her surname? Three years, she made it, since the break between her parents that had wrought the Schism with her half-brother that had sent her packing off to the Marine Institute at Monaco and thence to PEORCI in Aztlan. Sunnier climes both of 'em. Not the dreary desolation of a quasi-fjord in the wild west of Eireland, where the hills humped like tired giants on a bivouac, none-too-eager to rouse into mist and cold; and what threadbare scraps of foliage survived seemed as begrudged as the hair of the red-faced publican in what passed for a town two kloms back.

And definitely not that desolation waterlogged and pounded flat by the fringe of Hurricane Buckley a week-and-a-bit gone by. Eireland was still recovering from *that*. Communication was spotty even in the cities, never mind this far into the Gaelic outback, and transportation was worse. She'd hoped to arrive for this little rendez-vous last evening, grab a good night's snooze in Leenane's single inn, then rise sufficiently early to get her head straight at a reasonable rate and in peace.

Instead, her plane had been four hours late into Shannon (which only had two runways open); Dan Dooley hadn't had a spare rental car until this morning—and that

only because she'd spent most of a stressful night playing phone tag with a pair of diplomats, neither of whom she knew more than slightly—and three bridges on her intended route were now harping in architectural heaven.

Still, red tape had been sliced, bureaucracy cleared away (and at least one road opened, she suspected), and she'd finally arrived an hour ago—to an empty inn, desolation, and despair—in dread of a pair of reunions she did not expect to enjoy even slightly.

Sighing, she rose from the rough stone wall beside the N59, and wrapped her orange nylon windbreaker more closely around her compact body, squinting through a drift of fog that had wandered up from the bay, where it splashed and splattered at the base of a short run of cliffs a hundred paces to the left. A break in that same wall twice that distance behind her showed where a car had plowed through, gone airborne, and sunk. Bits of black metal and plastic still glimmered there, sole remnants of a stolen Citroën commanded by certain . . . beings with very bad intentions toward her troublesome only brother. And if Kev hadn't found the balls to engage his adversaries in the game of chicken that had forced them through the wall, he might well have been killed; no one would have learned the preposterous things they now knew; and she wouldn't be here trying not to shiver, catch cold, or scream.

Maybe she should retreat to the little red Ford Ka back at the turn-aside, crank the heater onto HI, and grab some Z's.

Maybe she should forget the whole thing. What, after all, did a well-educated marine biologist say to an equally accomplished mom who had conveniently neglected to mention she'd been sired by something that couldn't exist?

Never mind keeping an eye on a brother who wasn't speaking to that same mom, and probably playing referee 'twixt the twain.

Never *mind* doing both in front of a pair of high-ranking diplomats, while awaiting what was essentially another.

And *absolutely* never mind that she was about to become an ambassador of sorts herself.

First Ambassador to the North Atlantic, perhaps. But was she Eireland's envoy, or Aztlan's?

She returned to the car.

An hour passed.

Mom didn't show, which made her two hours late.

Fatigue overrode stress, and Carolyn dozed.

When she awoke, it was to rain and a gleaming black Humvee III bearing down on her, with more lights ablaze across its blunt prow than existed in some towns hereabout. She promptly sat bolt upright, reached for the highly-illegal Ruger automatic under her seat (last week's activities having made her paranoid), and didn't relax until a familiar, if nervous and over-amped, voice blared from out of the glare, "It's okay, Cary, it's us!"

Kevin.

She relaxed into the seat, but her fingers still shook as she opened the door.

The Humvee was disgorging its passengers as well: three of them, bulky in dark rain gear that reminded her unpleasantly of certain other bulky personages and gave her the willies all over. The driver paused in the act of unfurling an umbrella to reach back inside and kill all but the parking lights, and it was then that she saw that the vehicle bore government plates: Ministry of the Interior, if she wasn't mistaken. At least it wasn't Fish and Game—though that might've been more appropriate.

And by then she'd composed herself sufficiently to venture out to meet them.

The slimmest of the three men, though not the shortest, reached her first, and there was no mistaking that preposterous shock of carrot-colored hair nor the fading blue blaze that bisected it. Nor, of course, the face beneath it, that might have been quirkily handsome in a sharp-nosed, long-chinned way, had it not been quite so narrow or inclined to foolish smirks.

"You're here!" Kevin cried inanely, looking not at all a man of thirty-three, much less a world-famous (and world *saving*, if the truth were known) novelist.

"Been here," she drawled back, and reached out to give him a hug, though they'd only been parted two days—Kevin had left Aztlan on Tuesday to check on the small castle from which he'd been shanghaied in the middle of the recent hurricane. He'd also needed time to think; probably as much as she, for all he was better programmed to accept the unacceptable. His grip tightened, then unwound. He scowled over her shoulder. "Where's Mom?"

Carolyn shrugged. "Not here—obviously. And unreachable by phone for the last two days."

Kevin's scowl deepened. "Typical." Then, hastily, with too much apology: "*Not* a criticism!"

She ruffled his hair, for all he was her older brother. "It was her idea," she reminded him gently.

"She owed you," Kevin growled. "And don't look at me like that. I promise to be good when I have to. But she's not here—yet. Besides, she's not exactly been a model of support to you either."

Carolyn checked her watch—she'd had to stop wearing a time stud because certain recent activities kept compromising its attachment point. "Yeah, but she should've got here by now—or sent word. She had the embassy numbers."

"Speaking of embassies," Kevin broke in. "We're probably creating some kind of incident by keeping the guys waiting in the rain." He indicated the Humvee. "Roomier in there than in that little red baby-buggy; plus we've got fresh coffee and embassy chow."

She eyed him skeptically. "*Whose* embassy? Are we talkin' Guinness and fresh salmon here, or black drink and fry bread?"

"Your choice," Kevin snorted. "You eat, we'll lick our lips hungrily."

The remaining two men met her at the AWD, looking at once tired, puzzled, irate, and relieved. Ignoring protocol (she was, after all, half Eirish), she greeted the one on the left first—because she knew him better.

The Honorable Chief William Red Wounds, Kituwah Ambassador to Aztlan, looked absurdly glad to see her

for someone she'd only met twice. She tried to return the favor, though he made her a tad uneasy, mostly because of who he was—she wasn't used to running in diplomatic circles or associating with famous Native Americans. More to the point, though, he was the highest ranked person on earth, so far as she was aware, who knew about . . . certain things. And the most receptive believer in others. "*Siyu*," she began—"Greetings," in Cherokee. It was a courtesy one of her cadre of unlikely new friends had taught her. For his part, Red Wounds grinned like a boy: yet another incongruity; the guy was over fifty. Then again, wide-cheeked features, inky hair, and ruddy coloring didn't jibe with the expensive Irish wool sweater or emerald corduroy jeans peeking out from under his Driza-Bone.

"*Siyu*, m'lady," Red Wounds gave back, sparing a twinkling glance at his companion. "It's damned hard to say ma'am in a country like this," he added. "Cheapens the experience."

His companion smiled in turn, but Carolyn sensed a certain unease, as though he were in over his head but didn't want to admit it. He was the one she didn't know save from articles in assorted Aztlan telezines and the receiving line at the lone embassy ball she'd attended back there. His name was James O'Neal. His title was Eirish Ambassador to Aztlan. He was here because Red Wounds knew him, trusted him, and had needed someone with his connections. But more importantly, O'Neal had a strong interest in folklore in general and that of his native land in particular, and, mostly under Red Wounds's tutelage, was open-minded about the mystical and arcane.

Physically, he split the difference between Kevin and 'Wounds, with craggily handsome features, bright blue eyes, and dull red hair worn long in a tail. A bit of prowling in the Net had revealed that he was forty-five and twice divorced. Though rather short, he was fit for his age; an astonishingly dapper dresser even in foul weather; and had a fair reputation both as a horseman and a race car driver. He was also, oddly, a staunch en-

vironmentalist, which was one more reason he was present, since it was reports of a heretofore mythical "endangered species" that had prompted this meeting in the first place.

"Ms. Mauney-Griffith," he murmured, taking her hand gallantly. "Nice to meet you again. And welcome to my humble Humvee."

The Humvee (refitted in full Connolly leather by Vanden Plas, she noted), was indeed roomier than the subcompact Ka, warmer, and more luxurious than many executive offices she'd seen. It had all the expected electronic amenities, including CD, fax, shredder, and phone. But the connections were not, apparently, any better than elsewhere. "Just tried Shannon again," O'Neal informed them in a truly delightful brogue, as the last door slammed, sealing them all inside. "Nobody there can even tell me if your mom's plane has landed."

Carolyn rolled her eyes. "I don't know whether to be angry or grateful; whether to wait on her, or deal with the other thing now."

"You've had a tough day," Red Wounds agreed. "Shoot, just gettin' here's a good day's work for most folks."

"Including us," Kevin noted, as he unscrewed a thermos of coffee and poured into exquisite china cups.

Carolyn was wondering if she should continue making small talk when O'Neal solved the problem by coding certain numbers into a laptop along with his fingerprints. An instant later, paper began unscrolling from a slot in the back of the console. "If this was a Bond film," he observed wryly, "I'd have handed you a red leather dossier embellished with gold stamps and seals. Alas, things of that ilk attract too much attention and are a pill to dispose of besides. But what we've got here is as much hard info as I—and one exceedingly trustworthy assistant—have been able to amass concerning the . . . phenomenon. Most of it's based on what your brother told me, since you and I haven't had the pleasure of extended converse on this—or any other—topic."

Carolyn scanned the pages as they appeared, on one

level seeing pretty much what she'd expected, including Kevin's take on the matter essentially word for word the way he'd told it to her, with her own slant rendered only slightly less accurately, for all it was at second hand. There was also a list of references, and a short appendix of "Other Possible Contacts," subdivided into "Hearsay," "Sightings," and "Matings."

She frowned at that last. "Matings" was a cold term for something that had resulted in a for-real human being, namely her. And certainly not an accurate reflection of how that coupling had actually been. Or how it had been when she'd . . . dreamed it.

O'Neal was looking at her with eager interest as she finished, and her female aspect acknowledged that he was sure enough a charmer. "I'd like a full report from you too, of course," he said. "I shan't pressure you, though, given the agenda you're tryin' to juggle."

She managed a smile—and spoiled it by letting her gaze veer from O'Neal's face to the Humvee's clock.

He saw her. "She's over two hours late now."

Kevin was chewing his lip. "So . . . which do we do?"

O'Neal regarded him with tolerant humor, and Carolyn recalled that the Ambassador and her brother had met a number of times. Kev was, after all, the latest jewel in Eireland's literary crown. Expatriate American jewel, to be sure; then again, the diamonds in the British regalia had come mostly from South Africa. "Kev, my lad," the Ambassador confided, "family's one thing, the fate of nations is another altogether." He paused and studied Carolyn seriously. "Uh, that is assuming they have nations—or *a* nation. You don't happen to know, do you?"

Carolyn shook her head. "I know what you do: a dolphin delivered a message to me three days ago saying that my heretofore unacknowledged kin desired to have speech with me. Subject: whether to reveal their presence to the world at large. Having no choice, I agreed. Somewhere in there I called Kev and you two gents, then Mom called me. Somewhere a decision also got made. I'm here. Mom's—apparently—in transit. She'll live if I have

to make her wait, though I'd rather not. God knows she's used to it: she was in labor with me for two days.''

Kevin cocked a brow. ''I wonder if that's another function of—''

''Possibly,'' Carolyn snapped, and checked the clock again. Then found her gaze drawn back to Ambassador O'Neal. ''So what's it going to be, sir? How far does all this go?''

O'Neal shrugged. ''That's what I'm here to find out. On one level, I'm simply hanging around 'cause I've always been one to chase rainbows and search for crocks of gold. On another, I'm hoping to prove that my esteemed colleague here is either crazy as a loon or thinks I am, in which latter case I may just claim insult and try to start a war. And on *another* level, I'm here because it's not often one gets to be present when the fundamental basis of reality—either one's own, or the world's at large—gets shaken to its complacent core.''

Red Wounds downed his coffee and sighed. ''Well, as my . . . 'colleague' so aptly noted, your mother is now over two hours late. Shall we go see if we have better luck with our other appointment?''

Kevin sighed in turn. ''One wonders how they tell time, given that they've neither clocks nor chips in their heads.''

''*That you know of*,'' Carolyn corrected. ''But you're right. Besides, I've gotta do something soon, or I'll scream.''

''I think,'' O'Neal suggested carefully, ''that a stroll along the shore might be in order.''

Fortunately, only a fine cold mist fouled the air when Carolyn eased under Kevin's brolly a moment later, with the Humvee's document shredder making contented munching sounds behind them. And it didn't take long to make their way along the highway to a gap in the stone wall that let onto a narrow lane slanting down to the right. ''Fancy getting my Merc along this,'' Kevin told O'Neal as much as Carolyn. ''Poor old thing'll never be the same!''

''Teach you to drive the biggest car in Eireland,''

O'Neal chuckled—possibly to inject some levity into what was turning into far too grim a day.

"Biggest standard sedan," Kevin corrected. "There's—"

Carolyn started to tell them to hush; that such trivialities were . . . well, really *trivial* in comparison to what was afoot. But her mouth froze as she opened it.

They were no longer alone.

She hadn't heard the sound of the approach, though she hadn't really been listening, and the wind was fierce along here, never mind the patter-tap of the mist against the hood of her windbreaker and four people's labored breathing.

On the other hand, flippers weren't exactly the quietest means of land locomotion, and seals were famous for grunting like old men whenever they exerted themselves.

This seal, however, had simply appeared from behind the last remnant of piled stone wall at the root of the lane—not far from the clifftops—and was now calmly hunching toward them in that awkward arch-and-thrust gait pinnipeds used ashore. *Grey seal,* she classified automatically. *Halichoerus grypus.* Rare in these parts, and listed as endangered throughout the British Isles. This was a particularly fine specimen: young, sleek, and most likely male. She estimated its weight at 170 kilos: the low end for that sex and species.

"That our boy?" Red Wounds wondered behind her.

"Right brand," Carolyn replied, not looking at him. "Beyond that . . . I only know the process, as it were, not the application. Kev's really your man there."

"The one I saw was like this, at the end," Kevin acknowledged. "That is, Fir was. I . . . prefer to think of him as a person."

They had come to within four paces of the seal now, and Carolyn's biologist persona kept wondering when the beast was going to act like the wild animal it obviously was and beat feet—flippers, rather—out of there. Instead, it fixed them with keen, if wary, dark eyes, and remained in place, as if daring them to come closer.

Carolyn did, and O'Neal. Kevin and Red Wounds stayed a pace behind. Finally, when Carolyn was close

enough to reach out and tweak the creature's pointy black nose, it gave a muffled growl-bark-grunt, twisted its head down, and calmly set its sharp little teeth into the dappled hide of its left front flipper. Blood showed there, and pink-white flesh beneath, and then the seal began to worry at that rent, until it became a full-fledged gash more than a foot long. And then some automatic reaction seemed to kick in, and the seal's whole skin began to split and draw away from that fissure, so that, less than a minute later, it was not a grey seal that sat staring at her, but an appallingly handsome, dark-haired young man. The lad—he looked about seventeen—rose from where he'd crouched, drew the now entirely separate sealskin up with him, and grinned at her expectantly. His dark eyes were wide and feral.

Carolyn had seen enough ingratiating male grins for one day, but couldn't help grinning back anyway—though not so much at the young man as at Red Wounds's and (especially) O'Neal's expressions, when she caught them from the corner of her eye. The elder had eyes the size of saucers; the younger a mouth one could have spelunked in. Kevin was simply looking smug and trying with little success to suppress a guffaw.

Carolyn recovered composure first and told their perplexed-looking visitor, "You'll have to forgive us, but we're not exactly used to meeting selkies."

"Nor selkies humans," the lad gave back, in a voice deeper than she'd expected, which, given how young he looked, provided some needed credibility. Now if only he'd put on some clothes. On the other hand. . . .

Carolyn cleared her throat. "Ambassador O'Neal, Ambassador Red Wounds, allow me to introduce . . . uh . . . forgive me if such inquiries are rude . . . but what *is* your name?"

"Connor," said the boy who was also a seal. "Humans do not bark well, so I am told," he added with another grin, and Carolyn wasn't sure if he was trying to be flip or amusing.

"Remember Columbus," Kevin advised Red Wounds under his breath.

"I *am*," Red Wounds muttered back, without a trace of humor. "Every *second*."

Kevin turned pale.

"It is a pleasure to meet you," the selkie went on obliviously, extending his left hand, then peering at it a moment and swapping it for the right. "Is that correct?" he finished.

"Doesn't matter," O'Neal murmured, as he took the hand. "I hope this is a propitious meeting for both our kinds."

"That is our wish too," the selkie responded gravely. "Still, you know this is a risk. I have been asked to trust all four of you—and yet, my kind is taught to fear yours."

"Except my mother," Carolyn countered softly.

The lad's face clouded. "Except her."

Red Wounds looked at O'Neal, who looked at Carolyn. "Well, frankly I'm not certain where to start," he mused. "But seems to me we'd all be more comfortable some place warm and dry. We've got clothes," he added, to their visitor. "If you need 'em."

The selkie glanced absently down at his sleek bare body and shook his head. "I thank you for the offer, and indeed there will be time for such things. But for now, I am bid say that my folk request the presence of Carolyn in their own place as soon as that may be."

Carolyn grimaced and checked her watch. A glance up the hill showed no additional cars.

"My mother—" she began.

"Is still not here," the selkie informed her. "Nor is she within the range I can search with my mind."

"I'd prefer to wait, though," Carolyn insisted. "She's part of this too. In fact, she's the reason I'm here."

"Which we know," the selkie assured her. "Indeed, I was told exactly that—by your sire."

Carolyn swallowed hard. "My . . . *sire*?"

The lad nodded. "He it was bade you hasten. He

would not say how quickly, only that little time remains.''

Carolyn was shaken to the core. ''Until . . . what?''

''I could tell you,'' the selkie replied, ''or you could see for yourself. Which would you find most convincing?''

''It's their call,'' O'Neal told her gently. ''Whatever you choose, we'll be here.''

''But Mom . . .''

''We'll deal with her,'' Kevin assured her. ''I'll be absolutely as polite as I can—not that I'll need to, with O'Neal here to charm her. And 'Wounds.''

''Good point,'' Carolyn conceded, then looked back at the selkie. ''So what did you have in mind?''

''I suspect you already know,'' the selkie smiled. ''It would be best accomplished on the shore.''

Carolyn nodded stiffly—and, brother and ambassadors in tow, followed the naked boy toward the cliffs.

Chapter II:
Touchdown

(Aztlan Free Zone)
(Thursday, September 8—dawn)

Thalo had just lost the city and now feared he'd lose his breakfast as well.

Aztlan, which had been visible as a glittering smear playing hide-and-seek among the mountains along the horizon, had disappeared again as the Delta 787 descended through yet another layer of the thin clouds that were totally at odds with how one's first approach to the New World capital ought to be. Unsullied sunshine would've been ideal, with good old Sol unveiled in all his rising red glory to send beams lancing across pristine blue Caribbean water, pure white beaches, and buildings so new and clean and sparkly they were like faceted jewels cast upon a carpet of well-watered moss.

Instead, there'd been clouds and haze, never mind the bloody Sierra Madre Oriental, that blocked most of what view the overcast permitted. They were close suckers, too; and more than once Thalo had expected to hear the shriek of tortured metal against one of those barren peaks and find himself sharing space with his own private mountaintop. And that wasn't even counting the updrafts and downdrafts, which prompted pitching and yawing, which in turn precipitated—to his great chagrin—nausea. Which pissed him royally. He'd been looking forward to this too long, dammit—and to have it consummated beneath sullen skies while clutching a barf-bag . . . well, it just didn't jibe with his romantic soul. Twenty-four years

that soul had been romantic, the last three of which had focused on Aztlan's particular siren call. And now here he was on the long awaited first day of the rest of his life, and things had gone to hell.

"Ladies and gentlemen," came the pilot's smooth Alabama drawl over the intercom, "we are beginning our final descent into Aztlan International Airport. Normally we would be landing in fifteen minutes; however, Aztlan Control has advised us that, due to a large amount of priority diplomatic traffic, we will be placed in a holding pattern where we may remain for up to an hour. In the meantime, we will be offering complimentary drinks and snacks. We would also advise any of you who are unfamiliar with the layout of Aztlan International to consult the plan you will find in the pocket on the back of the seat ahead of you. We apologize for this delay and hope you'll fly Delta again soon and that your stay in Aztlan is a pleasant one."

"Yeah," Thalo grunted. "Right." An hour's hold, huh? That meant more circling, which meant more banking, which meant—on the landward side—more nearbrushes with the capricious winds that haunted the *cordilleras*. His stomach could *not* abide that, not an hour's worth. Sighing, he rummaged through the duffle bag between his feet. As a rule he avoided chemicals like the plague, but nausea was nausea, which could lead to embarrassment, which was worse. So it was that he found his stash of Dramamine—lodged between his copy of Linda Schele's latest update of *A Forest of Kings* and J. Thomas Smith's *Manifesting the Green*, which works neatly bracketed his passions: Native Americans and environmentalism, respectively. And of course here, where rampant deforestation had helped spell the demise of Mayan civilization, and where a consortium of nervous New World governments and megacorps were now trying to rise above their profligate roots while preserving the convenience of cities, the confluence of those two elements was ideal. Except that they needed to work on the weather.

Abruptly the plane banked. The portly St. Paul busi-

nessman who'd been dozing beside him for the last two hours twitched in his sleep but didn't awaken, for which Thalo was grateful. Unfortunately, *his* stomach *was* awake and didn't like the maneuver at all. His gorge promptly rose. A sour taste flooded his mouth. He fought it down, swallowed hard, then rang the stewardess for water and chugged the entire cup along with the Dramamine.

Probably he should've tried to nap, but the view (aided by the binoculars he'd retrieved along with the pharmaceuticals) was irresistible. The city had reappeared: a neat gridwork of well-planned avenues bracketing beautiful buildings with plenty of green space between. Just now, he had an excellent line on St. Tekawitha's: determinedly traditional Gothic in its form and proportions, though wrought of modern materials, a tad less ornamented, and with stubbier towers than the prototypical medieval norm—though it was still the tallest structure in the city. And even as he watched, those towers rose taller, as a phalanx of lasers secreted behind the limestone ramparts awoke and projected another fifty meters of phantom spires.

Which was odd. According to what he'd read, they only did that during Mass and on high-holy days. This was neither. In fact, as he strained his eyes, he could make out a pair of ghostly flags flying from both towers: those of the Aztlan Free Zone and the Vatican. He wondered why both were at half staff.

And then the plane banked again, the image fragmented in the heat-haze aft of the engine, and he was forced to close his eyes or vomit. When he opened them again, the cathedral was gone.

The landing, if fifty-five minutes later than scheduled, was as painless as the last leg of flight had been nerve-wracking. Indeed, Thalo never felt the usual jolt when the tires touched down. Aztlan International was supposed to have the smoothest runways on earth, paved with a special resilient synthetic Goodyear had patented—and donated, along with twenty years of upkeep.

He believed it. And wished he trusted the company's intentions. Unfortunately, it was a mega, and he knew megas all too well. There was a lot of guilt-money in Aztlan.

His seat had been well back—three rows behind the wings—so he had time to establish his land legs before deplaning. That he had only two small carry-ons helped; the rest, save his backpack and a couple of suitcases below, would be coming later, with his folks and Sara.

And then he was shuffling along the flexible connector twixt plane and terminal, and finally in the terminal itself. Space roared around him, a welcomed balm after the claustrophobic jet. The crowd, as though sharing his relief, dispersed into the carpeted vastness. A low pyramidal dome rose above: white sandcrete beams supporting panels of bronze mirror glass alternating with Hopi solar cells. The walls bore bas-relief Mayan motifs in some gold-toned alloy set into more white sandcrete. An electronic sign over a series of square archways opposite scrolled up directions in nearly two dozen languages, notably Spanish, English, French, Portuguese—and, for courtesy, Kìché, the "official" Mayan tongue.

All of them said "Customs." Smaller letters pointed to individual portals: USA, Mexico, Other North America, South America, and simply "Other."

Thalo chose USA and shuffled—as did the bulk of his fellows—to the nearer of the three arches with that designation. There were, he noted, a great many guards about—he assumed that armed men in identical tan pants and tunics under deep red serapes were guards, anyway. Certainly, they had guns—which surprised him. Aztlan was supposed to be excruciatingly law-abiding, with little crime—or reason for it—fast justice, and what convictees emerged set to work for the public good. Nonsporting guns were illegal save for security personnel. And the Canadian Mounties, who had the police contract for the place, were both efficient and incorruptible. It therefore bugged him that two of them bracketed each exit.

Fortunately, he had nothing to declare, and his bags made it through fine. And then he found himself facing

an elegant young black woman with silver dreadlocks
who perused his passport for a long moment then regarded him skeptically. "I take it that the black hair is
new?" she asked in an equally elegant Jamaican accent.
"And that the handsome copper paint job is neither natural nor a tan?"

Thalo raised startled eyebrows toward the invisible
layers that played across his forehead and tickled his
newly dyed ears and the nape of his matching neck. "Uh
. . . yeah," he grunted irritably.

"Contacts too?"

"Yep."

"How old *is* this picture?"

He shrugged. "Year—and a half. Got it when I went
to Italy after college."

She peered at him sharply. "Did you visit the Vatican?"

"N-no," he stammered back, cursing himself for being
nervous—and impatient—and self-conscious. "I mostly
saw the countryside. I don't like cities."

"Aztlan, as you may have noticed, young sir, *is* a
city."

"It's different," he countered. "Plus . . . sometimes
you can't help it."

She scowled, then inspected his passport again, oblivious to the line forming behind him. "It says here you
are a Native American. You will forgive me if I suggest
that you do not, in any nonsuperficial way, resemble
one."

Not for the first time, did Thalo curse the nordically
fair skin, blonde hair, and green eyes (dyed, dyed, and
contacted, just now) he'd been born with. He was only
an eighth Native, granted—Lakota, to be precise—but
that was enough in Washington's eyes to grant him the
BIA card he sported in lieu of the actual passport Oyate,
the Lakota neo-nation, had refused on more grounds than
nonresidency. It would have been nice if great-grandpa
had passed on more identifiable ethnic genes than a rangy
build, high cheekbones, and average, for a Native, height.

"Well I am," he growled back, as his temper kicked

up several degrees on the simmering scale. "I've got my card—"

"No need," the woman gave back. "We are simply being . . . careful."

Thalo grunted.

"And your reasons for visiting Aztlan?"

"Job," he said tersely. What was the deal with all this grilling anyway? This was, after all, *almost* his native land.

"Where?"

"Cherokee Embassy—that is, Kituwah Embassy, I think they call it here. I've got an internship."

"Is that all?"

Thalo shrugged helplessly. "Well, I suppose I'll do the usual thing: look around a bit, see the country, all that."

"You have a contact person here?"

"Thunderbird O'Connor. He's Cultural Attaché— something like that."

"You do not know?"

"We've never met. I was hired through the Net."

The press of people behind him had grown considerably. There was a bit of grumbling and—alas—a fair bit of giggling as well. *Well, fuck 'em,* Thalo thought. *They'll feel the lasers soon enough.*

The woman frowned, then turned to a small terminal beside her. "You will excuse me while I confirm your employment."

"Do I have a choice?"

The frown deepened as the woman punched more buttons, visited him with another long searching stare, then sighed. "You have arranged lodging for four. There is only one of you."

"My folks and sister are coming down next week. She's—my sister's—retarded. There's a clinic here doing work on her condition."

"The Aytchaycee Center?"

"Excuse me?"

"Aytchaycee: Aytch-Ay-Cee, for the founders: Heaton, Arnold and Caldwell."

"Oh, right. So you know it?"

"My brother went there," the woman murmured, for the first time showing cracks in her officious facade.

"It help?" Thalo couldn't resist asking.

"Did no harm."

He shifted his weight. "Is that all? I mean . . . is this normal, or do you"—anger got the better of him and he vented what had been seething in him for what felt like hours—"do you always treat new arrivals to the Inquisition?"

She eyed him levelly. "We do when the Archbishop of Aztlan has been found dead under suspicious circumstances on the eve of a major address and every second arrival here contains some head of state, high ranking flunky, or self-important diplomat!"

"Ohhhhh," Thalo mouthed silently.

The woman stamped his passport and returned it. "You may go . . . Mister John Gordon."

"Thalo," he corrected automatically, as he pocketed the document and pushed through the chrome metal turnstile.

"Thalo?"

"It's a kind of green."

The woman smiled, all attitude fallen away. "Like the true color of your eyes?"

"Like the party," he corrected again, then retrieved his bags and fled—only to slow abruptly when an even dozen guards swivelled their potent-looking rifles his way. Somehow he contrived a casual pace and tried to look neither sheepish, guilty, nor irate as he pushed through one final turnstile and entered the main concourse. At which point the woman's remark finally registered.

The Archbishop of Aztlan was dead! No, not just the Archbishop of Aztlan, he amended: *Archbishop Blackmer*—Green Francis, the Third World's champion, defender, and friend. His number one hero since his teens, and someone he'd hoped to see—meet, even—while here.

All at once he wanted to hit something—hard. Preferably something complicated, electronic, and expensive.

He settled for the wall beside the nearest relief. A guard glared at him as he raised bleeding knuckles to his lips. It was time, he concluded, suspect stomach notwithstanding, for a beer.

He drank Dos Equis because he wanted to hold off sampling the assorted local brews until he could savor them at a less stressful time. He drank it in a quasi-Cuban bistro called *La Casa de Castro* because (as he discovered too late, which was to say, after ordering) alcohol was forbidden in the concourse proper. He soaked up what he quickly determined was too much booze too early in the day with an iguana po-boy sandwich (now that his blessedly resilient tummy had got its act together), since he'd always wanted to try that dish. And he garnished it with key lime pie and coffee because he liked them.

Unfortunately, none of those things assuaged what was threatening to become a full-blown depression. This was supposed to be *fun*, dammit! He was not supposed to arrive in the world's neatest city to rendezvous with an ecopologist's dream job pukey, pissed off, and robbed of the view, only to find that his hero-of-heroes had flat-lined. Fortunately, the tables at *La Casa* sported those neo-tech keypads that broadcast radio into your watch-chips, which, as it happened, was as much hard-wiring as Thalo had—or desired. The trendy had chips clipped into their optic nerves and God knew what else, all for info-stim.

Which disgusted him. Shoot, he'd have had his watch chip removed had his parents not refused to pay for the operation, which was far more than the implant. And as for getting one of those tattooed body-phone things, no way! Tattoos were fine (he had several himself: Lakota motifs in bands around his wrists and biceps), as was piercing and scarification, because those things had ancient precedents. Chips in the skull and circuitry in throat and ears did not.

But then he found the local Green band and finally got the lowdown on Francis.

Fire: that much was certain. The Archbishop had been praying and his gauze cassock had caught fire from a candle and he'd been unable to extinguish it. Trouble was, he seemed to have made no effort to that end—had apparently neither tried to remove the robe nor roll on the floor. Analysis of the burns during autopsy had indicated that his cuffs had ignited first, and that death had come as much from shock as from smoke inhalation or other lung damage caused by breathing flames. There was even some indication that he had deliberately *held* his hand in the fire, perhaps as part of some meditation rite, several of which he was known to practice; circumstances clearly indicated that *some* ritual had been attempted. Only one thing was clear, L-GRN said: It *had* been an accident, *not*—as CNN had first reported—a suicide. The Vatican had squelched *that* line of speculation in a hurry (no doubt, Thalo thought sourly, to save face—not that he for a moment suspected that his hero would ever do such a thing, no matter what the symbolic value). There *was* talk of assassination, however; when it was pointed out that the Archbishop never locked his palace, that he had any number of enemies both political and corporate, and that it would have been perfectly possible for someone to have crept up behind him and held his hands in the fire until he was satisfactorily ablaze, any bruises accrued thereby being conveniently masked by blisters and charring. Trouble was, there was no sign of a struggle, which surely there would have been. And, more importantly, no sign of anyone entering the palace on the surveillance monitors. Yeah, Thalo (and most of the world press) thought that far too complex a theory, even if the time elapsed between the Archbishop's death and the discover of his body (by his cook) did allow tampering with all manner of recording devices.

The bottom line was that, in the absence of any better explanation, the world was prepared to believe the most upbeat option: Archbishop Francis Blackmer had been victim of a freak accident, nothing more. Besides (as someone in the Parisian press recalled), hadn't Martin Luther himself died on the john?

Thalo punched off the broadcast in disgust, snared the last morsel of lizard from the table where it had fallen, and rose. He still had a few days' grace before he had to report to his new job. And though he'd planned to use that time seeing the sights (mostly museums, the zoo, the aquarium, and the botanical gardens), now the mere idea of hanging around the city—*this* city, where his hero had died—appalled him. Half an hour into his visit, and already he was fed up: with snotty officials, with supercilious security guards, with impatient and rude fellow travelers, and with the oppressive omnipresence of tech, when Aztlan was supposed to be human-friendly.

Impulse said to ditch it all and go back home. Logic said that was stupid and unworkable. Regardless of his own plans, there was still the matter of his sister, who really *did* need the treatment the—what was it? Aytchaycee?—Center might provide.

Besides, he'd had these moods before, knew roughly how long they lasted, and how to effect the cure.

Forget the Museum of the Americas, the Zoo, the Western Gallery of Art, and St. Tekawitha's (forget that last especially); he'd retrieve his camping gear, store the rest, and take a taxi (better yet AFZoRTA, the rapid transit system—or a rent-a-bike—or best of all, simply his thumb) right on out of town and go online with some serious Greenery.

He was already striding toward Baggage Claim when he saw the girl.

He wasn't sure if she was actually pretty or merely enticingly exotic. Short, round-face, black hair and eyes, dark skin: those were the basics. Local Indian, probably. But her forehead and cheeks were patterned with subtle, featherlike tattoos in something on the gold end of the metallic spectrum, the color but half a tone off that of her skin, so that the effect was rather like damask. Plain, beige jeans and tunic accented it with their austerity, except that the color of the ink was picked up again in a chain-mail sash and, in brighter mode, in an ornamental net woven into her hair. She was also barefoot, and seemed to be determinedly involved in handing out sticks

of incense and some sort of fliers. And normally all that would have attracted him—but he'd already had enough interpersonal interaction for one day, with more to come. Thus, he casually veered away when she pointedly angled toward him.

Her smile—a very pretty and unaffected one— promptly wilted, and her eyes went dull and sad.

Already feeling terrible, guilt got the better of him, and he accepted both stick and sheet with a muttered, "Thanks . . . sorry, but I'm in a bad mood . . . not your fault." The paper, he noted automatically, was marked as recycled. The incense looked expensive.

"Lots of folks are," the girl replied, in very good English. "Bummed, I mean. About Green Francis."

He perked up at that particular appellation, since its use practically guaranteed that whoever uttered it was either a violent opponent of the late Archbishop using the sobriquet derisively, or else one of the Faithful. The girl's looks, dress, and flyer strongly suggested the latter.

"I sure am," he admitted finally—shyly; he'd always had trouble talking to girls, especially perky, open-faced ones.

"So come to the rally, then—the one on the flyer."

Thalo stared dumbly at the sheet in his hand. Sure enough, it announced a memorial gathering to be held in Blackmer's honor at the famous Lady Xoc Park. The sponsoring agency was a Green group called Outer Earth, of which he'd heard many good things, and which he'd been intending to investigate more thoroughly when he got time—until he'd heard it had dissolved. Obviously it was back together again.

And then he caught the name of one of the featured speakers-cum-performers and his excitement level maxed to overload. "Jesus Christ," he gasped. "They're having the fucking *Hero Twins*!"

The girl nodded solemnly. "They sponsor Outer Earth—help sponsor, anyway."

"Oh jeeze," Thalo breathed again. "Oh jeeze!"

"So you'll come?"

He swallowed hard. On one level he badly wanted to:

it sounded interesting—and, more to the point, like somewhere he could meet like-minded folk. And it would certainly connect with his need to mourn. The Hero Twins were a *great* band too; God knew their odd blend of classic European music, traditional Kîché rhythms (they claimed to be full-blooded Maya), and old-fashioned high-energy rock 'n' roll, with a blatantly pro-environment message thrown in, was irresistible. On the other hand, he'd just exchanged one city for another and hated to limit his time in the Mexican wild. Plus (and here he confronted a conflict of priorities that had confounded him since he'd gone Green three years back), however good the Twins were, they played loud electric music—which was a waste of resources. Which wasn't Green.

''See you there?'' the girl prompted hopefully, at which point he realized he was gaping at the flyer as though he couldn't read. He blinked up at her, but she was already moving toward another mark.

''Maybe,'' he called back. But she was thoroughly involved with the serious-faced Oriental girl who'd sat three rows up and two over on the plane.

The irate *blatt* of a horn at close range startled him, and he jumped sideways to avoid an electric cart transporting a phalanx of old folks to some probably expensive destination. The maneuver cost him his balance, which he corrected by grasping at the first thing he came in contact with, which proved to be the moveable rail beside a slidewalk. It immediately protested the impediment with a loud, ''Please do not interfere with this railing, it is not a toy,'' followed by the same in Spanish.

That convinced him. He growled at the officious machine, resettled his bags, and strode off in search of his backpack, a store room, and the straightest route out of town. Half an hour later, he had changed into hiking togs, stuffed his faithful Mountainsmith with camping gear, and had a line on the cheapest place to buy trail food. Five minutes after that, he was marching through the vast parking lot of Aztlan International heading west—toward the border.

Chapter III:
Sage Advice

The raccoon tore the larger front claw from the lobster-sized crawfish on which it had, for some time, been dining and looked up at the slender young *Ani-Yunwiya* man squatting sky-clad and impatient across the meter-wide stream before it. Without shifting its gaze, it dabbled the still-twitching limb in the water, then poked a dainty handlike paw deftly within the raw ends of the joint to draw out a shred of white meat filigreed with red. This too it washed and ate silently.

The young man sighed.

The raccoon's mask wrinkled in something very like a frown. It flung the empty claw down in disgust.

"You should know by now—*human*," it hissed, "that there is no need for hurry here. You have all the time you need for anything worth doing. And since the only thing you can possibly do here is learn, you have a great deal of time indeed."

'Bird—whose physical body slumped inside a sweat lodge in a certain obscure valley a few hours west of Aztlan—didn't reply, though he straightened and tried to look more attentive, just cognizant enough of the fact that neither this interview nor the primeval forest glade in which it transpired was conventional reality to wonder if an incorporeal projection of himself could blush, as seemed, by the heat rising up his cheeks, to be occurring.

"Red becomes crawfish more than men," the rac-

coon—the Ancient of Raccoons, more properly, whom 'Bird had met thusly once before—continued. "But since your impatient exhalations have spoiled my meal, we might as well get on with that for which I summoned you."

"But I thought *I* came here," 'Bird blurted, unable to lie in this place where dreams were the surface world.

"*You* decided you needed to go *somewhere*," the Raccoon growled. "But *I* heard you wandering among the *nowheres* and called you here."

"Where I have learned nothing," 'Bird grumbled, "except how you eat crawfish."

The raccoon's whiskers twitched. "You did not observe how I, whom you might well consider a god, yet remain true to my essential nature in spite of that fact? That though I speak, I am obviously a beast? I go bare, I hunt, I eat what I am designed to eat. Whatever I am *besides* a raccoon, I am *also* a raccoon."

"Which means, in effect, that you think I haven't been true to myself?"

"Which means, in *fact*, that *you* think you have not been true to yourself. Have you not spent most of your life denying many important things about yourself?"

"Like these dreams?"

"Do other men have them?"

A shrug. "I don't know. Most either don't, don't recognize them for what they are, or . . . deny them." He admitted that last reluctantly and his cheeks warmed again.

"Do not deny them!" the Raccoon spat. "That is your first lesson."

"But I thought they were sendings from . . . dolphins."

"And the vision you had as a child of Aztlan as a finished city, when it was not even begun? Was that also sent by dolphins? They did not know you then, young Thunderbird. You were too far inland for them to sense, much less ride."

"I . . . hadn't thought of that," 'Bird conceded. Nor had he, mostly because he'd spent the few days since

that last sudden glut of medicine dreams slipping back into his habit of explaining them in terms of mundane reality. Dolphins—*sentient telepathic* dolphins, granted, but dolphins all the same—projecting them into his mind while in a receptive state seemed marginally viable; they'd even admitted as much.

The Raccoon clearly had more esoteric notions. It patted the litter of crawfish shell strewn across the sand. "And what do you learn from this?"

'Bird started to shake his head, then paused. They were dealing with symbols here. So what could a half-eaten crustacean signify? "It's hard on the outside and soft within?" he ventured at last.

The Raccoon nodded. "But what does *that* mean?"

'Bird scowled. "That I—or maybe someone with influence over me, someone with watery connections, say—like Carolyn—is hard on the outside and soft once you get past the shell?"

"Which? Or both?"

Another scowl. "Well . . . I like to think I don't have a shell. But maybe it's another reference to what we were talkin' about, like . . . the shell of my own disbelief—in magic, I guess—that makes it hard to access the actual me."

"And?"

'Bird shifted. His thighs were getting sore. Probably his physical thighs were too; he hadn't danced in nearly a week. "Well, if it also applies to Cary, then it could mean the same thing for both of us, seein' how she doesn't want to believe in magic either. But she seems like a . . . a harder person than I am, so maybe it's a hint that she *is* soft on the inside and I need to keep that in mind."

"Very good. But what about the most obvious thing? What about the fact that the crawfish is being eaten?"

"Well, it's kinda what they're designed for, isn't it?"

The raccoon splashed water in his face. "It is not! They are designed, as is obvious, *not* to be eaten—not by the primary predators in their own world. They are difficult to find, dangerous to catch, and not the easiest

of meals to digest unless you shuck them first.''

'Bird's face broke into a smile of realization. "Ah, but you're not of their world, so they don't anticipate you and can't really defend against you.''

"So you have a brain after all!''

The smile widened into a grin.

"And what does this mean?''

The grin vanished. "I guess it means that everyone . . . oughta remember that no matter how good you think your defenses are, there're always predators from . . . other realities; that can swoop on you and . . . have you for lunch!''

"And were you not nearly skinned alive by what you could term predators from another reality?''

"Yeah,'' 'Bird acknowledged. His body—his *real* body—still bore a puckering scab in the hollow of the right clavicle where the silver tattoo of his body phone had been reamed out with the tip of an obsidian knife, not to mention a line composed by turns of scab, scar tissue, and stitchery from the top of his sternum to his navel, courtesy of a pair of what he and Stormy had taken to calling *werkas* in lieu of the more accurate but cumbersome were-orcas or shape-shifting killer whales. It was only his great good luck—if it *was* luck, given what he'd learned lately—that his own handsome Cherokee hide hadn't joined a dozen nameless others in a suit of human skin that, when properly prepared and donned, allowed certain fanatical members of the orca lunatic fringe to assume human shape and walk on land as men.

"So what you're sayin','' 'Bird mused at last, "is that no matter how well armored you think you are, there'll always be another . . . raccoon?''

The Raccoon regarded him seriously for a long moment, then returned to its meal. "It would seem,'' it said between bites, "that you have learned something after all.'' And with that, it suddenly batted at something invisible (to 'Bird) in the water.

Spray splashed up, then rose higher, briefly blinding him. When he wiped his eyes clear again, it was to gaze not upon the intimate primeval glade in which the audi-

ence had occurred, but at a tiny crack of true daylight
beyond the now-cold rocks of a stone pit: there between
the blanket-cum-door and the wattle-and-daub wall of
John Lox's sweat lodge. And instead of the crunchings
of crawdad shells, came the last fading beats of steady
hypnotic drumming, and words sung softly in Navajo.

"Thunderbird O'Connor," a voice called: old, but
strong and sure and vigorous. "Thunderbird O'Connor,
born to the Western Woman, born for the Wolf Clan,
come out and greet the day."

'Bird did, slowly, stiffly (he had, after all, been sitting
in the same position for an entire day and night). His
back popped as he pushed aside the blanket and rose to
his full lanky height. Muscles tensed and stretched along
the long arms and legs and hard, spare torso of a dancer.
His eyes teared at the light, though the sun hid all but its
forehead behind the high stone cliffs toward which the
structure faced. It was soft dawn here in Lox's valley,
but the cliffs behind him already blazed red and gold and
mauve. And it was still cool in the half-shadows, with
the barest trace of mist rising from the thread of stream
thirty meters to the north. Goats bleated. Wind soughed
through willow withes along the shore.

His stomach growled.

A drumbeat punctuated it. Silence for a moment.
Somebody snickered.

'Bird finally managed to stop rubbing his eyes long
enough to make out two shapes standing before him. The
left-hand one, which had laughed, was the closest thing
he had to a brother. They even looked alike—superficially. Certainly they were within fractioned sims of a
height, within grams of identical weight. Both sported
thick black hair to their shoulders, rangy builds, dark
eyes, and bronze skin. But where 'Bird was mostly Cherokee—*Ani-Yunwiya*, more properly; or *Kituwah*, to use
the old ceremonial name—and Cultural Attaché to the
Kituwah Embassy in Aztlan; Stormcloud Nez, his quasi-
doppelganger, was Dineh-ne-Navajo mixed with Makah;
mostly, by exposure, the former. He was also Assistant
Deputy Chief of Security at the Dineh Embassy three

blocks down Sequoya from the Native Southeastern Confederacy Compound of which Kituwah was part.

The other figure was shorter, heavier, and enough older to show more grey hair than black, though his face was surprisingly smooth, and his movements sure and agile. His name was John Lox—*Hosteen* John Lox, to include the honorific to which he was entitled. He was Dineh, a hand-trembler, and, at the moment, a *hataalii*: a Singer, or medicine man, for lack of a better term. But where Stormy had greeted 'Bird with laughter that spoke of two years' camaraderie; Lox greeted him with something far more immediately relevant: a cup of hot, sweet coffee.

'Bird took the battered enamel mug gratefully and paused to savor the aroma, which hinted at a more exotic blend than basic Maxwell House—which it surely was, coffee being Lox's preferred compensation for his services.

The old man eyed him narrowly as he drank. 'Bird scalded his tongue and winced. The cool morning air brushed him. His saturated, superheated skin steamed.

"You doin' that to impress us?" Stormy chuckled. "Or is it just native skill?"

'Bird glanced down at his sweat-sheened arms. "I had another one."

Lox's face went hard and intense. "I'm not surprised."

'Bird slumped down on a log and stretched his legs before him, careful not to disturb Lox's nearest sand-painting. "Does that always happen during Ways?"

Lox joined him. "Let's just say that it *can* happen. Any time you're in an altered state of consciousness you're receptive. And if there's anything out there wanting to be received . . . or if you are wanting anything sufficiently hard . . . sometimes things happen."

Stormy poured himself a cup from the battered pot by the fire and slumped down on 'Bird's other side. "Wanta tell us about it?"

'Bird frowned. "Hell, man, *I'm* still tryin' to figure it out! I mean, I don't mind tellin' you, but . . . well, this

just doesn't seem like the right time, what with you gettin' ready to start your own Way.''

Stormy looked crestfallen, but shrugged. ''No big
deal.''

'Bird flopped an arm across his shoulders. ''There was
a raccoon—*that* Raccoon; I'll tell you that much. And
there was a . . . warning—basically that there's always
more than one predator.''

Stormy grunted. ''Which means we aren't done with
our finny friends.''

'Bird vented an exasperated sigh. ''Who knows?''
Then, to Lox: ''Any ideas?''

''Always,'' Lox replied promptly. ''But not when we
are about to purify young Stormcloud here.''

Stormy stared at the cup in his hands. ''Think it'll
work?''

Lox's face was neutral. ''Ask your buddy.''

'Bird started. ''I . . . don't know. I honestly do not
know! I mean, something obviously happened—the medicine dream and all. And I certainly feel lighter and more
centered and more . . . pure. But I *always* feel like that
after a sweat. As for the earlier rituals''—he recalled
most of a week spent in a larger structure listening to
Hosteen Lox sing and pray and chant as he carefully
drew sand paintings on the floor—''Well, I've never
even *been* to a Way, much less been the recipient of
one—I guess this counts double for the one we talked
about last week and never got around to. Which basically
means that I couldn't turn off my anthropologist part. I
mean, I was genuinely interested and sincere and all—
but maybe in the wrong things.''

''You also had a vision.''

''Is that a problem?''

Lox shrugged ''It should make no difference. All that
matters is that the *chindi* ignore you.''

''That's the idea, don't forget,'' Stormy added. ''Or,
as a friend of mine once put it, 'To invoke the templates
of creation by re-enacting the relevant aspect, thus mending the flaws in it.' Which in the real world means getting
you back on an even psycho-spiritual keel so you don't

get sick—pardon the New Age mumbo-jumbo.''

"Trouble is,'' 'Bird countered, ''I'm not sure it matters. I'm not sure there *is* anything after death, and even if there is, that only the hateful parts of the dead survive and make folks sick. At least I'm not sure at my center. I guess this is kind of an aftershock of my meeting with Mr. 'Coon: this brutal honesty. I'm afraid I may have wasted your time, Hosteen Lox.''

Stormy snorted derisively. ''Well at least *I'm* satisfied. I've done what I could to keep my best buddy safe. Now I only have to deal with whatever weirdnesses have designs on me!''

"And another Way,'' 'Bird reminded him.

"Another Way,'' Lox echoed. ''You are certain you still want this?''

Stormy nodded. ''If I'm to be true to myself, my people, and my heritage, I don't have any choice. A man comes close to death—violent death, like I did—you do a Way so you don't get sick. That's a fact, and a good Dineh doesn't argue with it. Doesn't matter if the dead weren't human. Shoot, what makes someone human anyway? Is it the form—two arms, two legs, head on top, no tail, stereo vision, sparse body hair? Or is it something deeper? Speech, abstract ideas, history, love, hate, sacrifice, creativity? If it's that, anything sapient could qualify that embraces, or tries to embrace, all those things. The point is, me having been around not just dead people, but dead selkies, dead dolphins, and dead . . . orcas, and having killed—murdered, or whatever—a couple of the latter myself, puts me in very deep shit indeed. I mean, some of those guys had no love for me to start with— the orca-guys, for instance. And they certainly wouldn't have good intentions toward me if enough of their *self* survived to haunt me. They hated *people*, first off—that whole weather war deal last weekend was a response to us polluting the seas—and they have to have hated me and 'Bird and Cary on top of that, since we stopped 'em.''

Lox grunted irritably. ''Sounds like you're trying to convince yourself of what you already believe. The bot-

tom line, as I've told you, is to play it safe. You do a Way, you can't go wrong. One, you're doin' what you oughta do, and that can only help down in your deep part. Two, whether or not there are *chindi*, you're covering your ass. Three, it's what I think you oughta do, and regardless of whether I'm a man of power or just some crazy old Navajo, I have to think that any kind of belief is stronger than none. Therefore, if *I* believe it'll help, and *you* believe it'll help—or want it to, which is basically the same—then it can't do any harm.''

"Yeah," Stormy muttered. "Right."

'Bird smirked grimly.

"What's funny?"

"You. You were so hot to get me over here after I found that skinned guy last week. And now—"

"A lot's happened in a week."

"I know. But I grew up with a different set of givens; I'm not *supposed* to believe. This is *your* world, man. 'Sides, fooling with . . . with unseen powers is new to me. You've always been more open."

"And," Lox inserted finally, "we can sit here yakking the rest of the day, or we can start living it." He slapped 'Bird's naked thigh. " 'Bird, my lad, technically you're not done yet. You still need to wash off the sweat, since it came out of you and therefore contains a lot of you, and if you get rid of it, it'll help confuse the *chindi*. And since young Nez here needs to be clean to start with, I'd suggest you boys grab a dip while I rustle up 'Bird some chow—sorry Stormy, but you and me still gotta fast."

Stormy's stomach rumbled obligingly. "Tell me about it!"

Lox's eyes twinkled. "No need."

"Wish I could stay," 'Bird told Stormy nearly an hour later, as he gave his chest a final swipe with the clean but ragged towel Lox had provided and tugged a sand-colored tunic over his head. The stream glittered behind him. Green strands of willow limned patterns of dark and light across the bare stones further back. A goat drank upstream, beyond the pool.

Stormy wrapped a towel around his waist and sank down on a convenient boulder. "It'd be nice," he conceded, "but there's nothing you can do. And since this one'll take longer than yours, and I know you need to get back . . ."

"I don't *have* to."

Stormy cocked a brow. "No, but every time I look at you, you're beating an imaginary drum and half-assed dancing."

'Bird looked startled. "I am?"

"I didn't say what you had to get back for, did I?"

"My real job's not that bad."

"But it's not what you live for, anymore than totin' a gun around Dineh-Land's what *I* do."

"Bein' a grown-up's a bitch, ain't it?"

"Hell if I know. Never been one!"

"Sure you don't want me to hang around?"

"What would you do besides keep the fire hot and fidget? Lox won't have time to talk to you, and I won't be available."

"Maybe the *chindi* . . . ?"

Stormy's eyes went cold. "Don't even *think* it!" And with that, he collected his clothes, rose gracefully, and fell into step beside 'Bird as they trekked the short distance back to Lox's hogan, two dozen paces west of the sweat lodge. Lox met them there with a bag of ham biscuits for 'Bird. Stormy fished through the pile of clothing, finally locating his jeans. More fumbling in pockets produced a small plastic card. "Take care of my baby," he sniffed, as he passed it over. "Don't drive 'er above, say, eighty-five."

'Bird took it with a wicked grin. "Kliks, or MPH?"

"Either."

Lox cleared his throat and glanced meaningfully at the sky, as though seeking confirmation that it was time for Stormy's Way to begin.

'Bird reached over to give his friend a hearty hug. "Take care of yourself, man. And if a 'Coon shows up, kick his fuzzy butt and tell 'im we're *both* higher up the

food chain than he is, and that I've got a recipe for raccoon chili I'm just aching to try out.''

Stormy rolled his eyes. "I'll let *you* tell him!"

'Bird simply grinned again and searched his pack for the obligatory gift for the *hataalii*: a hand-sized wooden clan mask in the style of the last-century master, Davy Arch. Lox nodded his appreciation, and, per Navajo form, 'Bird left without formal goodbyes.

Half an hour later, with a klom of winding, rocky trail in his wake,'Bird reached the crest of the ridge that overlooked Lox's valley. He didn't bother to check back; better to forget that world for a while: hogans and sweat lodges and subsistence farming and goat pens. Ahead— a smudgy gleam on the horizon beyond the Sierras—lay the real world, *his* world, like it or not: Aztlan, the Queen City of Tech. "Tech," 'Bird grumbled in disgust, as he sidestepped a skittering scorpion on his way to the gold-toned clump of oversized-soapbubbles-on-wheels that was Stormy's new Jeep Juneau. "Can't live with it, can't live without it."

The card started the Jeep promptly, with a near-inaudible whir of alloy pistons and cams. A verbal reminder followed—in Stormy's synthesized drawl—that one of the glassy doors was ajar. 'Bird grimaced and reshut it, reached up to pop the roof hatch, and was on his way, big tires crunching softly across the rocky road, all but the worst jolts filtered out by sophisticated air/oil springs.

He relaxed into the well-bolstered bucket. The return to Aztlan would take a couple of hours, but there was no need to hurry; he wasn't due back at work until the morning. Shoot, he might even dance tonight if they hadn't found someone to fill in at the 'Wheel. "Radio. On," he called, as an afterthought.

"*. . . the funeral will be held at St. Tekawitha's,*" a smooth-voiced announcer was saying, with the merest trace of Latino accent. "*Pope Michael is expected to officiate, though there is still no confirmation from the Vatican.*"

'Bird froze abruptly. *Something* important had obvi-

ously happened while he'd been incommunicado in Lox's ruthlessly tech-free valley. More specifically, someone important had evidently died. Someone with sufficient clout that the Pope himself was coming to town to officiate at the funeral.

Which could only be—another chill wracked him—one man.

"Louder," he told the volume. Then: "Search."

Two stations later, his suspicions were confirmed: Archbishop Francis Blackmer was dead. There would be a state funeral. Everybody who was anybody was expected to attend.

'Bird groaned—and drove faster. Unfortunately, though not quite "somebody" himself, he did work closely with "somebody"; specifically, the Honorable Ambassador-Chief William Red Wounds—who was at present, and very inconveniently, AWOL in the backwoods of Eireland trying to make sense of the selkie situation.

Which meant that Deputy Ambassador Mankiller was, for the nonce, in charge of whatever ceremonial response Kituwah would make. And since ceremonies fell under culture, and he was Cultural Attaché . . . well, he was suddenly looking at a busy couple of days.

Reflexively, he reached for the phone to check in, then changed his mind and told it, "Off. No messages." The last thing he needed right now was orders he couldn't respond to—which the Embassy was bound to have stacked up and waiting.

Better he should plan in peace—and for that, music would be ideal.

Perhaps Stormy's new Hero Twins CD.

Chapter IV:
Imram

*(Killary Harbour—County Galway—
United Eireland)
(Thursday, September 8—mid morning)*

There was far less wind at the base of the cliffs west of Leenane than at their summits, and a marginally less fitful drizzle, though the spray splattering the rocks on the thread of rocky beach mostly compensated for the latter. Still, Carolyn couldn't suppress a chill at what she was about.

Shape-shifting, some called it—*skinchanging. Lycanthropy.* It all boiled down to one thing. You performed certain overtly absurd acts, and equally unlikely effects resulted. Trouble was, it ran counter to every law of both physics and biology she'd ever studied. Physics said production of mass required energy, and destruction of mass released it. So where did the energy go when a 170 kilo seal became a human half that size? How did chromosomes designed to produce *Homo sapiens* likewise accommodate the outward form (at least) of *Halichoerus grypus*? Tests might show—or might not. Anything conclusive would require multiple samples from someone fully human, someone half selkie like herself, and someone selkie born.

Her scientist aspect was intrigued as hell. But did she truly want to know? She loathed being poked and prodded, as had happened a week ago, at the dawn of the . . . *change*. Did she want to perpetrate—or perpetuate—such

activities? Science might give answers, but wasn't mystery better? Weren't dragons more fun before they were dinosaur bones and overgrown monitor lizards? Unicorns misrepresented rhinos? Mermaids dugongs? Sasquatches alien spies instead of surviving gigantopithicines?

And then she stubbed a very physical toe on an equally tangible rock, and pain replaced philosophy. By the time Kevin had steadied her from behind, and she had steadied herself against the naked boy's sleek warm (a tad *too* warm) shoulders, the time for speculation (it wasn't like she hadn't rehearsed this a thousand times anyway) was past.

Connor had led them considerably west of the spot where Kevin had witnessed the death of the selkie messenger he'd only known as Fir: he who, fearing he wouldn't otherwise be believed, had lured Kev to Leenane, revealed his true nature—and been murdered before he could do more than utter the cryptic phrase, "You are the Word, she is the Way, I don't know who is the Singer." They'd solved that riddle now—Kev, herself, and 'Bird O'Connor, respectively—but in exchange, had acquired more questions than anyone could process in a lifetime.

The cliffs were barely head-high here, merging into the rolling hills and hollows more typical near Leenane. The wind was fiercer. Carolyn shuddered. Kevin was panting a lot, while both Ambassadors maintained a carefully tactful silence. Connor was like a schoolboy on holiday—until he crouched abruptly at the base of the cliff, pushed a driftwood stump the size of his torso neatly aside, and reached into the crevice thus exposed. An instant later he withdrew two damp-looking masses of gray-white-pink, stood, and solemnly presented one sodden pile to Carolyn. She accepted it without flinching (though the idea of handling freshly flayed skins still gave her pause—because she knew how some of those skins were acquired). Connor studied her seriously for a moment, then lifted an inquiring brow.

Carolyn puffed her cheeks. "I've never done this with

. . . sealskin,'' she confessed. "Only dolphin. Is there any difference?"

The selkie shrugged. "I have only worn this kind of skin. It is the only kind we ought to wear. You are different. The same, yet different.''

Carolyn spared a glance at her three full-human compatriots, and it occurred to her that though all five of them passed as the same species, fundamental differences separated them at the deep-structural level. Or maybe even at some level below that, that bubbled up from the implicate order and wrought essential alterations though no mechanism could be observed; the same way one subatomic particle could be at two places simultaneously, or—apparently—one set of genes produce creatures with utterly dissimilar forms.

Connor coughed beside her. He looked impatient. "You think too much," he murmured. "The air *is*; it does not need a 'why' or 'how.' So for the sea. For your kind and mine.''

"It's my job to ask 'why' and 'how,'" Carolyn sighed, as she shook out the skin to its full dimension, noting by the nipples that it was that of a female. "If your kind seeks commerce with mine, you'll have to get used to questions. They're like breathing.''

"You do not all think that way," the selkie countered.

Another, resigned, sigh, and Carolyn spread her skin across a large flat rock, unzipped her windbreaker and threw back the hood, then sat down to attack her boot laces.

"A gentleman would not observe this," O'Neal informed Red Wounds. "And last time I looked, being gentlemen was a big part of our job descriptions.''

"I'd as soon you didn't," Carolyn agreed over her shoulder as she turned away. "Trouble is, it'd be hard for any reasonably curious person to resist.''

"You can watch me," Connor volunteered, striding past her, to halt somewhere behind. The men followed obligingly. Carolyn quickly stripped, leaving her clothes in a neat pile she consigned to Kevin on peril of his life.

And then it was time. Steeling herself for yet another

variation on what was still a mostly unfamiliar drill, she retrieved the skin, flung it capelike across her shoulders, took one final deep breath, called, "Here goes, guys"— and stuck both arms into the gaping, bloody pockets that had once housed a seal's front flippers.

Warmth met her, and a tingle like the buzz of an electric razor; and with them came an impression of tiny sparks arcing between her skin and the seal's. And then those minute bolts seemed to solidify into millions of minuscule threads, each with a hook on the end which pricked her. She swallowed hard, for that tingle was seeping through her skin to assail her muscles and bones with an unpleasant squirming sensation not unlike the muscular equivalent of nausea. Suddenly those threads contracted, drawing her newly fluid flesh away from its proper form and molding it to another. She was cold as hell, and it came to her first that she hadn't felt cold either time she'd shifted to dolphin shape because she'd always been immersed in warm Caribbean water; and then that it was probably due to the reaction itself drawing energy from her skin to seal that alien bond.

At which point a wash of heat flowed up through what had been her hands and arms into her shoulders, from which poured down her back and gushed up into the dome of her skull. More prickling followed, then a sharper heat and another round of that screwy muscle nausea—and she could no longer stand upright. Her vision had gone weird (skewed from red toward blue), and she could smell all manner of unlikely things, notably an ozone-stench something told her was the scent of the *change*.

All at once she fell to all fours. What began as a sigh of relief emerged as a bark—which surprised her. Another bark replied, replete with subtle undertones she couldn't—quite—understand. She blinked and twisted around, to see her companions barely more composed than at Connor's initial shift. Kevin was first to recover and bent down to pat her on the head—which prompted an odd mix of emotions indeed. "Not bad," he observed. Then: "Okay, lads, it's cool." Another head slid into

view: grey and pointed. It nuzzled her in a way that wouldn't have been proper had they both been human, and a grunt carried with it a thought: *Well done, but hurry. There is little time.*

And with that, Carolyn Mauney-Griffith, who now wore the shape of a female grey seal, licked her brother's trembling hand, turned awkwardly on unruly flippers, and followed another seal, whose name was Connor, across two meters of rounded stones; twice that again of mist, spray, and foam; and into the cold waters of Killary Harbour, whence they turned west toward the open sea.

Carolyn had no idea how much time elapsed between the hour she entered the harbor and that when Connor confirmed by a mixture of barks and thoughts that they were now in the North Atlantic.

It wasn't as though she didn't have about a million things to puzzle at already. Like how she somehow *knew* that the bottom was dropping away and the shore no longer rolled along to either side. Possibly that was due to some subtle shift in density, clarity, or speed and temperature of the currents, or to all of those things combined—but how could she really tell? And while she'd hoped to make a visual survey of the shoreline whenever she surfaced for air, then check the time by the sun, and thereby arrive at an approximation of where their nebulous destination lay, that plan had long since gone awry—because of another perplexity.

Connor's thoughts. Specifically, selkies' particular brand of telepathy. Selkies *were* telepathic: Kev had told her as much. And though they could obviously speak when in human shape, she'd sensed from what brief converse she'd held with Connor that it was not their preferred form of dialogue. Obviously a sentient race that spent much of its time underwater would need an alternate to verbal discourse, and telepathy was a reasonable choice. On the other hand, verbal speech was one of the things that separated the merely humanlike—such as chimps and yetis—from the fully human. Well, except that dolphins were obviously intelligent too—possibly

more so than men, or at least more mentally accomplished—yet they favored telepathic converse almost exclusively. Sound for them was roughly equivalent to human gesturing; true depth lay in their thoughts, which were a tapestry of shadings, nuance, and image sequences so vast and complicated that swimming with them was like immersing oneself in a thick stew of information in which one could lose all sense of physical surroundings in the limitless landscapes of the mind. Life at sea provoked a sort of sensory deprivation, she decided. And dolphins compensated with a constant stream of complex babble.

Selkie thoughts were simple and direct. There were shadings of emotions, true, but none of the intricacies that made swimming with a pod of dolphins such a marvel.

On the other hand, she'd always felt out of place among cetaceans: the stranger in the strange land—the odd being out. A child trying to understand Dostoyevsky or Tolstoy or Greenstein or Wu. Welcoming, the dolphins back at PEORCI might've been, but their warmth carried an implicit *noblesse oblige*: the hospitality of aristocrats to poor strangers come despondent to their door. Swimming with the selkie was like hanging out with home folks—and that from mere snatches of contact.

I would speak more, came Connor's thoughts when they surfaced out of sight of land, with only choppy waves, dull sky, and persistent mist to mark the upper sky from the lower, *were your thoughts not dancing so wildly there is no place for mine to lodge.*

Sorry, Carolyn told him, punctuating her remark with a yip that somehow seemed appropriate. *It is hard to get used to—for me. You were born to it.*

Yet I had to learn.

Somehow I thought we would speak more. That you would ask questions—

Why me and not you? You are the new thing here.

I—Carolyn paused. *You are right. But there was so much to notice, and I was trying to observe it all, and understand, and be sure I did not forget—*

You think too much, came Connor's thought again—
with a mental chuckle.

And you do not? Carolyn gave back. *I think all the
time . . . Is it possible you do not?*

*It is not wise to become so absorbed in oneself one
forgets to keep watch. Eat or be eaten: that is the most
ancient rule. You, who dwell on land, no longer need
fear that. Death finds you by chance; it does not seek
you out. It is different with us—in this shape, it is different. Dolphins may discuss philosophy while they swim,
for their minds are more . . . dense than ours. We do
not—when puzzling out the "why" of our existence can
cost us that existence. It is not all worry, though; as you
will see if you follow me!*

Follow the leader?

Or tag.

You know that game?

The selkie nipped her—and dived. *You're it!*

Whereupon Carolyn forgot about time and distance—
and even danger, save when Connor warned of the presence of sharks and krakens and other predators—and
gave herself over to testing the limits of this marvelous
new body and exploring this fine new world (which was
as different now, experienced in seal shape, as was dolphin perception of it from human) with a companion with
whom it was remarkable fun simply to *play*.

The upshot of which was that she knew only that it
was daytime and that she was marginally tired when Connor led her to the surface, told her to take the deepest
breath she could imagine, then another deeper still;
waited until she had acquiesced—and dived.

Pale water became dim water became black. Cool became cold became frigid, then stabilized. Pressure rose
in her lungs and would have become unbearable, had not
new instincts asserted themselves. Her heartbeat slowed.
Her limbs felt distant—doubtless a function of more
blood being shunted to her heart and brain. It was best
to be mostly seal now; best to keep a thread of consciousness fixed on Connor and move with him, that tenuous contact all that kept her human half . . . awake.

And still they dived, at an angle, until they reached a layer of muddy ooze.

How—? she began, when the eerie cold silence became too great.

Silence! It is easy to miss, even if one knows the way, and I have not been this way often.

And longer yet they swam.

Ah! There it is! came Connor's thoughts at last. He sounded vastly relieved.

Carolyn's nose thumped into his back above his flukes, where he had halted; yet even knowing he was there, she could make out nothing. No wait! A blacker blackness showed there, and if she strained, she could barely discern a rough circle of luminescence at an angle to the sea floor just beyond. The blackness—Connor—was moving too; and she had no choice but to follow, noting an upward slant in the bottom, as though they approached a hill.

A hill indeed—once, the selkie agreed. *On land—when the waters were lower.*

So we're still on the continental shelf?

A thoughtful pause. *I think that is what your kind call it. We call it the Lesser Deep. We do not often fare into the Greater—nor can we, at its deepest.*

And then the selkie swam more swiftly. She followed, saw the dimly glowing ring grow closer, then rise around her as she passed through. It was like runway lights: a ring of luminescent sea life defining an opening. Clever. And of course she found herself wondering what *sort* of sea life. Most of the bioluminescent species she knew moved. These did not.

Sponges, Connor supplied spontaneously. *They are . . . transparent. They capture—what do you call them? Plankton? that glow, and from them construct their own light. They are extinct now, save where we live.* He swam faster and with more confidence. They were in a cave, apparently—or a tunnel—or a tube. Probably a lava tube; seals were known to frequent such places.

Seals. . . .

These *weren't* seals, dammit! She was letting the fact

that they wore that shape prejudice her. Selkies were at
least as much human; that their culture had never inter-
faced with her own didn't change that. No selkies lived
on land—as humans—as far as she knew. But they *did*
live, presumably, in some way that provided knowledge
of man's world—which was best experienced in man's
shape. And they knew terms like *extinct* and *plankton*
and *continental shelf*, and had names like regular folks.

More thinking, Connor chided. *But you will find your
questions answered very soon. For now, I will only say
that we lived above during the . . . ice age. We found
places to dwell below ground. Eventually the seas swallowed them. They swallowed us too. But we learned how
to retain heat and light and air.*

Carolyn found it nearly impossible to remain "silent,"
to restrain a whole new flood of questions. Eschewing
the conundrums of shape-shifting itself, or the new world
it was allowing her to visit; every comment of Connor's
seemed to open up vast new vistas of knowledge, whole
new opportunities for scholarship. Already she could
think of a dozen topics for PhD dissertations—though
she doubted they'd be written without selkie consent. Not
given the hush-hush atmosphere that surrounded this affair.

She chuckled herself at that. All her life she'd heard
conspiracy theories: secret societies that manipulated history, events, even whole epochs, without the world the
wiser. And here *she* was on the razor edge of one. Forget
academia; all she needed for fame and fortune was the
tabloid press.

Abruptly the tunnel floor began to slope upward, and
then upward far more steeply. A surge of relief reached
back at her from Connor, but before she could ponder its
source, her nose poked into the air of what she knew
immediately was no tunnel.

She inhaled gratefully, felt an odd twitch as her meta-
bolism speeded up. Heat washed her like a fever, and she
inhaled again; caught the scent of mustiness, fish, salt,
and sea shores.

Her next impression was of dimly lit domed silence in

which the gentle lapping of water against dry land was the only sound, and yet so subtle it was like non-sound. As she thrust her head higher, she saw that they had surfaced in the middle of a pool maybe twenty meters across, completely bordered with white sand twice that distance again, and with the ceiling roughly ten meters higher and apparently of natural work. Beyond the beach, an assortment of irregularly spaced and sized openings gaped. Most were unobstructed, but a few were closed by flaps of fabric that looked suspiciously like blankets and quilts. Light came from a single smokeless torch at one end of the pool, and a half-dozen mirrors that gleamed with what she supposed was reflected sunlight, uncannily bright, as though they also housed their own fire.

They do, Connor told her, as he arched toward shore. *But we did not make them—nor can anyone else, any longer.*

Carolyn followed dutifully and, once she'd heaved herself up onto the sand, was both relieved and perplexed to be back on land. She was, after all, a terrestrial creature, occasional dolphin or seal incarnations notwithstanding. Trouble was, she preferred to navigate on *two* legs.

And so you should, came Connor's thought, responding to what she'd assumed was a private musing—she'd *have* to learn the etiquette of that. A glance his way showed him savaging the same flipper he'd worried at before. She followed his example—only to find that it hurt! Of course it did! Teeth were teeth, meat was meat, and nerves did their job regardless. Besides, she'd done it before: when she'd put off dolphin shape—except there you had to gnaw the inside of your mouth. That had hurt too, but she'd discovered afterwards that her pod mates had dulled her pain response. Apparently they hadn't wanted her fear of *changing* to discourage her from helping them.

But it certainly hurt now! And she was on the verge of asking Connor to do the deed for her, when his voice—his *human* voice—startled her from behind. "I

cannot," he sighed. "It is part of the Blessing: that you must do it without aid. It has to do with pain prompting the release of certain chemicals necessary to the Change."

Which was all very well for a cocky lad like him! On the other hand, she was a woman; and women were designed to withstand pain—like childbirth. All right, by God, she'd show them! And with that, she let instinct take over and slashed ruthlessly at her flipper. Blood showed. Pain flared bright, then more pain, and more blood, and finally came the return of that odd tingle; only this time it heralded not tension but relaxation, as though her borrowed hide was releasing its hold on the underlying flesh and allowing it to lapse back into its familiar form.

Cold flowed across her skin. She felt uncomfortable on all fours. Her senses realigned—and she was human.

She rose to find Connor grinning at her. She glared back, though none of what she'd just suffered was his fault. Still, it was irritating to endure such agony, then be leered at by someone who looked like a lad of seventeen, with all the testosterone overload that implied. He was a boy, she a woman—a good-looking woman, so she'd been told. She was also naked. And no attractive naked woman could be completely at ease around a bare-assed adolescent male.

Fortunately, Connor was no longer watching. Having ascertained her success, he'd gone prowling up the shore. A moment later, he retrieved something from a flat-topped stone, just at sitting height. A long tunic, as it turned out: rusty brown, and of a style that had been current three years back. There was also a towel: white, with the Dublin Hilton logo. He presented both to her with a shy smile she managed to return. "Thanks," she added, when she recalled the option of speech. While Connor made a point to gaze elsewhere, she dried herself and slipped the garment on. Then: "Uh, if it's not rude to ask: where *is* everybody?"

"Waiting discreetly," Connor replied promptly—and surprised the hell out of her by twisting around and vent-

ing a bloodcurdling high-pitched howl. "*That* should bring him," he laughed.

"Him?"

"Your escort. Listen with your mind, and you can sense his approach."

"I can't—"

"Not without learning, Con!" a new voice called, with more than a trace of friendly sarcasm. Echoes made it hard to tell from which opening the voice had issued; but Carolyn only guessed two archways wrong. She started up the beach to meet the newcomer, but Connor (who had *not* dressed) restrained her with a hand on the shoulder. "No," he whispered. "You are the guest. It is for him to approach."

By which point her contact was barely three steps away.

Another dratted boy! Didn't these folks have adults? Preferably adult women, so she wouldn't have to go through the nudity-taboo song-and-dance every time she shifted shape. On the other hand, male seals were dominant. As—dammit—were male humans. She was doubly doomed from the start.

At least the newcomer wasn't threatening. He looked even younger than Connor, for one thing: a well-grown, if slender, fourteen; though he had the strong chest and shoulders logic (and Kevin) suggested were normal for selkie kind. He was also . . . prettier than his comrade, had longer, darker hair, and—blessedly—wore a low-slung kilt that was really little more than a crimson towel secured jauntily at one hip by what was she realized with a start was either an antique pennanular brooch such as were the pride of the National Museum, or a damned fine copy. She wondered whether such garb was normal or a concession to human prudery.

The boy smiled broadly. His teeth were very white, with good canines. There was something familiar about him. But then he spoke and the memory dissolved.

"I wrap myself because I am of . . . siring age but have not yet sired," he explained offhandedly, having evidently chosen that perplexity from among the scores

whirling through Carolyn's mind. She had to stop herself from launching into a dialogue on nudity taboos versus body taboos versus puberty taboos there on the spot. To cover, she coughed.

The boy looked stricken. "I am sorry," he blurted out. "I forget myself. I have confused you when I should have comforted you. Still, our folk have little cause to perfect the art of greeting as the land-kin practice it." He extended a hand—the correct one. "I am Sean," he continued, with a small, stiff bow. "In the name of the folk of the sunset hill, I greet you, and welcome you to our . . . sanct—sanctum." An awkward pause, then, shyly: "I *also*, myself, am pleased to meet you, Caro— Uh, which name *do* you prefer?"

"Cary'll do fine," she informed him, encouraged by the informality in evidence here, and grateful that no one seemed to stand in awe of her—though why she should've expected that, she didn't know.

So what role *should* she play? Lost child returning home? Aloof, accomplished stranger come to change the world? Or what? "I am very pleased to meet you," she hedged finally, wondering what Red Wounds or O'Neal would have thought of her performance, and what they'd have done in her stead. Which prompted an image of the two of them presiding over embassy balls in stolen Hilton towels.

"If you would, please follow me," Sean said suddenly, motioning toward the archway by which he'd entered. "Our father is anxious to meet you."

Carolyn froze in the act of turning and stared at him. "*Our* father?"

The selkie boy raised a wry eyebrow. "Did Connor not tell you?" he asked innocently. "I am your brother."

Chapter V:
Identity Crisis

(West of Aztlan—Mexico)
(Thursday, September 8—midday)

I swore I was gonna do it, Thalo told himself, as he wiped sweat off his brow for the fifth time in two minutes. *I swore!*

He would too: this protest trek into the wild—the *Mexican* wild, in fact; over two hours having passed since the taxi he'd been forced to hail had dumped him at the border. Not his preference, that, but AFZoRTA had proved intractable, no bikes were available at either Hertz or Avis, and hitchable traffic all seemed to be heading *into* town. Maybe he should've taken that as an omen; this was turning into far more of an undertaking than anticipated.

It was hotter than he'd expected, for one thing, here on this ascending pig-trail between the first of the Sierras, and his system was still running on Midwest acclimation. Which meant that the backs of his hands, his nose, forehead, and the semicircle of skin between his hair and the Mountainsmith were all turning a nice shade of red beneath their Lakota-look dye. He'd been a fool to forget sunblock and the fact that dye didn't work like actual melanin. On the other hand, he was here to grieve, and mortification of the flesh went along with that—which was good, because his flesh was sure enough being mortified.

Besides the ever-present sun (Where were those damned clouds when you needed 'em?), there was wind-

borne grit that got into eyes already smarting despite RayBans, clogged nostrils that felt bone dry, and found its way beneath the pack straps and the drawstring waistband of his jeans to chafe tender skin raw.

And the air was dry, too: *damned* dry. That was the worst thing. Back in Minni you took a certain amount of residual sogginess for granted. You did not take into account the fact that a fair bit of a person's daily water ration was inhaled, nor that saturated air wasn't nearly as likely to suck your skin dry as lo-hu stuff like Aztlan's.

Basically, he was thirsty as hell. Fortunately, he was an Eagle Scout (if a city-bred one, which had limited his opportunities), had read *some* of the guides about backpacking in Mexico (just not recently; this was, after all, an impromptu pilgrimage), and remembered that rule number one was "always take too much water."

Thus, he'd drunk until he sloshed, back at the borderbarrio that clumped around the northernmost of the three major highways that drove into Aztlan from Mexico, and had crammed the pack full as well. He also had an electronic divining rod if things got desperate. Even if it *was* tech.

He didn't think he'd need it. The plan was to walk as steadily west as possible (straight into the mountains) for eight hours, with thirty minute breaks every two hours and shorter ones more often; give himself time to find a campsite (preferably with water), pitch that camp, and then cruise on the Green until he crashed. He'd sleep as late as he liked, then trek back in the morning. Surely he had enough water for that; he'd just have to be careful not to chug it like an alky swilled brew.

Sighing, he paused to clean his shades, then re-donned them, sparing a final moment of this latest break to take in the view. It was pretty damned good, actually; with almost no trace of tech to spoil it. Oh, more contrails drifted across the startlingly blue sky than he'd ever seen, almost a spiral mandala of them (which reminded him *again* of what he'd already heard too often that day: that Green Francis was dead and the world's elite were beat-

ing a path to his wake) but contrails were a given, no matter where you went.

Eschewing them, however, he'd seen two pop-tops in the last ten minutes, three cigarette packs (all busy biodegrading), and half a dozen beer bottles: two Corona, one Guinness, and one each Bud, Moretti, and Kirin, and that was it, for tech. He'd picked up the first two from habit, and buried the rest.

Otherwise . . . well, the mountains were . . . mountaining nicely, rising to left and right along what was probably a defunct quarry trail (the stone for Aztlan had to come from *somewhere*); and the vegetation was hanging in there. Trouble was, it was mostly scrubby dry grass, assorted succulents, and a fair bit of actual cacti.

And of course, as he recalled yet again, as he watched a hand-sized scorpion skitter away while he wet his whistle with Kroger Perrier, there was the wildlife.

Lowlife wildlife, most of it was, and not so much present as there by implication—or imagination, which was better or worse, depending. According to what he'd read, the area should be rife with lizards, tortoises, and snakes (which he'd made more than one mental memo to research thoroughly before making another foray out). And there really *were* tarantulas. Lots and *lots* of tarantulas, including the fine big gal who'd made it halfway to his knee (*outside* his pants) the last time he'd paused for a piss. That had *not* been cool. Sure, he'd met a few in pet stores, and a less-than-stable friend had even owned one, which he'd allowed to sit in his hand exactly once. Trouble was, the things were cold, which fuzzy critters weren't supposed to be. And they had little beady eyes (and lots of 'em), when most of the animals he was into had big ones. And while he knew logically that what the ignorant called vermin were important to the ecosystem, it was still hard to equate them with carrie-meggies— *charismatic megafauna*—basically big impressive mammals that were often attractive in the bargain. Like lions (still a fair number), tigers (might last out the century— in zoos), and bears (flourishing, because they'd eat human garbage).

It was sad, though, he thought, as the trail steepened, that he was probably one of the last people on earth to touch a live black rhino. He had (it was one of his most treasured experiences), in a private nature reserve a friend had got him into. It had felt like an old suitcase and smelled like mildewed socks. And the look in its little eyes had seemed infinitely sad (more likely bored, but there was that romantic inclination), as if the creature knew it was one of the last.

Sigh.

He had just crested the latest of the numerous small gaps that pierced this portion of the Sierras, and was sullenly confronting the fact that his chosen path ran steeply downhill to parallel an actual (if semi-paved) *road* for most of a klom, when a cloud of dust and the muffled crunch of tires on gravel signaled the approach of a vehicle there. His first impulse was to retreat over the rise and lie low. Instead, he continued defiantly down the hill, noting that his path and the vehicle's would likely coincide, and hoping that if it bore natives, they'd prove friendly. Shoot, maybe they'd have some sunscreen on 'em. And a hat—yeah, one of those big sombrero-jobs like you saw in movies. Now that'd be *tres* cool—if it was a real one and not too touristy. He quickened his pace.

He could see the vehicle now, running interference for the dust cloud it was raising. Sunlight gleamed off fresh gold paint and mirror glass. *Jeep*, he identified. *Juneau. New.* One of those neat little jobs that looked like soap-bubbles on wheels, the cabin being the biggest, with a stubby hood and rounded fenders (each of which sported smaller bubbles housing various lights), filling out the corners. There was music, too: the Hero Twins's last CD but one, if he remembered right.

So intent was he in perusing the approaching vehicle, however, that he neglected the pig-trail path. The result was that he stumbled on a rock (or was it an armadillo? *Something* had scampered away), and sprawled forward into the only patch of cactus for half a klom on either side.

"Shit!" he spat, as he sought to right himself without becoming hopelessly impaled. "Damn!"

Brakes squealed. Gravel crunched. The music waxed, then faded. A rounded shadow occluded half the cactus and the road. The low hum of an IC engine ceased, followed by the popping of cooling alloys. A door hissed opened. Footsteps approached: light, soft ones.

Thalo saw nothing—because the pack was balanced wrong and kept pressing him cactusward, which let the blessed succulent get its literal hooks into his tunic for real and good. The stuff was like bloody *Velcro*, he concluded—and embarked on a more vigorous approach to extrication.

"Got a problem?" a voice inquired helpfully, from less than a meter away. Try though he might, Thalo's view was restricted to dusty calf-high sneakers that might once have been white, with baggy beige jeans tucked into the tops, and a small knife sheathed in the right-hand one. He swallowed—then coughed, for his throat had gone dry—again.

"Or you cool?" the voice amended. Only then did Thalo finally conjure sufficient presence of mind to realize that the person was male and spoke English with a definite American drawl—probably from the South.

"Hot, actually," he managed, as the latest flood of forehead sweat chose that moment to assail his eyes. The stuff stung like fire. He blinked and tried to wipe them—only to find himself unbalanced again and perilously close to crashing down across the main mass of the plant.

"It'd help if you'd lose the pack," the man observed. "I'll hold, you do the buckles."

Thalo saw little point in arguing and a slew of reasons to assume the guy was right, and did as coached—one-handed, while supporting himself unsteadily with the other. His burden abruptly lifted, he made short work of freeing himself. Unfortunately, his last tug sent him scooting backwards on all fours, which abraded his palms badly. He sucked the right one. And gazed up at his benefactor. "My fault," he grumbled. "Shouldn't have been in such a hurry to flag you down."

In reply, the fellow squatted, which took him out of line with the sun, whose disk he'd eclipsed with his head. And Thalo realized with a start that he had evidently been rescued by a genuine Native American—one more blooded than he, at any rate, if the dark skin, black hair, and facial structure were any indication. The man's clothing betrayed nothing: merely jeans and tunic of loosely woven hopsack clones beneath a worn, rust-red serape. A gold stud winked in one ear. His teeth were very white. He moved gracefully, and was altogether quite good-looking—in a late-twenties way.

"Whatever," Thalo muttered finally, stretching to retrieve his pack. The visitor regarded it with a critical eye Thalo found disconcerting.

"Goin' campin'? Or been campin?" the man asked. "Prob'ly goin'," he decided. "Too much water otherwise, and your clothes're too clean. Plus, you're not nearly red enough."

Thalo felt himself blushing beneath the dye and sunburn. He wondered what color that produced—probably one that glowed. This guy had his number sure enough, and the stupid along with the rest. "Speaking of which," he ventured, "sunburn, that is. Do you . . . that is have you got . . . Oh, fuck, man: you got any sunscreen I can borrow?"

The man laughed, though his overall expression remained grim, as though some large dark something troubled him. "Sure," he replied. "It'll cost ya, though."

Thalo's heart sank. Here it came: his money—a blow-job—his *life*; who knew what that price might be. In the end, he simply didn't reply.

"Ride back to town with me," the man said eventually. "That's my price. You don't belong out here—yet. Hot off the jet, aren't you? From the States—probably a cold rainy one, to judge by your smooth skin, your clothes, and your shoes. Been here no more'n a day, max. Saw the sights and decided to play nature boy in the great Mexican outback without doin' your homework. Trouble is, folks from the Motherland think it's like the Smokeys

down here, and it's not. Folks from the dry states generally do all right, the rest . . . fuck up.''

Thalo regarded him sourly. ''I appreciate what you've done,'' he gritted, picking at the first of several spines that ornamented his left wrist. ''But don't lecture me. I'm an Eagle Scout, and an—''

''Indian?'' the man finished. ''Native American? Or would you prefer to be defined by tribe? The tattoos look Lakota—'cept they didn't *use* tattoos. The design on your pack's either bad Navajo or worse Hopi. Your accent's urban Midwest.''

''Lakota,'' Thalo gritted again.

''Ha!'' the man snorted, and rose, ambled toward the Jeep, popped the passenger door, and rummaged around inside, to return a moment later with a small plastic bottle. He tossed it to Thalo.

Thalo watched it land beside him, but made no move to retrieve it. ''If I accept this, does that mean I'm committed?''

The man nodded enthusiastically.

Thalo rolled his eyes, but picked up the bottle, flipped the cap, and squeezed a dab of white cream into his palm, which he proceeded to rub along his burning forearms. ''I take it you're local?'' he asked resentfully.

''No, but I *am* a real Indian, which you almost certainly are not.''

''So what's *your* tribe?'' Thalo challenged, surlier than intended.

''Cherokee, most folks'd say. We call it Ani-Yunwiya or—''

''Kituwah,'' Thalo supplied eagerly. ''It's an old ceremonial name they resurrected to identify their nation when it finally got recognized.''

Another nodded. Then: ''*You* got a name, White Boy?''

''Thalo.''

''Thalo? Like P-T-H-A-L-O? Like the pigment?''

''Lose the 'P'; otherwise, you got it.''

''That your real name?''

Thalo shook his head. ''It's my Movement name. The

Young Greens where I went to college decided to come up with new names; you know, like in the Catholic church you get a new one when you're confirmed? To signify rebirth, and all? Well, I went with Thalo—'cause it's a kind of green.''

"I . . . see."

Something about the man's tone bugged Thalo. It was bad enough being caught at an awkward moment, but to have that happen in front of a for-real Indian . . . well, he might never live it down, but would just as soon be about trying. Too, the man seemed disinclined to take what were to him serious intentions as seriously as they required. Never mind that he kept staring at him, as though trying to decide if they'd met. Maybe they had; he'd been to a lot of pow-wows, and watched everything about Natives he could find on the tube. "So what's *your* name?" he asked finally.

The man hesitated the barest moment. " 'Bird."

"That's it?"

'Bird chuckled. "You're an Indian. You know how we are about names. That's as much as I feel like passin' on right now."

Thalo decided not to press the point. "Where does this trail lead?"

"West," 'Bird grunted, still with that disarming twinkle in his eyes. "East'd be *much* better for you—for reasons I've already stated."

Thalo frowned as he attacked his face and neck with the sunscreen. "Can't," he muttered tersely. "I know I promised—but I can't."

"Why not?"

"I'm in mourning."

"Mourning . . . ?"

"For the fucking Archbishop of Aztlan, *okay*? For fucking Green Francis—Bishop Green Jeans—whatever you wanta call him!"

'Bird's face stilled abruptly. "Yeah, I just heard about that. Bummed me too. He was a great man. I take it you admired him?"

Thalo was surprised to find tears welling in his eyes. "You could say that!"

'Bird patted him on the shoulder. "Lots of us down here did."

"It's such a waste," Thalo spat, "such a goddamned waste!"

"Yeah," 'Bird agreed. "And your little memorial jaunt here reflects admirable intent—but it's still plain-ass stupid, with no more gear than you've got."

"I was only gonna be gone a day!"

"Gets cold at night, though. And lots of things like to crawl into warm sleeping bags."

Thalo swallowed.

"Tell you what," 'Bird announced. "Since you're a fellow Francisite, I'll do you one favor—Indian to Indian," he continued in a tone that, though mocking, was not without sympathy. "You climb into this little Jeeplet here and ride back with me, I'll show you a place they've got good Native food and entertainment. Guy there knows this area real well and'll give you the full download."

"Oh yeah?"

"Guy named O'Connor. He's kind of a . . . kinsman of mine: traditional dancer at one of the ethnic *divertos* down in Sinsynsen, if you've ever heard of that."

"Sin, synthesis, and sensation," Thalo quoted the tourist guide he'd worn out prepping for this trip. "But who's this O'Connor guy?"

A brow lifted delicately. "Like I said, a dancer . . . a drummer. Sometimes a singer. Why?"

Thalo retrieved his pack and rose. " 'Cause that's the name of the guy I'm supposed to be working for—*Thunderbird* O'Connor. Kinda pretentious sounding."

The other brow joined the first. "Actually, it's pretty common, 'least up where I'm from. There was a fad for it 'bout thirty years back—fellow named Kirkwood Thunderbird O'Connor was a major activist 'round the turn of the century, which you prob'ly already know. Lots of Native kids got named after him, 'specially if they

were O'Connors already. You do know why they called
him that, don't you?''

'' 'Cause his dad liked the cars and collected 'em,''
Thalo replied. ''Was supposed to have had about fifty
when he died—of which five ran.''

''The fifty-seven, the sixty-six, the seventy-one, the
ninety-nine, and the aught-three, as I recall.''

Thalo eyed him warily. ''Not bad.''

A shrug. ''One of my buddies did a paper on it for
Journal of Cherokee Studies. I had to read it about a
zillion times.''

Silence.

''You said something 'bout workin' . . . ?''

Thalo was already on his way to the Jeep, though his
chauffeur hadn't moved. ''Internship at the Cherokee
Embassy. Fall quarter watching that culture up close.
That Thunderbird guy's supposed to be my boss.''

''Ever met 'im?''

Thalo shook his head. ''Job was posted in the Net. I
applied, he netted back. We've never spoken 'cept on the
glass.'' He hesitated with his hand on the passenger door.
''That offer still stand?''

''I made it, didn't I? And a couple of digressions back,
you accepted. Unless you want me to reclaim my sunscreen . . . along with the skin that goes with it.''

''That's fine,'' Thalo conceded. ''Plus, there's always
a chance you might be right. 'Sides,'' he added, ''any
fan of Green Francis is a friend of mine.''

Chapter VI:
Free Parking

(Aztlan)
(Thursday, September 8—early afternoon)

Roughly three hours into what he'd taken to calling "the harrowing of Thalo Gordon," guilt at ignoring his diplomatic duties got the better of 'Bird and prompted him to ring up the Embassy. Thalo had ducked into a McDonald's 'Bird had deliberately overshot, and 'Bird was supposedly circling the block while the kid cleared his kidneys for the third time in as many hours. In fact, he'd parked down the street, left the vehicle idling to preserve the AC, and told the phone, "On: Thunderbird O'Connor to Kituwah: Priority one."

A voice promptly fuzzed out of the stereo speaker, the distortion likely due to the number of circuits in use, courtesy of the Green Francis chaos. Good thing his body phone was a mass of scab; otherwise it'd be burning a hole in his tunic from sympathetic overload. "'Bird," the voice—female—rasped. "Where the hell are you? We've been lookin' all over—"

"Figured as much," 'Bird broke in. "I've been walkabout."

"*Again*?" The voice was cold as ice. *Wilma Bloodworth*, he identified through the static, his least favorite of the Embassy's three receptionists.

"'Wounds authorized it—as you know."

"You could've still checked in! We've got a crisis here."

"As opposed to somewhere else?"

"You heard?"

"Not when you wish I had, but let's cut the crap, okay? Has anybody got hold of 'Wounds? And what's the deal with our response?"

The woman took a deep breath—'Bird was, after all, her superior. "Nobody can find the Ambassador, thanks to that damned hurricane in Eireland. We've dispatched a courier to chase him down, but meanwhile . . . we're coping. Mary Jane's in charge."

And mostly stalling, 'Bird thought with a smirk. The deputy ambassador, Mary Jane Mankiller, was at odds with Red Wounds on virtually every important point. Which meant she was going bonkers now: forced to act, while knowing that anything she did would probably be wrong in her boss's eyes. 'Bird and she didn't get along. "She need me to do anything?" he asked anyway.

"Not so far as *I* know," a new voice inserted: Holly McClure—his *favorite* receptionist; they'd even gone out a couple of times. "We've sent official condolences to the family, the Cathedral staff, and His Holiness; but there's a standard form for that, and we just fill in the blanks. We've requested download on funeral arrangements, but nothing's been released except that the Mass is to be at St. Tekkie's. Aztlan's high-honcho of protocol was down in Caracas at a heraldry symposium, and is having to do everything by fax-'n-phone from his jet. Which means he's stalling too. Frankly, 'Bird, nothing's getting done anywhere."

A glance in the mirror showed Thalo prancing down the sidewalk, his eyes (no longer RayBanned) wide with understandable wonder, given that they were across the street from Colombia's pyramid, which had double doors five meters high, plated with genuine Amazon gold. "But you don't need *me*?" 'Bird repeated.

"Unless you feel like kicking some very important ass."

"Might get my sneakers dirty," 'Bird laughed. "But I tell you what; if anyone asks, tell 'em I'm . . . researching at home. I'll check in later, and be ready to roll with the sun."

"Sounds good."

"Catch you."

"You wish!"

"—Again."

"Better be better'n last time, then—or at least last longer!"

"Which time?" 'Bird snorted. "I'll admit I had to work on number four, but I *had* been dancin' all night . . ."

"It showed."

At which point Thalo arrived, eager-faced and grinning. 'Bird told Holly "bye," and the phone "off," and the kid—it was hard to think of him otherwise, though he was only three years younger than 'Bird—opened the door and bounced in. "So, where to now?" he asked breathlessly, passing 'Bird the large box of fries he'd acquired along with a burger. Which latter 'Bird considered a good sign, since it proved he wasn't a vegan, which affectation he loathed. He helped himself to a handful and pondered. "Let's see . . . we've done the World Pool, the Big Four 'mids, and the Museum of the Americas. We've cruised the zoo and a piece of *El País*, and I've pointed out where you're gonna work. What does that leave—besides the Cathedral?"

Thalo's brow crinkled. "The aquarium?"

The idea made 'Bird shudder. They had dolphins there—and more to the point, orcas. He didn't think he could look either in the eye just now. Never, he suspected, in the case of the latter. "Uh . . . actually, we're goin' the wrong way for that," he hedged. Which was true.

"So . . . what about Lady Xoc Park? There's supposed to be some kind of rally there for Green Francis."

"Know it well," 'Bird chuckled. "Got laid there one night—twice—Brazilian girl and her twin brother."

"You do guys?"

"Not by preference, but sometimes it happens. You?"

"I . . . have." Thalo settled back in his seat as 'Bird urged the Jeep up to speed on one of the wider boulevards. "So . . . is this *the* Lady Xoc?" he asked eventu-

ally. "The park I mean? Like, is it named after the famous one?"

"Is there another?" 'Bird wondered, genuinely curious. "I'm rusty on my Maya history."

Thalo shrugged, but seemed glad for an opportunity to show off—given that 'Bird had been leveling his Indian wannabe karma every chance he got. It was impossible to resist, dammit. The kid was *so* earnest—and *so* obviously (and innocently) a fool when it came to that. They'd make hash out of him at the Embassy if 'Bird didn't toughen him up first. Not that he wasn't having fun along the way. He still hadn't revealed his own identity. He was saving that for last.

"The one I know," Thalo replied, "was the principal wife of a major Maya king, depicted in a number of significant pieces of art. That's the short form."

"And the long one? We've got a ways to go."

Thalo puffed his cheeks. "Long form is that she was married to Shield-Jaguar, who was king of Yaxchilan for about a zillion years. Among other things, he used her to legitimize the succession of his son, Bird-Jaguar, by another, much younger, wife named Lady Eveningstar. Did the old tongue-piercing bit and the whole nine yards— You know about that, don't you?"

"I'm not entirely ignorant," 'Bird retorted dryly. And launched into a discussion of classical Maya political intrigue that kept them testing each other, with neither clearly the winner, most of the way to their destination.

"So that's how you got this job of yours, huh? By knowing all that obscure stuff?" 'Bird asked as they slowed to turn between the replica stelae that marked the entrance to the park.

A shrug. "Didn't hurt I guess. I just hope they don't give me too much shit about . . . other stuff."

"Like what?"

Thalo's face colored beneath his bogus tan. "You know: the dye job—my hair. I mean, it all seemed cool back in Minni. But here. . . . I don't know how it'll fly."

"Till it lands," 'Bird assured him with a wink. "Now, let's go find this rally, then zip back and get your stuff.

By then it'll be time to eat, if you still want to check out that *diverto* I told you about.''

"Let's wing it," Thalo countered. "Run on Indian time, and all.''

'Bird smiled fiendishly. "You got it."

Ten minutes later they'd found the Outer Earth Rally. It was impossible to miss, actually; 'Bird had but to follow the hordes of young people shuffling, skating, boarding or biking along; many dressed in shades of green; most sporting black arm bands, and not a few equipped with those new Sony headsets that bypassed your eardrums and fed music straight into your aural nerve, thereby allowing maximum volume without damage. 'Bird hated them—as he hated most frivolous uses of tech; even Stormy's neat little wheels, if the truth were known. Earnest young Thalo had nothing on him there.

"Wanta get out?" 'Bird asked, when they found themselves becalmed by a phalanx of pamphleteers blocking the road ahead. He felt sorry for the inhabitants of the next car up. Japanese tourists, or he was a Swede.

"I'm not sure," Thalo responded, which surprised 'Bird. He'd expected an enthusiastic *yes*—which would've given him a chance to beg off his offer of dinner and powwow with the Embassy at length before heading down to Sinsynsen to moonlight at the club. "I mean . . . I'd like to, but—" Thalo broke off, gnawing his lip.

"What?"

A frustrated sigh. "Oh, it's just that . . . Dammit, I get caught in these crazy conflicts in situations like this. Like, on the one hand, I feel like I oughta go 'cause of mourning, and all; and 'cause I like the music and could probably meet some neat folks and stuff. But on the other hand . . . my conscience really bugs me at things like this. I mean, there's so much . . . waste. All that paper: fliers and disposable cups and all. And the music . . . I mean, I *love* loud music, but to be loud it has to be electric, which is a waste of electricity, which is a waste of fossil fuels a lot of the time. And—"

"Aztlan runs on solar and tidal power," 'Bird cor-

rected smoothly. "Only time we run fossil is when we buy from outside, and that's only during the hottest months when the AC goes overload. Most buildings have Hopi cells, as I'm sure you noticed—and you know how efficient those suckers are. Street lighting's about all that comes to mind otherwise, and even that depends in part on Hopis."

"In that case," Thalo grinned, "why not?"

'Bird took a deep breath. "I'll tell you why not," he said slowly, suddenly all business—might as well download the hard stuff now and get it over with. "And it's got nothing to do with the motivation for this little gathering, which is a good and honorable thing, nor with any disrespect for Green Francis, nor anything like that."

Thalo scowled. "So what's the deal?"

"Fraud," 'Bird replied flatly. "I don't know what you know about the Twins, besides that they're one of the five most popular bands on earth, and have political clout like nobody's seen since U2 and Geldof and those dudes got cookin' fifty years back. But the fact is . . . they're fakes."

"Fakes?" Thalo gaped. "What the fuck do you mean by *that*?"

"What I said," 'Bird retorted. "Oh, they do their own music; nothing bogus there. And all that about studyin' for years and playin' six instruments each is documented: they're genuinely good musicians—and reasonably responsible for filthy rich tweenagers: they've got a good political conscience, which is to say I mostly agree with 'em. And they really are twins—identical, down to their dozen toes apiece. But they absolutely are *not* Maya, which is what they claim to be, and base a big hunk of their popularity on. I know,'cause a friend of mine checked. Shoot, they're not even Native—no more'n anybody with Caribbean roots is. They're Puerto Rican if they're anything: born in New York City."

"You're full of—" Thalo began. "—putting me on," he finished lamely.

"Got no reason to," 'Bird shot back. "But since you're here under—well not false pretenses, since I'll

accept that you really are an eighth something, though you're still tryin' to be something you're not—I figured you'd appreciate knowin' that I'm an equal-opportunity wannabe basher.''

Thalo's face had grown dark. His lips were trembling with something between disappointment and raw fury. He also looked suspiciously like he was about to cry. 'Bird wondered if all that emotion was directed toward him or his musical heroes. ''See the thing is,'' he went on relentlessly, ''I'm a for-real Indian, which is both good and bad. You're a for-real romantic, which is also both good and bad, and I can't really blame you for wantin' to be Native—or for being a fan of the Twins. But if you're gonna like the Twins, it oughta be for the message and music alone, not 'cause of what they claim to be, to make themselves exotic. That's a crock, m'lad. They used to play *divertos* down in Sinsynsen all the time a few years back, for not much money at all. And then somebody pointed out that they had six toes on each foot, like some of the Maya nobility used to have. And then somebody else mentioned that they looked sorta Maya 'round the profile . . . and the next thing you know, they've hocked everything they own, flown to Thailand for cheap plastic surgery—including implants to change the shape of their skulls to something more Maya—and *voila*! Instant deposed preColumbian nobility.''

The scowl returned. ''So you're saying . . .''

''That a lot of their mystique is based on misinformation. Lies, if you prefer. I just think you should know what you're gettin' into. You want 'em for the music, fine. Or for the message. But not for the Native American thing, 'cause, boy-o, they ain't it. They'll give you the form, but they flat ain't got the substance. You wanta understand Native Americans, you ask me or the folks at that embassy you're gonna be workin' at. End of rant.''

For a moment Thalo simply sat in stunned silence, mouth agape, eyes wide and unfocused. Abruptly his jaw hardened. He punched the door release. ''Okay,'' he spat, as the door swung open. ''I probably was dumb to head out into the mountains like I did, and for that I owe you;

and ditto the sunscreen. But the rest . . . well it's like this, man: I'm not a kid, no matter what you think. My life's not been as easy as you evidently think either—my folks aren't that well-off, and I've got a retarded sister—but I make my own decisions. I get the facts, and I decide. You've made your point. Fine. I'm makin' mine: I'm outta here.''

And with that he stepped out into the thickening mob, pausing only to snare his backpack from the footwell. The door didn't slam behind him—but only because it had been engineered to preclude such things.

'Bird rolled his eyes as he watched his incipient employee vanish into the Green. ''Cocky little shit,'' he muttered, then returned the Jeep to Drive, executed an illegal U-turn, and retreated back the way he'd come. *Cocky little shit, indeed.* Yet by the time he reached the gate, he was laughing. Young John ''Thalo'' Gordon hadn't seen the last of him by a long shot. Not when the kid pranced into his new employer's office tomorrow morning and found Thunderbird Devlin O'Connor grinning back at him from behind a sign that said CULTURAL ATTACHÉ. Should he wear war paint? he wondered. Or merely a tomahawk and feathers? A black scalp with blonde roots might be right interesting. Or would've been three centuries back.

Oh well, 'Bird sighed, as he left Lady Xoc, bound for a nap at home and then a night's dancing, *those were the good old days.*

Chapter VII:
The Old Folks At Home

(The North Atlantic)
(Thursday, September 8—mid-afternoon)

. . . your brother.

The memory of those words rang in Carolyn's ears more loudly than the actual footfalls of the kilt-clad selkie boy prancing along the narrow passage before her, his waist-length flag of blue-black hair switching across the small of his back with the careless, sensual abandon of someone who was young, handsome, strong, and smart—and knew it without conscious vanity.

. . . your brother.

It shouldn't surprise her, really. Mom had produced two children by as many sires: one selkie, one human; there was no reason to assume that her father hadn't been similarly prolific. Male seals had harems, after all; and male humans would assemble them given half a chance. If her progenitor was true to either his species or his sex, he could've populated half the west coast by now, with pups and bairns alike.

But one brother was enough, dammit! Even someone as maintenance-free as Kevin (eschewing his opinion on Mom's infidelity, which had begotten the Schism—and last week's crises, of course). And even if Sean was innocuous for his kind, it would still require major mindset reprogramming if she was to accept him as part of her life.

Worse, he seemed to have accepted her just fine, if the stream of thickly accented chatter he'd maintained while

she followed woodenly behind was any indication. She'd tuned him out—not from lack of interest, but for pure self-preservation; there was such a thing as info-overkill.

Sighing, she shook her head, told that aspect of herself that was still chanting *brother, brother, brother* to shut the hell up, and tried to rouse the observant scientist she'd trained to be—and to revive the diplomat she'd stumbled into being as well.

Unfortunately, there was little *to* observe at present, save dry walls of glistening stone that bore the marks of selective smoothing and squaring; a ceiling that rose and fell like the undulations of a sea snake; and occasional niches bearing clumps of that glassy luminescent sponge set in pools of scummy water (to keep the glowing plankton alive, Sean had already explained). The floor was simply white sand that didn't jibe at all with the igneous stone elsewhere.

"You think a lot," Sean called back. "I can hear you wondering, yet as soon as one question forms, another thrusts it aside or argues with it."

Carolyn was chastened. But since all information was valuable at this point, it didn't matter where she began. "Your language . . ." she ventured. "You speak—"

"—English, most often, for that is the language of knowledge, which we value because we have so little. Gaelic, too, for the sound: the poetry; and because it is the tongue we *ought* to speak, living where we do. Neither is difficult to learn if a native speaker is nearby, for the meanings come with the words, and so the two twine in our heads. But among ourselves, we speak mostly mind to mind."

"And you also talk to dolphins?"

"Aye—and to their kin: the great whales, and the evil-water-ones—what do you call them?"

"Orcas," Carolyn supplied. "Killer whales."

"And killers they are," Sean agreed, his pace never faltering. "But so are dolphins, sometimes. Myself, I have seen clans of them batter other dolphins with their heads, injuring them so badly inside that they cannot live, and then cast them, dying, on the shore."

"I've heard of that," Carolyn acknowledged. "But it's hard to reconcile with what I know about dolphins—the ones I've studied, and the ones I've—"

"—Been?" Sean finished for her. "It must be the same for you then as for me now: I think you think too much, and if I let myself, I could become lost in your thoughts. But dolphins think more than humans: more often, louder, and in greater numbers at once, so that at times they are almost one being, or at least their . . . edges blur. If you were with them, you could not have helped but think as they did; therefore you thought what they wanted you to think."

Carolyn broke stride at that. It had never occurred to her to doubt the veracity of what she'd been told when she'd twice donned dolphin skin. But had it all been true? It had seemed reasonable, and surely she'd have sensed blatant lies. But belief was not truth. And perhaps what she'd been told had merely been belief. Christ, perhaps that whole weather-war thing had been a set-up! Perhaps she hadn't sided with the good guys at all! Maybe the militant young were-orcas *hadn't* been bent on destroying human civilization.

Except that her very existence was the result of some master plan concocted between selkies and dolphins to facilitate contact with humans. Dolphins, it seemed, could "speak" to selkies; selkies to men. But fully human minds could not, apparently, receive dolphin "transmissions." And selkies . . . What was their problem? Why couldn't they function fully as men and work the will of their dolphin allies as easily as a half-breed like herself?

"*That* riddle you will soon have answered," Sean told her. And with that, he stepped deftly into a higher, narrower passage that opened to the right. Carolyn followed dutifully, and saw that the end was occluded by some sort of glimmering curtain.

Pearls, it turned out, and diverse small discs of carved shell strung on what was clearly monofilament line, to comprise a series of veils, each separated by a pace or so. Light showed beyond, and they tinkled softly as Sean

pushed through, making a soothing almost-song as they resettled in their wake. The boy stopped with one veil remaining. "Our father awaits beyond," he murmured. "Do not fear him, for though you have never met, he loves you as he loved she who gave you life."

Whatever Carolyn expected, it was not what greeted her when, after one final steadying breath, she followed her brother through that last and thickest barrier.

Her first impression was of Tolkien's illustration of Smaug's lair. Certainly there was an enormous rocky chamber, with a high domed ceiling and irregular shelves of raw stone bracketing the walls. But instead of a "vast, red-golden dragon" sprawled across a mound of jewels and coins, a vast number of people of all ages and sexes lolled on cushions and pillows of every description, ninety percent of them stark naked; their common physical denominators those of height (about two meters), build (slim-muscular), and length and color of hair— mostly waist-length, dark, and with jewel-toned highlights. A few, like Sean, wore kilts; but nearly all the women went bare-breasted.

And there were also a fair number of seals—mostly pups and old bulls and cows; the former often nestled in the arms of a selkie; the latter draped languidly between.

And then there was the treasure.

That selkies were apt pillagers was already evident from what Kevin had told her about Fir's eclectic apparel, and from what little she'd observed here. And God knew enough went into the sea or could be found nearby, that an accomplished sneak could satisfy any reasonable need by availing himself of what fell to hand. But when "fell to hand" encompassed loose piles of what were likely Armada-era doubloons, racks of Waterford crystal, and chests of golden brooches, chalices, plates, and croziers that Vikings had plundered from Irish monasteries a millennium back; never mind Art-Deco sculptures that had clearly come from some drowned luxury liner of the last century—perhaps the *Lusitania* herself—all mixed with high-tech gewgaws that smacked of sunken sub-

marines, and even a pile of automobile badges and mascots . . . well, it frankly fried the brain.

Indeed, it took her a moment to note that there was also a bed (Napoleonic, though the linens evoked the much-abused Hilton)—and that it held the oldest living man she'd ever seen.

Though shrouded in a thick velvet tapestry to just below his clavicles, Carolyn wished more of him were covered so that she didn't have to gaze upon the ravages of age that had turned what had obviously been a strong man's muscles to hanging bags of flab, and smooth, clear skin to wrinkles so dappled with age spots, moles, and . . . *excrescences* it was like looking at a map of the moon. Never mind the shadowed face that drooped and sagged from its skull as though it had been wrought of wax and left too near a flame. At least the man still had all his hair—a luxuriant wave of white tinged with other colors like mother-of-pearl, that flowed down the near side of the bed to the floor. A matching beard would've been a mercy, for it would've obscured much that was otherwise revealed.

But then a young woman moved from where she'd crouched beside him, a priceless goblet in her hand, and when she did, the man's face came fully into the light. And Carolyn saw that, in spite of the bags and wrinkles and hollows, his dark blue eyes still held joy, and his lips were as firm, red, and sweetly smiling as a boy's.

The eyes brightened when they found her; the lips twitched. The voice was a hollow whisper in the oddly dry air: "Daughter!" And again: "Daughter—you have come!"

Somehow she was beside him; grief, wonder, and a thousand other emotions thick upon her tongue. "It's what I'm supposed to do, isn't it—according to the songs?" she gave back, with an eloquence she usually lacked on such occasions. "I'm the child of a selkie and a mortal; and all those songs end with the child returning to the sea."

"Where bad things happen," the old man chuckled.

"Or perhaps where the selkie's child learns how slippery age can be."

Carolyn swallowed hard. Her father was right. When she'd heard that her "sire" wanted to see her, she'd conjured images of someone like the man she'd called "Father" for more than twenty years: a crisp, precise American academician in his middle fifties. Her dolphinborn vision of her begetting, however, had shown her selkie-sire to have been no older than Connor: seventeenish, max. Add that to her own thirty, and you got late forties.

Not far more than twice that age.

The old man smiled. "You forget, lass, that we are both men *and* seals. When we wear men's shape, we age as men; when we wear seal shape, we age as seals. A year in fur is more than two without it. If a selkie would live long in years, he must wear man's shape as much as possible."

"But you can't," Carolyn guessed. Or was it a guess?

The old man shook his head. "To shape-shift properly, we must practice that art constantly or our instincts war with themselves and we go mad. And of course, it *is* a pleasure to be a seal. You have felt the sea in your blood, have you not? The . . . oneness with the world that can never come to one who swims in air alone."

Carolyn nodded. "I . . . think I've always felt it. I know I never feared the water, and could swim before I walked."

"And now study the sea and that which dwells within it."

"And find there's even more to study than I'd thought—and that to study it as I should, I may have to—"

"—Betray your kin and their ancient privacy?" her father concluded. "Oh, fret not, lass, I could hear you thinking it—we all could. But we could also hear you thinking that you should not think—or do—such things. Fortunate it is that I am old, to put up with all this . . . *thinking*!"

Carolyn blushed, confounded at having her innermost

thoughts laid bare. "How old *are* you?" she blurted.

The selkie wrinkled his already rugose brow. "I was born thirty-eight winters ago—so they tell me, for lately I have spent much time in my other skin."

"But why? If you age faster as a seal—"

"Life is not always a blessing," the selkie answered. "We come to our growth quickly; for human babes, though beguiling, are too much at risk in our world. Yet therein lies our curse, and one reason we have brought you among us."

Carolyn felt an odd chill at the word "curse," as though it carried an actual weight of dread, not the superficial triviality that rode with it in her primary reality. "Curse?" she echoed warily.

"Yes, daughter, the *selkies'* curse. Not seduction or abandonment, or even premature age—but ignorance. As I have said, when we are seals, we age as seals, and likewise when we are men. But also we learn that way; thus, when we are seals, we learn seal things at the rate seals do. But human things . . . it is hard to explain. Imagine that you are a child of two or three. You can walk, you can speak, you can reason a little. But then imagine that—as must happen—you put on another skin and become a seal. That seal would be your equivalent physical age: a mere pup. But then suppose you spend six months in sealskin, learning the arts of hunting and swimming and evading enemies. Then you become human again. Your body will have aged a year during that half year's time—but your mind will remain where it was in terms of human learning, and must pick up where it left off. You can see where this is leading."

Carolyn puffed her cheeks. "Basically, it means that your physical development quickly surpasses your mental. You'd be children in adult bodies."

The selkie nodded back. "We can control it with careful regulation in the early years. But the problem remains: the curse of ignorance."

Carolyn scowled. "I'm not sure I understand."

"Tell me," the selkie said, "how long has it taken

you to become as wise in the ways of your world as you are?''

The scowl deepened. ''I'm not sure I'm wise even now ... but I went to school for ... about twenty years.''

''Twenty years to learn what you need to know to make any mark?''

''At least.''

''And how many years lived to make *anything* useful? To learn *anything* new? To live at more than a basic level?''

''Fifteen, maybe ... if you're really bright. But even then, anything you did would probably be amateurish.''

''It would take one of us two or three times that long— in your years.''

Finally Carolyn understood. ''Which is why you don't have much technology: nobody lives long enough as human to create any. You have to import it. And your learning too, I bet—though I gather most of you can read.''

''Aye. But by the time we can grasp those concepts that are expected of adult humans, we are already middle-aged. By the time we know enough to accomplish anything, we are old. And with fewer years between age and youth, we recall the latter more vividly, and thus hate old age more—''

''—And so spend more time as seal toward the end,'' the woman who had been serving the selkie broke in, ''to hasten death along.''

Carolyn caught her breath. It was too much to grasp: to accept as a given that between birth and death were less than half the years any of her kind now expected. And that fewer yet of those years could be spent doing the two things humans most revered: learning and creating.

''Primitive is the word, is it not?'' her father inquired.

''Which isn't necessarily bad,'' Carolyn countered.

''But frustrating, all the same, if one would change things and cannot. Or have things and be denied them.''

Carolyn gestured at the surrounding splendor. ''You don't seem to be doing too badly.''

A tired shrug. ''I have never seen a movie, driven an

auto, or keyboarded more than a line with my own hands.''

''But why not? You can live on land, you could do those things.''

''And have men see adults with the knowledge of children, and yet expect them to act as adults? We would be branded fools or mad—and ridicule hurts selkies as much as humans. Fir, as you would have known him, knew more than any of us about the wonders and perils of your world—yet he did not know enough to fit. Though he shielded his thoughts, he left a trail of improbabilities anyone could follow. Certainly the evil-water-ones could.''

Carolyn gnawed her lip—she'd picked up the habit from Kevin. ''Okay, wait a minute: you say you're stifled because you don't *live* long enough to *learn* enough to function in our world on our terms. But the were-orcas must have the same problem—yet they seem to get along just fine.''

''They live longer than we and age more slowly,'' the selkie gave back. ''And they co-ride with your kind more easily. Effectively, they learn as you do. Oh, we can read the thoughts of men if they are near the sea, but the evil-water-ones and their kind are much stronger and more adept, and can read much further inland. I—''

He broke off as a coughing fit wracked him. Red oozed from the corner of his mouth and trickled down the furrows of his neck. The woman dabbed it with a towel.

Too late Carolyn tried to shield the thought that came into her mind.

''No need to deny the truth,'' the selkie gasped at last. ''I am dying. My choice is whether to die as man or seal.''

Carolyn went numb. In spite of her trepidation, she'd come to love this old man in the mere minutes she'd been near him. That he loved her, she had no doubt: it was a sort of warmness in her head when he spoke. And now she was about to lose him. She wasn't ready. She just wasn't ready!

''I regret it too,'' her father acknowledged. ''And

though you expected to come here as an ambassador, to help us determine our role in the dry world, that was partly a deception. Still, I would have it that our kinds work together as best they can, and as individuals will it. Yet that will not happen without aid from your kind. More to the point, it will not happen unless one of us goes among you a longer time than any has, and learns as much as he can as quickly as he can, and so helps us know your world as well as he can, so that we can make the right decision about revealing ourselves.''

Carolyn studied his face. There was more: something he wasn't saying—or feared to say. Suddenly she knew, though whether it was logic, intuition, or yet another aspect of telepathy, she had no idea. ''Someone wants to do that, don't they?'' she gasped. ''Someone who can stay longer than usual.''

''Which means someone with years left to live,'' Sean inserted, speaking for the first time. ''Someone young enough to be—what is the word? Flexible.''

Carolyn stared at him aghast. ''You!''

Her father and brother nodded as one. ''If you are willing,'' the elder said, ''I would send my youngest into the dry world with you. He learns quickly and knows as much about your world as we have been able to teach him. He adored Fir, and was his best, if most reckless, pupil. For that one's death alone, we owe him.''

Carolyn didn't know what to think. The last thing she'd expected was to be placed under family obligation—which, as both a Southerner and an Eirishwoman, she took very seriously indeed. But the last thing she needed right now, with everything unraveling and world-changing events forcing her this way and that, was a sidekick. Worse, a teenage *male* sidekick, with all the hormonal chaos that implied; worse still, one who wasn't even vaguely socialized, as far as the givens of her world went. And worst of all, one who was even younger mentally than he looked.

Sean obviously read the unease on her face—if not straight from her mind. ''You don't want me.''

A deep breath. ''You'd know if I lied,'' she replied,

"so, no, I don't want you. Actually," she amended, "it's not that I don't want *you*; it's that I don't want anything complicating my life right now."

"You have a brother," Sean retorted. "He is not of my blood, yet we would call him kin. Perhaps he could—"

"He might," Carolyn found herself saying. "He's more flexible than I am: more tolerant, since he's basically just a big kid himself."

"Is it the fact that I am . . . male?" Sean asked pointedly.

"That doesn't help."

"I would work very hard," he persisted. "I would try very hard not to . . . embarrass you."

Carolyn rolled her eyes, wishing Kevin was here—or anyone she could consult for advice.

"Sean is like you," her father whispered. "There was a reason for your begetting. And so there was for Sean's. He is fully selkie, but we have kept him in human shape absolutely as much as we dared; indeed, he has spent more of his life human than anyone his age ever has. First it was our choice, then it became his. If you deny him this, his life will have been in vain. By our standards he is nearly an adult. One child he must sire, and then can do as he will. You know what will happen then: He will go to land. In spite of our efforts, he will not fit. He will become unhappy. If he stays, he will go mad. If he returns, our kind lose something precious we have long worked for."

Carolyn gnawed her lip again. "Not much choice there."

"Guilt-trip," Sean cried suddenly. "Is that not what you call such things?"

"Yeah," Carolyn chuckled in spite of herself. "And we usually say 'isn't that,' not 'is that not.' It's called a contraction. If you're gonna live in our world, you'll have to learn such things. You're gonna be weird enough."

Sean's face brightened as though the sun had risen. "You mean you'll take me?"

Carolyn started, having no idea when she'd changed her mind. "It seems," she conceded, "that I will."

"That is all I wished to hear," her father sighed, extending a withered hand. She took it reflexively. "Sean," he called, and the boy took the other. "Maevyn," he rasped at last, to the woman who'd been tending him. She eased onto the bed beside Carolyn and stroked his brow. "I have done what I was born to do," he said— and closed his eyes.

It was as though a small, brilliant light blinked off in Carolyn's head, one she hadn't been aware was present, but which had given comfort and solace in this strange land. All at once she was crying. A soft hand on her shoulder was Maevyn's, a firmer one was Sean's. He was sobbing. When she looked up through the burning glimmer of her own tears, it was to see his and Maevyn's faces likewise streaked with wet. Connor moved from where he'd been standing silently by the entrance. "A selkie is dead," he announced simply. "He died as a man, which not even Fir was brave enough to do."

And with that he bent his head and vented a low, wretched-sounding moan. Others echoed it, and the chamber slowly filled with a sad, growling sigh that gradually rose to a high-pitched keening. It was like the earth music, Carolyn decided: the infra-sound dolphins and orcas tapped to empower their magic. Which made her wonder if selkies likewise had magic—beyond their very nature, of course.

"Not now," Sean warned gently. "Now is the time to feel."

"You're right," she acknowledged, and meant it. It was while she sat holding the hand of a dead man and crying silent tears, that she realized she had never known her father's name.

Chapter VIII:
Bread and Circuses

(Aztlan: Lady Xoc Park)
(Thursday, September 8—dusk)

"Helluva show; right, man? *Helluva* show!"

Thalo glanced around from reflexive politeness, though his attention remained fixed on the granite platform fifty meters away, where the latest speaker—a minor functionary at the Ukranian Embassy, whose vestigial arms were eloquent legacy of parents who'd lived too near Chernobyl—had just departed to thunderous applause and chants of "Green way, all the way! Green way, all the way!"

The kid who'd accosted him sported Asian features beneath green spray dye he'd likely acquired at a booth atop the square step-terrace that comprised the Lady Xoc amphitheater. A silk fig leaf the size of his outspread hand hung crookedly across his otherwise bare crotch, while a beautifully executed dragon tattoo, rendered in brilliant metallic gold, crawled up his belly, across his right pec, and clawed at his jaw with silver talons, before coiling its sinuous neck across his forehead to rest its maw on the opposite cheek. The dye hadn't stuck to it, and the effect was like cloisonne. "*Helluva show!*" the fellow repeated. His eyes were glassy; clearly he was high, whether on emotion or chems wasn't evident. Maybe something in the dye; "surfing"—surface absorption—was pop these days.

"Yeah," Thalo yelled back, courtesy of the waxing decibels of U2's ancient anthem, "Pride (in the Name of

Love),'' on the PA. He finished with a reassuring grin
and returned his gaze to the stage, which a troupe of
bronze-skinned roadies in gym shorts, green Outer Earth
T's, and black bandannas were hastily redressing for the
next act—speaker or performer: one never knew, which
upped the excitement. The Twins still hadn't shown, but
the rally would disperse at ten, so they were bound to go
on soon. Meanwhile, there'd been scads of surprise appearances by other celebs, including Jenny Bender, late
of Placenta Pie; as well as a plethora of notable speakers—like the sixteen-year-old Dalai Lama, the High Shaman of the Reformed Native American Church (who'd
had everyone in tears by the end of his tribute), and the
Chief-Pretender of the Upper Amazon Republic, which
Brasilia still hadn't recognized. Shoot, even without the
promise of a free concert by the world's premier eco-
rockers, this would've been an uplink—definitely better
catharsis than fucking around the Sierras being pissed.

Thalo sighed, stretched, and stole a swig of Perrier
from the copious supply in his pack. It had been a hot
day even for Aztlan, and his surplus water had won him
scores of ''friends forever''—since the fountains cost six
bucks a minute (coins only, please; the Creditor having
flatlined three hours back when a chiphead had tried to
bypass it); the donated Coke was long since depleted, and
Pepsi had lasted barely longer. A topless girl in a tie-
dyed sarong, with green feathers woven through her inky
hair, peered at the canteen hopefully with large dark eyes
that matched her nipples. He extended it silently. She
accepted with a smile, drank sparingly, and rewarded him
with a smooch on the chin.

''Hey, bro, what's your tribe?'' someone else slurred,
from where he'd displaced Dragon Boy (or was it Fig
Leaf Lad?)

''Lako—'' Thalo began, then paused. The speaker
(shirtless, as were most males hereabouts and over half
the women), looked about twelve, with the obligatory
black armband augmented with feathers and leaves, and
a black plastic miter displaying an impressive spray of
same. ''Revlon,'' he grunted finally. Maybe that 'Bird

guy had been right: maybe he really was a fraud.

Not that he wasn't in good company, the free-party fringe having shown in force, along with the opportunist entrepreneurs, local and mega alike. *And* the Twins' army of groupies, none of whom seemed remotely "Green." On the other hand, plenty of sincere folks lurked about too, the majority older than Chief Blond Eagle there and less inclined to show the world how weird they were in the guise of how concerned. Most wore standard street attire—loose jeans and tunics (where the latter weren't doffed in the heat)—and few sported either exotic hair-dos, makeup, dye jobs, or tattoos. More to the point, their expressions displayed a focused intensity when the speakers held forth (on everything from water pollution, through jungle deforestation and endangered species, to paeans in praise of Green Francis) that was not present in the more mercenary revelers. More than one cheek showed tear stains, and many an eye was red with weeping. Most, he noted, wore Outer Earth buttons or equivalent insignia.

In this lull between acts, Thalo found half a square meter of unclaimed turf, flopped down, and bent himself to perusing the Outer Earth brochure he'd acquired upon arrival. He knew the name, of course: from the Net, friends in the Great Green Whole, and assorted newszine reads. It did good work, too; having risen from the ashes of the Greenpeace scandal a few years back. They'd played it close at first, hoping to achieve accommodation with govs and megas alike. But then someone had said too much to the wrong Third World bully, and the head of the whole shebang had conveniently OD'd soon after.

Unfortunately, instead of rallying, the organization had fragmented among competing leader-wannabes. Thalo had thought it defunct. Now, so the flyer explained, it had reformed with new financing from the Hero Twins, and seemed bent on taking a more radical stance, especially on towing a hard line with megas—mostly EEC and P-Rim megas, granted (the EPA having put the fear of God into the Northie ones twenty years back), but a hard line nonetheless. And with Green Francis coming

online on the same side (though he was leery of endorse-ments), things had looked really good—until today.

Thalo still didn't know what to believe about what was increasingly being termed the Archbishop's assassination, but the prevailing notion mid-crowd was that a mega had maxed on him and had him flatlined in such a way as to resemble an accident or—better—suicide. Hyundai was mentioned, because he'd opposed a major dam they were building. Georgia Pacific was a popular candidate as well, courtesy of its predilection for employing "private security forces" bigger than some national armies. Thalo was trying to stay open-minded.

—And was wondering if he ought to go questing for a loo, since the roadies seemed to be taking their own sweet time setting up for the next act, and the U2 ("Sun-day, Bloody Sunday") was just *too* loud, when a scream a dozen yards to his right segued into a chorus of yells, first of surprise, then of outrage, finally of pain, all sprin-kled with confusion. He was on his feet with the rest of the sitters-around, and by craning his neck (though short for a Northie, he was tall for this mob), saw that the Mounties had arrived *en masse* and were closing down the dye-vender. An ambulance had accompanied them, blue-and-red lights sporadically visible beyond the sur-rounding arcade, and he could *just* make out a team of paramedics ministering to someone on the ground. A lull in the music clarified the jumble of voices sufficiently for him to hear hysterical female screams of "Gotta help 'er! Gotta help 'er! Gotta help 'er!" In the wake came other info-bites, in Spanish, Kìché, and English, prominent among them the phrases ". . . in the dye . . ." ". . . close down . . ." ". . . the hell you will . . ." ". . . *convul-siónes* . . ." and "Mega-scum! *Muerte a todas las me-gas!*"

"*¿Qué pasa?*" asked a tiny woman in a striped serape who appeared, as by magic, in front of him. She kept jumping up and down, but even so, wasn't nearly tall enough to see.

"Dunno," Thalo told her. "Looks like somebody got

hurt, and they had to call an ambulance, and the cops got dragged in.''

She gaped blankly. ''*No hablo inglés.*''

''Fucking Mounties,'' someone else spat. ''Fucking everything up.''

''They gonna arrest that dye-dude?''

''Somebody said there was Nirvana in it. I think that girl had a reaction.''

Thalo scowled. Drugs were *not* cool—not when one could alter consciousness by nonchemical means if one had the patience to learn the techniques and the endurance to suffer the rituals. For that matter, free highs and cheap energy were equally nixers—cheap power in the sense of that derived from the most available, as opposed to cleanest or Greenest, sources, anyway. And of course the last thing the Movement needed was a contingent of druggies undermining their credibility.

''*Oh fuck, there's a gun!*''

Thalo's heart turned over—until he saw that what had been mistaken for a weapon was in fact the nozzle of the dye pump, which a wild-faced woman had commandeered and was training on the Mounties. One got it full in the face and fell, clawing at his eyes (you were supposed to close 'em when being dyed). His partner made for the nozzle-wielder. A club flew. The shouting redoubled on both sides. And then came the free-for-all.

—An amoebic one, as it evolved, because all at once the violence was washing toward Thalo at an alarming rate. Scores of people wired to the hilt by grief and raw-nerved from too much heat and too little drink (and possible contact with the suspect dye or the skin of the those bearing same—Nirvana could give a fair jolt even contacted dry) abruptly gave their angst free rein. A few even tried to resurrect pit-diving: launching themselves atop their fellows and trusting the pack to see they didn't ground-out.

Thalo felt himself jostled every which way—save away from the chaos, which he'd have preferred. A fist grazed his cheek, though by intent or accident was un-

clear. Green and black flickered across the sky, along with Mountie scarlet. A naked teenage boy slammed into Thalo's chest, shoved by a woman twice his size. Blessedly, neither wore a trace of dye. And then he heard a furious but relatively calm voice growling "Oh fuck! Oh fuck! Oh fuck!" And glanced around just as a phalanx of sturdy lads and not a few women, all in Outer Earth T's, wedged through the crowd and began hauling at anyone who showed the smallest sign of combativeness. "Not here!" someone snapped. "You don't pull shit like that when Outer Earth's runnin' the show," another voice echoed. "Cool it . . . *now!*"

Thalo's impulse was to get the hell away, but that wasn't viable in the press of bodies, half of whom were trying to embrace the action, half trying to escape. For his part, he thought the 'Earthers had the right idea. A pro-planet rally was not the place to start tripping—or bashing one's fellow man if someone tripped anyway. And with the eyes and ears of the World-at-Large sharp-focused on Aztlan just now (and on this rally; Thalo had counted a dozen network portas around the arcade, and had himself told an earnest young woman from TV Buenos Aires that he thought Green Francis's death was "really, really bad" and "really, really sad," and that the rally was "a really good idea"—and that he was sort-of from Minneapolis), the last thing any responsible organization needed, was to look . . . irresponsible.

Which left being trampled, squashed breathless—or helping. Without being truly aware of his decision, Thalo found himself wading forward in the wake of a burly 'Earther intent on subduing a probable Mexican even larger than he. The Mex swung a fist, connected, and leered like an ape, even as he shook his hand in pained surprise. The 'Earther staggered, shook his head, and stomped grimly back into the fray. But when Mr. Mex would have launched another blow, Thalo was behind him, neatly restraining the arm with one hand while twisting the free one up between the shoulders with the other.

"Thanks," the 'Earther panted. "I got 'im."

"Don't think so," Thalo gritted back, "he's a strong 'un."

"I'll help, then," the 'Earther replied. And together, they escorted their struggling quarry to where a second cadre of 'Earthers, in company with a crew of Mounties, was spraying bursts of sweat-smelling smoke into the faces of anyone who seemed remotely rambunctious. Slow-smoke, Thalo identified: a fast-acting tranq designed for crowd control, much as tear gas had been years before, though friendlier. It was the first time he'd been around any.

Mr. Mex took a prime dose full in the face, and Thalo's 'Earther companion slapped hands across both their noses just in time to block debilitating whiffs. "Need to keep your fight-or-flight," he explained a moment later. "If you're gonna keep on helping out, anyway—which I hope you are. We're outnumbered, in case you didn't notice. I'd hate for the Twins to come on and find everybody flatted or binding wounds."

Having finally found a focus for a day's frustration on top of a day's nervous energy, Thalo accepted eagerly. All he'd needed was something to do—something responsible. This was it. He lost all track of time, and all count of the free-for-allers he and Big Earth (as he called his de facto partner) grabbed from behind and hauled protesting to their rendezvous with Mr. Slow. Before long they had a system going, almost a dance. Thalo was grinning like a fool. Big Earth grinned back. Once Thalo glimpsed the girl he'd seen at the airport: the one with the flyers and damask tattoos. His grin widened when he caught her eye, then maxed to overload at the appreciative look she returned, whereupon she was swept away by the mob.

He and Big Earth had just deposited Trouble Number Nine with the Slow-Smoke brigade, when the thundering U2 cut off in mid-note; a shriek of feedback tore through his ears like the slash of an electronic whip; and a furious male voice yelled with the slow precision of absolute command, "This bullshit ends *now*!"

The voice had come from the stage. Thalo whirled

around, but it was hard to focus through the mass of craning heads.

"*Now!*" a nearly identical voice repeated. "Or we won't play."

Another shriek of feedback, and the crowd began to quiet. Yells became grumbles, became growls. Became reverent silence.

"Ladies and gentlemen—if that's what you *hombres* still are," came the voice of the emcee, whom Thalo vaguely recognized as a former MTV VeeJay, "you've heard how they sound when they're pissed. Now hear how they sound when they're making the best god-damned music on planet earth! Ladies and gentlemen; *damas y caballeros:* The Hero Twins!''

The explosion of applause and cheers exploded through merely loud into white noise. Thalo shouted with them, in need of release as much as any. A dozen breaths passed before he realized that one of the feather-clad figures on stage had laid down a chord on a synthesizer that was rising in both pitch and volume to drown out the most orgiastically enthusiastic ovation.

The mob quieted. The chord—organlike—hung in the air as though suspended. Thalo recognized it instantly: "The Great Gates of Kiev." Originally by Modest Mussorgsky and then brought into the repertoire of rock by Emerson, Lake and Palmer back in the last century; the Twins' version transcended both—in part because it used instruments neither earlier performers could have accessed, and partly because the Twins had voices so perfectly harmonious that Greg Lake's provocative vocals paled in comparison.

Nor was the song inappropriate. Lake had found words for the music back then, and Thalo, like everyone else his age, knew them by heart from the Twins' rendition. Part of the chorus fit the Francis situation perfectly. He screamed it with the rest when it came around: "death is life." And closed his eyes in ecstasy as the song thundered on.

The Twins had just begun their trademark shift from classical European rhythms to traditional New World,

when someone nudged Thalo's side. Big Earth was pointing at his canteen with eyebrows raised, while sketching
a question mark in the air. Thalo nodded.

Big Earth drank copiously—not that Thalo cared. He
had just retrieved the canteen when another nudge, followed by a fumble of movement, snared his attention
once more. His new comrade was skinning out of his
Outer Earth T. Thalo shrugged, but as he turned away,
Big Earth caught his arm and thrust the garment upon
him. "You earned it," he shouted, then fished in the
pocket of his jeans and handed Thalo a sheet of paper.
"We could use more folks like you. If you feel like joining up, fill this out and leave it with one of our ushers
when you split."

Thalo was already prowling through his pack for a pen.

Chapter IX:
Nightmoves

(The Medicine Wheel, Sinsynsen)
(Thursday, September 8—evening)

No, you fool, that foot doesn't go there! 'Bird chided himself, as his weight came down wrong on a moccasined toe and threw his balance off. *Nor there either—* when the correction veered perilously close to a stagger.

It was useless. No way he could salvage this set, and if he screwed up much more, there might not be another. No, scratch that; his reputation as an eagle dancer here at the 'Wheel was solid enough to weather a ragged round. He just didn't like having ragged rounds—because, this one excepted, he never had them.

Tonight . . . he didn't know what had got into him. The Drum was fine: Maza-Kute, the same lads who'd seen him through that great set the night he'd found the skinned man, which had initiated the recent craziness. The crowd was more than usually appreciative too, and even included a corps of the World Champion Na Hollos who'd hung around after stealing the Hugh King Cup at last week's Toli Championships. Sure he was tired—but no more than at other times (unless—dreadful thought— old age was ambushing him, which wasn't likely at twenty-seven).

But actually (as he masked *another* misstep with a flourish of the eagle-feathered wings strapped along his arms), he really did know what the problem was. Three things.

The death of Green Francis was most obvious; then

again, everybody in town was bummed about that, including one member of the Drum, who'd asked to be excused; and a good third of the audience, to judge by the black and green armbands in evidence. 'Bird had one too, and more green and black limning the painted spirals that adorned most of what skin showed beneath feathers, fur, and fringed leather.

Another was that damned medicine dream. Those things irked him on principle because they didn't fit his worldview: namely the Western consensus reality called, more or less, scientific rationalism—and this dream bugged him more than he wanted to admit. And though he'd managed to sublimate it during his tour-guide session with wide-eyed young Thalo, he'd been reminded of it in force as soon as he'd entered the arena, in the form of a fat *turista* in a wildly incongruous fur coat and black shades that made her look remarkably like the Ancient of Raccoons—especially when she had the audacity to order lobster.

Which had to be an omen.

Just like the green pigment he'd borrowed from another performer when his own supply proved insufficient was one.

Pthalo green. As in bright, smug, full-of-himself, naive Indian-wannabe John "Thalo" Gordon.

Who'd managed to entertain him with his guileless (and selective, it appeared), ineptness then surprise him with his knowledge of arcane tidbits of Native lore, then impress him with the passion and sincerity of his convictions—and finally piss him off royally with a recurrence of the arrogant "attitude" 'Bird suspected kept the lad eternally on somebody's shit list.

Like his, at the moment. And even worse, he was the reason the kid was down here! He'd hired him, for God's sakes, so maybe his continuous fuck-ups (he'd just lost the beat again) were the gods getting back at him for that trick he'd played—was still playing—on a well-meaning kid. Shoot, he could imagine Green Francis's ghost huddling with the Ancient of Raccoons over mugs of black drink and beer, pointing at little Thunderbird where he

marched (stumbled, rather) his hour upon the earthly stage, and giggling as they turned the joke back on him.

Which was not an image to be contemplating when the dance brought him back in view of the Raccoon Woman. She grinned lasciviously. 'Bird glared back—another no-no during a serious dance—then forced himself to blank his mind to everything but the Drum. And, because dancing was ninety percent reflex anyway, managed to avoid any more missteps, whereupon the crowd deigned to reward what really had been a shitty performance with its customary roof-shaking ovation.

He bowed, sweeping his arm-pinions along the earth floor, then gestured to the Drum, who likewise rose. "Ladies and gentlemen, *damas y caballeros*," the emcee intoned, "Thunderbird O'Connor!"

'Bird barely recognized his own name, so mortified—and preoccupied—was he. Somehow, he escaped the arena at the foot of the semi-circle of stone terraces that comprised the *diverto's* dining area. "Sorry," he told Elena Murray, the stage manager, as he slipped past her on his way to the dressing room.

"It happens," she replied frankly. She too had been weeping, to judge by the film of mascara staining the plump cheeks beneath her brown eyes. "I'm half-Greek," she'd informed him earlier. "We cry a lot. I cry even more—and will until this is over." It was only later that he'd recalled that she was Presbyterian, not Catholic.

"I'll do better tomorrow, I promise," 'Bird assured her through an apologetic smooch he stepped back to bestow.

"You've got company," she called as he resumed his retreat. "Said he was a friend of yours, so I let him in."

'Bird nodded absently, wondering who, since Stormy was in mid-Way by now, 'Wounds was in Eireland, and he didn't have many other buddies.

He found out as soon as he slumped into the mirror-walled cubby that comprised his personal corner of the male performers' dressing room and saw the slight, handsome, Latino-look young man lounging on his makeup stool. "Rudy!" he exclaimed. It was Rudy Ramirez,

whom he'd met during that mess with the werkas. He was a co-worker, chum, and ('Bird suspected) sometimes lover of Carolyn Mauney-Griffith—whom (excluding medicine dreams) he hadn't known until last week either. Cary had been in the thick of things—she was, after all, a marine biologist with a specialty in cetaceans—but Rudy had been mostly on the side. He was a kind of third-in-command, primary-backup, jack-of-all-(especially electronic)-trades out at PEORCI. As for his part in the conflict between the werkas and the local dolphins, which had seen 'Bird function as Singer to Kevin Mauney's Word and Cary's Way . . . he'd mostly been there to bring the raft and provide moral support; his debriefing had come later. And, except for taking part in one ritual; guarding the beacon fire while 'Bird, Kev, and Stormy half drowned ferrying a water drum out to sea during a quasi-hurricane; and seeing about a zillion dead adolescent orcas come floating to shore the morning after, he'd had little contact with the really arcane stuff. Certainly he'd neither seen Cary change skin nor almost lost his own.

Still, he was a nice guy, 'Bird liked him as far as he knew him, as did Stormy; and Cary liked him as well. Besides, he'd been a comrade in adversity, and that of itself was a bond.

" 'Bird!" Rudy cried, extending a hand, then pausing as he noticed the costume and makeup. "Uh, that *is* you under all that war paint . . . ?"

"Not war paint," 'Bird corrected reflexively, as he commenced doffing his gear. "But it's a common mistake."

"Sorry! And sorry to surprise you," Rudy went on quickly, as he backed into a corner, which, given his trim size, he fit neatly. He plucked at the hem of his shorts. That, and a slight tremor in his Spanish-accented voice told 'Bird he was more wired than he was admitting.

"No problem," 'Bird assured him. Then, deliberately: "You want to, you can give me a hand with these feathers. They get hung on each other if you're not careful."

Rudy obliged. 'Bird had asked partly because he really

did need the help, as clumsy as he'd been; and partly to give the guy something to do besides fidget, which seemed his inclination. Too bad he didn't smoke.

"Good show," Rudy observed too casually. "Not that I haven't seen it before, or anything. In fact, it was me who got Cary down here the night all *that* happened—not that I knew anything about it . . . then."

"Fate," 'Bird said, bare-torsoed.

Rudy sat. "I don't believe in fate."

'Bird regarded him keenly, sharp eyes made even more piercing by bracketing black makeup designed to evoke the eye patches of peregrine falcons. "I didn't either, until last week. I still don't want to. But it'd probably help both of us if we did."

Rudy suddenly looked as though he were about to cry. He bit his lip. "Nobody around to talk to about that stuff," he burst out. "Nobody but you and the Ninja Queen—Mary Hasegawa: mine and Cary's boss—and she wasn't *there*, man. She didn't *see*. And you can't talk to somebody who didn't see!"

'Bird nodded. "I've had the same problem—'cept I've got Stormy."

Rudy shrugged. "Yeah, well, it really got to me tonight, and I . . . I just had to talk to somebody. Cary's out of the country, so I figured I'd take a chance and—" He broke off, too many words battling for priority on his tongue. " 'Bird," he managed finally. "Are you doing anything tonight—after you clean up, I mean?"

Sleeping, 'Bird nearly replied. Courtesy of Thalo he'd barely managed a nap since the inception of the Way more than a day ago. But Rudy was—almost—a friend. He *was* a nice guy who was unhappy and in need of company. And, 'Bird admitted, he wouldn't mind having someone to decompress with himself. "Gotta shower," he found himself saying. "You feel like hangin' 'round, we can go somewhere—long as it's not here. I—uh—wasn't all that hot tonight, and I'd hate to hear what folks're sayin'."

"Fine," Rudy sighed, handsome face brightening beneath his tan. "That's cool."

'Bird paused before shucking his breechclout. "You got a car?"

Rudy shook his head. "AFZoRTA."

"We'll take the Jeep then."

"Thought you didn't drive."

"Don't own a car; don't like tech—but sometimes you have to deal with 'em. Sometimes they're even convenient." 'Bird replaced the breechclout with a towel. Rudy looked discreetly away—which was pointless, given that they'd been naked as jaybirds together during Carolyn's cleansing ritual. The guy had a nice body, as 'Bird recalled. "Ten minutes," he warned, from the entrance to the cubby.

"I'll be here," Rudy replied to 'Bird's reflection.

After three successive *divertos* proved too noisy and another seated them too near the obligatory salt-water aquarium-wall, they headed for Rudy's apartment. Somewhere along the way three mugs of Tecate had been consumed apiece, resulting in what was to 'Bird a mild buzz, but which prompted Stormy's Jeep to vent an electronic admonition the last time he inserted the card: *"This vehicle senses potentially hazardous amounts of breath alcohol. Compensation mode has been engaged. Any increase in breath alcohol will result in deactivation of this vehicle."*

Which meant that it would automatically lower accelerator inputs by fifteen percent, filter out sloppy steering, and damp any sudden applications of either that or the brakes. A top-speed governor had also gone online. If they drank more, it would warn them again, very firmly, then relentlessly slow to a stop.

'Bird was both irked and impressed. All that on a humble Jeep—what must something really high-tech have? And how high tech was it, for Stormy (who liked his brew) not to have bypassed it? Rudy, more jaded, took it in stride. Or was even more preoccupied than 'Bird thought—since he returned from his local Kroger with two sixes of Bud in lieu of the requested Corona. *Oh*

well, 'Bird concluded wryly, *it'll all be piss in an hour anyway.*

"Hey, what's this?" Rudy cried a moment later, as he sought an AWOL bottle that had rolled beneath his seat. 'Bird caught the satiny gleam of blued steel in the hand his companion withdrew from those dubious reaches: Smith & Wesson .38, he identified. Part of Stormy's permanent (if illegal) stash. "Put that back," he growled. "Stormy'll have my head if anything happens to one of his toys."

"Mine," Rudy protested in a bogus pout. Then, seriously: "Actually, I'd feel a lot better if we had this around tonight."

'Bird grimaced and pried the weapon from his fingers one-handed (after first setting the safety—Stormy's hideaways were always live and loaded). "Not a bad idea, actually," he conceded, "but *I'll* do the totin'."

By which time they'd reached Rudy's apartment. It was small, almost an efficiency, and sparely, if comfortably, furnished in a mix of trashy make-do and elegant conquest-era antiques that complemented the white sandcrete walls and beamed ceiling. It was also nicely located, being the projecting, semi-detached corner of a tumble of cubes (like the old Habitat complex the Israelis had built at the Montreal World's Fair last century). And since trees were a priority resource in Aztlan, there were a lot of them on this particular site, and it was at the end of a cul-de-sac in the bargain, *Casa Ramirez* was actually fairly secluded. "I can sunbathe nude," Rudy confided as he shucked his serape by the door, "and nobody cares."

"Prob'ly like the view too much," 'Bird shot back with a smirk. "God, I don't believe I said that!" he added quickly.

"Well, you *have* been drinking . . ."

"Sleep deprivation," he countered—and yawned abruptly. The air smelled of incense, sweet and pungent. Smoke drifted from a small brass burner by the door. 'Bird coughed.

"Sorry 'bout that. 'Earthers were handing it out free

down by my bus stop. Figured I'd give it a try."

"Strong stuff."

A shrug. "Want some coffee?"

"We're not *drunk* yet!"

Rudy laughed and skinned out of his gold-toned skin-shirt and sneakers, which left only tight white shorts. Already barefoot, 'Bird doffed his tunic and relaxed into the comfort of a white beanbag on the floor, stowing the pistol beneath. Rudy popped a cap and passed him the bottle. He rubbed the bottom across his bare chest; it was wonderfully cool. Rudy grinned, but his eyes were troubled.

"Talk," 'Bird said finally. "You wanted to talk."

"Yeah," Rudy sighed, all pretense of frivolity fallen away. "Trouble is, I don't know if I can."

'Bird took a long swallow and forced himself to more focused awareness—which took some effort. The incense didn't help. "So maybe you oughta start with what's buggin' you most."

Rudy claimed the bean-bag opposite. Their feet brushed. "Sorry," Rudy grunted and eased his away. 'Bird didn't bother.

"I think," Rudy began eventually, "it's the 'on guard' thing. I dunno. It's weird: it's like"—he swallowed—"it's like this dream I had when I was a kid: I was in the town I grew up in back in Spain, and it was a really little town, and it was dark and nobody was out on the streets. But *I* was out, and a couple of blocks from home, and I had a radio, and I heard on the radio that a werewolf was loose in town. And all of a sudden I wanted to get home so bad I couldn't stand it—only there was this thing loose somewhere, and I knew that it and me were the only things outside, and town wasn't that big. But anyway, I was trying to get home, only I didn't want to walk down the streets,'cause then the thing would see me, and I didn't want to knock on doors . . . I don't know why. So I started taking back ways and stuff, except that was bad too, 'cause that's where the thing could hide. Except that way I had somewhere to hide too . . ."

"So did you make it?"

"I dunno. I woke up. I was scared as shit, man!"

"So you're sayin' . . . ?"

"That to do my job I have to go in the water—it's what I've been trained to do, and what I love to do. And I'm used to knowing what's out there, and that some of it's dangerous—sharks and stuff; even orcas you don't want to mess with. But now . . . all *that's* still out there, only some of it's more than it used to be. Like, dolphins are intelligent and are thinking about me. And orcas are probably thinking *bad* things about me 'cause they know I know about 'em. And now when I see an orca—I've only seen one, and it was on a remote—it's like the werewolf thing. In that dream I saw a dog . . . only I didn't know whether to trust it to be *just* a dog—and that's the bad thing: not being able to trust what you used to trust."

"Plus there may still be some on land," 'Bird finished, reminded of the warning from *his* dream: that there could always be another predator. "We have no idea how many were-orcas—*werkas*, me and Stormy call 'em—there are. I've seen as many as four together, and Stormy killed two and wounded another—'course they might've been part of that bunch that kidnapped Kevin. But we don't know how many were the same ones, or how many others there might be. We think it takes at least four human skins to make one an orca can use to change shape, and it takes that many *every time*,'cause they don't know how to reuse 'em. But we also don't know how long they can play human before they have to return to their own form—which Kevin thinks they have to do to stay sane—assumin' they *are* sane, which I doubt. But anyway, accordin' to confidential police records, there've been almost sixty skinned corpses found in the Zone in the last two years—which means there could be as many as fifteen of 'em, if they didn't shift but once. But the bad thing is, that's only the tip of the iceberg. See, 'Wounds got me and Stormy into records all up and down the coast—Miami to Caracas, includin' the Caribbean—and the total of skinned bodies, or those too gone to tell if they'd been skinned: burned and stuff—found over the last couple of years, which is how long we think the

werkas have been doin' their nasty thing, is more than
three times that. Two-hundred-nine, by last count.''

"Jesus!'' A pause. Then: ''And *nobody* knows? That's
hard to believe.''

''Yeah, well, people sure don't *like* to believe it—or
what it implies—so they bury the reports, or lose 'em,
or whatever. And of course there's supposed to be no
crime in Aztlan—certainly no sensational crime—so the
Mounties suppress the hell out of it, and chalk up what
they can't to the Xipetotec folks.''

''The resurgent cult of the flaying god,'' Rudy said,
nodding.

'Bird wondered how he'd managed to be so eloquent,
when his senses seemed so muddled and his eyes so hard
to focus. He stretched languidly. A foot touched Rudy's
leg. He left it. Rudy mirrored his gesture—and, coinci-
dentally, eased closer. ''It scares me,'' Rudy whispered
at last. ''It means you can't trust *anybody*!''

''Not quite,'' 'Bird murmured—the dim light made
that seem the preferred mode of speech. He was lazily
comfortable, in spite of the subject matter, and perhaps
that made it easier to speak of unpleasant things. ''It's
really pretty easy to spot 'em, leastwise when they've
changed—only, you've not seen any, have you? Well,
basically, they tend to be big and bulky—conservation
of mass, I guess—and they've got sort of . . . unfinished
faces, though we think their features are a mix of their
victims'. But like I said, they're big and tend to wear
floppy oversized clothes—as, unfortunately, do most big
men 'round here. But the main thing is the way they
move: It's a big leap, I guess, from swimmin' to walkin'
on land—and while people swim sometimes, and get
used to bein' in water, orcas *can't* get used to bein' on
land. Which means werkas move funny when *they* do:
they're kinda clumsy, and tend to move slowly, like
they're afraid of losin' their balance—falling's gotta be
a weird idea for 'em. And since they're used to usin'
their fins all the time, they make these . . . swimming motions with their arms when they're just standin' around.
I'm sure it's reflex, and I'm sure they'd try to stop if they

knew they did it, but it's a dead giveaway. Trouble is, by the time you're close enough to catch it, it's too late—as I well know.'' He ran a finger down the scar that bisected his torso meaningfully.

"Too bad about that," Rudy yawned. "Messed up a nice body."

"I'll live," 'Bird sighed. "Mostly it follows the line of the muscles. Where it doesn't . . . maybe I'll get it fixed."

Rudy finished his beer with one long swallow. "Want another?"

'Bird chugged his in turn. "Sure."

Rudy padded off to the refrigerator and returned with two more frosted bottles. He passed one to 'Bird, but instead of reclaiming his old place, dragged his bean-bag next to 'Bird's and sank down beside him. "This stuff scares me," he repeated simply. "Sorry. But . . . I just need to be close to somebody right now. Don't worry."

"That may be the best defense," 'Bird chuckled. "Safety in numbers and all. In fact . . . it might be best not to sleep alone."

Rudy's breath caught. "How so?"

'Bird eased an arm behind his shoulders and stroked his hair, where it had fallen into his face. " 'Cause that's how they get you. They get folks who aren't all there mentally: crazy folks, retarded folks; maybe folks in altered states of consciousness. Like when you're asleep, maybe: I know the dolphins got at me a couple of times through medicine dreams."

Rudy shivered, the goosebumps plain across his bare skin. "What about being stoned? Or . . . drunk?"

"I don't know," 'Bird replied frankly. "See, I tend to be around people a lot, and I've got a well-secured apartment at the embassy. But you: you're in the water a lot, and you live by yourself in kind of an isolated place—"

"And like you said," Rudy mumbled sleepily, "I maybe ought not to sleep alone."

And with that he reached over and kissed 'Bird (who'd been absently stroking his hair all that while) in the hol-

low between his chest and neck and shoulder. 'Bird giggled softly—and reached down to untie the drawstring of his jeans. Something wet fell on his shoulder, as the warm, smooth body shifted beside him and fingers brushed his belly just left of the scar. It took him a moment to realize that Rudy was crying.

Chapter X:
Finn's Wake

(The North Atlantic, west of Eireland)
(Friday, September 9—morning)

The smoke from her father's funeral pyre was still merging with the morning fog when Carolyn broke surface at last. The sea was featureless: dead calm, though she suddenly loathed that phrase, having seen death closer than most folk nowadays. The fog seemed to hang suspended a meter above her head. *Weather magic*? she wondered, as she would not have a week gone by. Dolphins could manipulate weather. Selkies and dolphins were allies; perhaps someone had called in a marker. Or maybe it evinced some uniquely selkie art *she* might someday command.

When she stopped hurting. For now, she paddled in place, half herself, half seal—in mind. Physically, she was totally pinniped, having at last night's wake been gifted with the skin she'd worn to the selkies' hold. Skins were inherited, she'd learned, through lineages both seal and human. Hers had graced a female pup of the bull seal whose hide her late father had worn when he'd first seen Carolyn's mom. *That* pelt had burned with him: had pillowed his head where he lay atop the pyre in the uppermost vaults of the uncharted sea mount that twice daily raised its peak above the waves in a finger of sodden stone no more than twelve meters across.

Precious wood burned too: one stick ferried to that long-drowned land by every member of her father's clan, to honor one who'd been called chief, and might have

added *Ard Rhi*: high king, had he desired that title. Age had sufficed, it seemed; he'd been the oldest selkie on earth. No other clan—and there were a few, secreted beneath cliffs and rocks and skerries, here and Scotland as well—had spawned his like. Already his name had grown: *Finn the Far-sighted*, they called him, who in his youth (so Maevyn, his last and most tenacious mate, had confided with a laugh), had been styled Finn the Randy, for his penchant for tumbling women.

A head broke surface beside her: a round, whiskered knob craning above cold, still water. Another joined it: smaller, less dappled, shorter of nose. *Connor*—she named them as they rose—*Sean*. Cousin and brother.

He lived in water, died on land, and fire sends him to the air, Connor mused. *They should have called him Far-*Traveler.

Carolyn resisted the urge to discuss funeral customs among the selkies of western Eireland, and again felt a pang of frustration. They needed an anthropologist for this, not a marine biologist! All *she* could do was swim, identify fish, puzzle about the mechanism by which transparent sponges in symbiosis with an obscure genus of deep-sea plankton produced sufficient light to illuminate a labyrinth of caverns, and observe a heretofore uncatalogued species of kelp that discharged vast amounts of oxygen to augment air vents atop the holds when seas ran high or storms drowned the skerries utterly.

Besides . . . it *hurt*! True, she'd barely known Finn, but she'd felt genuine affection for him, and he, seemingly, for her. And if he'd also made her a pawn in some complex para-human conspiracy, and had likewise manipulated her, still, he'd also bequeathed a legacy of wonder the like of which no one with her background had ever known.

A nudge at her shoulder was Sean: playful when he should've been serious.

Being good at what you are is *serious*, Connor informed her—and dunked her. Abruptly they were playing tag: plunging through the skimpy waves, then dodging deep and arrowing up again, all unexpectedly. Carolyn

was least successful. Still, one didn't learn the subtleties of three-dimensional tag in a minute. And somehow, amid the play, the pain diminished. When she rose again, the plume of smoke was gone and the fog was dissipating. Blue sky gleamed overhead. Connor nipped her neck (which gesture vaguely alarmed her—it could've been taken as a prelude to mating), and struck off toward where the sun now shone fitfully through the haze. *Not with kin*, he chided.

Incest is best, Carolyn teased back from reflex—prompting a twinge of concern lest that comment be misconstrued. Happily, her intent had ridden the words, and Connor understood. *Besides*, he confided, as she caught up with him and Sean, *your mother is surely waiting*.

Carolyn started at that. She'd totally forgotten the rendezvous she'd preempted in favor of pinniped caprice. And now there'd be more crises to hash out—beyond establishing *exactly* what her mother had known about Carolyn's sire; and why she, a happily married woman with three advanced degrees, dual citizenship, and a bouncing (and full-human) son, had felt compelled to dally with a mere *boy* who shouldn't exist, at the risk of her marriage; *then* concealed that dalliance for over twenty years, and its preposterous repercussions even longer.

Perhaps she will want to be my mother too, Sean mused from below, sounding more the near-child he was than the chattery info-maxed adolescent he'd affected yesterday.

Maybe, Carolyn agreed off-hand. *But for God's sake, don't bring it up!*

Do not fear.

Hmmmm, she continued, as Connor set a feverish pace, aided by westerly winds, *we have* gotta *get you on the Net.*

Net? The word carried a surge of instinctive alarm from Connor and Sean alike.

Not that *kind of net! Network: Everything in the world worth knowing, and a lot that isn't, all tied up in glass and plastic ready for your touch. Why, you can—*

Nets have claimed many of our folk, Connor broke in. *They are not our greatest friend.*

I'm not surprised, Carolyn gave back. *And speaking of that: what happens when . . . one of you 'dies in fur'—is that the term? Do you turn back, or what? I mean, Fir was killed while in the act of Changing—and kept on.*

Likely because he had already willed it so, lest being found in human shape with his skin nearby raise unwanted questions, Connor replied. *Our kind have that much control—that much "will power," you would say—though once fully Changed, he would have remained so in any case, with no way of showing he was other than he seemed—unlike your orcas, apparently, perhaps because they must wear multiple skins at a time, and none of them freely given. Fir, though—they could have cut him up and used all their machines on him, and it would have revealed nothing. The Change comes from . . . somewhere else.*

Father said it came from belief, Sean appended. *And from something he called the . . . implement—something.*

Implicate order, Carolyn supplied. *I don't really understand it, but it's basically the idea that there may be a . . . world below or around or between or within or some other weird way connected to our world, out of which generative orders of various types unfold; and that things that have no rational explanation by the rules we know come from there. I'll show you some books on it sometime—but be warned, it's hard going.*

I will—that is, I'll *look forward to it,* Sean replied promptly.

No doubt, Carolyn "chuckled" back, *you will.*

Roughly an hour later, Carolyn once again surfaced to smoke on the horizon. But it was the eastern horizon now, and beneath it lurked a blue-green darkness that could only be forested land. *Probably some poor old fisherman trying to hang on to tradition,* she reflected. *Poking up his peat fire 'twixt commercials on his cable TV.*

Your kind burn many things, Connor grumbled. *When you must hoard fresh air in your dwellings, you learn*

not to squander it. Finn's pyre was a very great honor— and a terrible risk.

Keeping warm isn't squandering, Carolyn shot back.

Perhaps it is someone's funeral.

The Eirish don't usually burn their dead, Carolyn replied. At which point a thought struck her so forcefully she strangled, as human instincts made her gape. *Sean?* she ventured carefully, fear clotting in her heart. *You know what Father said about us aging faster as seals, which makes us die young—from my point of view . . .*

Yes—I mean yeah.

Well . . . how does that apply to me? I didn't become a selkie until I was grown. And I have no idea how old my seal-self is—how many years it's got left. So will I age like you lads, or what?

It was Connor who turned to face her, round eyes serious—a disquieting effect in a nonhuman head. *I—we— do not know. But Finn and Fir and I have spoken of this, and they thought your mixed blood would help. Certainly you are as wise as any of us in your knowing. Still . . . I cannot say—save that Finn's father thought you would not. That was one reason you were sired: so that someone of selkie blood would live long enough to accomplish something.*

So basically I need to watch it, Carolyn concluded. *Or maybe,* she continued with what would've been a laugh had she been human, *I should con a Galapagos turtle out of its shell and spend weekends that way to compensate . . .*

A kraken would be better, Sean advised. *They live forever—of course you'd have to talk it out of eating you first.*

Ever talk to a kraken, boy? Connor snapped.

No. But—

Well, I *have: tried to. It was like sticking your mind into cold fire mixed with blazing hunger and vicious hate. I don't recommend it.*

I thought krakens only lived in the Antarctic, Carolyn broke in. *They need cold deep water. Warm water doesn't*

contain enough oxygen, so they suffocate. The ones we've found have always been dying. And—

Thought, Connor observed wryly, *is often a far cry from truth.*

And how big were these krakens, anyhow? Sean wondered.

Carolyn tried to shrug—and failed, lacking viable shoulders. *Over fifty meters, by report. Of course we've only assumed that from tentacle fragments . . .*

Fifty meters! Connor snorted. *Must have been a young one!*

Hush, Con, Sean cautioned. *You're scaring her.*

He was too! And for the first time she actually pondered the fact that she was in the cold north Atlantic, not the friendly, warm Caribbean, where she'd spent most of her wet-time before the Change. Suddenly she felt very small, very human, and very . . . edible.

Land ho! Connor proclaimed, then nodded with his nose—and nipped her.

Carolyn knew something was wrong as soon as she drew close enough to shore to see how Kevin was sitting. His shoulders slumped; his head and hands hung slack, as though his joints had all dissolved. She wished she could see his eyes. Impulsively—and in spite of her unease, she noted how she woke that new skill by reflex— she sought his mind, seeking to relieve her own anxiety that much sooner.

But Connor was there blocking her. *No,* he cautioned. *Your brother is sad enough; to approach him thus would only disturb one who needs no more concern.*

But . . .

No!

Carolyn's response was to growl at him—and swim faster.

Meanwhile, Red Wounds and O'Neal were picking their way down the strand, each clad as they'd been the day before. She was relieved to note that the former carried the canvas tote in which she'd stowed her clothes, along with another she didn't recognize.

But where was Mom? Surely she'd arrived by now, what with two diplomats pulling strings.

Still, she was coming from some nameless part of the Third World, and even ambassadorial strings could get snarled among tree stumps and telephone poles if one fared too far afield.

On the other hand, it was cold and rainy; and Nuala Griffith was famous for her loathing of both. "Someone lost my application to be born in the Sahara," she was fond of saying. "Next time I'll stand there playing moldy-oldy rap songs on my harp until Saint Peter sticks on all the right seals to get me into someplace hot."

So Mom was probably up in the Humvee with the heat on high, drinking dapper Mister O'Neal out of hot coffee, warm Guinness, and cold soda in precisely that order. No chance of any salmon surviving, unless Kev had zipped off in the Ka to score more.

I will go first, Connor advised. *I will see that your clothing awaits.*

Clothing . . . ? From Sean. *Why . . . ?*

But Connor was already a diminishing dot amid the rising surf of a changing tide. Kevin, who'd been gazing vaguely out to sea, perked up when he saw him, and Carolyn *sensed* his relief even at that distance. Red Wounds saw him too, clutched O'Neal's arm, and pointed. Both increased their pace.

Connor had made landfall by then, with Sean right behind, and as Kevin rose and stalked toward them, Connor ducked his head and worried at a flipper. A moment later, the skin began to loosen and slough away. He caught it as he rose on two legs, thin sunlight glistening off smooth, wet skin—by which time Kevin had arrived. He looked tired and impatient. She tried to read his face and failed. "It can wait," she heard Connor tell him. "Give her time."

Time for what? she wondered, pausing in the shallows to assail her own flipper. Best to do it that way: turn off your human aspect, pretend your limb was prey, and chow down. Hopefully, by the time the pain hit your

brain, the Change would be in full swing. 'Wounds and O'Neal had turned their backs already.

Actually, it was easy not to think—probably residual numbness from her father's death. And the chosen appendage really did seem remote, even if the pain was far too real as she tasted blood and saw it drip upon the rocks to mingle with the sea, as her father's ashes were now dissolving in it—what weren't spread across the sky.

And then the small lightnings struck, and she felt a peculiar deconstriction as her surrogate skin loosened and fell away. By the time she stood again, Connor had retrieved her bag, opened it, and was shaking out jeans, a baggy sweater, and a towel. "I'm back," she announced, as she applied the last with vigor. "Whatever's up can wait 'til I'm dressed. We've *gotta* work on the etiquette o' this," she added with a forced chuckle. "Turning your back's a helluva a way to say hello."

Kevin glanced around as she dragged the sweater over her head, yanked it down as far as it would go, and stepped ashore. It felt odd after all that swimming, her ears compensating for movements that did not exist. She snatched the jeans and tugged them on.

Connor had likewise found jeans, as had the now-human Sean, who was pondering the confluence of drawstrings and his sparse pubic hair. "Should've brought the velcro kind," Kevin sighed. "Lucky I didn't know Con's size and picked up a spare."

Carolyn waited for Sean to "arrange" himself, then motioned him forward, holding him by the shoulders before her. He was taller than she, she realized—probably about 1.7 meters. Then again, everybody was—except some selkie women. "Guys," she proclaimed, "I've acquired a ... protege—kind of like an exchange student ... without the exchange."

O'Neal's brows were already rising as he turned. Red Wounds remained grimly passive.

"Gentlemen," she continued. "Allow me to present Sean ... O'Finn. He's the youngest son of the late chief of a major selkie clan, and he's gonna be staying with me for a while. Oh, and Kev," she appended, "you'll

have to be 'specially nice to him, 'cause . . . he's our brother.''

Sean was obviously trying hard to look solemn and adult when he wanted to grin and ask questions. He thrust out a hand—first at Kevin, then at Red Wounds, then got confused, stuck out both, and stared forlornly at all three men.

''Family first,'' O'Neal advised smoothly, tipping his head toward Kevin. Kevin shook hands, then muttered a gruff, ''What the hell?'' and gave the boy a hug. Sean did grin then—and had to be restrained from embracing the ambassadors when Carolyn, with one hand still firmly on his shoulder, introduced both men in turn.

''And of course you remember Connor,'' she finished. Then: ''So what's up? Who died?''—that last too flippantly.

''Death's a cold thing,'' O'Neal murmured darkly. ''This'd go better in the 'Vee.''

''Vee?'' From Sean.

''Humvee: high utility military vehicle,'' O'Neal explained, aside, as he led the way back up the beach. ''You can drive it sometime, if you like.''

''Not!'' Carolyn countered, and blushed at that burst of maternalism.

Sean started to reply, but Connor silenced him with a glare, and the company trudged on in silence, in which, however, one thought chimed like a marker buoy in that cold and misty air.

Someone had died.

''So who died?'' Carolyn repeated, when they were once more ensconced inside the Humvee—it was tight for six, even when three were fairly small, and Kev and 'Wounds averaged out to two standard guys.

O'Neal nodded to Red Wounds, who cleared his throat. ''We got the word right after you left,'' he began. ''We had no way to contact you. But . . . Archbishop Blackmer died yesterday morning.''

''God, no!'' Carolyn gasped. She'd met the archbishop a couple of times, and had heard him speak—though not

at church—several more. She basically agreed with his agenda, if not his timetable or methods. And she firmly believed in freeing the seas from the tyranny of pollution, as did he. "The planet's lost a friend," she added dully.

"Which was the headline in yesterday's *New York Times*," O'Neal observed. "We got ours by fax."

"What happened?"

"Short form: he set himself on fire while meditating. Was wearing one of those flimsy gauze robes, got too close to a candle, and *poof*! He was in his private chapel, which had no sprinkler 'cause it was made of solid stone with nothing worthwhile to burn."

"Except the world's foremost churchman," Red Wounds appended, "His Holiness notwithstanding."

"There'll be a state funeral," O'Neal continued quickly, as though this were something he'd rehearsed countless times and was glad to have over. "It'll be back in Aztlan, though he was from . . . Tennessee, I think."

"Which brings us to the problem," Red Wounds rumbled.

"You've gotta go?" Carolyn wondered if she was relying on logic, intuition, or telepathy.

Red Wounds nodded. "We basically have to leave *now*. O'Neal's generously offered his private jet."

"No problem," Carolyn sighed. "You guys do what you have to, Kev and me'll come when we can—assuming you don't have other—uh—orders."

Kevin vented a long shuddering sob, and Carolyn realized he was weeping. "It's . . . not as easy as that, Cary," he whispered.

She felt a sudden chill. "What?"

"Blackmer was bad enough," he replied. "But it gets worse. For you and me, it gets worse."

Carolyn thought of the phrase that had haunted the trek up here. "How *much* worse?"

The reply came so softly she had to read his lips for confirmation—or was that his mind? He gripped her hand—for himself as much as her, she sensed. Then: "Mom."

Her nails pierced his palm, but he didn't flinch. Some-

one—Red Wounds—had an arm around her. She was aware of other closenesses: Connor and Sean. The latter, especially, seemed very . . . present. And *very* sympathetic. No way he could fake such raw emotion.

"How . . . ?" she demanded. "*How*?"

"Plane crash," O'Neal answered. "She made it to London fine, tried to catch a jump-jet to Shannon, but they were rerouting to Dublin, so she conned her way onto a relief flight. Old plane. Old pilot. Guy got lost and actually flew out to sea. He caught it, but by then he was out of fuel. He evidently blacked out at a crucial moment and . . . crashed on landing at Shannon. No survivors."

In spite of the Humvee's efficient heater, Carolyn felt as though she was frozen in ice. But at least ice would numb. At least, finally, she would not have to feel. She didn't dare *let* herself feel. One death in the last day had been bad enough, and that someone she'd loved, however briefly she'd known him. Two—no, three—was intolerable! It ran against the rhythms of her life as she'd long since established them in her singleminded pursuit of self.

"I'm sorry," Sean murmured into her ear.

"I too," Connor echoed faintly.

"Dad had her will," Kevin managed. "It's all worked out, nothing for you and me to do but be there. But it's gonna be a little freaky, Cary; not what you'd expect."

She regarded him through tears she hadn't felt begin. "How so?"

"She asked to be buried in Georgia."

"I've arranged to drop you off on the way," O'Neal added.

Carolyn didn't hear him. All she heard was Kevin crying.

Chapter XI:
Early Bird

(Sequoya Avenue, Aztlan)
(Friday, September 9—07:50 hours)

Thalo was not as alert as he would've liked when the white-and-gold AFZoRTA bus hissed to a halt at the covered sandcrete stop across Sequoya Avenue from the Native Southeastern Confederacy Compound's north gate. He shook his head to clear senses dulled by dearth of sleep, and rubbed his eyes viciously—courtesy of the dry, grit-laden air, which had yet to make peace with his contacts. Shoot, he'd considered ditching the colored ones, since he'd pretty much decided that the Lakota look that had seemed so convincing back in the States wasn't going to fly where half the population had Native blood and the rest saw it often enough to peg fakes at thirty paces. God knew the elegant, leather-suited woman next to him in the aisle had just doubletaked, then raised a bemused eyebrow.

Oh well. . . .

A small army was apparently disembarking—slowly. Thalo used the downtime to straighten the gold-braided bolo-tie that, with a long-sleeved black silk shirt and tan hopsack vest-suit, reflected local business wear. No three piecers here, where even vests and ties were only worn for special occasions—and initial contacts, for which they were deemed a courtesy.

A yawn ambushed him as he inched ahead. He really had *not* had enough sleep. Announcements to the contrary, the rally hadn't wound down until after midnight,

and it had taken forever to make his way through the exiting mob (reports said thirty thousand). And when he'd finally reached the rough stone arcade that rimmed the amphitheater, it had been no easy task to locate an 'Earther sufficiently unharried to accept the membership application he'd spent half the Twins' set completing. Probably he should've waited—except that he tended to procrastinate where paperwork was concerned, and the Earthers had been so *damned* impressive that Priority *numero uno* had quickly become joining their ranks.

Still, it had taken a while to hand off the form, and a longer while to work his way out of the park. That accomplished, he'd discovered that he had no idea how public transport functioned in Aztlan at night, nor where his motel was. The former he solved (to the dismay of his conscience) with yet another taxi (at least Aztlan's were all electric); the latter via the vehicle's NavCom and the driver's access to the Net.

That had been followed by the obligatory (and much delayed) check-in call to his parents. They'd been asleep—and irate—but after they'd finished berating him about yesterday's unscheduled walkabout, they'd mostly wanted to know if he'd located the apartment they'd be renting upon arrival, and whether he'd contacted the Heaton-Arnold-Caldwell Center. Not wanting to lie (they were actually fairly *good* folks, as practicing adults went), he'd explained about the rally, and emphasized how bummed he was about Green Francis and how everyone else in town was too. *That* had gotten through. His folks had also been bummed. His mother had even wept.

And then he'd reached the motel, and his father had told him to get some sleep. He had, determined to compensate for his indulgences by reporting to work one day early.

If he could ever get off the effing bus!

Eventually, he gained the exit, and disembarked in something between a bound and a bounce. The doors thumped shut behind him, leaving a cloud of dispersing AC as the big Mercedes diesel hustled the vehicle up to

cruise, where the electrics would sustain it.

"Wow!" he yipped, from pure astonishment, as he got his first good look at his place of employment. True, 'Bird had cruised it yesterday, and it had been impressive even then. But that, it appeared, had paralleled one of its short sides. Now he confronted a long one—and the place was bloody *huge*. A full block it stretched, in either direction, the whole enclosed by a cream sandcrete wall twice his height, sloping inward toward the top and decorated with meter-wide bas-relief world-circles at four-meter intervals. A quartet of impressive 'mids showed above, through a smattering of treetops that promised shade within. And straight ahead was the gate. Fortunately (and unlike some he'd seen), it was humanly scaled, rustically detailed in wood carved with slightly whimsical organic designs, and altogether inviting, in contrast to the intimidating wall.

Without further ado, he jogged across the street, only to be caught up in the surge of bodies from a bus that had come the other way. *God*, he realized with a start, *these were people with real, professional lives—and he was one of them!* He'd been so ensnarled in anticipation of an internship at a for-real Native embassy that the fact of it had been obscured. True, he'd amassed a brainload of book smarts, especially about what had once been called (unfortunately, he thought) the Five Civilized Tribes, four of whom (the Creeks and Seminoles having merged), along with the Tunica/Biloxi and Yuchi, comprised the Native Southeastern Confederacy. And he knew a fair bit about pre-Columbian meso-American as well. He'd also been to powwows, cruised the Net till his eyes teared, and been to movies—even tried to hang out at the Oyate Consulate in Minni. But he'd never actually considered that he might one day *use* that research and be paid for it. Nor—until yesterday—had managed significant contact with any real Natives. And whatever a pill that 'Bird guy had been, he'd known his stuff Native-wise. But he'd also known how it fit into the World-at-Large—and how Thalo, with his pretentious dye-job, would be a jarring element, and probably subject to rid-

icule, on top of being green (in the old sense) as well.

Still, as his dad was fond of saying, an hour from now it would all be over. And with that firmly in mind, he let the crowd surge past him and found himself alone on the sidewalk.

Well . . . not entirely alone.

A tan-brown flyer rippled and flapped against the Compound's pristine walls a few meters down from the gate. Another mirrored it a dozen paces further. Thalo couldn't resist wandering down to inspect the nearest. A familiar logo appeared at the top: the polar-projection world map, counterchanged along the yin-yang line, of Outer Earth. The accompanying text asked a number of pertinent questions about the reader's eco-political beliefs: "Do you *enjoy* looking at trees? Do you find clean beaches appealing? Is your health important to you? Do you want to live to a ripe old age—and enjoy the world you find there? If so . . ."

Quotes by Movement notables followed, including several by the late Archbishop. A few were fresh from the rally—and probably hadn't been rehearsed then. Finally, there was a short paragraph saying that if you agreed with any of the above, Outer Earth had something for *you*. At the bottom was a simple version of the complex membership form he'd already completed.

At which point the flyer promptly freed itself from the wall and drifted away down the sidewalk. Thalo followed, as much from aversion to litter as anything. Retrieval proved elusive, however; indeed, he was beneath the second flyer before he captured the first. Panting lightly, he scooped it off the pavement and was already retracing his steps to the gate when something caught his eye. Though it still bore an Outer Earth logo, the second flyer's text was different. And since he was sympathetically predisposed anyway, he read it.

He also read the third, which was different again.

A half dozen more brought him to the end of the block, where he paused. Was there any point in pursuing variations-on-a-theme around the corner? Intending to arrive at work early, he was now late. On the other hand, he

wasn't technically due to appear at all, nor had he announced his intention to arrive. Therefore . . .

The latest flyer was still being installed—by a slim young woman in a beige wraparound skirt and emerald-and-gold serape: Outer Earth's colors. Her hair was twined with feathers, and she was juggling a mass of flyers, old-fashioned masking tape, and an esoteric-looking staple gun.

—Without much success, since even as he watched, several flyers escaped and pirouetted further down the walk. She chased them. He followed. Their hands met on the last one, and then their eyes.

"You!" they exclaimed as one.

And laughed as one as well.

It was the girl who'd accosted him at the airport, then glimpsed again at the rally.

"Saw you last night," he grinned, flopping against the wall, arms folded across his chest.

"Saw you too."

"I know," he replied, blushing. "I . . . uh, tried to catch up with you, but then the Chaos Beast arrived."

"*Muy mal*," the girl sighed, in Spanish. "I was afraid that would happen. Still, we got hold of it."

"Yeah," Thalo agreed. "I, uh, helped."

A brow shot up. A smile appeared—quite a dazzling one. He was trying to construct a non-frivolous reply when the girl froze where she stood, brown eyes utterly blank—only for a second, as it evolved, for an instant later, animation returned.

Thalo scowled. "Something wrong?"

She shook her head. "Twinges," she dismissed, off-hand. "I get them sometimes, when I work too hard, or—"

"Which you did last night, I bet," Thalo broke in.

"—If the rest of you 'Earthers did as much as the ones I saw."

The girl nodded. Then: "Speaking of work; looks like you've got on First Day duds."

Thalo glanced down at his black-and-tan finery and straightened his tie from reflex. "Uh . . . yeah, actually."

"Where?"

Thalo went suddenly shy. "Uh . . . here, actually." He jerked his thumb toward the compound wall that now seemed to be propping him up. Certainly his knees were weak. It had just been too long, he decided, since an even vaguely pretty female had paid him any mind—especially when he didn't have water.

The eyebrow lifted higher. "The Native-South Compound?"

He nodded smugly. "Internship in southeastern culture. Kituwah hired me—Cherokee, that is. That's what most folks call 'em, anyway."

"I know."

Thalo's tongue became paralyzed.

The girl came to his rescue. "Most of us down here know Ambassador Red Wounds—he's kind of a celebrity 'cause he's so flamboyant. Kind of a rebel, too—for a diplomat. And greener than most, of course."

"H-how do you know?"

A shrug. " 'Earth's got probably the largest D-base in town excluding the Mounties, the Big Four E's, and the automotive megas. He's definitely a good guy."

Thalo yawned unexpectedly—and blushed again. "Well that's a relief."

The girl paused on the verge of resuming her task. A dull white sedan had pulled up opposite, Thalo noted—because it *wasn't* sparkling clean, expensive, and brand new. Nor a taxi. Incongruity attracts attention, he concluded—and recalled his bogus skin tones and hair. "What about Thunderbird O'Connor?" he mumbled.

The girl started, then relaxed again. "What about him?"

"He a good guy too?"

"I . . . don't know," she said with an odd tremor in her voice. "I've only heard of him—seen his name on lists, actually. Red Wounds is the one we keep up with."

"I . . . see," Thalo mused, though he didn't.

"You going to be working for him?" the girl asked casually. "Red Wounds, I mean?"

A shrug. "I don't know. It wasn't him that hired me.

But from what I hear, everybody there's pretty laid back.
They don't stand on ceremony—folks have easy access
to the Ambassador, and stuff like that. All I know is that
I got a letter from him saying welcome aboard and not
to be scared to approach him 'cause of who he was. It
sounded sincere.''

"It fits," the girl affirmed. "Oh, and by the way, I'm
Verde."

"Verde," Thalo echoed stupidly. "Spanish for *green*,
right? I'm . . . uh, Thalo. John Gordon, actually, but I
prefer Thalo."

"That a Movement name?"

"Uh, yeah, actually. Young Greens back home."

Before she could reply, a car horn beeped plaintively
across the street: the dingy electric. One dark-tinted window powered half down, revealing a shadowed driver. A
hand gestured—at Verde, who grimaced and hurried
across the pavement, barely missing a rental Caddy that
turned the corner too fast.

All at once Sequoya was a flood of traffic. Thalo was
forced to watch helplessly as his erstwhile companion
(whom he'd been working up nerve to ask out, assuming
she was unattached) was co-opted into another conversation. *Who was it*, he wondered, glaring at the anonymous sedan, *who could command Verde's attention so
completely*? Too bad he wasn't a superhero: one with X-
ray vision to plumb that vehicle's depths. Alas, all he
could see of the driver was a clumsy bulkiness, shades,
and either a hat or tunic hood. And he only caught those
because the man glanced his way. A flash of chrome on
a passing vehicle dazzled his eyes right after, and he
blinked, briefly lightheaded—evidently the sun bouncing
off all these white buildings, mirror surfaces, and metallic
finishes could catch you out down here. His eyes watered
lavishly, and when he looked back, Verde was gone.
Swallowed by the sedan, he assumed.

Which was just as well: she'd surely have turned him
down. Sighing, he unstuck himself from the wall,
brushed sandcrete dust from an inky sleeve, and eased
back around the corner. A dark lad in official-looking

livery was already removing the flyers there, rubbing absently at tape-residue with a tawny hand. Thalo grunted a greeting as he strode past. The lad glared, then giggled and went back to his cleaning.

The Gate Guard—a stocky Seminole woman named Mozelle Worth (so her gold ID badge proclaimed)—made short work of pointing him to the appropriate mini-'mid inside, and a moment later, Thalo found himself beneath the forward facet of a slanted, bronze-glass pyramid-cum-dome, striding up a wide flight of red marble stairs toward the low-slung wooden kiosk at the top. A sign there said "Information"—in English, Spanish, and Cherokee. Two women manned it: one—older and heavier—looked like thunder; the other—younger and slim (her name proved to be Holly)—did not.

Holly pointed left down a gallery that overhung the entrance level (which was given over to exhibits and displays), then told him to turn right at the end. Before Thalo knew it, he was there. Gold letters set in frosted glass beneath a design from a Spiro shell gorget said CULTURAL AFFAIRS.

The sign on the desk within said THUNDERBIRD O'CONNOR.

The man leaning back in a chair behind that desk, with his bare feet crossed precisely in its center and his hands laced behind his head said "Hi, Thalo!" And looked entirely too smug—and too familiar.

"Well," continued the man Thalo had stalked away from yesterday in self-righteous indignation, "it's good to see you again. Have a seat. You look . . . pale. Could I get you anything? A podiatrist, perhaps? Or would you rather keep your foot *in* your mouth until it's thoroughly digested? It'd help if you soften it by gnawing."

Thalo turned scarlet. Heat blazed up his cheeks. Had he been able to move, he likely would've bolted. "Sorry," he managed eventually. "Sometimes . . . I'm a fool."

"So am I," O'Connor laughed. He swung his feet off the desk and strode gracefully across the room. "I did a *bunch* of stupid things not a week gone by." He paused

by a built-in cabinet to the left of the door. "So tell me, Mr. Gordon; would you prefer Dos Equis, Corona, or the Ambassador's homebrew? Oh, and you can lose the tie, the vest, and the shoes; you've made your impression; I'd rather deal with the guy inside."

"Brew," Thalo managed weakly, already tugging at his tie, even as he pried off his loafers. "Homebrew."

"Good choice," 'Bird said—and passed him a brimming mug. "Now then," he continued. "What do you know about Catholic funeral rites as they relate to native southeastern tattoos?"

The beer tasted like sweet nutty heaven. "Well," Thalo (barefoot now) began carefully, "if you're talking about Green Francis, I doubt they're gonna burn him. As for tattoos . . . didn't the southeasterners mark important occasions with 'em? So maybe if they respected someone enough, even if he was from another tribe, they'd . . . do something like that in his honor."

"Possibly," 'Bird nodded. "Anything else?"

They were still discussing the matter eight mugs and two hours later. The pile of reference books around them on the floor reached to Thalo's ribs. Perhaps, he'd decided three beers back, this wasn't so bad after all.

Chapter XII:
Dead End

(Kituwah Embassy, Aztlan)
(Friday, September 9—late afternoon)

"So, how's the Green Kid doin'?" Holly asked, as 'Bird padded by the reception desk for the fifth time that afternoon. She smiled while awaiting his answer; her partner-in-info did not.

He smiled back. He'd have to ask her out again soon, if for no other reason than to atone for tumbling Rudy Ramirez the night before. Of course he and Rudy hadn't done it four times in one night—exactly. On the other hand, they'd been drunk—by the end. At which point he realized, by Holly's raised eyebrows, that he hadn't replied. "Thalo? Oh, he's fine. He's in the library surfin' for visuals on funeral tattoos—any tribe."

"Like a good little puppy," Holly laughed.

"Kinda like a beagle, actually: quiet and wise and assertive by turns. And loyal—*very* loyal."

"Cute too—if he'd lose the paint."

"God, don't tell him *that*!" 'Bird cried. "He saw some girl three times for five minutes total and thinks he's in love."

"Ah! A man of expansive passions! And loyal, you say? Hmmm."

'Bird's growl was curtailed by a phalanx of phone calls. Nor could Holly foist them on her dour compatriot; that one had full ears too. He filled the downtime with a trek to the commissary for tacos, choosing the hottest sauce he could find. Thalo liked 'em that way, huh? Well,

he'd see how Betty Mather's patented Bottled Hell filled the bill! Probably make the kid's ears smoke, his scalp steam, and pop his eyes right out of his head. Maybe he should get his camera.

He was still pondering that possibility when he passed reception again. A glance at the big clock behind it showed sixteen-hundred: later than he thought; an hour until closing, in fact. So much for tacos: too close to dinner for spicy snacks." 'Wounds still hidin' out?" he asked Holly.

"Not as of eleven-hundred our time," she replied. "Courier finally found him 'round then, but he already knew about Archie. Said he'd be on his way as soon as that Carolyn person returns from whatever screwy errand him and O'Neal sent her on, which apparently involves a boat. 'Course we didn't find all this out until ten minutes ago," she added. "Seems telecom in Eireland's even more screwed than we thought, and the poor guy had to try three towns before he got patched through—those folks need *dishes*, man—and then there was the small matter of the wreck."

'Bird rolled his eyes. "Forgot which side to drive on?"

"He'd only been over there a month! And most of that was in Dublin; he hadn't driven much. Besides . . . he was my brother."

"Ooops!"

Holly shrugged. "Live and learn. He's gotta do a lot of the latter."

"Like our friend Thalo."

"Speaking of whom . . . He came up for air a while ago and asked me if I thought you'd mind if he invited you to dinner sometime. Seems he's feelin' guilty about something."

'Bird grimaced wearily. "I'd as soon not—today."

"Oh come on," Holly chided. "He can't be that bad."

"He's not. In fact, he's right good company—as long as you keep him off his little Green hobbyhorse, which is pretty damned hard, since practically everything connects with it some way. But the fact is, I just need to go

home and decompress. I still haven't recovered from that Way, see. And then there was last night . . ."

"What *about* last night?"

A shrug.

"I tried to call you. You weren't home."

"Got drunk and spent the night there."

"Which means you weren't at a *diverto*."

'Bird shifted his weight. "So it would . . . appear."

"Anybody I know? Or would like to?"

"Don't think so. And probably. Very good-looking, but kinda freaked by some things. Mostly I stayed over for comfort."

"Yours or . . . his?"

"Both. And how'd you know?"

"You don't hedge when it's a woman."

'Bird snorted and noted the time again. "Actually, I need to call him. I left something over there—one of Stormy's G-U-N-S he found under the seat and made me take in for security. But since I've gotta pick up Mr. Cloud tomorrow, and he's bound to check first thing, I guess it'd better be there. I—"

The phone rang again—twice. Holly rolled her eyes. Her counterpart scowled. 'Bird passed Holly the bag of food, typed a note onto her memo pad—*"tell Thalo I went home and to lock the office door when he leaves— see how long it takes him to figure out he's been de- serted—and give him the tacos if you feel really mean. See y'all in the morning."*—and padded, still barefoot, down the stairs.

"Phone. On," 'Bird yawned a moment later, when he found himself becalmed in the Vehicle Gate while rush hour did its thing beyond. The Jeep's AC was on as high as it would go—which wasn't sufficient. "Thunderbird O'Connor to Pan-European Oceanic Research Institute, Inc.," he continued. "Seeking Rudy Ramirez."

"Pardon?" the phone replied.

'Bird repeated himself more slowly.

"Mr. Nez has programmed that name to its colloquial

form," the phone intoned primly. "I will respond to PEORCI, porky, *por qué*, or 'why?' "

"But not the *real* one?" 'Bird spat, forgetting he addressed a machine.

"I do not recognize—"

"Thunderbird O'Connor to *porky*," he snapped, suppressing an urge to call the machine a bitch, since it would doubtless reply there was no such person. "Seeking Rudy Ramirez!"

He drummed his fingers anxiously while he waited, wishing the phone didn't override the radio. Traffic inched forward a meter. He was beyond the wall now, with his right signal on, angling onto Sequoya. Eventually someone picked up. A woman: by her uniform, some sort of info-jock. "I'm sorry," she panted. "Rudy's not . . . that is, Mr. Ramirez wasn't scheduled to work today."

'Bird started. "Oh, right! I forgot. Sorry. Bye."

At which point 'Bird found himself sucked into rush hour traffic, which made him nervous as a cat. Two blocks later, a light caught him, and he phoned Rudy's apartment. His phone was very polite (more than Stormy's, anyway) when it informed him that Mr. Ramirez was presently unavailable but would be glad to receive any messages.

"Rudy, you lazy slut," 'Bird began. "You can't be that hung over, so if you're refusin' my call 'cause you couldn't respect yourself this mornin', remember it was you came lookin' for me. But seriously, man. I'm on my way over to pick up something you probably noticed I left and shouldn't have—nod-nod wink-wink. If I find you, fine. If I find you *en flagrante*, I'll take pictures. If you're not there . . . call me and leave a message 'cause I'm gonna go back home and flat. Catch you later—if you're lucky—or I am."

Rudy neither picked up nor returned the message. 'Bird searched for a place to turn around. Trouble was, he'd let himself be maneuvered into the wrong lane and was now being forced onto the Beltway (what came of driving so rarely), and would have to loop halfway

around the city to get off anywhere useful. And since Rudy's place was only a block off the Beltway anyway . . .

Besides, the radio had seen fit to spice the traffic report with the heartening news that due to unprecedented use, telecom circuits were packing up, but that Comunicaciones Azteca was buying time from one of Colombia's sats, and the situation would be resolved soon.

That was why Rudy hadn't called back.

Twelve minutes later, Rudy's exit appeared on the horizon. The Jeep's NavCom (which Stormy never used, but which Thalo had activated because he thought it was neat, and which 'Bird couldn't figure out how to cancel) promptly advised him to choose the righthand lane and prepare to exit in thirty seconds at present speed. The lane was clear, it added, though another vehicle had entered the outer safety zone and was closing.

"Fuck you!" 'Bird yelled, then set his jaw and swung over. A stab of brakes when someone cut him off, a swirl around an elegantly arching ramp, and he was back on surface streets, recalling again how much he hated driving (though he'd done a shitload of it lately, most in this very vehicle), and why he usually walked or took AFZoRTA.

A liquor store loomed ahead to the right. He turned into the drive-through and picked up a twelve-pack of Anchor Steam, adding a six of Sweet Georgia Brown Ale as an afterthought, since Thalo had never tasted any Southern brews and was curious.

Before he knew it, he was easing into the cul-de-sac fronting *Casa Ramirez*. Rudy's bike was there, but that didn't mean anything, since there were zillions of shops and restaurants in walking distance, and it was close to dinner time—never mind the multiplex theater one block over.

Nor were the lights on.

He knocked tentatively.

No one answered.

Another knock, louder; then the bell.

Still no reply.

"Rudy?" he called. "Hey Rude-Boy, it's me!"

Silence.

"Slithey toves," he told the speaker by the door, in his best bogus Ramirez, on the off chance the lock might be gullible.

Apparently it was, for the bolt released with an audible snap and the door popped back from its seals. So maybe Rudy *was* home and asleep—or in the bath, or whatever.

But then 'Bird caught the faint reek of something unpleasantly organic issuing from inside—and suddenly had a very bad feeling. Folding the hem of his baggy tunic around his hand, he twisted the knob, wondering if he ought not to zip back to the Jeep for one of the dozen-odd weapons Rudy hadn't found, much of it treasure-trove from Stormy's assault on a werka lycanthropy lab.

It didn't matter anyway, for a gust of wind thrust the door from his hand, revealing what lay beyond. "Oh shit!" he gasped as light flooded the room. Then: "Rudy, oh shit, man . . . *no!*"

Denial meant little, however—when someone's brains were splashed across the sandcrete wall behind his head, while a security-issue Smith & Wesson .38 still lay in lifeless fingers, and blood had dyed a white futon scarlet and rust.

"No!" 'Bird managed again—and was violently ill all over the jade plant in the corner. As he wiped his mouth on his sleeve, it finally occurred to him to wonder why Rudy had done it. *When* was fairly obvious—from the smell, the amount of dried blood—and the crusty semen on the guy's belly, which he'd noted when he got up that morning. 'Bird had showered before leaving his friend (still snoring) on the futon where they'd wound up. Rudy would surely have done the same upon rising—which meant he'd died that morning.

So why . . . ?

Well, it wasn't shame or remorse; Rudy made no secret of the varied ways he swung, and nobody in Aztlan cared anyway, since everyone under fifty did much the same.

Fear?

Of what?

Guilt?

Again, for what?

Betrayal? Some secret he'd dared not reveal?

No, dammit, there was just no good reason!

Best to call the Mounties and get it over with. It wasn't like he wasn't used to them, after all; not after last week, when he'd been—briefly—Murder Suspect One.

He had almost reached the Jeep—no way he could stay in *that* place, with Rudy's dull eyes staring at him in frozen horror—when he noted a disturbing anomaly. Nothing much, really; nothing most people would've noticed: merely a dark smear gleaming on the pavement in front of Rudy's house—barely a car length in front of the Jeep. Trouble was, it hadn't been there when he'd left that morning. And since the Aztlan DMV was picky about things like leaky battery packs and tended to catch them at inspection, it was already odd that way. But for that much fluid to have accumulated, a vehicle would've had to stay in one place a good while—as if, for instance, the driver had been watching. And since anyone parking in front of Rudy's for either a visit, a delivery, or a maintenance call would surely have discovered the body . . . well, you had to wonder.

Slowly, and very aware of where he put his feet, 'Bird eased closer. And felt his heart bolt into his throat. *Casa Ramirez* lay across the road from a vacant lot, which, unlike Rudy's block, was mostly bare of trees. Its sandy soil was therefore free to blow into the street—which it had, mounding in tiny dunes along the curbs. But Rudy's place was on a cul-de-sac, plus the weather had been calm today (until just now) so there'd been nothing to disturb the drifts—or impressions left therein. The Jeep's tracks were clear indeed, both going and coming. But other impressions displaced the earlier set: those of the leaking vehicle, which seemed to be a smallish sedan. More to the point, footprints showed as well: precisely where someone would've stood if he'd stepped from the driver's seat into the road.

Human tracks—but very large ones. And since both

'Bird and Rudy were middle-sized, as was most of Aztlan's population . . . well, it just made him uneasy. Werkas, however, *weren't* small, presumably because of some rule governing how far one could diverge from one's primary mass when shapechanging. Werkas also had big feet—all the ones he'd seen did. Nothing conclusive there either, but something else to consider. And then he found two things that utterly convinced him. One was the neatly stripped skeleton of a good-sized fish lying where the probable driver would've dropped it. Again, no big deal—save that it had been eaten raw. Careful to leave no prints of his own, 'Bird squatted to inspect it, probing it with a stick. Which was when he found the final proof of werka involvement. It glittered there under the tail like a sliver of dusky diamond.

Obsidian!

A flake of black volcanic glass no larger than his fingernail. And werkas used obsidian knives in their flayings. He'd never been sure why—unless it was that the things didn't rust, were sharper than regular steel, and were basically untraceable if homemade, which wasn't hard to do. But he'd also heard it suggested that they used them—had their controlled human minions use them, rather—to divert suspicion onto the newly reformed cult of Xipetotec.

But Rudy's skin was intact . . . so what was a fragment doing here?

Filleting fish, if the cuts on the carcass were any indication. A born carnivore like a werka would surely be frustrated as hell by the limits of human dentition. And even if they favored raw flesh, they might still need to cut it. But obsidian was fragile; whoever had sat watch here could easily have dropped their edge, shedding a flake unaware.

Suddenly it was all too clear. Sometime after he'd left, at least one were-orca driving a leaking car (perhaps they didn't know the law, or the vehicle was stolen, or they were afraid to deal with the intricacies of maintenance or the people equipped to handle it) had parked in front of Rudy's house. He'd watched for a while, eating fish, then

launched one of those little psychic probes and determined that Rudy wasn't in his right mind (which in turn implied that they'd both been under surveillance, which gave him the willies well and good); and then, when the time was right, had simply taken over Rudy's beer-befuddled brain, and made him stick Stormy's pistol in his mouth and pull the trigger. Which neatly implicated 'Bird, Stormy, or both.

But why?

And equally to the point, why Rudy and not him—or both of them?

Because Rudy knew too much?

'Bird knew too much too, but offing them together might not have been viable. Or might've been too suspicious. Killing Rudy first would divert the blame. He was the easier target too, because he lived alone in a secluded area; and in fact, 'Bird's showing up there might well have been a lucky—for the werkas—coincidence. Otherwise . . . Rudy could easily have been found flayed, instead of messily lobotomized.

But it was still perverted, sick, disgusting—and scary as hell. The question was: what should Thunderbird O'Connor, incipient murder suspect, do?

Chapter XIII:
Scene of the Crime

(Aztlan)
(Friday, October 9—late afternoon)

Rudy Ramirez was dead.

'Bird knew that objectively—he could see the poor guy's corpse through the open door—but he still did not believe it. You couldn't just hang out with a guy one day—see him warm and alive and moving, then know him as intimately as a person could: touch him and taste him and watch him breathe and sweat and cry—and then edit him neatly out of your life. No one *human* could. And 'Bird was suddenly very conscious of being human—though not the way most folks defined it nowadays.

Not like werkas.

Werkas were intelligent. They had history, philosophy, and poetry—and a grounding in science sifted from hominid minds. And they certainly had cognizance of their own mortality, and of the complex mechanisms that defined the world, including plots and stratagems. They could even—now—walk as men among men unmarked by the inattentive.

But they *weren't* human. 'Bird had wrestled with that a lot lately: he and Stormy and John Lox had. And the only workable solution seemed to be one his father had used to defend capital punishment for murder: that by deliberately depriving a person of their right to existence, one implicitly relinquished any claim to equivalent

honor. And if that made the state *de facto* nonhumans
. . . well, what else was new?

One thing alone was clear: much as he wanted to, he
couldn't report the crime—not when there were sure
signs of werka involvement. Convincing as they might
be to the initiated, they weren't what the Mounties would
consider first. No, what *they'd* see (as would he, had he
been in their shiny black boots) was either a murder or
a suicide, and the last thing he needed if werkas were out
killing folks who knew too much was to be "held for
questioning"—not only because he'd be unable to act
freely, but because it left him a sitting duck. And even
if he retrieved the gun, no way he could recover the bullet, which would be traceable—straight to Stormcloud
Nez—who was a friend of Thunderbird O'Connor—
who'd been observed with Rudy Ramirez at a dozen locations last night in increasing degrees of inebriation.
There'd also be DNA to trace; Stormy's Jeep too, if anyone had seen it. And while his friend had an alibi named
John Lox, it was shaky—because Lox's compound didn't
officially exist, and needed to stay that way.

Even worse, not only was 'Bird implicated, but Stormy
was as well—as jealous lover (though they'd only fooled
around, as buddies do) who'd caught 'Bird and Rudy
together and decided to off the competition.

God, what a sordid mess!

Meanwhile, he was standing with the door wide open,
acting suspicious as hell, just as half the city headed
home. And even if Rudy's neighbors hadn't yet noticed
anything odd (sandcrete made excellent sound insula-
tion), no way they'd remain blind forever.

Yeah, he concluded numbly, he'd loitered 'round here
long enough. Rudy was dead, and there was nothing he
could do about it save wait for the police to contact him,
or contact them himself, neither of which would give him
what he needed.

What he *needed* now was time: time to determine who
knew what, who *might* know what, and who could be
trusted with what if they didn't know already.

Unfortunately, all his key advisors were out of reach.

Stormy and Lox knew everything, but were inaccessible by telecom—and 'Bird hated to disturb Stormy's Way. He might have to, but only as a last resort.

Mary Hasegawa (who knew very little) had returned to Cadiz to get her head straight, so she was hopefully safe for the nonce—but also out of the loop.

And Carolyn, Kevin, Red Wounds, and Ambassador O'Neal were playing "take me to your leader" with selkies. Too bad, because 'Wounds would know how much about the werka situation would be safe to tell the Mounties. They knew about the flayed bodies, dammit. And they knew that most of them had been skinned by people who couldn't realistically have done it. Beyond that . . . 'Bird had no idea *what* was known. 'Wounds probably did. And Ambassador O'Neal. Beyond them . . . well, if 'Wounds knew, he wasn't saying, even to 'Bird whom he trusted like a brother and loved like the son he'd never, after three marriages, managed to sire.

But again, 'Wounds was in Eireland. Worse, as of an hour ago, he was *incommunicado* in Eireland: unreachable by phone or fax without elaborate patching. Or else he was already in transit (the High Chief in Oklahoma had left word for him to "get his butt" back to town for the funeral), and neither way would he be able to talk freely.

'Bird couldn't call direct anyway. His body phone was kaput. Stormy's car job wouldn't connect anywhere Kituwah's main lines wouldn't. And if he went back to the Compound and tried to invoke diplomatic rerouting through the Eirish Embassy (who might have contact with O'Neal via "Above-Top-Secret" channels), it still left him open to apprehension (home base being the first place anyone seeking him would look), as well as presenting the problem of explaining to Mary Jane Mankiller why he was in trouble he could discuss with 'Wounds but not her. She wouldn't actually try to stop him, but she could sure slow things down a lot.

Still, there was one person who might be able to get hold of 'Wounds in a hurry . . .

Ambassador O'Neal's son Bryan was deputy legate at

the Eirish Embassy and a sometime drinking buddy of
'Bird's. Bry knew *some* stuff because his father knew
some stuff and the two were very close. And even if he
didn't, he'd trust 'Bird to use their secure line without
comment. What he would say then, and to whom, he
didn't know; maybe by the time he got there he'd have
a plan in place.

All of which deliberation required no more time than
it took to retrieve Stormy's pistol (no sense making it
easy for the Mounties, though he almost lost his gorge
again when he had to touch Rudy's fingers), wipe his
prints off the door and attendant areas, relock it, and return to the Jeep. He wished he could do something about
the puke on the jade plant, but that would take time he
didn't have.

With luck, he'd be on the phone to Eireland ten
minutes from now. After that . . . Well, he supposed he'd
get the hell out of Dodge.

Courtesy of traffic, it took twenty minutes to even
reach the Eirish Embassy, and 'Bird cringed every time
he saw a cop. Though music might have soothed him, he
kept the police band open, lest there already be a call out
on him. There wasn't; merely endless info-babble about
what Lord-High-Mucketty-Muck had just arrived at
which airport, where another VIP motorcade was heading, and who had requested extra security because they
hadn't brought enough of their own. It was odd, though:
circulating through this mass of folks all intent on their
individual, mostly unremarkable, lives, and knowing all
the *very* remarkable things occurring invisibly. "The
creature walks among us!" he snorted. "There's a killer
on the road," he continued, quoting the old Doors song
Rudy had played for him.

His brain was squirming like a toad, too. But at least
he had a plan.

Sort of a plan—as he eased the Jeep into a VIP Guest
slot in the forecourt between the inner and outer gates of
the embassy. The building itself was green—of course:
the requisite pyramid, wrought of emerald glass, with

ne'er a trace of orange save where lines of Hopi cells edged the facets with a gold-copper gleam. And the friezes set into the buttressed outer wall were a deft fusion of Aztec scrollwork with Celtic, of feathered serpents with attenuated birds. The Norwegians next door had something similar but in wood. It was very nice—if you weren't in a hurry.

'Bird, however, was out of the Jeep very quickly indeed, checking the motor pool across the way for Bryan O'Neal's classic Dodge Viper (which he drove "because there are no snakes in Eireland and I thought I should sample one while I had the chance"). Happily, it was there: low, green, and venomous.

He'd almost reached the inner gate, and was scanning the four alert-looking Lads-with-Uzis who secured it for someone he recognized, when he noticed something he should've noted sooner. A swath of blood stained the hem of his tunic, likely from where it had brushed against Rudy's leg when he'd retrieved the gun. No way these new guys would admit him after hours with something that suspicious showing, either. Fortunately, there was a bus stop down the street, and they had public loos. He'd zip in there and either wash the stuff off or abandon the garment entirely. Probably ought to clean up anyway. Trying to look as though he'd just remembered something pressing; he executed a smart about-face.

—And had just strode through the outer gate onto the sidewalk beyond when a man stepped from the shadows of one of the buttresses that braced the walls between the friezes. 'Bird started reflexively (*God, he was wired!*), but continued on, intending to ignore the guy—except, he realized too late, the fellow had been slumping and was much taller than he'd thought. Larger, too! *Uncomfortably* large, in fact. And his hands were making stirring motions!

"Oh fuck!" 'Bird spat—and bolted. His reaction was a trifle slow, however, and somehow in the act of spinning around, he made eye-contact with the "man" (heavy-featured and too-smooth beneath long dark hair). The eyes were dark—inhumanly so—as though the pig-

ment of four separate brown-eyed people had been concentrated in two irises—and suddenly 'Bird couldn't look away. His body slipped slightly apart from him, like that strange time-attenuation that can manifest during a major accident. It was an adrenaline push—but he only knew that subliminally. What he knew much more imminently was that he had to escape *right now*—and that the fastest way was to run across the street.

The taxi that came hurtling down on him wasn't real and never had been. And then it was.

He was aware of one blunt pain biting his left thigh—and then he was free and flying. And on the ground again, while an assortment of brand new agonies stair-stepped down his shoulder into his torso. Various bits felt strange and numb, but at least, after two false starts, he was breathing.

The vehicle screeched to a halt twice its length beyond. Footsteps slapped toward him. "Stay down," someone called—a woman with a Mexican accent. "You . . . I am sorry."

But 'Bird was already rising, dusting himself off and inspecting for damage. Except for a troubling in his thigh-hip interface that didn't want to support as much weight as it was supposed to, he seemed fine. Bruised, scraped, and beaten, but otherwise intact.

"*Señor*, are you hurt?" came the woman's breathless cry. "I am so, so sorry." She thrust an arm under his, though he was already standing shakily. The man—werka, rather—was nowhere in sight.

"I'm . . . *bueno*," 'Bird told her absently. He brushed at his tunic and tried to hide the bloody hem with his arm.

"You are certain?"

"I play *anetsa*; I'm used to that kinda thing."

"But . . . I could have killed you! I was slowing for a fare—I *thought* for a fare. I had my foot on the brake, but you moved *so* quickly. *Señor*—"

'Bird shook his head. "Don't worry; I'm insured.

Right now . . . I've got something important to do.'' And with that he limped away.

Not to the bus stop, however; no way he'd isolate himself with a werka lurking around. But not to the embassy either, because he was even more suspect than heretofore and the guards would be bound to ask too many questions before they'd even begin to believe he knew Bryan.

Nope, he was going to do what he should've done in the first place: go where there was no need for deception, smoke screens, or lies.

He'd fill up this nice little Jeep—on his own cash, to complicate tracing—and take the fastest way out to Lox's. If Stormy's Way wasn't finished, tough; they could always do it over. Besides, according to Stormy's worldview, 'Bird had been exposed to Rudy's *chindi*, which would have to be dealt with anyway. In the meantime . . . he could plot strategy. He could consider options . . .

Not until the third traffic light did he realize what one of those considerations would be.

He'd been accosted by a werka. He'd inadvertently made eye-contact with the thing, and it had promptly taken over his will long enough to send him sprinting into traffic.

Trouble was, he'd been stone cold sober (if amped on adrenaline); certainly sane enough to plan. Therefore, no werka should've been able to influence him—they hadn't before, when they'd had him in their literal hands, otherwise he'd be dead and his skin a werka's thigh, or whatever.

Therefore something had changed.

But what?

The light turned green. The street ahead was clear. He availed himself of that respite to drive faster.

Chapter XIV:
Coasting

*(Cumberland Island, Seminole/
Creek Coastal Protectorate)
(Friday, September 9—sunset)*

Carolyn loved the beach at sunset. There was always something calming about the vastness of sky and sea, but twilight added its own fascination. Perhaps it was the way wind stilled, or the fading light both warmed and softened. Certainly color was a factor. More shades showed this time of day than any other, and more richly. Blue-gray waters gained shimmering highlights of crimson and gold. Dingy white foam became pink filigree. And the clouds . . . One never knew *what* one would see, courtesy of last year's volcano. They were indigo now, where they rose above the forested dunes behind her—and orange, burgundy, and scarlet the very hue of heart's blood, all limned and shadowed with black like a funeral shawl.

In spite of her sorrow, Carolyn smiled. A single tear slid down her cheek, where, clad in a loose black wool tunic and grey linen jeans, she sat barefoot on the pristine sands of the sole remaining unspoiled island of the string that bejeweled Georgia's coast. Not Georgia's now, however; Cumberland was a protectorate of the Seminole/Creek arm of the Native Southeastern Confederacy, that also embraced what was increasingly known as Kituwah, where Red Wounds and her new friend 'Bird O'Connor worked. 'Bird would enjoy this place; with its

marshes, live oaks, and palmetto hells it was wild enough for him. In fact, excluding the airstrip where Ambassador O'Neal's generously donated Gulfstream had parked them that afternoon; a small clump of cabins on the south end, which were doled out to researchers; a rambling wildlife/forestry/ecology lab ten kloms up the coast (conveniently unstaffed now, courtesy of a funding dispute); and the odd decaying farmstead (abandoned since the Creeks had evicted their owners), there was little sign man had ever trespassed. Well . . . except for Dungeness, the Toad-Hall-style mansion a Carnegie heir had built last century, the scorched ruins of which in their own odd way actually accented the surrounding woods. Carolyn still couldn't believe she was here—eight hours ago, she'd been in Eireland. But Mom had been amazingly well-connected and had cleared this little shindig long ago, via a former classmate who was also Seminole. He'd been researching conches; so had she. Dad—Kev's dad—had been working on them too. The rest was history.

And that was what all this was about, wasn't it? History had brought Mom and Dad together, and a secret alternate history (with Mom's passing, forever lost) had sundered them again—along with her and Kevin. Today they were reunited; and with Mom lying in a coffin back at the cabin where the others were well into the wake, was there really any reason not to likewise seal the Schism for good? Kev had sided with Dad when Mom had admitted that Carolyn wasn't his; she'd gone with Mom. They were over it. It only remained to determine where Dad—Floyd, she preferred to call him—fit into her life. It wouldn't be hard. He wasn't demanding. She was used to going her own way. He'd hurt her by hurting Mom, but she understood his point. Men were like that, even now. Floyd was a generation older.

Sighing, she leaned back on her hands, watching the sky grow darker. A few gulls stirred the air. Frogs—she'd never bothered to learn what species—chittered in the woods. A feral pony wandered from the nearest gnarl of live oaks and cropped placidly at a patch of sea-oats.

A wisp of Spanish moss was caught on one ear and dragged across the sand. She giggled. Mom would have too; Mom, who'd chased her own stars the last few years, would've reminded her that she was Eirish and born to laugh and drink and party.

So maybe it was time to get at it. Fences needed mending with all the men in her life—which was now all the family she had, Mom being an only child of only children, born late in life to boot. Men. Dad—Floyd. Kev. And now Sean. Each splendid in his own special way; each bowed by a common grief.

Abruptly she rose and strode back to the trail among the trees that, by excising a finger of beach, would shorten her solemn journey. The forest rose before her: a lacework of tiny black leaves, outrageously twisted limbs, and delicate tendrils against a violet sky. Though it was Floyd's country, not her own, it was easily as romantic as the bare rolling hills of Connemara. Sean thought so too: that new brother of hers. He loved it. Then again, Sean, aflame with adolescent curiosity and wonder, loved everything. He hadn't slept at all on the flight.

As she reached the trees, she glanced at the sky one last time. A contrail gleamed there: a jet rising from Brunswick Airport on the mainland. She wondered if the Ambassadors were on it, wending their way down to Aztlan for the Archbishop's requiem, leaving O'Neal's private jet, with pilot, completely at her family's disposal. Blackmer would be buried tomorrow with the eyes of the world upon him. Mom's funeral—not a burial—would likewise be at dawn, with five people attending, max. And then both the larger world and the smaller could return to the business of living.

Carolyn heard the racket before she arrived, and couldn't believe that three grown men and a quasi-teen could make so much noise. Music. Laughing. Talking loud, with Mom's bier right in the middle. Male bonding through and through. All it lacked was Rudy, 'Bird, and Stormy.

No, she amended instantly, that much testosterone in one place would surely provoke an explosion, especially as she suspected that all three of the latter had designs on her for more than a one-time tumble. Someday she'd have to choose. It would be a tough decision.

Twisting to avoid a particularly pendulous tendril of Spanish moss, she pushed aside a meter-wide fan of palmetto that thrust brazenly into the sandy trail and finally caught sight of the cabin. It was made of sandcrete, tabby, and cypress in roughly equal thirds, in a style Kev had christened Bombadil/beach-bum/chalet. Which mostly meant an assortment of high-peaked roofs, many windows, and wraparound porches, on the eastern kink of which the men were arrayed. Kevin and the pilot (Liam Kelly was his name: a cheerful, straight-backed young officer O'Neal had coopted from the Eirish Air Force, whose short-cropped hair glowed like russet velvet in the waning light) had taken positions on opposite sides of the bier-cum-kitchen-table and seemed bent on ringing the plain pine coffin with a rampart of Guinness bottles, to which Floyd, at its foot, was also, in his own slow way, adding. Sean wasn't. Admirable for a lad his age, he hadn't yet reconciled the taste of beer with the need for being cool. Carolyn remembered those days with more than a trace of pain, since it was Mom who'd taken her aside when she'd turned seventeen and told her that whether or not she liked the taste, she ought to have a head for her native brew. They'd gone to a pub in Cong (where the lead guitar player from U2 still sometimes hung out) and got drunk as skunks. Looking back, she was amazed Mom hadn't let something slip about the selkie.

She was close enough now to catch conversation, such as it was—it seemed, yet again, to have lurched onto the selkie/dolphin/orca interface. Both O'Neal and Red Wounds knew the whole tale now. Liam, after O'Neal had sworn him to Above-Top-Secret security, did too. As of an hour before her solo down the beach, so did Floyd. He'd taken it with amazing calm. If he was hurting for more obvious reasons, it didn't show. She suspected it

would soon enough. Neither she nor Kevin was inclined to push him.

Floyd was the first to see her and saluted her silently as she approached. She nodded back and eased past Sean (sprawled on the lower steps clad only in a pair of Liam's boxers—a compromise between modesty and, for him, excessive heat) onto the porch proper. Conversation dissolved for a wary instant, but she shook her head, appropriated a Guinness from the cooler by the door, twisted off the cap, and tossed half of it back, then grinned appreciatively.

Kevin raised an eyebrow, and smirked.

Carolyn lifted both of hers and killed the bottle, then reached for another. Tension broke; talk revived. She didn't join in, simply content to *be*. Eventually, propped against the peeled cypress trunk of the corner post, she dozed.

When she awoke, it was into soft night. The stars were out, and the sky had shifted from violet to royal blue, the sea to grey and silver. Gleaming shapes sported offshore: dolphins. She wondered if they sensed her presence and what she was about—and what she'd wrought with their Caribbean kin.

Kevin and Liam were well into their cups now, sloppily and slurrily drunk. Sean and Floyd, who'd joined the boy on the steps, were conversing animatedly. She rose, snared another Guinness, and claimed the top board to listen.

Floyd patted her knee. She ruffled his hair—still thick and red, without a touch of grey, just as his body was remarkably lean and fit for an academician pushing sixty; wire-framed glasses being his sole concession to age. "So," he began brightly, "I was just askin' your fine new sibling here some stuff I don't know if you've thought about—and before you get puffed about me ignorin' your Mom in favor of my own selfish interests, remember that she always said learning was the best thing you could do, and you took knowledge where you could—so think of this as carryin' on her work."

"No problem," Carolyn murmured—and meant it.

"Really. It'll take my mind off . . . things."

Floyd stared at her uncertainly, then nodded. "What we were talkin' about, actually, was selkie blood—genes, whatever. I was wonderin' if it carries the potential to shift to *any* shape, assumin' you've got the right kind of skin, or if you're limited to seal."

"Dolphins too," Carolyn reminded him. "In my case, anyway. 'Course you knew that. And orcas can turn into people."

"But is it genetic? Or is something else involved? Like, could *I* do it—with proper instruction, I mean? Not that I'd want to, you understand."

Sean frowned. "I am . . . not sure. I know that it is— it's—not just automatic. The skin has to be taken from a live seal, for one thing, and we bond with it in our heads when we do, so we can both share and lessen its pain. That helps the whole thing, I think." He bit his lip thoughtfully. "In fact, that may be why the evil-water- ones—uh, the orcas—have to have fresh skins every time they Change: because they do not bond with the people they skin. There is no permission given, or sharing."

"But I didn't bond with the dolphin whose skin I wore, either," Carolyn countered, intrigued in spite of herself. "Nor the seal whose skin you gave me back in Eireland, which you said is mine forever."

"—As long as you wear it occasionally and keep it fresh." Sean spared a glance through the door to the re- frigerator, where a second cooler, filled with salt water, housed both her skin and his. "As for the dolphin, I doubt it gave the orcas permission, but it seemed to know about you. Likely it recognized Kevin and risked it. I do not know."

Floyd puffed his cheeks. "So the seal thing may still apply only to selkies. But to understand that, we need to know where selkies come from, which we don't, 'cept that they used to live on land, back in one of the inter- glaciations."

"There was . . . coupling," Sean admitted. "That is all I know. It was long ago."

"Science says that's impossible," Floyd snorted.

"Science isn't everything," Carolyn countered. "Oh, I used to think that, granted; and I still think everything's ultimately part of some vast pattern. But I also think—know, now, I suppose—that there're forces in the universe inexplicable by conventional science. Like I *know* telepathy works, maybe 'cause thought is electrochemical, and neurons are designed to send and receive, so it's only a leap of degree, not kind, to extend that to thoughts from other minds. But there's also just . . . the power of belief—or desire. That's what magic is, I think: desire focused to a fine point and thrown home. And if you believed you were going to change shape, or desired it—"

"You would," Kevin inserted from the porch. (Liam had evidently maxxed his limit and was out of the loop— so closed eyes, gaping mouth, and steady breathing attested.) "But orcas know more about telepathy and magic than we do," he went on, "and they were going nuts trying to learn how to Change without renewing their skins. That's why they captured the selkie that died right before Stormy saved me."

Again Sean's brow wrinkled. "Perhaps," he suggested slowly, "it is like this. Selkies are stronger telepaths than humans—except Carolyn. And dolphin-kin are stronger than we. So perhaps there is a fine balance. Orcas have trouble Changing because they are—they're—*too* strong. The strength of their minds—their belief, or whatever— overpowers the effect. Humans cannot shift because they're not strong enough. We're in between."

"But there's more to it than that," Carolyn shot back. "I had to die—twice—for my selkie aspect to manifest."

"So there's something biochemical too," Floyd mused. "Maybe death triggers the release of chemicals that activate others—or that's how it works in half-bloods."

"Something I've been wondering," Kevin broke in again, "is—well, two things actually. Actually a bunch of things. One is . . . do you look exactly like the donor? I mean, given that the only pattern you have for looking like a seal comes from a particular seal, would you then

look like that seal, down to its specific arrangement of spots, or what?''

''Good question,'' Floyd agreed, and looked at Sean. ''Any notions?''

''Not sure,'' Sean replied. ''Never thought about it.''

''Were-orcas just look weird,'' Carolyn observed. ''Kind of bland and unfinished.''

''Generic human?'' From Kevin.

''Or combo human,'' she gave back. ''If you morphed a bunch of human faces together—and remember, orcas need more than one skin to make enough to cover 'em— wouldn't you get bland?''

''If I had my PC here, we could check right now,'' Floyd sighed. ''I could scan us all in, and—never mind.''

''Actually, that brings me to my next question,'' Kevin went on excitedly. ''Since orcas can put on human skin and thereby gain our shape, what about someone like Cary? If she put on human skin—just for the sake of argument, sis, I'm not suggesting you do it!—One: would it work? Two: would she look like the donor? Three: what if the donor was the opposite sex? And four: would she share any of that person's memories the same way she picks up animal instincts when she becomes one of them?''

''Whew!'' Carolyn breathed. ''As Sean's folks say, you think too much, lad! Trouble is, I've wondered those same things.''

Sean's eyes went wide with alarm. ''That is forbidden!'' he spat. ''It is beyond evil! Beyond wrong! Without permission no one would think of such a thing, and no one has ever been permitted. Death is the natural end of things. To continue beyond . . . *that* way would be wrong!''

''Why? If someone wanted to continue?'' Carolyn challenged, only then realizing that the discussion had crossed from science into the misty realm between ethics, philosophy, and theology.

Sean shrugged uncomfortably. ''Actually . . . I don't know. And now that I think about it, perhaps permission doesn't matter if the Changers are the same—like dol-

phins and orcas are much alike. Men and seals are not, and selkies began as men.''

Carolyn scowled. ''So you're saying human and human without permission, or human and selkie, or . . . selkie and selkie?''

''You *really* need permission,'' Sean repeated. And that was that.

''*I* need something to eat,'' Floyd announced, rising and stalking toward the door. ''I also,'' Sean echoed, and joined him. Carolyn followed, running a hand down the coffin as she passed. Propped in his chair between the bier and the wall, Liam was snoring. ''Goin' for a walk,'' Kevin called, and steered for the beach.

There being no moon—yet—and them having left no lights on, it was dark in the cabin's common room/kitchen. Built before voice switches became the norm, the place had an actual pull chain depending from a ceiling fan in the center. Floyd was still flailing for it while Carolyn angled toward the pale rectangle of the 'fridge, when Sean, roughly between them, froze abruptly and whispered a desperate ''*Oh no!*''

Hand already on the appliance door, Carolyn twisted around; having picked up both Sean's comment and mental thrill of alarm. Unfortunately, she couldn't tell which of the ensuing vivid impressions came from him and which from a number of *presences* outside that were far more sinister. ''Watch it, Dad, something's up,'' she hissed—and wrenched open the refrigerator door. Light lanced across the wooden floor, just as Floyd found the overheads.

Light—then dark again, as a sharp report sounded outside, light flared brighter than the sun, and the room plunged back into gloom. The contrast—dark, light, then brighter light, and dark once more—blinded Carolyn, but that didn't stop her ducking below cabinet level. Reflexes she didn't know she had went questing along with Sean's and impacted other consciousness: ravenous angry ones that vaguely evoked dolphin thoughts, with nearly as many weaker ones, which, though more human, seemed curiously veiled, like faces overlaid with masks designed

for others. For an instant she touched all that, but it was too much—too violent, strong, and scary. She retreated, blinking and gasping for breath. The stench of ozone filled the air, and she had barely sense enough to realize that someone had blown the transformer, when chaos erupted.

"*What the fuck?*" Floyd spat, even as she wrested him to the floor. Sean was a boy-sized blur scooting around the room's perimeter.

She screamed—just as the thud of heavy feet sounded from all directions at once and both front and back doors were suddenly full of enormous bodies. She smelled marsh mud mingled with unwashed flesh, and managed a murky glimpse of at least four large men fumbling around—apparently the flash of light had done them no good either, and they were as blind as she, perhaps, having been closer, even blinder. She bet on that and shoved Floyd toward the door to the adjoining room, even as those shapes converged on her. As for Sean . . . she had no idea. What mattered now was escaping from what had to be were-orcas, their mind-numbed human minions, or both. No time to wonder where they'd come from (beyond the sea, which was a given); no time to question why neither she nor Sean had sensed them; no time to curse herself for not having anticipated this attack. No time to do anything but flee. And Kev—and Liam: Both had been outside. What of them?

And then she reached the door, thrust Floyd through, and shot the bolt behind.

Heavy bodies hit immediately, and more thumping sounded outside. Only then did she recall that the porches ran all the way around. Fortunately, the only windows on this side were high and narrow; maybe too high for big clumsy were-orcas. On the other hand there were more of them and they were stronger and meaner. Belatedly she remembered that they had some ingrained taboo about killing humans directly, thus their use of mind-raped surrogates, but that was cold comfort just now. She only hoped they didn't have weapons—she hadn't seen any. They'd have to have come up the land-

ward side of the island, too, otherwise their approach would've been noted by the offshore dolphins.

At which point something shoulder-solid slammed into the door. The hinges creaked. Wood splintered. Another blow—she didn't know what would happen. "What's goin' on?" Floyd panted from the floor beside her. Being a couple of senses shy, he'd experienced a mere shadow of what she had, and probably had no idea what was actually occurring.

"Were-orcas," she rasped. "And some guys they're controlling."

"But what do they want?"

"They tried to skin 'Bird alive, for one thing!"

"Well *fuck* 'em, then," Floyd cried recklessly (or drunkenly, which was much the same)—whereupon he stood, fishing in his pocket. Something gleamed in the hand he withdrew: the dark metal and carbon fiber of a military handgun. "Took this off Liam,'cause he was flashin' it around too much," he explained. "Loaded son-of-a-bitch too!"

And before she could stop him, he aimed directly at the door and fired. Flame spat red sparks across the gap between him and the portal, and the report well-nigh deafened her as he pulled the trigger thrice. A scream followed, then a scurry and a thud, whereupon something else hit the door even harder. It exploded inward in a confusion of boards, nails, and splinters; and hard upon it came something large and dirty that sprawled gasping on the floor, clutching a bleeding chest.

She spared it barely a glance as she leapt over it into the common room—just as two more figures dove for the back door at once, colliding before both got through. More shots thundered in the bedroom, and a check showed Floyd peppering the walls like a pro, the heavy-caliber rounds making small work of sandcrete and cypress alike. At least one more attacker was hit outside, to judge by the resulting high-pitched scream.

A noise behind her made her spin around again—to see Sean crouching on the counter by the sink with a butcher knife in his hand with which he held off two

assailants. He saw her too—and slashed out. One was hit, and screeched, then fell, clutching a spouting neck. The other backed away. "If you cut their throats, they'll Change!" he yelled savagely, and even in the gloom Carolyn caught the wildness in his eyes.

It sounded like sense to her; so she grabbed a segment of the shattered door that had flopped backward into the room and advanced on the remaining attacker. Caught between them, he—it—growled, then feinted toward the door. Sean was there before him, more quickly than she could've imagined, and two swipes of steel opened first its throat, then its gut. It gurgled and collapsed. Two shots spat in the other room, followed by a cadence of thumps on the porch, then one more.

Then silence, marked only by three frightened people's ragged breathing. "Everybody okay?" Carolyn panted.

"I am!" Sean cried instantly, dancing past their fallen foe to rejoin her in the center of the room.

"Yeah," Floyd echoed from the doorway. A fumbling followed, but a less threatening one, and a circle of light appeared. "Flashlight," he called. "Be there in a sec. Think they blew the transformer." He too was wild-eyed, his lips curved in a feral grin.

"Nature red in tooth and claw," Carolyn quoted inanely. And rushed to embrace the man who'd been her father in fact, if not biology, among the bodies of the slain.

"We got 'em!" Sean was crowing. "We got 'em!" He brandished the knife like a saber, lithe body splattered with gore.

Half in shock, Carolyn flopped down on a sofa and watched numbly as the flashlight beam prowled the room, revealing one corpse after another. As best she could tell there was one in the door between the rooms, and one right beside it—the ones Floyd had shot; one near the back door, whom Sean had nearly beheaded; and another that, not quite dead, lay crying in the corner between the sink and 'fridge. Abruptly Sean burst by her, screaming like a crazy man, and stabbed the knife into its neck. "God, Sean, no!" she cried helplessly. But it was too

late. He hopped back, grinning even more maniacally, then grossed her out entirely by licking the dripping blade. Only with difficulty did she recall that, though overtly fourteenish and very smart, he was younger than that emotionally and had spent nearly a third of his life in the guise of a carnivore. As if reading her thoughts, he spoke. "They kill us. They herd us into the sea and ambush us there. They snatch us off ice floes. We never get to kill them! But now I have."

"Were they all . . . orcas?" Floyd asked. He set the flashlight beam-up on the counter and began fooling with a hurricane lamp he'd found on the mantle. The light, reflecting off the white ceiling, brightened the room enough to show three of the four bodies writhing in a slow dance of death. And even as she watched, at once fascinated and disgusted, their skin drew away from their wounds and darker flesh showed beneath. More and more it split, as what were clearly three adolescent orcas sloughed off the trappings of humanity and let their true shapes show. Dead, though. If not now, then soon: suffocated by the weight of their own bodies. The fourth—one of Floyd's—didn't Change. Though as large as the others, he was clearly human. Black. Probably some poor old wino from Brunswick or Jacksonville.

"I will check outside," Sean volunteered, already moving toward the door.

"Be careful," Carolyn advised absently.

And then it struck her so hard it was like a physical blow.

Outside!

Kev was outside. And Liam—who, however drunk he was, could not have slept through all that.

A frantic rush to the porch proved it empty save for the casket on the table-bier and the fortress of bottles around it. Liam was gone.

And as far as she could see up and down the beach there was no sign whatever of Kevin.

Chapter XV:
Fiddler's Green

(Aztlan Free Zone)
(Friday, September 9—dusk)

"Please insert your credit card before exiting," the taxi intoned silkily, as it glided to a halt in a spacious, oak-shaded turn-out on Aztlan's hilly western fringe. Thalo started, having slipped into a doze courtesy of too little sleep the night before and too much work today. *An hour more of the latter than he'd planned on, too!*— thanks to 'Bird O'Connor's dubious sense of humor. *That* still burned him: being abandoned in the library to see how long he'd stay before realizing everyone else had split. At least the research had been fun—and they *were* dealing with a deadline: trying to contrive a formal, yet culturally correct, response to the assassination by noon tomorrow.

Trouble was, everyone who knew anything (like 'Bird, damn him!) had to have every detail approved higher up the food chain. And the fact that the Ambassador was apparently becalmed in some podunk airport on the Georgia coast (which made no sense at all) didn't help, since Deputy Mankiller either made decisions no one liked or deferred them until his arrival. The result was like running in mud—in the midst of which 'Bird had abdicated without so much as a howdy-do.

The nice receptionist—Holly—had extended sincere, if slightly smug, sympathy and offered to buy him a steak to salve his wounded pride—and tongue, since the promised tacos had proved inedible. Alas, he'd had to decline

169

because the dinner slot was already occupied. The nap had bridged the gap between.

"Please insert your credit—" the taxi insisted, and this time the driver twisted around.

"Okay!" Thalo grumbled, but did as told. Circuits clicked. The fare display flashed a number that was bound to prompt parental commentary, but he confirmed it anyway: bird finger on the approval pad. The door hissed open. He hopped out, fishing in his vest pocket for a certain flyer—which he found just as the taxi whisked away. A sick twitch promptly twisted his tummy.

This couldn't be right. He gazed at the flyer, then at the meter-high cast-aluminum numerals set into the high wall before him, then at the flyer again.

Definitely the same.

But . . . this was no club house, civic center, or high school auditorium, such as Green groups used back home.

This was a palace! A private estate, more properly; for the wall (actual *stone* in lieu of the ubiquitous sandcrete) which towered an arm's reach above his head, was breached just left of the numbers by a wide, gateless gap flanked by what were *not* reproduction Maya stelae, beyond which a driveway dove through what most towns would have considered an adequate park toward a series of terraces and colonnaded neo-Maya buildings that shone pink with sunset afterglow a quarter klom away. There was even a small step-pyramid rising above the roofs at the far end, authentic down to the wedge-roofed temple up top.

He had just turned away in disgust, torn between hailing another taxi and scoping out a phone by which to find a rent-a-bike, when a vehicle eased up beside him. New sedan. Indeterminate make. Electric. Packed to the gills with people. A window powered down as it angled into the drive. Only then did he note the Outer Earth logo painted (*not* decaled) on the door.

A dark young man with a shock of metallic gold hair that matched the studs outlining his nose, stuck his head

out and called cheerily, "Goin' to the meetin', mate?"

"O-outer Earth?" Thalo stammered—and felt like a fool.

"You got it."

"It's . . . here?"

"Yep. Climb in."

An instant later, Thalo was sharing tan velour upholstery with three young men his own age; a boy barely into puberty, who (by the way they snipped at each other) was the driver's brother; and two women: one—the driver—a tad on the heavy side and rather sour looking; the other, topless save for silk fig leaves cupping her breasts and the obligatory black arm band, quite attractive.

"This isn't . . . private, is it?" he ventured as the car halted in a paved courtyard fronting a second gate, this one closed but also made of stone—stone Cosmic Monsters, in fact, snarling at each other across a rift of light, while their bodies twisted off around the walls. There also appeared to be a doorman . . . or gatekeeper, or guard, or something—and, to judge by the dark-skinned, bare-chested boy marching smartly toward the car, valet parking. None of which he expected from Outer Earth. "Uh, whose place *is* this?" he asked the burly black lad on whose tree-like thighs he perched.

"Twins," the leaf-topped lass supplied.

His reply turned into an awkward cough, which he hoped sounded genuine. *Twins? Like the* Hero *Twins?* Well, they *were* major sponsors of Outer Earth. But . . . they were also Rock Stars, for Chrissakes! World-class, card-carrying celebs. They owned jets and sold out coliseums, were on the covers of 'zines and had cartoon series based on them. *Fortune* had ranked them among the hundred richest entertainers on earth, and closer to one than a hundred. People like that didn't share their space with the proletariat.

"They don't own it," Leaves told him, as though that explained everything. "They just borrow it when they're in town."

At which point the driver shut off the power and every-

one disembarked. Thalo wished he'd thought to change into something more casual than the semi-dressy black-and-tan togs he'd worn to work. Not that anyone had said anything, but already self-conscious about his dye job, corporate drag put him over his pretense quota. Impulsively, he unbuttoned his shirt and pulled out the tail. The chubby driver stared at his chest appreciatively. Being firmly on the slender side, he had no idea why. Perhaps she was counting hairs. It would take her all of two seconds.

Surprisingly (to Thalo) they passed this second gate without the doorman (a tall, heavy-set man in a hooded grey overcloak) giving them more than a vacant stare. There was something vaguely weird about him too, but Thalo couldn't say what, save that it had to do with the way he moved. He glanced back impulsively and decided that, eschewing the fellow's imposing size (which made sense if he was also a guard), the only things really out of the ordinary were his arms. They hung loose at his sides—almost *too* relaxed—yet his hands moved constantly: slow stirring motions, as though he were nervous.

"You came!" a familiar voice cried, jarring him from his reverie. A *female* voice! Thalo's heart leapt. Women rarely paid him any mind, and he was commensurately shy around them. He was therefore almost always taken aback when one noticed him, and more so when one actually sought his company. He was, he noted absently, standing in a square-pillared arcade which enclosed a rectangular courtyard in which a profusion of exotic plants frothed over sculpted heads the size of small cars. He blinked: it was dark in there, even for the time of day; into which gloom the rest of his party had dispersed in no obvious direction. Which was fine—because he'd correctly identified that voice as the girl with the gold damask tattoos: the one from the airport, the rally, and the embassy walls that morning. Verde.

"Hi!" he called, grinning as he located her—lighting the contents of one of the meter-wide stone braziers that smoked between every third set of pillars.

She foisted her electric torch on a dusky female com-

panion, muttered something inaudible in passing, and pranced over to join him, looking younger than he recalled—and genuinely glad to see him. She threaded her arm through his, which really did surprise him. Or maybe that was normal for her culture—whatever that was; he had no idea about either her origin or background, though her skin-tones suggested the tropics. It also occurred to him that it might be impolite to inquire.

"You look shocked," she laughed, in perfect, unaccented English.

Thalo shrugged and inspected the floor—sea-shell mosaic in Maya motifs gridding square flagstones—"I . . . uh, I wasn't sure I should be here."

"Why not?"

" 'Cause . . . Well, it's this place: the . . . Hero Twins' place, right? I guess I just figured it'd be something simpler. More down to . . . earth."

Verde steered him along the arcade with gentle pressure of her hand on his arm. "It doesn't cost us anything," she chuckled. "The Twins' record company pays the bills, and its president uses it once in a while. And since they support us . . . well, it just saves us money. Besides, the guys like to take care of their friends."

" 'The guys?' You call the *Hero Twins* 'the guys'? Jesus!"

"They're famous. They're also folks. That's what they like about Aztlan: they can be themselves down here, pretend they're just normal guys like everybody else. After all, they're hometown boys. I—"

Thalo tuned out the rest. First because Verde's comment didn't jibe with 'Bird's diatribe about the Twins being Maya wannabes who hailed either from Puerto Rico or one of its mainland colonies. And second, because she hadn't removed her arm, and in fact seemed intent on snuggling closer. Which might still be cultural, since (excellent English notwithstanding) Verde was not from the First World. God, but he wished he felt more at ease around women!

They had turned two corners now, into the arcade opposite that into which he'd entered. The light was better

there, and he caught the boom of music from somewhere further in what now seemed less a dwelling than a labyrinth. The song was one of the Twins' early pieces, but in a new arrangement with more drums, sparer guitar, and heavier bass. A march become a dirge. There were odors too: smoke from the braziers most notably, which seemed to include something akin to incense or copal; but more subtle scents as well: the spice of conifers and the heavy perfume of tropical flowers he couldn't identify. And of meat cooking, like an afternoon barbecue back in Minni.

Abruptly Verde froze—so forcefully Thalo flailed out to keep from falling. "What—?"

She was staring at him intently, twin furrows between her brows, which folded the damask tattoo in on itself so that she seemed to wear a pair of gilded exclamation marks on her forehead. Or antennae. "What color are your eyes?" she demanded.

"Green," he replied from reflex, though in fact they were contacted brown. But then he was looking in *her* eyes—which really were brown—and forgot about explanations. In fact, he seemed to have gone entirely blank—odd, but not unpleasant, as though he'd closed the mental equivalent of an outside door and scurried off to do errands in his hypothalamus. The sensation lasted no longer than it took to recall that he, an admitted romantic, was actually doing one of the most blatantly clichéd romantic things one could do, and then wonder if he should bother to fight the blush warming his cheeks, before Verde uttered a clipped, "No, they're brown," withdrew her arm, and continued without him. He had to run to catch up. "Verde . . . !"

She spun around; face, for the briefest instant, utterly vacant, as though she'd never heard of him; then filling all in a rush with recognition and apology. "I'm sorry," she gasped. "I told you about the stress-thing."

Thank God! Thalo sighed. He hadn't committed some stupid faux-pas and screwed things forever. "But . . . what's so stressful, all of a sudden?"

She froze again. "It builds up," she answered, with

none of the animation that had earlier colored her voice. "And then it kicks in and I can't stop it. As to why . . . Mostly it's just . . . planning."

Thalo started to reply, but a crowd of chattering 'Earthers (full members, by their T-shirts, which apparently one couldn't acquire casually—which made him appreciate the one he'd been given even more) engulfed them. He lost Verde's hand entirely (when had he taken it?), and didn't catch up with her again until the lot of them were making their way through another archway, beyond which a second courtyard sprawled, filled equally with young people cooking at long grills in the corners and young people consuming the results thereof. The food smelled heavenly—enough to make him forget the steak he'd refused.

But he forgot all about food when he saw who was stretching out a hand in greeting beside the arch.

Medium height, stocky build, black hair, long nose sweeping in one imperiously smooth arc back to an odd-shaped, slightly flattened skull, the effect accentuated by jet black hair pulled into a top-knot and adorned with feathers. Heavy jade earrings. Bare muscular chest. Elaborate white breechcloth studded with more jade and other noncrystalline gems. Six-toed feet thrust into complex sandals.

A Hero Twin.

Blowgunner. Jaguar Deer. No one ever knew which was which, save that one was supposed to have had a vestigial tail removed, with attendant scarring. Still, exact identity scarcely mattered when that hero—that semilegend, that international mega-celeb—was standing a forearm's length away, grinning at him (with *very* white teeth) as though they were ancient buddies.

Thalo took the proffered hand numbly, vaguely surprised to find it warm—perhaps he'd expected cool, like the pictures in the 'zines. Or the poseable action figures. Or the carved Maya kings on the stelae, whose very image they were.

"Nice to see you," the Twin murmured, shaking Thalo's hand enthusiastically. "You're new, aren't you?"—

With a glance at Verde, who'd wound up beside him.
"Friend of Verde's maybe? She's a jewel. Jade and Emerald. Hard to resist. And your name . . . ?"

"Thalo."

"Ah . . . like the pigment."

"You got it."

"You have . . . another?"

"John . . . Gordon."

The Twin's brow wrinkled slightly. "I've heard that
somewhere."

"Application," Verde supplied, easing closer. "He
filled one out last night. And didn't *tell* me," she added,
with a mischievous grin.

"Ah," the Twin smiled in turn. "I see. Well, that's
where I've seen it then. Which means he made the list."

"What list?" Thalo wondered, as Verde gently urged
him past the beaming Twin.

She gave him a cryptic smile. "You'll see."

He stared at his hand, which had just gripped another
that made music heard 'round the world. "Yeah," he
whispered, "I guess I will."

There was food in abundance, which Thalo ate with
relish; and drink (beer, water, and wine, but no soda)
which he drank with barely more moderation, given that
he was young, on his own, and the fare was both excellent and free. There was music from a group of Austra-
lian aborigines who did amazing things with wooden
drums and a didjeridoo. There was even conversation,
though much of it was muted by the event which hung
like a pall in the mind of "every right thinking Greenie
on Earth," as someone put it. And there was a quite
amazingly large crowd—several hundred min, equally di-
vided between established 'Earthers and curious neo-
phytes like Thalo himself. How one told—well, the
T-shirts were one thing, but there was also a certain confidence about the way the established members moved,
the same confidence that had brooked no nonsense at the
rally.

Thalo felt as much at home as being in a completely

new city among total strangers allowed. Though a vast majority of ethnic, national, and social backgrounds were evident, their overriding goal—their sense of mission—united them. For the first time in months he felt free to voice pro-Earth sentiments without fear of censure (what he got for moving back in with his folks after college). It was, in short, a blast.

Only one element disturbed the ambience (eschewing the persistent incense, which made him sneeze and frame questions about air pollution he never got around to asking). "Who *are* those guys?" he asked Verde, when they'd deposited their earthenware plates and metal cutlery in the designated bins (no paper trash for the Twins, nosiree).

"What guys?"

Thalo nodded toward a series of archways to the left, then toward the low stage from which the meeting was about to be conducted—with the entire membership ensconced on the ground or assorted artfully placed boulders, tree-trunks, and shelves of stone. The figures in both places stuck out like sore thumbs, both by their size—tall and heavily built—and their hooded cloaks, which were marked contrast to the amount of bare, young, and mostly well-shaped and nicely-tanned flesh around him. "Them: the ones in the cloaks. There were a bunch of 'em at the rally, and they're all over everywhere here. Are they—"

"Guards," Verde replied shortly—for no reason he could determine, given the conversation they'd been having about whether the new president of Hopi Solar was a Good Guy environmentally. "Roadies," she continued with no more warmth.

He stared at the nearest curiously, taken aback when the man scowled at him and swept away. "So what's the deal?"

Verde regarded him blankly. "What do you mean?"

A shrug. "I dunno. They're just . . . odd. It's almost like they were mass-produced. And they're so big, and . . . not old, but not young either. They just don't fit. It's

like everyone else 'round here's really alive, and they're kinda . . . dead.''

"No they're not," she retorted. "You just have to get to know 'em.''

"*You* know 'em?" Thalo gaped, recalling the way someone very like them had summoned her away that morning.

"Yeah," she grunted. "The Twins've volunteered their services to Outer Earth until this stuff with Bishop Green Jeans is over. Now hush, things are about to get going.''

He did. It all made perfectly good sense. He coughed, sneezed again, and breathed deeper.

Thalo didn't remember a lot about the ensuing meeting, save that he agreed with most of what was said (much of which was about Green Francis and how they couldn't let his death be in vain, nor the environmental causes he'd so tirelessly espoused left to lie fallow), and was suddenly amazingly sleepy. In fact, he actually caught himself nodding off in the middle of it, and more than once started awake, to Verde's consternation. "Sorry," he murmured, through a lull in the latest address. "Didn't get a lot of flat time last night.''

"May not tonight, either," she laughed, with a cryptic coyness that surprised the hell out of him, and evoked a not-so-surprising twitch in his groin.

And then, without him being quite aware of it, courtesy of fatigue, good food, and a few brews too many (which he didn't intend to let recur), the meeting adjourned. Happy chaos followed with more food eaten, more drink imbibed, and more conversations downloaded. There was music too: nonstop and louder; and the incense, now that he'd got used to it, seemed to impart a delicate drifty languor that made him wonder if that was how people who smoked cigarettes felt. It wasn't bad, actually. And Verde was a marvel. Of course he knew no more about her than when they'd met—because every time he tried to direct the conversation that way, someone would hail her or engage her in conver-

sation; and often as not, it was someone with something interesting to say, some tidbit of insider info about the funeral, the Movement, or which muckety-muck had just arrived in town, where and how long they were staying, and what pressures might be brought to bear on them to propagate the Cause.

The upshot was that Thalo was more than a little surprised when, after they'd been deserted by a lanky Icelander who'd related all kinds of interesting gossip about who *really* ran his country's fishing industry and how bogus their use-to-waste ratios were, Verde drew him into a small frescoed room that opened off the inner arcade.

One of the Twins sat there, sprawled easily in one of two vast papa-san chairs, while a mug of what smelled like exotic coffee steamed on the stone floor beside him. The fellow grinned smugly as Verde thrust Thalo forward, and actually laughed aloud when she uttered a giggling, "You asked for 'im, you got 'im," and gave him one final shove, which nearly put him in the rock star's lap. He righted himself just shy of grabbing the fellow's knee for balance, and mumbled an awkward, "Sorry. I'm a little buzzed."

"Don't blame you," the Twin replied casually, "if the last few days have been as bad for you as for me."

Thalo had to work to connect the statement with a reasonable reply. "You mean Green Francis—I mean, Archbishop Blackmer?"

"Exactly. But don't just stand there, grab a seat. I don't bite. I don't do anything you don't do except spend more money more flashily in more places in front of more people. Our hearts beat exactly the same."

"One of the guys," Thalo burst out.

"I hope so. Me and my brother, both. Fame's fun. Friends are better. Being famous with friends is best of all—which is not to say that we're friends," the Twin went on. "Not yet. But I *am* saying there's a bond between us that could forge that kind of closeness. You can't make that happen, of course; it has to evolve—"

"Like in that song of yours," Thalo exclaimed, as he

flopped down in the second papa-san and tried to look both relaxed and attentive.

"Which one? Out of curiosity, I mean. Not that I'm fishing for compliments, it's just fun sometimes to see if people get what we mean. If we're saying the right thing the right way, in other words, or if the message is going wrong."

" 'Blood and Scars.' It's one of my favorites, by the way."

"Glad you like it." A pause for a sip of coffee, then a long sigh. "And I'm truly sorry to make this so brief, since we seem to be on the fringe of a wide-ranging conversation, which is definitely a good sign; but the fact is that I *did* send for you. Well, not me, actually, it was the Board's decision. It was just my choice to talk to you direct. But . . ." A pause. "Let's cut the crap, Thalo. You helped us out at the rally, right?"

Thalo nodded.

"And you filled out a membership form?"

"Yep."

"Which speaks well of you right there," the Twin confided. "You did the long version and didn't leave anything out, which is damned impressive, given where you were—I've been after them to trim it. But anyway, you heard Verde refer to a list when we met up front? Or maybe that was my brother," he amended slyly.

Another nod.

The Twin smiled. "Well, to make a long story short, that application, along with over three hundred others in various stages of chaos, was reviewed by four distinct levels of our organization between then and the start of tonight's meeting. We made a list, then we made shorter lists, and finally an even shorter one. You made every cut. And . . ." He paused for effect. "We'd like you to join Outer Earth—and not as a rank-and-file flunky, either; as a member of the local governing board."

Thalo was stunned. For a moment he could neither speak nor—almost—breathe. "Me . . . ?" he managed finally. "But you don't know anything about me."

"Ah, but your application gave us access to people

who do—who accessed others, who put us in touch with your files in assorted places, which include copies of everything you've written on environmental topics since you were sixteen, plus your college record, plus the activities you were engaged in then. You get my drift.''

Thalo found his breath. ''All that?''

''Connections help,'' the Twin said simply. ''And money doesn't hurt.''

''But—''

''No buts, Thalo. You don't have to join, of course; or you could join at a less . . . responsible level—I realize this is a lot to dump on you in a hurry. But we need good people, man. Right now especially we do. The world's eyes are on Aztlan, and their ears are on everything that's ever been said by, about, in favor of, or against Green Francis. And we just happen to be the world's premier eco-rockers, at the right place, just as Outer Earth conveniently has more influence than ever before . . . And frankly, it's an opportunity we can't pass up. See, we're still a young group. We're undermanned, though not, I'm happy to say, underfunded. And unfortunately a lot of our personnel have more idealism than dedication. Unless you lied on your application and half your academic records, you're different.''

''Whew!'' Thalo breathed. ''That's a lot. Thanks, by the way . . . but— Well, just . . . whew!''

''We really do need you, Thalo.''

Thalo's grin was as infectious as the Twin's had been. ''And I'm ninety-nine percent sure I'm your man. I just need to get off by myself for a while and think.''

A casual shrug. ''Fine. The sooner you reply, the better, but take your time. The only thing I ought to add as maybe a kind of bribe is that we're having a formal initiation tonight—around midnight. If you respond by then, we can do you up right.''

Thalo's face was serious—as much so as it could be, given how elated he was. ''I'll be there.''

The Twin nodded, rose, and extended a hand. ''I've got other new blood to meet.'' He sighed. ''And much as I'd like to continue this, I'd best get to 'em. But one

thing . . . when you come back . . . Well, it's an authentic
Maya ritual. We'd prefer you fasted until then. And don't
drink anything except water or black coffee.''

"Or black drink?" Thalo ventured, with a grin.

"Yeah," the Twin grinned back. "Now, take care, and
hope to see you later.''

Verde met him outside, her face ablaze with an infectious smile. "So you're in, huh?" she cried, hugging
him. "Great. I knew you were one of us when I saw
you!"

"Yeah," Thalo laughed, through a yawn. "I reckon
I'm gonna do it. The initiation, I mean. Uh . . ." he added
shyly, "you don't happen to know if there's anywhere
to flat around here, do you?"

An eyebrow shot up meaningfully. "There's crash
space in one of the side halls: futons on the floor. And
actually," she continued, "I could use a nap too!"

"*Only* a nap?" Thalo chuckled, with a leer.

"Only a nap," Verde replied firmly. "Fasting includes
that too."

Ten minutes later, in an alcove off a low, cool room
centered by a softly splashing fountain, Thalo fell asleep
on an enormous futon, with Verde curled trustingly at his
side like a loving sister. From somewhere came the sound
of slow, rhythmic drumming. The air smelled of incense,
thick and sweet.

Chapter XVI:
Last Ditch Effort

(Martinez Amoco, Aztlan)
(Thursday, September 9—evening)

Meth splashed 'Bird's hand: a jump-start shock of cold he needed, given how sleepy he'd become. The nozzle promptly locked down and wouldn't be bribed with trigger-finger nudges, as incorruptibly insistent as the Jeep had been about needing a refill *now*.

Uppity tech!

A cool breeze caught him wiping his hands on his jeans—dress Kleins he'd worn to work—and made him wish he hadn't tossed his blood-stained tunic into the public squeezer happily crunching between the pumps. *He* was hungry too, but assuaging that could wait until he'd blown town—as though that were likely anytime soon.

Thanks to the French! It was their pres's motorcade that had prompted the roadblock which had first slowed him then provoked the detour from which only recourse to the Jeep's NavCom had extracted him. Alas, the thing knew locations, not traffic conditions, and he'd lost an hour covering barely a quarter of the distance between the Eirish Embassy and the Beltway—by which time his four-wheeled steed was pleading for sustenance. He'd acquiesced—here—and committed a third of his paltry cash reserves to satiating the beast.

It was full now, so he replaced the nozzle and secured the cap. A pause to retrieve his serape and assess the

chaos out on Bolivar (creeping), and he stalked off the pay the piper.

The piper sold him coffee—two jumbo cups (the second on standby in the Jeep's built-in thermos)—and the biggest bag of Ruffles in town, along with a stash of Butterfingers and a half gallon of mango juice. He was back underway in two minutes—if five kloms per hour could be construed as traveling. Perhaps he'd have been wiser to take AFZoRTA to the border and walk.

And then traffic stopped entirely.

"Thank *God*!" he sighed half an hour later, as he finally got to drive over thirty for the first time since leaving the station. He eased up to a careful cruise and watched the wall of taillights ahead recede along the Beltway: a Thunderbird—irony there; he'd piddled along behind it for four exits now and knew its license number from memory. Miraculously, his lane was almost empty—and remained so until he crossed the Tlaloc Street overpass, when cars began merging in on him from the entrance ramp. He swung two lanes over, realizing too late that Tlaloc was the main north-south artery that serviced St. Tekawitha's, which would be hosting a nonstop flow of memorial services right up until the funeral itself. What had assailed his flank were the refugees from the latest feeding onto the Beltway in bytes. He found more at the next interchange. He found the T-bird too: becalmed in the center lane. The radio, which had been sort-of numbing his nerves with "Evening Classical," suddenly produced a tired-sounding woman who revealed that "a bus bearing pilgrims from Guatemala has just crashed on the Beltway between Tlaloc Streets and Hillerman, resulting in gridlock. Anyone leaving Cathedral Square by car is advised to seek alternate routing."

"Now you tell me," 'Bird growled. And advanced another whole meter.

Customs at the Mexican border were no problem—hard to believe, given the complications of the last four hours. (Had it actually taken that long to cross one-third

of the city?) Now, however, with the western arc of *El País Verde* looming behind him, dark beneath a starry sky; and the elegant glass austerity of the visitors' arcade a low glitter closer in, he dared a relieved sigh. If the Mountie band was reliable, Rudy still hadn't been found. (*Christ, he hated leaving him like that!*) Or perhaps an ordinary murder was unworthy of attention when there were celebs to be shadowed, made way for, and guarded; not to mention turbulent traffic to be untangled, and the still-evolving plans for the actual funeral. Compared to those, the death of a mere "nice guy" was small potatoes.

A lot they knew! The same beings who'd murdered Rudy had also orchestrated a quasi-hurricane that, had it been fully realized, would effectively have leveled Aztlan! There'd have been no warning—no early tracking— because the whole mess had been conjured spontaneously from the subtle huge powers of earth, sky, and sea by a cadre of militant young orcas bent on blasting technization back to the stone age. Of course it might also have saved Green Francis, but one could spend a lifetime playing *might*.

'Bird had to *act*. He had fuel, food, and caffeine to sustain him for the rest of the drive. A couple of kloms of border grunge to navigate (efforts to suppress the clot of overpriced businesses and substandard housing along the thoroughfares into the Zone being at best a holding action), and he'd be home free. The mountains would soothe him; the natural world would salve his soul (he was starting to sound like Thalo!), and maybe—finally— he could get his head straight. Two hours from now he'd be hashing all this out with Lox and Stormy.

Two hours . . .

Ten kloms down the road he saw the Eagle. It was an old one, so battered around its plastic grill that even in the mirror the radiator showed when light caught it right. What looked like a defunct railroad tie doubled as front bumper, and it was missing one low-beam entirely, with the other scarcely better—which perhaps explained why,

having swept out of the obscurity of one of the frequent side roads, it now hung so close behind him. It was riding his brights to compensate for its own inadequate ones. Mexicans did that sometimes, still (according to an article Stormy had quoted from *Road & Track*) the worst drivers on earth.

Jesus, those fuckers were close, though! Really close. Too damned close, in fact. And, macho man or no, he tapped the brake three times.

The Eagle didn't budge.

In no mood for games, he brushed the brake again— four times. And wished he were driving something besides Stormy's nice new toy. A last-century Buick, say; with bumpers like chrome I-beams. Maybe a little body contact would get those assholes' attention!

Fortunately the highway had straightened into a two-klom stretch of four-lane stabbing deep into the Sierras: a chance to build distance from his troublesome tail. Outbound traffic being light, he floored it. The Jeep surged forward, as though compensating for all that stop-and-go. In no time, he'd savaged the speed limit. The Eagle faded to a dim-fasciaed blot. Faster still, and he'd have dared more yet, had a certain turn not been easy to miss even in daylight. There was the landmark already: a snarl of trees uprooted by a 'dozer and left to rot like a pile of weeds beside a garden.

Closer, and . . . *now*!

He braked hard and turned right, tires skimming slightly as they passed from pavement to gravel too fast for tech to counter. Still not as fast as he'd have liked (not in Stormy's wheels, though), but a decent clip all the same—especially around the rim of a defunct stone quarry. Half a klom to go now, before the penultimate leg. That the final one would mean a nerve-wracking scoot up a rutted mountainside—in the dark with him dog-tired—didn't bear contemplation. Not when the thigh that had played point man against a taxi was starting to protest his inattention, never mind the half-healed wounds that remained from last week's misadventures. Grimacing, he slowed again, searching for the turn.

—Found it . . . and . . . left.

Dirt road. Empty.

Good.

Not-so-good was that a glance in the mirror showed someone eating his dust: someone with nothing special in the way of lights. And since he'd long since determined that no respectable patrolman would be caught dead in anything that decrepit . . . Well, he had a sinking feeling he knew who his shadow was.

They'd done the same to Kevin a week gone by, then tried to run him off the road by bashing him up the butt. But they hadn't reckoned on the rock-like solidity of a mid-Seventies Mercury, or the commensurate fragility of a half-century newer Citroën. In large mass versus smaller, physics sided with the heavy guns.

Trouble was, the Eagle was bigger than the Jeep: easily as sturdy, and thirty percent heavier. And equipped with a wooden bumper that meant business sure enough.

And it was closing. 'Bird mashed the gas and switched the traction control to MAX, not trusting himself in gravel. Meanwhile, the landscape was wrinkling into the dry foothills of the Sierras. Mountains humped against the sky; the road was a rough-scaled snake twisting among them.

He managed another two kloms before they caught him: a sudden blaze of light in his mirror from hand-held spots. *They were trying to blind him!* And it was already taking all he had to maintain control, courtesy of a set of rocky ruts worsened by the almost-hurricane.

In spite of his efforts, he smacked something hard enough to ring resoundingly underneath. The springs bottomed. "Sorry, old girl," he muttered. "Don't tell Mr. Cloud!"

But he truly could go no faster—not without ripping the suspension right off the vehicle, which would put him on foot in the outback. And while he trusted his outdoor skills more than those of the selectively inept werkas, there was (as best he could tell) a car full of them, and only one of him—tired, stressed out, and with a newly bummed leg in the bargain. Best to stick it out in the

Jeep as long as possible. The road would improve past the gap of the long hill he was navigating.

If he got that far.

The Eagle was *right* on his bumper again, and he wasn't at all certain that last jolt hadn't been contact with its battering ram. Where was James Bond when you needed him? More to the point, where was that tricked-up Aston Martin? An oil slick would be mighty fine right now. Or a trail of spikes. Or a smoke screen. Unfortunately, though he surely had something about that would serve, he didn't have time to fish for it. And the derringer under the seat was out, because he needed both hands to fight the wheel. Ditto the tainted .38.

Besides, it might not *be* werkas back there. And if he shot at the wrong folks . . .

At which point the surface improved and he stomped the accelerator mercilessly. The Jeep responded with a jerk and another metallic crunch, and the traction control lights flickered like a pinball machine, as did the neat little diagram that told how much power was going where.

It worked, though; the Eagle was falling back, victim of being a sedan instead of an SUV. But the difference wasn't that extreme—if you weren't trying to conserve your vehicle, as 'Bird still was with Stormy's.

Nor if you were willing to suicide, as the werkas who'd played chicken with Kev back in Eireland had done.

And all at once the mirrors were full of lights, and that latest bump had really and truly been contact. "Sorry," 'Bird told the Jeep again.

Another jolt, and the rear hatch began to rattle—probably sprung. At least the road was smoother and straight. He fumbled under the seat for the derringer, hoping like hell it was loaded. It usually was, but no telling . . . Had it! No, that was the seat adjuster. Further back then, steering with one hand . . . *Thunk!* . . . and he lost the wheel but caught it again, all the while tugging against the velcro that bound the holster to the underside of the seat, while the seatbelts tugged at him.

Another jolt. Metal shrieked, and the Jeep skittered sideways. "Traction control malfunction," it informed him calmly. "Please reduce your speed or this vehicle will compensate automatically."

"Fuck you too," 'Bird growled, hating tech more than ever, especially officiously helpful tech. Then: "Damn!"—as the hardest impact yet sent the vehicle halfway 'round.

He had the gun now—if he could find time to use it, given that the Jeep was careening downhill with a mini-gorge on the left that might be a riverbed, and a wall of raw red rocks on the right.

Something darted through the glare ahead: armadillo. Reflex shifted his foot to the brake, even as self-preservation yelled *no!* and his thigh told him all that right-and-left down in the footwell was not what it needed. And that moment of hesitation proved his undoing.

With his foot off the gas, engine braking slowed the Jeep. The Eagle *didn't* slow—and dealt him the hardest blow yet—just as he was coming up on a right that was always sharper than expected.

Either luck (bad type, for him) was in effect, or the impact was precisely timed; but either way, the Jeep gave up trying to maintain forward motion and skidded sideways: tail going left just as another impact caught the right rear fender and spun it on around.

'Bird saw a variety of things, many of them unexpected and most of them unpleasant—flashes of very hard rocks, mismatched headlights, scrubby treetops, the road, the rocks, the headlights, and then treetops again. He also *said* a number of remarkable things which were lost in the Jeep's running commentary on its operating condition. And then the view was mostly headlights and branches; and a final nudge found the Jeep teetering on the brink of the long slope at the base of which those same trees were rooted.

For a long breathless moment it hung there, suspended, as the belts alternately loosened and tightened; and then gravity won, and the Jeep slid off the bank. For an in-

stant, 'Bird thought it was going to remain upright and the two of them would simply embark on a long bouncing slide down to whatever glittered below. It did—briefly—but then, inexorably, he felt it tilt further and further, and saw ever more horizon through the left-side windows, and then they were rolling. Mostly it was loud and most of that volume was a roaring gritty crunch, punctuated by an occasional shatter. Light did the flashing thing—on the dash, across the landscape, and behind his eyes as well. He closed them, which was wise, as safety glass was raining everywhere from a canopy that had been mostly glazing and was now largely reinforced air.

It didn't hurt much—perhaps because so much of him hurt already. And then, thankfully, the barrel rolls ceased with the Jeep upright. Except that the bank was even steeper here, and it promptly slid straight into the thickest tree for probably five square kloms. 'Bird tried to steer with the one hand that was still in the general area of the wheel, but failed. The Jeep struck dead center—and stopped for good. The airbag, having finally been placed in the situation for which it was designed, obligingly deployed, confronting him with a wash of white plastic like a vast tongue lolling from the steering wheel. Fortunately, he had sense enough to recall that the vehicle still bore most of a tank of meth and had suffered multiple shunts up the rear, and with that firmly in mind wormed his way free the belts very quickly indeed, thrust through what remained of the door (it had been two-thirds glass), and fell an unsuspected meter to rocky ground. Blessedly, the Jeep didn't follow, firmly wedged as it was between bank and tree.

He made it four meters before his weakened leg ambushed him. He flailed, rolled, and caught up against a rock, which knocked what little sense remained in his head clean away. Blackness replaced it.

When he regained consciousness, it was to find himself propped against the same boulder that had brained him, with a half dozen ominously large and loosely-clad shapes clustered around, two meters away at best. Most

had their hoods up, but the one just left of center had lowered . . . his, and 'Bird's suspicions were confirmed. The face was too bland, the features too smooth and unfinished, the eyes too dark a brown. And of course there was that damned stirring: arms perpetually in motion.

And then that one grinned ('Bird half expected to see sawblade teeth instead of normal human incisors, canines, and molars), licked his lips, and stared at his companion to the left with what 'Bird could only term unholy glee.

"I have never tasted human flesh with a human tongue," he told his accomplice casually. "Have you?"

Chapter XVII:
By the Skin of Their Teeth

(Cumberland Island, Seminole/ Creek Coastal Protectorate)
(Saturday, September 10—past midnight)

Carolyn slapped the mosquito that had just stabbed her hand, leaving a bloody smear across her flesh—and wished it was every were-orca that had ever lived or would. "Fuck," she spat under her breath, "fuck, fuck, fuck." She pounded a fist against the trunk of a convenient live oak for emphasis.

"I do not understand," Sean murmured, padding up behind her from where he'd been relieving himself in a patch of palmettos beside the trail. "Fuck means coupling, which is good. Why use it for something bad?"

" 'Cause if someone makes you do it and you don't want to, it's the *worst* thing than can happen," she retorted. "It's called rape: you lose possession of the most personal part of yourself."

"Then what the orcas do is rape?" Sean wondered, even as he eased past her and commenced surveying the trail. "The mind is more personal than any part of the body, I think. And they take control of that."

"Only when nobody's home," she shot back, at once irked by the boy's endless questions and grateful for anything that might, however briefly, take her mind off . . . everything.

"Liam was home," Sean persisted. "He'd just gone to sleep."

"Which was enough," she snapped, wondering if Floyd was having any luck finding a functioning phone from which to apprise Red Wounds and O'Neal of their situation. The one at their cabin had blown along with the transformer. The others in that complex had been neatly sliced. And the plane was on the airstrip, which was near the lab—roughly eight kloms up the island. Maybe *that* phone was still connected; Floyd had gone to check. Not for the first time did she curse her inability to wear a tattooed one, but salt water played hell with the circuitry. Sean, being what he was, didn't have one, and Floyd had never felt the need. They had limited range, and few cities were equipped to handle the extra load.

"Fuck," she said again—louder.

"It is bad," Sean agreed, laying a hand on her shoulder. She flinched, still unaccustomed to his elevated temperature, then relaxed and ruffled his hair. "Sorry. I'm just worried."

"We will find them. It is an island. We have heard no boats or planes. They must still be here. When Floyd returns, we will search more carefully."

"It's him I'm worried about!"

"He has the gun. You have me—and magic."

"That's what *he* said," she snorted. "But I still want him back right now." And with that, she strode into a patch of moonlight glimmering ahead, and stared at the sky accusingly.

The moon had risen—finally—which meant it was something past midnight. Which meant she, Sean, and Floyd had been tramping around the Cumberland wilderness for over four hours.

Vainly, apparently, since, ignoring two sets of footprints they'd quickly lost, they'd found no sign of either her brother or the Eirish pilot. Once they'd established that all three orcas in the cabin were dead, and a poor mind-raped black man with them, and then confirmed that two more unfortunate humans lay dead on the porch (by the remains of their uniforms and the whisky stains thereon, a pair of Peruvian sailors from King's Bay off

on a bender), they'd begun the search in earnest. The last
they'd seen of Kev, he'd been heading for the beach. The
attack had come seconds later, but the were-orcas had
apparently marshalled their forces behind the cabin, so
that no one had seen them assemble, then rushed around
to assail both doors at once. Kev might've caught that,
or might not. His prints were ambiguous: an amble toward the shore, then an accelerated pace that could be
equally indicative of fear or overloaded nerves. They
vanished at the waterline, which again meant little, and
reappeared further up the strand, angling toward the
woods. But the forest crept close to the shore there, and
in the dark it was impossible to tell if he'd been accompanied or was still innocently alone. "We need 'Bird,"
Carolyn had growled in frustration. "Or Stormy."

Floyd had then suggested, reasonably, that if Kev *had*
heard the shots he'd have returned if he could. Barring
simply barging in, which he obviously hadn't done, he'd
have reconnoitered from the woods until the coast was
clear, which their subsequent actions certainly indicated
it was. The implications of that line of reasoning weren't
encouraging, which was why they'd turned their attention
to Liam.

The pilot was an equally hard call: they'd left him
flatting on the porch, propped against the wall in his
chair. The invaders would've had to pass right by him to
get in the front door. Possibly he hadn't awakened, but
he hadn't seemed so far gone he'd have slept through the
ensuing noisy carnage, nor sat idly by had he roused.
He'd done neither. Instead, his tracks showed in the sand
beside the porch, as though he'd simply walked off. Like
Kev's, they ran to the woods and vanished. Maybe in the
daylight someone could've followed him, but not at
night, with Floyd's sorry flashlight the sole illumination.

Which brought them back to the present.

A rustling in the woods put Carolyn on guard, but it
was only a deer bounding away. Sean's ears were
sharper, however, and he yanked her into a patch of
shadow, brow puckering as he reached out with his
thought. "Floyd," he whispered, and she relaxed. It was

him sure enough, pacing stolidly up the trail behind, flashlight a bright glow in one hand, Liam's pistol (freshly reloaded from the pilot's duffel) a dark blot in the other. "Any luck?" she asked shakily, as he flopped against the tree.

He shook his head. "Liam's locked the plane up tighter'n a tick, and you apparently have to have a remote to unlock it—which is evidently still on him. I couldn't find anything to pry with, and could barely get at the door if I had. As for the lab, the outside lines were cut like the others, and I can't work a shortwave, assuming they've got one—which I should've thought of earlier; comes of relyin' on phones all the time, I guess. And before you ask: no sign of Kev or Liam."

"At least *you* made it," Carolyn sighed. "That's something."

Antsy as ever, Sean had been prowling further down the trail. The path was wider there, and in the waxing moonlight, the pickings might be better—assuming there was anything to pick. "Here," the boy cried abruptly. "Tracks: three sets!"

Carolyn had to race Floyd to his side, and squatted down to examine what he'd found. He really had struck pay dirt. Kev's sneakers were easy to spot, from their distinctive tread and narrowness. Liam's, too, were plain enough: standard light-issue military, with striated soles and solid, serviceable heels. But with them, often atop them, blurring them into obscurity, were the tracks of a very large man, unshod.

"Looks like we've found our boys," Floyd agreed, relief making his voice quiver.

Carolyn studied the tracks, then followed them a short way onward. "Yeah," she acknowledged upon return. "And it looks like they're all together."

"How can you tell?" From Sean.

" 'Cause the big guy—who has to be a were-orca in human shape—has a long stride; only every now and then he shortens it, as though he were following Kev and Liam and had to slow to keep from running into 'em."

Floyd exhaled loudly. "So they've been captured?"

She nodded. ''Probably at least one were-orca stayed behind when the others attacked, or changed his mind when he saw Kev leave. But he also saw—or sensed—that Liam was drunk, and thought fast—I mean, *I'm* thinking this, and they're as smart as we are—and he figured that Kev might or might not know what was up, but that he'd be more likely to trust Liam than him. So he took over Liam, and somehow the three of 'em got together.''

''At least they're still alive,'' Floyd breathed. ''I hope.''

''I bet they've got Kev's hands tied—maybe tied him to Liam. That's what I'd do.''

Sean had been standing very still with his eyes closed. All at once they started open. ''I have been seeking them with my thoughts all this night—though I cannot seek far that way, in this body, or for long at a time. But I just touched . . . something. Fear, very strong, or pain. I know which way to go.''

''You lead,'' Floyd charged. ''We'll follow.''

Too many minutes later, they burst through undergrowth half a klom south of their cabin and found themselves staring up at the ruins of Dungeness. A terrace had been built on this side, presenting a head-high rampart that rose from a patch of palmettos twenty meters off. Beyond it, rearing into the starlit sky like the frantic fingers of some giant whom the sucking earth had otherwise claimed, were a fantastic jumble of chimneys, fireplaces, and sections of shattered wall. The place had been *enormous*: far larger than Clononey, Kev's tower-house in County Offaly, and dwarfing Holybrooke hall, where his solicitor's folks lived.

''He is there,'' Sean announced. ''Only go slow, for . . . something is wrong.''

''There's a fire!'' Floyd added, pointing into the ruins.

Carolyn squinted but couldn't see a thing. Damn Floyd and his superior height. Shoot, even Sean was taller than she—and he was just a lad.

The boy tugged her sleeve and pointed to the left. ''Stairs.''

"Should we sneak?"

Floyd shook his head. "Probably too late now. 'Sides, there's more of us than them."

"Three," Sean supplied. "And two run away. The other—" He broke off and sat down abruptly, curled into a tiny ball. Sobbing uncontrollably.

Carolyn was beside him in an instant. "Sean? What is it? What's happened, lad? What's wrong."

The boy removed his hands from his face long enough to meet her eyes. His features were wild with some strange intense emotion she couldn't identify. It beat off him like waves: like heat from a flame. She reached out to touch it, to understand—

"No!" Sean shrieked, sounding utterly wretched. "Please, no. I am sorry—I did not think—I could not control—I should not have said—"

"Sean—"

"See—if you must," he managed finally. "You have to know. But see with your eyes only; the rest . . . I cannot say."

Floyd was already moving. Like a man possessed, he was striding through the palmettos toward the stair. The gun gleamed, where he held it straight ahead. Carolyn hesitated between ministering to Sean and following. "Go," the boy gulped. "I will be fine. In a moment, I will follow."

Oblivious to the way the hard-edged fronds ripped at her legs, Carolyn ran to join her father. He was halfway up the steps now, and the fire-glow was stronger, issuing from a defunct fireplace in the heart of the ruins, sheltered on three sides by intact walls. It was a wonder they'd even seen it.

Ignoring caution, Floyd paced ahead. Ash crunched underfoot, still a factor after all these years, all these seasons in which the ruins still hadn't been washed entirely clean. A small animal skittered out of the way. A bird called: a chuck-will's-widow. The cry made Carolyn shudder.

And then Floyd reached the fire, and for the first time in her life, Carolyn heard him scream.

"*Noooooooooooooo!*"—a forlorn sound in the night. She froze. What could be so bad that it thrust Sean into fits of frantic denial? That made her calm, rational father scream like the terminally insane? Without deciding, she moved. Without intending, she saw, too soon, what lay there.

They'd found Kevin all right, and, aside from being naked, he didn't look that bad—initially.

Lying on his back, he was spreadeagled on the sooty stone, arms and legs bound by ropes to pitons driven into cracks once filled with mortar. Something dark shimmered like silk beneath him, and it took her a pair of breaths to mark it as blood. More darkness pooled beyond, and his skin looked oddly rough. But then she realized what she saw, and before she could stop herself, before she could even feel loss or remorse or denial, she was hurling the contents of her gut on the ancient, haunted stones.

They'd have one more ghost now, she thought grimly. And this time she was ready.

"They've skinned him," her father moaned, from where he knelt beside his son's body, screening the worst from sight. "They've skinned my boy alive!"

And with those words, it became real and final. Which, oddly enough, made Carolyn feel better able to cope, though part of her knew she hovered close to shock. Still, she needed proof; had to see, to touch, to confirm. Swallowing hard, and with her gorge revolting at every step, she eased around Kevin's bare feet and crouched opposite her father.

"He's *still* alive," Floyd said numbly. "You can feel his pulse and hear him breathing."

"Oh God, no!" she gasped, and sat down with a thump. It was the hardest thing she'd ever done to examine Kevin's body, but she was a biologist and more qualified than her father to assess what had been done, what his condition was, what his chance of survival might be.

Well, they'd skinned him sure enough. Probably the were-orca had helped Liam stake him down and strip

him, then taken complete control of the pilot for the actual flaying. 'Bird had said they'd started on him with a cut down the center of his chest. It looked to have been the same here: an incision from just below the throat to just above his . . . male parts, then running down either leg to the ankles, and the same up top: slits across the chest and down each arm to the wrists. The skin had already been peeled back there, and hung in loose folds on the dirty pavement. But they'd arrived before the grisly work could be completed, because Kev's hands and feet—and, thank God, his face—were intact. To her chagrin, Carolyn found herself thinking about the times she'd been hunting, and the small animals she'd skinned. The torso and limbs were easy, though she seemed to recall having trouble with squirrel armpits. Hands and feet were not, and heads were hell, which is why she usually cut them off. And human skin was supposed to be fragile, it would be difficult to get it off intact. Sick thought though it was, she wondered exactly how much skin one needed to be useful? And vomited again, turning aside barely in time.

But Kevin really was alive. Blood bubbled from his mouth with every breath, and the exposed ropey muscles across his chest really did rise and fall. Steeling herself, she found the pulse in his throat and confirmed it. It was also racing like hell. But at least he was unconscious. He would die—he had to. But if he was lucky, he would know no more pain.

"I'll kill Liam," Floyd gritted.

That brought her back to herself. Carefully she laid a hand on his shoulder. "Liam didn't do it, do you hear? He absolutely did *not* do it. The worst thing he did was get drunk at the wrong time, so that one of those . . . *things* could take him over."

"Somebody has to die," Floyd gave back, through a round of shudders. "Somebody did this to my son, and that someone has to die. All of 'em have to die."

Abruptly, he was weeping. Only by main force did Carolyn keep him from flinging himself atop Kevin's body. Instead, she folded him in her arms and let him

vent his pain, which he did in long shaking sobs. Eventually she noticed Sean. He'd come up quietly and was staring at the body with clinical detachment. "He isn't hurting any more," Sean said in an odd voice that told her he was trying to avoid any show of emotion. "I felt it begin from afar, and I feared what might be happening. But he felt very little. He has gone to hide within himself. In a little while he will be gone. We should—"

Floyd glared up at him savagely, his body so tense it felt like embracing stone. For an instant Carolyn feared he would lunge at the boy. Instead, he shook his head. "I should yell at you and ask why you didn't tell us what was happening as soon as you knew. But you knew there was nothing we could do, didn't you? You let us hope a little longer. That was good of you."

Sean nodded mutely, and sat down at Kevin's head. "I didn't know him well, but I liked him. And he was, in a way, my brother. It hurts to lose a brother before you've ever had him."

"He's not dead yet!" Carolyn spat, through a surge of helpless anger.

"But what can we do?" Floyd countered desperately. "No way he can survive—not like this! Not that he'd want to—like this. Think of the scarring! Think of—" He broke off, sobbing. Then: "God, I can't deal with one of those—*things* touching him. Not my poor, poor boy."

"We still have to find Liam," Sean reminded them. "I will look for him."

"You do that," Floyd replied. "And for all our sakes, I hope you find him alive. But you both know I'm gonna have to stay here. I've got the gun, I can defend myself if I have to. But no way in the world, I'm gonna let Kevin die alone."

Carolyn's immediate response was to offer to stay as well, but then something told her that the aftershocks of the Schism were still not quite all settled, and that while there was nothing useful she could do here, finding Liam might save another life. And with that grim decision made, she patted her father on the shoulders and rose. He rose too—but only to remove his loose blue tunic.

That accomplished, he gently folded the skin back across Kevin's exposed muscles as best he could, ripped the garment's front from its back, and covered the worst of the damage with it. Carolyn found the remains of Kevin's clothes nearby, which showed signs of having been cut off after he was bound. She added them where she thought they'd do the most good: over her brother's hands and feet. Sean donated the tunic he'd donned earlier for protection against briars, as a pillow for his head.

"The more we wait, the worse it may be," Sean prompted, and turned to go. Moonlight silvered his bare torso, and here, among the ruins, he looked himself like a wraith. Or an elf: one of the *sidhe* come out of the hollow hills to gaze on human folly.

"I'll go with you," Carolyn called, only then making her decision. "If nothing else, maybe I can find some Spraskin. You need us, shoot," she added, to Floyd, then hugged him one last time and kissed his tear-stained cheek.

"Nothing will ever be the same," Floyd gasped, as he knelt again. And then, gently but firmly, Sean the selkie tugged Carolyn away.

Chapter XVIII:
Initiation

(The Hero Twins' Compound)
(Saturday, September 10—past midnight)

Night had transformed the Twins' Compound. Though the sun had long since set when Thalo had fallen asleep in what he'd quickly termed the ''low room,'' it had still been fairly early. Now, as he stood yawning at the foot of his futon, it seemed a different place entirely. The squat carved pillars that separated the sleeping alcoves had lost their too-new clarity and lapsed into mystery, as light from torches that hadn't been lit when he'd flatted made the warriors, kings, and ladies graven there seem to tremble with incipient life. A cool breeze was blowing, too; and the flimsy gauze curtains on that side fluttered. Unseen feet rustled on the meter-wide woven mats that framed the futons on three sides, or thudded against solid stone floors. But there was no slap of shoe-leather and rubber soles, only bare skin and hemp-rope sandals; and none of the distant rock'n'roll whose thumping had twined with his heart's to pace him stride for stride through forgotten dreams.

A sideways glance showed Verde still asleep. She made a soft mewing sound and rolled over. An arm flopped into the hollow that still retained a semblance of his form. He started to rouse her, then noted that other folk—including four women—were likewise emerging from their cubbies: stretching, yawning, and generally showing signs of having newly revived. Thalo *thought* at the time: closer to one than midnight. He also noticed a

subtle rumbling drone in his skull, as though, at some
great distance, vast blocks of stone were being dragged
across each other. His eyes felt heavy, but he was surprisingly clear-headed for someone who'd imbibed as
much as he had.

"You doin' the initiation-thing?" came a low male
voice close by. He squinted into the torchlit gloom and
found a young blond guy lounging against the next pillar
down, clad in a low-slung pleated Scots kilt and green-
bronze metallic skinshirt. He was scratching his backside
absently.

Thalo nodded. Another fellow wandered over: Mexican, or native Indian. A woman followed: European fair.
"You know anything about this?" someone inquired.

Thalo chose to assume that "you" meant him. "Not
a thing," he murmured, and wondered again when, exactly, he'd decided to go through with it himself. He took
a deep breath, noting that one thing hadn't changed: the
air was still heavy with incense. How much did a place
like this consume, anyway, if they always burned it at
this rate? Too much, he concluded—if it was the good
stuff, which only came from trees.

Again, he started to wake Verde, but paused, having
caught the cadence of multiple footfalls approaching
from without. There was a purposefulness to that stride
too: a stern formality that made him shiver. This was
great! This place, the meeting, the food. Verde. And now
to awaken thusly. It was like traveling through time; like
living in the age of the Maya.

As if to reinforce that illusion, the footfalls grew
louder still, accompanied now by a wooden drum and a
rattling jingle like sea shells chiming together. He tensed,
gaze probing feverishly through the flickering shadows.
Verde sat up and pushed her hair back from her face with
both hands. He saw her only long enough to flash her a
smile, which she returned tiredly, before his attention was
riveted upon the group of men who strode from an archway to the left to encircle the fountain in the center of
the room.

Two sets of six, they were tall and clad in exact rep-

licas of garb he'd seen in textbook after textbook, holo
after holo, on stela after stela. Bare-chested they were,
and bare-armed and -legged. All were dark-skinned,
which made their brilliant white kilt-aprons seem whiter
still. Dark knobby bands gleamed and glittered on wrists
and ankles, and on wide collars around their necks. Jade-
on-leather, if they'd recreated it right. And of course
there were the high-swept topknots decorated with shells
and jade and feathers that crowned their heads. Gold
winked here and there, and silver and copper with it.
Their eyes glittered wildly when the torchlight caught
them.

Behind them, at a respectful distance, came a teenage
boy with a drum, flanked by two girls carrying elaborate
fretwork rattles like lyres strung with cowrie shells. An
older man followed, dressed in a loose cotton robe. He
clutched a stick in each hand from which depended a
carved jade pot pierced with holes that leaked tendrils of
smoke and the odor of some strong resin burning. The
girls were naked, and barely old enough to have breasts.
The boy wore a loin-guard so skimpy pubic hair showed
above. His face was both feral and intense, as though he
took his role seriously indeed. The girls, by contrast,
stared vacantly, their pupils dilated as though they were
stoned.

Abruptly, two men stepped away from their fellows,
and they alone bore crozier-like staves of carved wood,
from the tops of which flew feathers and streamers of
bright fabric. As one they stamped those staves against
the floor, which echoed hollowly.

The other men—priests, or whatever—formed a line
and began to work their way around the room, starting
to the left of the arch by which they had entered, which
put Thalo next to last. At every alcove they checked for
occupancy, and, if empty, moved on. At those that were
inhabited, they stopped stone still, the boy beat the drum
and the girls shook the rattles, and whoever had flatted
there was absorbed into the file.

Thalo couldn't help but grin when they swept him up.
He flashed Verde a wink—she smiled back winsomely

and mouthed a silent "good luck"—then took his place behind the tall Icelander. Without a single word spoken, the priests marched them out of the room.

The journey that followed had the quality of a dream. They turned left immediately, then went up stairs, down passages, through courtyards, then up more stairs. At the end, Thalo and his fellow initiates—fifteen of them— were ushered into a spare, clean chamber with no more ornamentation than a low stone bench that completely encircled the perimeter save where the long sides were pierced by matching doors. Braziers flickered in the corners. The scent of incense was heavy, though the fumes vented through slits near the rough-beamed ceiling.

Thalo was trying to decide if they were supposed to sit or stand when another "priest" entered, this one even more elaborately dressed than the others—mostly in green feathers Thalo hoped were from farm-raised quetzals, as the wild ones were all but extinct. He carried a pile of pale fabric before him, which Thalo mistook for towels until he was given one. Only when he'd unfolded his and noted the arrangement of ties along the long edges did he realize what they were.

Loincloths. *Maya* loincloths.

The Icelander regarded his dubiously, but the hyper Latino in the corner seemed to know exactly what to do, and had already stripped to his briefs. They went too. Thalo grimaced and followed suit. The room filled with groans, sighs, and nervous chuckles—and the occasional frustrated curse. ("Damn, got the thing on backwards—I think—or can you do that?"—"Shit! It's twisted!"— "God, I hope I don't fall out."—And, from one of the women, "Well, I'll do topless if you will!") Thalo remained silent. Not that he wasn't uneasy, though no more than in any unfamiliar locker room; it was just that this ritual marked what was conceivably one of the crucial junctures in his life. And unlike most of his contemporaries, he believed in the necessity of rituals. He therefore tended to take them seriously, even when others didn't.

Eventually the last tie was knotted above the last bare hip, and the priests inspected each in turn. Save for one

lad who'd got his on inside out (you told by the pattern
woven near the edge), they all passed muster.

Silence invaded the chamber. From somewhere beyond
came drumming. A moment later, there was also song.
Thalo held his breath. Nervous. Expectant. A little giddy.
A little high, in fact, as though all this strangeness was
easing him out of himself. He raised a hand and marveled
at that movement: how it felt, how it looked, how the
vastness of air parted at his bidding. He grinned. And
inhaled. Probably there was something in the incense, he
decided, something that, in sufficient concentrations,
made you high.

Which *ought* to be pissing him, he realized. Still,
though he officially disapproved of drugs, he had, in fact,
tried drugs, and for most of one summer had been part
of a congregation of the Reformed Native American
Church, which used peyote as a sacrament. And of course
this *was* an important ritual. . . .

Someone coughed. Another scratched, the scraping of
nails against skin strangely loud. Thalo expected to hear
echoes.

Drums thundered. A rap sounded on the door. The
priests nodded at each other, then maneuvered the initiates into a double line. The door opened. Clean night air
rolled in.

Thalo walked out into the seventh century.

It could have been that, anyway, for the courtyard they
entered looked no different from the countless reproduc-
tions he'd seen in books, films, and VR sims. Oh, the
scale might've been a bit off—even media moguls
couldn't afford to duplicate full-size Maya pyramids—
but what faced them across a stone plaza maybe a half-
acre in extent and ringed by square-pillared colonnades,
was a fair copy of the main temple at Yaxchilan, from
the wide phalanx of steps marching up its face, through
the twin altars on either side of the stair head, to the
massive roof-comb on the sanctuary proper, that rose like
a crown above. The whole was lit by huge braziers, and
by the flare of those healthy fires the figures painted on
the facade seemed to stretch and strut and move. Or

maybe it was some subtle holo effect, like the towers at St. Tekawitha's. Did it really matter?

It did not, Thalo told himself eagerly, as he dragged his gaze from the building to survey what lay between.

Obviously the party had continued in his absence, to judge by the crowd jamming the plaza. Or maybe it wasn't the same group at all, for, discounting their age and the pervasive flamboyance of tattoos and hair, these people could as easily have been total strangers; Thalo didn't recognize one single face.

Of course it was hard to tell when those faces were contorted in a variety of private ecstacies, as the crowd— most of whom were obviously drunk, stoned, or both— whirled and twisted and cavorted, all to the pounding of unseen drums and deep-voiced singing from the depths of the dark arcades. If there were words to that song, he couldn't distinguish them, for they were no language he knew—not that it mattered. The sounds *were* the meaning. They said what you wanted them to say. Through them truth might, if you were lucky, be revealed.

Part of him rebelled at this. It was too unrestrained, too . . . orgiastic. Outer Earth was supposed to be a serious organization. But . . . wasn't seriousness a human construct? Man thought, but when he thought too much things went wrong. He thought, and he made machines, and those machines raped the land. He thought, and ideas were born—like slavery and revenge and jealousy.

Better one should simply *be*. Better one should step on the cogs of the cosmic clock. (Hadn't the Maya revered time above all things, and ordered their world through vast cycles of the same, so that act and world and time became part of one—not mechanism, but simply—existence?) Better one should ride the celestial flow.

The drumming grew louder yet. The singing matched it. Shell rattles commenced to jingle. The dancers spun ever more wildly. And then, so suddenly it was like the stroke of death—

Silence.

Two men strode from the single door of the temple. Each took a place behind one of the altars. The part of

Thalo that still dealt in concepts as mundane as names
identified them as Blowgunner and Jaguar Deer: the Hero
Twins.

They looked like Maya kings, like Eighteen-Rabbit
and Shield Jaguar and Great-Skull-Zero. Likewise they
resembled the priests who accompanied the initiates, save
that their garb was more elaborate, their feathers longer,
the carving on their jade pectorals finer, the gilding
thicker on their arm rings and leg bands, and the cotton
embroidery on their kilts more intricate. But the main
thing was their faces. Modern men they were—and yet
were not. Their solemn handsome visages, as alike as
sides of a scallop shell, showed the perfect stamp of the
Maya nobility, from their thick, out-thrust lips, through
their elegantly arched nostrils and strong-hooked noses,
right on up to the tops of their elongated heads, where
skull, hair, brains, and feathers seemed to merge and flap
away into the gathering night.

"Kings," Thalo whispered aloud. "They honest to
God really do look like bloody kings!" If he'd ever
doubted the Twins' boasts of being the true heirs to defunct Maya thrones, that moment dispelled them. He was
theirs. Body and soul, he belonged to them.

The drum sounded again: a single muffled thump that
nevertheless filled all the world. The priests at the head
of their group struck their staves against the paving stone
and the file of initiates marched forward. The dancers
made way for them, sometimes grudgingly, sometimes
gladly. Thalo saw mostly mindless, joyless madness in
their eyes. He didn't care. For himself there was madness
in joy. The file stopped before he knew it, so that he
stumbled into the woman in front of him. The priests
eased aside, then steered them into a shallow crescent at
the base of the temple stairs.

One of the Twins began to chant in what an increasingly distant part of Thalo thought might be Kìché. His
brother joined in, sometimes singing the same note,
sometimes one complementary. Occasionally they alter-
nated words in rapid succession, without in the slightest

disturbing the flow of the melody. At some point the other Twin took the lead, with his brother doing the augmentations. Through it all the crowd swayed, stamped their feet, and clapped their hands softly together. A few—a very few—tried to sing.

Thalo remained rooted in place, at once keenly aware of himself as an individual, even as his consciousness threatened to merge into what he could only term a vaster whole. He and his fellow initiates shared a dream, which was to revive and protect the natural world. The fervor of that dream had brought them, through many eliminations, together tonight, as parts of an incipient team. Already they had slept together, all unknown. They had shared anticipation and nervousness, had been naked together, marched together, and seen the wonder of the plaza together, and, crowning all, had witnessed the glory of the Hero Twins transfigured into kings. They saw the same sights with the same eyes now, and heard the same notes with the same ears. They inhaled the same incense and felt the same earth beneath their feet and the breath of the same rising wind. They were one now, never to be parted.

Just when Thalo thought he would discorporate entirely and explode away upon that wind, the drum thumped again, and silence returned.

The right-hand Twin stepped sideways, to come between his altar and the head of the stair. The left-hand Twin mirrored him precisely. "Tonight we expand the confraternity of the Outer Earth," they cried as one. Both mouths moved, though Thalo wasn't sure either spoke all the words.

"Tonight we perform the vision rite," the left-hand one continued.

"Tonight," the other went on, "we will materialize many ancestors and ask their aid in what we are about—"

"—And you initiates must prove your devotion by aiding *us*!" they finished, reunited.

There was murmuring in the ranks at that, though not from Thalo, who was utterly swept away.

"Brothers and sisters of earth," the Twins chorused. "Let us present your new kin!"

Wordlessly, the priests who ranked behind them moved in. The one on the left separated the youth on the extreme end. His opposite did the same. The right-hand fellow stumbled, face ashen and uncertain. His priest-in-charge steadied him with a hard grip on his arms, and urged him, with the other, toward the stairs.

"Come, brothers!" the Twins shouted.

Thalo swallowed hard. The time for the ecstacy of *being* was past. It was time to *do* again—whatever that entailed. He was, he sensed, one step closer to some great mystery.

Meanwhile, two more of his group had been sent up the steps, and then two more, and two more again—four times. Thalo suddenly found himself alone, looking up at his erstwhile companions who now formed a line between the altars at the summit. There'd been an odd number of them, he realized, as nerves made his semi-trance waver. But why did *he* have to be odd man out? Why did *he* always wind up alone? And him standing there in some stupid loincloth with his dyed hair and skin and contact lenses, with only a tiny fraction of Native blood in his veins, when in truth he was nigh as fair as the Icelander.

And then he felt a gentle pressure on his shoulders, and he too was ascending those stairs, a thousand ecstatic eyes fixed firmly on his naked back. He tried to stand straight and tall, and neither walk too fast, too slow, nor stumble. And then he was with the others, turning to face the crowd who roared their acclamation.

"He who waited longest shall now wait least," the Twins yelled, at which point the drum thumped again and the singing resumed. The priests, who had followed them to the upper platform, ululated. Two figures slid in beside Thalo: the Twins themselves, he noted, with a start. Turning their back on the dancing mob, they escorted him into the temple. Paintings brightened the walls: authentic copies of those on the prototype in Guatemala. A bench followed the perimeter, like that in the changing room.

An archway loomed opposite. They passed beneath. A door closed behind. And with it went all sound save those they made themselves.

Thalo blinked, for the air was thick with the harsh perfume of copal and some other resin. Torches flared on the walls between the braziers, which occupied the corners. A low stone platform a meter on a side occupied the center of the room, with another waist-high behind it, upon which, atop a white cloth, a number of objects were arranged.

"Anciently this was done in public," the right-hand Twin intoned, his voice formal, yet without the remoteness that had characterized it moments before. "Anciently this was the province of nobles and kings!"

"But we are *all* nobility now," the other went on. "And we do not wish to frighten our most promising prospects—"

"—yet we must know if you would truly dare whatever is required in order to free the earth—"

"—and for *that* you must dare the sacrifice."

"Sacrifice . . . ?" Thalo mumbled, suddenly aware that he was functioning on two levels again: one—entranced—moving slowly, surely, in precise response to the rite. And another who watched and analyzed. Even so, he wasn't sure which had spoken.

"Sacrifice," a Twin repeated. "If you do not know, we will show you."

Thalo—the inner Thalo—surveyed the objects on the table. There was a wide shallow bowl, carved from solid jade in the shape of a human skull, and empty. Balancing it on the other end was another wrought of quartz crystal, containing a number of tiny rolled scrolls of beaten-wood paper made from a tree whose name he could recall if he was sober. A third held narrow knives of flaked obsidian so obscenely sharp even looking at them made his wrists throb as though they were already bleeding. And a fourth bowl—of carnelian—contained a coil of rough-twisted rope, the strand as thick as his little finger.

And precisely in the middle, polished until it shone,

was a hand-long sliver of barbed and striated bone that could only be a stingray spine.

Abruptly, the clouds of muddle that had dulled his senses and deadened his intellect dispersed, so that inner and outer selves reunited. He swallowed hard—the inner self did, and the outer responded. A cold sweat shivered his body. He knew what this array was for—and the thought chilled him to the bone. This was the twenty-first century, for Chrissakes. Surely they didn't expect him to use this gear as, by its presence, was intended.

He twisted around, wild-eyed; body—if not mind—tensed to bolt. But the entrance—and the doors in the adjacent walls—were each blocked by one of the bulky guards. Though seemingly unarmed (they wore only loose hooded robes, that, if not Maya, were certainly not mundane), they were obviously impassible. Thalo discovered he was shaking.

"You know what this is for," the closer Twin told him softly, his voice soothing as a shower after a long day's hike. "If you are a man, you will do what is necessary. If you are not . . . we will do it for you."

Thalo's heart double-thumped. Already sweating, he flushed with heat. His head swam. His groin tightened to a cold dense knot. And though as terrified as he'd ever been, that terror manifested as a strange, numb calm—at which point his rational self retreated utterly, leaving the more pliable half-dazed doppelganger. "Tongue . . . ?" he heard himself say. "Or—?"

"You are a man," a Twin replied, with a wicked grin. "What do you imagine?"

He didn't want to imagine anything! Indeed, he was trying hard to drag what little active consciousness remained into Never-Never Land with the rest when the Twins slowly but inexorably forced him down into a spraddle-legged squat on the lower platform and placed the empty jade bowl between his thighs, inches from his groin. One handed him the stingray spine, the other fumbled at his garment. "I'll do that!" he snapped—shocked at the sound of his own voice. Then, "God help me," as he loosened the ties himself, and drew the crotch aside.

For a long moment, he stared at his penis. It was an unremarkable penis: a bit slender, perhaps, but otherwise normally sized. Now, however, fear had made it shrivel and his balls retract, so that it resembled some small shy animal hiding in a nest of dark hair. The Twins were staring at it, too, which didn't help at all. But at least that meant the skin was loose, which is what, so he'd read, was required. Holding his breath, he pinched up a flap along its upper curve (wishing his folks hadn't followed then-current fashion and had him circumcised). It was an awkward maneuver one-handed, and he lost his grip and had to try again. Finally, steeling himself, he grasped the stingray spine in his right hand, closed his eyes—and in one swift decisive gesture, forced it through the thin flesh.

It was the blood that got him, not the pain. And it would certainly have been better if reflex—self-preservation, probably—hadn't made him open his eyes. But when he did, and saw the spine transfixing his most intimate, must vulnerable part, with blood trickling out to either side, the world tipped sideways and he reeled. Someone—probably a Twin—braced him, while the other with a calm calculation that gave him chills shifted the bowl so that the blood that now drenched his wounded member, dripped into it. He leaned back against the taller platform, breathing hard, too far gone into shock to do more than sit and accept what had happened. And as he did, the pain, that had been in abeyance, raged out to fill the world. Distantly, he was aware of someone dropping the paper scrolls into the blood. And some part of him knew this was no perverse rite, but an ancient and honorable one, which the Maya kings and their ladies had practiced alike, with their genitals and their tongues; and that sometimes they pierced themselves not once but many times, and drew long thorny ropes through the wounds.

The world spun again, then stabilized.

"You have to remove it," a voice prompted gently. "And then you will be free."

He did.

The pain was epic.

But for some odd reason, the thing that occurred to him, before darkness claimed him utterly, was to wonder why he'd never screamed.

Chapter XIX
Frying Pan and Fire

(West of Aztlan)
(Saturday, September 10—past midnight)

The smallest of the six werkas clustered around 'Bird built a fire—a very bright one. The night being warm and the moon waxing, that puzzled him—until he recalled that orcas didn't depend on their eyes as much as humans did, relying instead on sonar. But these new bodies of theirs weren't equipped with echo-location, so that they were in effect as disadvantaged as a human deprived of sight or hearing would be. And with one sense down, the others would be commensurately more important. Thus the fire. "The better to see you with, my dear!" Or *find* you.

Or maybe it was merely raw instinct: fire to form a focus and a center and a . . . home. He wondered if the concept of home existed in his captors, who had three-fourths of the earth's surface to dwell in, and in three dimensions to boot.

One regarded him sharply, eyes glittering beneath its loose grey hood. "Home is where we live," that one rumbled. "You foul our home. Over and over, you foul our home. That is why you cannot continue to live."

'Bird started, having forgotten that werkas could read minds—strong emotions, anyway. He'd have to be doubly careful—or shield his thoughts, if that was possible outside fiction. "Yeah, well there's eight billion of us," he countered. "The last estimate showed less than a mil-

lion of you. And there're places your power can never reach.''

Now where had that *come from*? He'd determined not to say a word himself, to pick up as much as possible from his captors, and to try to escape—not in that order. And here he was in a pissing contest with the enemy! On the other hand, maybe he could learn something.

"We do not need to kill all of you," the one who had spoken retorted. "If we destroy enough, you can never rebuild. There is no cheap energy anymore, nor easily accessible food. If we upset the balance even a little, most of you starve. The survivors slay the others over what remains. The rest— It is as I said: You can never rebuild. You would be what you were ten thousand years ago. Hunter-gatherers, you call those ancient selves. Them we could abide.''

"I know someone you need to meet," 'Bird snorted. "You and he'd get along just fine!"

Before the werka could respond, another made a noise at it that sounded like a warning. The speaker growled back. "It will be dead soon, anyway. What harm if it knows?''

In response, the Warning-One growled again. The air went tight with tension, and something buzzed inside 'Bird's head. Almost words—if only he could grasp their intent. It hurt like a son-of-a-bitch too, adding to the pain already throbbing in every part of his body. Evidently he'd picked up the slop from some telepathic dressing-down. But why did they bother to speak at all among themselves?

"Keep wondering," the Chastened One spat—and fell silent.

For a time nothing happened. The werkas didn't move from their crescent around the fire, though every now and then the one who'd remarked about his tongue stared at him . . . hungrily. And in fact, the way they sat hunched over, with their long grey overcloaks obscuring the subtler shapes of their bodies and the peaked hoods overshadowing their faces, they looked like a circle of sharks

come to land and striving to sit upright. 'Bird couldn't stop thinking about teeth.

God knew it was better than thinking about himself—either his present condition (bruised, shaken, and abraded twice in one night, but basically intact), the situation he'd just abandoned (Rudy's murder), or his thwarted goal (contacting Lox and Stormy). He could walk—assuming his legs were untied—and his arms were basically sound. A rib might be gone, and he might well have a concussion, but he could deal with that. Pain was pain, but that's *all* it was. A warning. Not an end.

Eventually one of his captors glanced at his watch, then up at the sky, hood falling away to reveal a mostly bald head studded with tufts of hair in mismatched colors. Grunting like an old man, it rose. The others followed. 'Bird's brain buzzed again—or clogged, since more than anything else, it reminded him of how his nose felt when he had a rip-roaring cold. He had to work to keep his own thoughts intact. Evidently some discussion was underway on which there was strong disagreement, for he sensed a heat in some of the . . . emotions, he supposed they were . . . bouncing around. There were a lot of agitated gestures too, and what he assumed were directions being pointed out or alluded to; the whole punctuated by angry-sounding grunts, squeals, and hisses that were nothing like human speech. As best he could tell, some wanted to go ''back,'' some ''on.'' As for the rest . . . nothing.

Abruptly, the largest slapped the next in size across its heavy face—an odd motion, with the arm locked at the shoulder—and the contention ended, though 'Bird definitely picked up resentment. His brain abruptly unclogged, he gasped, then tried to mask it with a cough, and to think of nothing at all. But as Tongue-eater made to join the others, Leader growled and snapped an unmistakable ''No!''

The other wilted, the very image of a younger child denied some guilty pleasure by an elder.

'Bird caught one final flash of disagreement—or disappointment, it was hard to tell—so strong that he

winced, and then the . . . elder . . . five orcas turned as
one and trudged heavily up the slope to the waiting Eagle. He heard the engine crank, followed by the crunch
of gravel. Lights played over the cliffs, and he was angled exactly right to note that they didn't turn around, as
though to return to Aztlan, but continued the way they'd
come. Which told him something he'd as soon not have
known.

There were *plenty* of reasons to go back, after all, one
being that Aztlan was near water, which, he suspected,
was necessary to werka mental health. As for going on
. . . the only impetus the werkas might have for that, as
he understood their goals, was a certain hidden valley
where Stormy and John Lox were even now winding
down Stormy's Way. "Shit!" he spat, not caring if the
remaining werka heard.

That one, who'd been staring fixedly up the slope (and
who was still radiating an anger 'Bird could feel and
wished he didn't, since it made his already throbbing
head hurt worse) vented one final unintelligible remark,
turned, and stumped back to where 'Bird sprawled
against the rock with his feet all-too-near the fire. Ignoring him completely, it thrust a stick into the fire and
flopped down awkwardly, become at once an amorphous
pile of fabric with large hands and a head.

"Stuck with guard duty, huh?" 'Bird chided.

It glared at him. "You will remain silent."

'Bird glared back, having just that moment had an
idea. "Why? If you can hear my thoughts, which go on
all the time, what difference does my tongue make? Or
do you have a way to silence them?"

"Unconsciousness—or death."

"Do I get a choice?"

The glare intensified. "Best you keep silent, and your
thoughts as well."

Seeing no reasonable alternative, 'Bird tried—and almost succeeded, perhaps because he'd been dog tired
even before this latest misadventure. An incipient snore
awoke him. He jerked reflexively and shivered.

The werka blinked up from something it was fidgeting

with in its lap, then looked down again. Silence filled the night, broken only by the crackle of the fire, the pop of the occasional coal, and the werka's heavy, intense breathing. And one other sound 'Bird recognized from years of powwows and native-skill classes.

Antler against glass; he'd know that scrape-pop-snap anywhere. The werka was making a blade—probably one of those obsidian knives. He wondered why.

To his surprise, the werka looked at him. Perhaps it had grown bored or was still nursing resentment from being left behind. It vented a very human sigh. "We cannot make things," it gritted. "We envy you that. When we learned to put on your shape, making was the first thing we wanted to try. And since our oldest memories, the ones longest passed down, are of the First Men making tools, we tried to copy them. Only later did we realize that no one makes tools like this now. And that they are untraceable. And," it added, with a flash of too-white teeth, "glass edges are sharper than steel."

'Bird perked up at that. No way the anthropologist in him—or the curious human—could not be intrigued by that brief reference, not in light of the bargaining chip Carolyn had been promised the night she'd discovered her uncanny nature.

Most cetaceans were intelligent and telepathic, but, lacking any physical means of manipulating their environment, they'd had no choice but to hone their psychic skills. Like humans, however, they were curious. Eventually, they'd learned to tap into human consciousness and "co-ride" with humans ashore, experiencing life simultaneously with their hosts. They'd been doing that since man first arose, though limited to folks who dwelt along the coast, since telepathy had a finite range. But the clincher was that they never forgot! Good "adventures ashore" were recalled precisely and passed down from generation to generation intact. Human lives were therefore, in a sense, the cetacean equivalent of fiction, movies, or video. And they recalled perfectly things that were long since fallen into the shadows of human history. It was a treasure trove of knowledge past believing—if

it could be accessed. Carolyn was this moment taking the first steps to forge an accord between all the sapient peoples of the planet that might accomplish that goal. And *these* guys were out to destroy it? He couldn't allow that.

If only his captor would quit fiddling with that damned knife! It reminded him too much of a similar blade and how it had felt as one of the werkas' mind-raped human slaves had drawn it down the center of his chest, and what the intent had been.

"If I had been there, you would have been dead," the werka noted, with a grin.

For no more reason than to acquire even the tiniest fragment of useful information, 'Bird replied. "I thought you didn't kill . . . humans—not directly, anyway."

The werka stopped flaking. Fire flickered across its face, giving it—almost—cheekbones. "We do not. But there are *many* things I could remove from you without killing you; *many* things I could taste—and few of them would even render your skin unsuitable." And with that, it fell silent again. The flaking resumed.

'Bird was at a loss. No way could he lie here and let events take their course (and he still had to do something to save—if that was the operative word—Stormy and Lox). But how could he do anything when the werka could pick up his thoughts as plainly as if he had spoken?

How indeed?

Well, this nice fellow here had intimated that he could mask thoughts if he tried. Only how did he do that? How did he think yet not think? More to the point, how did he consider such basic notions as survival and such intricate things as plots without appearing to? Especially as strong emotions were broadcast most strongly—and what was the desire for survival if not a strong emotion?

And then he knew. Before he could even register that knowledge, he acted. Yet it seemed he did not act at all, merely surrendered to his body and let it take over. More than once he'd done that: keyed the breathing pattern, meditated, and slipped into a trance. And if he could send his essence into that place where the medicine dreams came from, perhaps there he'd be free to plan. Of course

there were dangers too: dolphins had found him there and planted dreams of their own. And werkas did their dirty work while people were in altered states, which what he intended most certainly was. But his captor was intent on its blade, and the trance shouldn't show on his surface mind, given that he'd already slipped into it, so that all these arguments were occurring as he drifted deeper into his own subconscious.

Drifting . . .

. . . Solidity formed beneath his feet. He blinked, and was in a forest glade—the same, in fact, where not two days gone by he'd communed with the Ancient of Raccoons. It wasn't there now—he sought it automatically— but the stream it had crouched beside was, as were the remnants of its feast: a plethora of empty crawfish shells scattered across the opposite bank. The predator had obviously found more prey—which was what had happened to 'Bird, save that he was the one who'd been found. He'd been too impatient, too eager to seek fast solutions to his problems. Had he gone slower, more thoughtfully, this would not have occurred.

But the problem was not what had happened; it was what would happen. And how did he decide anything without seeming impatient? More to the point, how could he do anything *but* hurry when amoral young sapients kept making remarks about relieving him of his skin? That poor crawfish had certainly lost its skin—and everything else! He didn't want to end up the same.

Which reminded him of something he'd been denying since his skin had first been mentioned. Something, in fact, he'd been denying since that night on the raft when he, Kevin, Carolyn, and Stormy—and poor Rudy—had sung up the counterstorm that had defeated the werkas.

Not shapeshifting itself, but what it represented.

Magic.

The manipulation of the tangible world by intangible means.

Which returned him to the battle he'd been fighting with himself since he was a child: how to rationalize the world of logic and science with his people's traditional

worldview which personified directions; ascribed sentience to everything; and used words, patterns, and rituals to produce results. Yeah, dammit, that was it! It was like Stormy had observed: Kevin wanted magic but didn't believe in it. He—'Bird—believed in what many white men called magic but didn't want to. Carolyn was somewhere between, and believed mostly, it seemed, in herself.

But if magic *was* real, then it was an option. And since his captor's perception of humans might not allow for that option, perhaps that was a vein he could mine.

Only what did he do? He considered the choices, but nothing came, given that he was tied up and didn't dare sing, since any sound would draw attention to himself. On the other hand—

The alternative was aborted a-borning as a more vigilant aspect of his consciousness went ascendant and yanked him out of the glade at the heart of his mind.

"What?" he almost blurted aloud. But then he knew. The werka had touched him—was in fact crouched beside him with one too-warm hand delicately cupping his throat below the chin and those over-large fingers pressing hard against the angle of his jaw. He had just time to wonder how they knew so much about pressure points—and any number of other topics—and yet so little about certain other things, when that pressure increased, and he felt his mouth pop open. The werka grinned and flourished the knife. "You fear this, do you not, little human? You fear it so much you hide in yourself from it. Shock? Is that what they call it? But fear is nothing to pain. And I have grown bored—and hungry."

'Bird could only gag and try ineffectually to struggle.

"You know what we are, do you not, little human? It is all in books and on film. But do you know that we—my kind—the wolves of the sea, you call us—often attack our larger kin? *Do you?*"

Somehow 'Bird nodded. All at once a dreadful image filled his mind, from the first thing he'd read about orcas. Or was that *his* thought at all? Was his captor maybe projecting? Did it even matter?

The werka's other hand was caressing his lips now, occasionally pressing a finger delicately inside. Once it brushed his tongue, and 'Bird couldn't ignore the flare of victory—and, worse, of hunger—that ensued. "Tongue," that one said. "We eat the tongue. We capture a . . . blue whale, and we rip off the lips and then we tear out the tongue—while it lives. I may do the same to you!"

The grip tightened. 'Bird twisted, but still could not work free. Slowly, inexorably his mouth opened wider. Fingers thrust inside. He thrashed more violently yet, and his tongue seemed to have a life of its own. And of course he tried to bite. But the thing was holding him so *tightly*! If only there were some distraction . . .

As if hearing him, the fire popped. A twig shifted. New wood slid into the flame. It blazed higher. 'Bird could feel that increase, subtle as it was. Its back to the fire, 'Bird imagined the werka felt it too, only more so. It shifted. And in that instant of relaxation, he bit down absolutely as hard as he could on the fingers fumbling in his mouth, at the same time jerking with all his might.

The werka snatched its hand away like a child from a vicious dog and slapped at him, even as it staggered backward. Not into the fire, though, as 'Bird had hoped, but a meter to one side, where it slumped down sullenly, nursing a plentifully bleeding hand. "Good teeth," it growled, but made no other move. 'Bird could almost feel its pain—and rage, so strongly was it broadcasting those things.

Which maybe meant it couldn't hear *his* thoughts. He relaxed the merest moment, for the plan he'd almost grasped while in the Racoon's glade had finally manifested—born perhaps, at the same deep level of his brain that could solve math problems while he slept.

Besides trances and medicine dreams, 'Bird had tried magic exactly once: when he'd sung the song Kevin had written to turn the werka's storm. They'd used Kev's words then, but part of the input had been his: how the Cherokee thought the whole world was alive, including such things as storms. And the way you turned a storm

was to personify it and remind it that its wife was off fooling around and it had better investigate. 'Bird doubted that, but no longer dared let himself doubt that when the formula that embraced that notion was applied something could happen. And if one could turn a storm, perhaps one could . . . redirect a flame.

Keeping his conscious mind as clear as he could, he drew just far enough into himself to hover on the edge of the trance. The words of the Storm Turning song waited there, clear as his waking self found them obscure. Effortlessly, he reshaped them, redirected them to another cause. And for good measure, he thought them—tried to think them—in Cherokee.

> *"Oh most noble fire,"* he began in that tongue. *"Oh most noble Ancient White and Ancient Red. It is good that I find you here so close; it is good that you warm my hands and my face and my mind and my heart. It is good that you are here with me, free in the wilderness, and away from the Long Man, your foe. But one sits beside you who is friend of the Long Man. He would give the Long Man dominion over us all. He would take us away from those fires my kind have raised with their knowledge, those fires that are heart-kin to you. He would destroy them: those bright fires of harnessed lightning, and those unseen fires that bind the world together. He would quench those upstart fires and only leave the old ones. Ancient White and Ancient Red, he would leave, whose work is mostly done. If the Long Man rules, and his larger, older cousin the Wide Blue Man called the sea, you would have to work hard again. Men would call on you all the time—for work in lieu of pleasure. But if you will work for me only a moment, perhaps that will not happen. Then you, Ancient Red, can rest and watch the deeds of your children. And my kind will turn to you for joy, not for work. That is all I have to say: I am Thunderbird Devlin O'Connor."*

And as those words came to him, 'Bird was aware on some level that he was softly tapping his bound fingers against the earth in that same odd rhythm the dolphins had sent him, to set the beat of the song they needed. And with the last of those words, he felt the force of his desire focus within him like a scarce-restrained flame of his own, and, finally, when he opened his eyes—break its bonds and fly.

The fire, which had lapsed back almost to embers, roared to life again. The werka started, its grey robes washed with crimson, its bland face with scarlet and rose. A hiss escaped its lips as the heat found it. And before 'Bird could consciously direct his thought, a flame had lapped toward it and found the hem of its overcloak. The fabric blazed up—more quickly than it should have—but 'Bird determinedly didn't notice that. And somehow in its efforts to rise (the wrong instincts probably kicking in there) the werka managed to step on the cuffs of its own baggy trousers and go sprawling. An arm fell full into the fire, and flame bit it too.

It screamed—and leapt to its feet, tearing at its clothes, beating at them as the flames took hold and flared higher.

But it was too late. Its hair had caught, and the light fabric of its tunic front blazed up into its face—into its mouth and nose. It screamed again—an inhuman note that rang in 'Bird's mind far more than his ears, as though it was ultrasonic. And then other things masked it: raw emotions slamming into his mind to overpower his own. Fear and pain. Fear and pain. All the world was fear and pain.

Fear and pain . . .

Fear and pain . . .

And then *pain . . . pain . . . pain. . . .*

And then nothing at all.

The relief was like an explosion, and for a long time-less moment 'Bird lay gasping. His mind was free of strain, his thoughts his own again. Compared to that, the agonies in his limbs were nothing.

And by the light of the still-flaming werka, with the stench of its burning filling the night as its true form

began to exude from what remained of its skin, 'Bird pondered what to do.

Escape, of course, and warn Lox and Stormy.

Yeah sure. With what?

It was with a ghost of despair already starting to hover over the field of his nascent victory, that his gaze fell on something glittering by the fire.

A freshly chipped obsidian knife.

In seconds he had worked his way to it. Another minute, and he'd fumbled it into his hands. Eighteen minutes later, he finished sawing.

The werka was a three-meter slug of charred meat. "This feast I give you, Ancient Red and Ancient White," he said formally, from his feet; bowing toward what embers remained, and making no move to extinguish them since there was no danger of them catching the surrounding brush. "Take it with my thanks, and I pray I never have to call on you again."

But then he looked at the Jeep—which was not wedged as tightly between bank and tree as he'd thought—and recalled what made that complex little alloy V-6 spin.

"Please remember me fondly," he sighed, "to your still-enslaved kin."

Chapter XX:
Out of the Woods

(Cumberland Island, Seminole/
Creek Coastal Protectorate)
(Saturday, September 10—the wee hours)

It was barely a klom of water, but it might as well have been a million miles.

Carolyn glared at it from the end of the weathered pier: at the moon-silvered waters of the channel between Cumberland's landward side and the mainland. And, more to the point, at the dozen-odd orca fins that flashed among the waves: a deliberate show of force—or intimidation. The grid was too regular for chance.

A chain of lights glimmered on the opposite shore, with a brighter bank further to the right. St. Mary's lay over there: still a sleepy tourist town in spite of a major submarine base just up the coast. It had a pier—and a ferry, and a consular outpost of the Native Southeastern Confederacy: Seminole/Creek Branch that screened researchers eager to work on the wilderness island. But between her mom's mysterious burial codicil and Red Wounds's considerable clout (the Seminole chief owed him a favor), the island would be closed for two days. No ferry would come whisking over with the dawn— which was too bad, because Kevin's only chance of survival lay on the mainland—not that she had any idea what she'd say once they arrived. Explaining how your brother came to be flayed while on an interdicted island with four other people wouldn't be fun. Maybe Red

Wounds and O'Neal could pull some strings. But in the great cold scheme of international diplomacy, Eireland and Kituwah were very small players indeed.

She doubted it would matter. Kev couldn't survive the night.

But he *had* revived—to everyone's surprise. She'd even been there, when the pattern she and Sean were weaving in search of Liam and the were-orca who presumably still controlled him took them by the ruined mansion. Kev had opened his eyes, stared glassily up at her and Floyd, murmured a liquid, "I have to live . . ." and passed out again. "He's a fighter," Floyd had said. "I always knew he was."

Maybe he *still* was. Sean was trying to keep tabs on him, but that was tricky because his power had limited range, especially now that Kev was unconscious again, and the selkie had no pain or strong emotion on which to fix. Nor did it help that he was also exerting a fair effort trying to locate Liam and that damned were-orca. Evidently the thing was shielding, and the boy had speculated that Liam must surely be sobering up by now, so that the creature would have to exert ever more effort to maintain control—which might, being tightly focused, function as a shield.

Carolyn both cared and didn't. It was dangerous to feel and think right now; it would be much, much better to *do*. "I still wish we could swim," she grumbled. "Anything but roaming around in the woods."

Sean slid an arm around her. His body heat pulsed through her. "You know we cannot. There are orcas out there. In human shape or seal, they would kill us. Even in a boat they would."

"Then why haven't they *done* it? Why attack at all? I don't understand."

Sean took a deep breath. "I think it's because of what you know. They do not want humans knowing about them, and now many do. They would change this, but they must kill you so as to leave no hint of their existing, or hints that would not be understood, since men do not

consider such things when they try to . . . discover crimes.''

Carolyn released a breath she didn't know she'd been holding. ''And a fair chunk of the folks who know about 'em are on this island.''

''Your mother too. She knew. And now she is dead.''

Carolyn's heart skipped a beat, though deep down she'd suspected and denied. ''The pilot . . . blacked out.''

''Flying over the sea . . . where there are orcas.''

''Oh my God!''

''You see?''

''But why haven't they attacked again?''

Sean shrugged, the movement hard against her side. ''Only one thing I can think of: They live long and lei-surely in a world of quick death with vast empty spaces between. It must affect the way they think. They can plan and plot, and have lived in human minds to know the complexities of such things. But they do not react quickly to sudden change. They are not—*aren't* adaptable. And because they live so long in each other's minds, they don't do well when forced to act alone. They could plan the attack on the cabin, but couldn't foresee that Liam would be drunk or that Kevin would go off alone.''

''Whew!'' Carolyn breathed. ''Thank God Liam didn't have the gun. They could've made him shoot us all!''

''Then made him shoot himself.''

A scowl. ''But . . . we'd *all* been drinking—''

''But they had not expected that. They expect humans to treat death a certain way and you—we—did not. And they already had people under their control and another plan in place. You see what I mean: they are not . . . flexible.''

''Yeah,'' Carolyn sighed. ''And another thing I see is that we're doing nobody any good standing around here. We might as well go through the motions, at least, of looking for Liam, then check back with Floyd.''

''*Dad*,'' Sean corrected with a smile. ''I feel your mind catch every time you call him anything else. And he would like that.''

Carolyn smiled back and ruffled his hair. ''Christ,''

she complained without malice, "you're like bloody Jim-
miny Cricket!"

"Who?"

"The conscience of a puppet in a movie. I'll tell you
when all this is over."

"If it ever is," Sean murmured.

"We have to get on with it." Carolyn released him
and started down the pier. Her footsteps echoed on the
boards. Waves splashed invisibly below.

Sean hung back.

She turned. "You coming?"

He shook his head. "I need to think. You go on, I will
follow. Never fear, they won't find you. The orca is
thinking only of Liam; he has no other choice. The cabin
is on the way. Meet me there—outside—I will find you.
I will only be"—he glanced at the sky—"two fingers'
movement of the moon."

Carolyn scowled at him. "We shouldn't get separated."

Sean looked as serious as she'd ever seen him. "Only
a minute. I . . . cannot think with your thoughts around;
even though you try to shield, they burst through. It is
like the noise the airplane makes: always there. I am not
used to it. But I have to think."

"You're sure?"

"I must, dear sister, I *must*."

Carolyn gazed fixedly at him for a moment, then
turned her back on the sea and the town beyond, walked
the remaining length of the pier, and once more entered
the forest.

The route back to Dungeness ran by the cabin, where
there was food Carolyn discovered she wanted. She
paused on the shadowed fringe of the skimpy yard to
curse Sean's quirkiness, but also to take a breather, given
that she'd been walking pretty much nonstop for close to
six hours. The eastern sky was showing the first pale
washes of luminous pink beneath its pall of midnight
blue. Dawn couldn't be far away, and— Well, all this
would go better in the light. It would also be more real;

for night wrapped the world with a glamour only harsh daytime could disperse. But she was up for some good hard reality now, and the cabin, for all its connotations, was something solid she could understand. Still, it was best to go forearmed, so she made a slow circuit of the structure from the shelter of the forest, determined the coast was clear, with the hurricane lamp still glimmering balefully through the windows, then angled in for a direct approach: front porch from the northeast.

She was shocked to see it look so normal, given what had happened there. The coffin was exactly where they'd left it, as was the bier and its rampart of Guinness bottles. Other bottles stood or lay about, including the one Kev had abandoned half full when he'd made that last fateful journey. It occurred to her suddenly that no one had thought to worry about her mother's corpse. Nor would Mom have been bothered by that apparent lack of reverence. The dead were dead. Assuaging that death was fine. But the living must always come first.

She stepped onto the porch—and froze.

Someone—or something—was inside! The door was open the way they'd left it, but through it, she could see a pair of legs extended at an angle between the floor and an unseen chair masked by that barrier. She squinted, and released the breath she'd caught. Fatigues. That had to be Liam. Which meant—

She froze all over again, this time with an actual chill. And hesitated, uncertain whether to investigate or get the hell out of there. But then she remembered that unexpected gift that had come to her with her selkie blood. Cautiously—clumsily, Sean would've said—she reached out with her mind, ready to retreat at the touch of anything too strange. And what she found *was* strange, though not in any way she expected: Not one alien mind dominating another, but two separate minds; one—the alien—registering simply as a presence that told her it was alive. The other— She was surprised she hadn't felt the backwash of that torrent of anger, remorse, and black hatred. Human thoughts, though; veiled with a vague

dullness that must be the world's worst hangover—but human.

Before she knew it, she had crept down to the doorway.

It was then that she heard the words. Or perhaps she'd heard them before and, tuned to more rarefied senses, simply ignored them. Now, however, they were clear: Liam's young tenor, his brogue thickened and slurred by shock and what sounded like simple fatigue.

"... you *made* me remember. You *made* me remember. You *made* me ..."

Carolyn briefly thought he meant her, but then, though the bulk of Liam's body was still masked by the door, she understood.

A were-orca sprawled in front of the sink. Like its now-deceased fellows, it wore loose, shapeless clothing but no footgear. Mud caked the khaki trousers to the knees, and a suspicious darkness Carolyn suspected was drying blood showed far too liberally on its hands, arms, and sleeves. To judge by its closed eyes, gaping mouth, and shallow breathing—and what her probe had suggested—it was unconscious.

A massive bruise across the right side of its forehead and continuing into the temple told her why, which was confirmed by the broken chunk of door-frame lying athwart its legs. The crucial throat skin was intact, however, which explained why it still held human form.

But Liam clearly thought otherwise, for even as she twisted around to check on him, the litany he'd been steadily chanting changed. "You *made* me do it. You *made* me do it ... but I *got* you, you son-of-a-bitch!"

Her breath caught again. The pilot slumped in the remaining kitchen chair, legs stretched stiffly before him. His clothes were torn, muddy—and caked with blood, whose origin she didn't want to contemplate. His hands were bloody too: palm-up in his lap, fingers curled like dying spiders. He was staring at them. That blood was old, already darkening into flaking stains that vanished under soggy cuffs. His face—Carolyn had never seen human madness, but it must look a lot like this: wild

eyes, taut muscles, cheeks and chin scratched and splattered with more of that awful red. And still he stared.

Carefully, so as not to alarm him, she eased closer. "Liam . . . ?" she called softly. "It's me, Cary."

His head swiveled toward her, slowly, mechanically, as though he had to think each element through before he could execute it. "He *made* me do it, Cary," he repeated. "But I got the son-of-a-bitch. I killed that fucker dead!"

"Yeah, Liam, sure," she whispered. What happened next, she had no idea. The important thing now was to get him away from the were-orca before . . . well, just before. Probably she ought to kill it like the others they'd hauled out the back door and left at the fringe of the wood. Or—

Steps thudded on the porch: carelessly quick and decisive. Someone light. *Sean*—even as his slim figure slipped around the corner to where she was poised in the doorway. God, but it must be nice to be that confidently fey!

"I've found Liam," she said, inclining her head inside.

Sean slowed, his eyes went empty for the merest second—and then, far too quickly for her to interfere, he was pushing her out of the way as he dashed into the room. Caught off guard, she staggered, only kept from falling by bracing herself against her mother's bier. When she righted herself, it was to see Sean in the center of the room facing the unconscious were-orca. Even in the lamp's faltering light she could tell that the boy's body was tense as a too-taut harpstring: legs wide-braced, arms curved outward at his side, fingers stretched wide. "You killed my brother," he spat at the unconscious figure. "I will not let you live. But I want you to know who brings your death. I want you to feel what he felt!"

"No, Sean!" Cary cried, oblivious to Liam's rambling monologue—at least, so far, *he* was harmless.

Sean turned savagely. "Why? He didn't care. Why should I?"

"Sean—"

"No, sister, this is for me. This is for Kevin and your mother and for . . . Trevor, that Kevin called Fir."

And with that, the boy leapt toward the counter, grabbed the same butcher knife he'd wielded in the initial attack, then darted back to squat on his haunches between the werka's legs.

Carolyn started forward, but a burst of anger from Sean made her halt. Maybe the boy was right. Maybe revenge did more good, ultimately, down there in the depths of the soul.

Sean was staring at the werka now, and she caught some of the backwash of that, unbelievable though it was—for the boy was willing the creature back to consciousness.

It twitched once, made to raise an arm, then paused as though uncertain—and the limb fell numbly back to the floor. It made a hollow sound. Carolyn felt a wash of panic—not from Liam or Sean—but from the thing itself. Curiosity made her reach out with her mind—and disgust made her recoil. It couldn't move.

"No," Sean gritted. "I have burned out the part of its brain that controls motion—I can do that when it offers no resistance. And now"—and she sensed that the words were for emphasis as much as information—"I will awaken it. And then I will skin it—alive. *Both* skins!"

"*No*, Sean!"

Again his anger lashed out at her—so fiercely it seemed to be her own, which perhaps, at some deep level, it was. Certainly she'd felt as Sean was feeling—still did, when she let herself. She had to keep reminding herself that though he looked like a sleek handsome teen, his emotions were years less mature. And then she recalled how strong her own childish feelings had been—and what they would've wrought had she had power to enforce them. Sean had that power: three kinds of anger to fuel revenge. Justice was a child's concept; mercy an adult's. Though she hated what it said about both of them, she couldn't resist him—not armed as he was.

"No," he told her. "This is for me."

And with that, he turned away and bent his will on the orca. She couldn't help but ride along—or read the backwash, she was never certain which, when emotions were

involved—and so was there when the were-orca's eyelids fluttered open. It blinked, looking strangely solemn, but fiery anger seethed there as well.

"You killed my cousin," Sean hissed, with an edge of death in his voice. "You killed my brother. You killed my kin."

Though it couldn't move, the creature's eyes glittered defiantly, red in the light of the rising dawn. To Carolyn's horror, it drew back its too-thick lips and laughed: a cold grim chuckle.

"Your cousins are nothing, little selkie," it rasped. "Now or later, we will kill you too. And everyone you know. Everyone who has dared to spy on us. We will find you in your sleep, in your dreams, when you drink too much. Endless are the ways we will find you, for we are patient, as you are not."

"But when you die," Sean countered icily, "you will know who it is that kills you, and you will die alone."

Another laugh. "It does not matter. I die. But then you die, and then tomorrow, a thousand thousand die and chaos rules, and—"

It broke off abruptly. Carolyn caught a wave of sick surprise, as though it had said too much. And with that came other images: Archbishop Blackmer's immolation. Aztlan thronged with people. Diplomatic motorcades. Countless people lying dead. There was a grim finality to it too, as though she gazed not upon a wish or a desire, but on a . . . plan.

"Christ," she shouted. "Sean, make it tell you more! Make it . . ."

But the were-orca had closed its eyes. Apparently its alarm at what it had inadvertently revealed had driven it into itself.

"I will find it!" Sean shrieked. "I will bring it back!"

"God, yes—please," Carolyn urged, and wished she was with him, dragging that thing's mind back to the waking world so that she could see the truth and *know*.

She *was*! Desire was action, and, wound tight by the events of the last day, her desire was strong. But then it didn't matter, because she and Sean had laid hold of the

were-orca's consciousness, which was both a wonder of complexity and a cesspool of hatred and loathing no human could have encompassed and yet stayed sane.

It resisted. She probed harder—and felt pain, and shock, and dismay. It fled. She chased it. Finally it could go no further. *Tell us!* she raged, while Sean reinforced her with his own vast store of power.

No!

Tell us!

No!

Tell us! Tell us NOW!

Resistance melted like a sandcastle before a wave, and before Carolyn knew it, she was through and sifting memories. Many there were, some quite appallingly wonderful in a purely positive way. But what she wanted lay deeper, a secret hidden in an alien mind as those minds had hidden in the human world.

Abruptly she found it—but even as she grasped it, it slipped away, went draining off into some cold empty blackness even she dared not invade. Yet she started.

No! Sean warned. *That way lies death. It has fled across the final threshold. You cannot follow unless you too would die, and me with you.*

But . . .

No, Cary, it is dead!

And with that Sean's mind cloaked her own and drew her back to consciousness.

"The funeral," she gasped, when she could speak again, as though to cement those words into reality before they too fled. "They're going to kill everyone who goes to Blackmer's funeral! And chaos will follow."

"But we don't know how," Sean groaned. "He died before we could find out."

". . . killed the son-of-a-bitch," Liam slurred. "Killed—"

"Yes, I know," Carolyn snapped. "We did too."

"And now," Sean said decisively, "we have one *more* problem."

Chapter XXI:
Vision Rite

(The Hero Twins' Compound)
(Saturday, September 10—the wee hours)

Fire—

—was Thalo's first thought when the fragments of his self reunited and informed him he was alive.

Fire—

—because this place where he sprawled spread-legged on his back was hot as hell, smelled of smoke, and was bathed with flickering red light.

Fire—

—because the first thing he fixed on when his eyes slitted open was flame, chaos, and more flame. He blinked and scooted up on his elbows. The movement jostled his penis—which seemed likewise infected with fire. He gasped, which forced the world into sharper focus. Shaking his head, he took stock of his surroundings. He was in a featureless room little larger than the futon on which he'd been flatting. It butted against one white stone wall; another, to his left, held a dark wooden door. A window lay beyond his bare feet, open on inferno.

No, not a window: a wall-sized TV—a very good one. And that was no true conflagration but an extension of the rite in which he'd recently participated. He stared at it stupidly, aware that he was more than a little muddle-headed, courtesy of too much booze, never mind whatever more subtle games had been played on his unsuspecting psyche. He tried to summon anger and couldn't find it, and then the image claimed him utterly.

The revelers in the temple courtyard were dancing, if possible, more frenziedly than ever. Many spun like dervishes, hair and clothing flying out at right angles from flailing limbs. Music pounded: drums mostly, but with a thread of melody that might've been one of the Twins' songs. Enormous iron braziers sent flames leaping three or four meters into the air, their smoke merging with the clouds that scudded across Aztlan's grey-gold sky, even as sparks vied with what few stars conquered a city's worth of light. Smaller burners puffed clouds of incense and copal—how well he recalled those odors.

The tempo increased, whipping the crowd to a fever pitch. Many doffed their clothes and danced naked, sweat sheening skin of every hue, natural and otherwise. A few coupled on the bare stones of the pavement or pressed against the massive pillars that supported the arcade along the plaza's sides. The fires basted all with a wash of scarlet: flashing limbs, bobbing breasts, the curves and clefts of buttocks. Sleek flesh (mostly), or shaking flab. Eyes sparkled. Teeth shone ghastly bright in feral grins. Tattoos danced reels across an integumentary sea.

The tempo increased again—then stopped abruptly, which seemed both a pattern and a sign. The dancing wilted. The camera panned toward the temple. Two of the bulky roadies emerged, sidestepping to flank a darkness that was maw and womb alike. Two more figures strode out behind: young, strong, and vigorous; festooned with jade, cotton, and quetzal plumes.

Blowgunner. Jaguar Deer.

The Hero Twins.

Each held an all-too-familiar bowl—which conjured all kinds of unpleasant memories. Yet still Thalo stared; no way he could stop, not now. That was *his* blood up there! *His* humiliation! *His* pain! He also had a notion what it would be used for, and having suffered, was determined to see it through.

And then . . . ?

Escape, emotion demanded. Get the hell out of here and tell Outer Earth to get fucked. Expose all this cra-

ziness and excess and put the organization back on sound footing.

Watch . . . ! Intellect replied. *Learn! Know!* And that argument was stronger.

After a pause during which the Twins flourished the bowls aloft while the crowd roared in anticipation, two priests separated from the stiff ranks standing like statues before the temple. Both chose torches from those blazing along the platform's rim and, moving as one, strode toward the matching altars. As one, they thrust those brands into hollows atop them. As one, flames roared on high. As one, they backed away.

The Twins remained unmoving, perilously close to those new infernos, bodies bathed with crimson so that their sweat-stained flesh seemed soaked with blood. Their ornaments glittered. A feather on one jade-crusted wristband ignited and crisped to air. The Twin ignored it.

The flames subsided.

"Your new kinsmen have made the sacrifice!" a Twin shouted.

"—They have given pain and blood to fuel this rite—"

"—Blood is life—"

"—Blood is power—"

"—Blood is strength to call the Ancestors to validate our claim—"

"—Let us see what the blood of our kinsmen buys!"

And with that, still moving as halves of one whole, they tipped their bowls forward and spilled rolls of bark paper soaked in the blood of fifteen young men and women into the fire.

Smoke boiled up instantly: thick clouds Thalo could almost smell as they rolled toward him—toward the camera, he amended. For an instant the plaza was obscured, but the oily billows quickly dissipated, replaced by strangely straight columns of dense white that twisted toward the sky, masking the tableau behind them.

Holographic augmentation? he wondered briefly. Like the towers at St. Tekawitha, perhaps? But no, he didn't think so. Real fire (which that patently was in the altars)

produced real smoke, and there was too much other smoke around for the laser beams needed to effect holograms not to be visible here and there, which they weren't. Plus, it . . . well, it just didn't *look* like holography, and the people in the plaza weren't reacting to it like holography, and—

At which point the drumming commenced anew, and the singing, and Thalo was caught up again. The Twins had joined in now, while the smoke continued to spiral and contort as though seeking to mold itself into some more tangible form. With every beat, it pulsed. And slowly the columns swayed toward each other, finally merging in an arch that framed the temple, high above the Twins' heads.

Thalo swallowed hard. He recognized this from an endless array of anthropology books, but had never expected to see it enacted; certainly not in the world's most modern city, armored with the trappings of tech. Magic was what it was (though one small part sat back and questioned and told him that the power of suggestion was mighty in its own right and had been used more than once tonight). But one didn't suggest to a camera. One didn't use high-tech effects to conjure a vision rite.

Magic.

That was one of the things he'd studied under the guise of ''primitive belief systems,'' and he neither believed in it nor scoffed; it had simply been absent from his reality. But 'Bird had skirted the subject earlier, mentioning casually that he'd had medicine dreams; and 'Bird, for all his head games, was a pretty straight shooter. The Lakota had certainly had men of power who'd predicted their resurgence. The Hopis . . . well, hadn't one of them been fasting for a Kachina Dance when he'd he'd suddenly scrawled certain odd symbols which, when deciphered, held the formula for the complex ceramics from which had come the solar cells that had bought their independence and fueled that movement for all Native tribes? Shoot, hadn't Montezuma himself known the vast convoluted cycles of time so intimately that when Cortez

arrived, he had no choice but to believe that arrival fore-told, his own demise ordained?

And Green Francis: the smartest man on earth, some had called him. But he was as staunch a Catholic as had ever lived, and that church was rotten with magic and mysteries, was in fact *founded* on mystery. And if Green Francis could believe in miracles, angels, and incarnate gods, Thalo could accept vision rites.

And then it didn't matter, because something was hap-pening.

The coils of smoke had merged inextricably now and looked thick enough to be solid. And in the heart of each, a darker core was forming and forcing its way up to their juncture—

—and bursting out, like a river of molten jade sprin-kled with powdered emeralds.

The vision serpent!

Conjured from blood by flame, its gullet the way to the Otherworld: to Xibalba and Hades and Hell. Or Tir-Nan-Og and Valhalla and Heaven.

As big as a tyrannosaur's, that serpent's head was (and did it wear a crest of plumes, or were those simply at-tenuated scales?); its eyes were long and glowing yellow.

It hung there for a long moment, suspended above the stairs, wavering from side to side as though assessing the crowd's worth before proceeding. And then, like a huge gate swinging wide, it opened its mouth. Darkness gaped within, but then that darkness was plugged by a paler shape that moved. Ruddy blots appeared on upper and lower lips, then gradually coalesced into what could only be fingers as, with agonized deliberation, a man pulled himself from that serpent's maw. Halfway out, he slid, and twisted his torso upright to face them, as the ser-pent's head flung back. Maya he looked, with the stamp of kings upon both his face and the elaborate jade or-naments that made the Twins' regalia look like plastic baubles.

The crowd roared. The drumming returned at a frantic pace. Thalo shivered.

"Behold our ancient kin!" the Twins cried.

''Behold the power of blood and fire and belief!''

''Behold the power that can save us!''

The Ancestor simply stared at them fixedly, interminably, with yellow eyes that exactly matched those of the serpent that had delivered him. No word he spoke, but Thalo had never seen such power as shone upon that face. And then he clapped his hands—a sound like thunder—and folded his arms before him. Then, as easily as his emergence had been difficult, he slid back into the serpent's maw. The serpent promptly closed its mouth and subsided into the smoke, which dissipated.

''Of this you will not speak,'' a Twin said quietly, but his voice carried throughout the plaza.

''Nor, beyond these walls, will you remember!''

''You have seen our power.''

''Let that power give you confidence in your labors.''

For a long still moment, silence reigned.

Silence . . .

Breathing . . . soft with wonder.

A padded stick fell gently onto a drumhead.

The tension dissolved.

A second beat—and once again drums thundered.

Wooden flutes piped strange melodies.

The dancing began anew.

The Twins watched for a measured time, then turned as one and returned to the sanctuary.

The camera panned back to embrace the dancers.

Thalo sank back exhausted.

Perhaps he slept.

When he returned to awareness again, it was to a clearer head and a dreadful uncertainty about the veracity of what he'd witnessed. What time was it? he wondered: more proof that he was sobering up. A thought told him: a bit over an hour since he'd impaled his dick on that stingray spine and passed out. *God, that'd been stupid!* Sure, he'd had no choice . . . but couldn't he have resisted? Made a break, or something? So why hadn't he? To prove to a bunch of too-rich poseurs that he'd pay any price to join their elite?

Well screw 'em! No way in hell would he be part of

an organization that perpetrated such preposterous—and risky—acts on its acolytes, vision rite or no. What in the world could he have been thinking? He was basically a serious person and fairly conservative in his private life, for all he was also impulsive and subject to grandiose passions. It was the booze, had to be . . . and maybe the incense. Certainly he'd been maneuvered into a suggestible state by . . . something. Probably a combination of somethings: food, drink, pervasive incense, music, group karma, the Twins' extravagant charisma . . .

And he'd gone along with it, and here he was: stashed away in some cramped little cubby with his dick going up in flames, and who-knew-what transpiring on the screen. More dancing, it appeared, more singing—a lot more coupling. Always more, more, more. Where was the *earth* in all this?

He scooted back, trying to sit upright—and pain flooded up from his crotch. He'd been denying it, he realized; fearing to check . . . down there in dread of what he might find. Swallowing hard, he eased aside the towel someone had wrapped around his waist and regarded his wounded member. It no longer bled; that was some relief. And it bore the unmistakable sheen of Spraskin across its upper curve, so he'd at least been given minimal attention. But Spraskin contained an anesthetic; therefore, it shouldn't be hurting like it was. But then he recalled that he'd been out over an hour, that the painkiller wore off after a while, and that it really wasn't so much a sharp bright pain as a distant throb.

So what did he do now? Obviously they'd put him here for a reason. But what? The Twins' hints suggested that all his fellows initiates had been subjected to the same rite as he. And if *he'd* known what it was going to be, he'd have bolted right then and there; therefore initiates were not returned to the temple plaza. Yet they still had a right to partake of the ritual, thus this fine big TV—likely one of many.

"Yeah," he muttered. "Thanks a lot! I pay the cover charge and everyone else gets to see the show."

As for the show itself . . . he didn't dare think about

that. In fact, it hurt to think about anything, and worst of all, it hurt trying to decide what he really *did* think about the enigma he'd just witnessed—and another now facing him.

Had he really seen the vision serpent?

Did he stay with Outer Earth?

They needed him—they said. They'd sounded sincere.

But did he need *them*?

Well . . . they certainly had power; that much was obvious. Or magic—or something they called magic—or led folks to *believe* was magic. But why hadn't he caught wind of that before? Surely hundreds of fervent young people couldn't all keep a secret that big, if the rite had been enacted previously, as seemed likely. So what bought their silence?

Fear?

God knew *he* was afraid: of what he'd seen, what it implied about the nature of reality, and what it said about Outer Earth.

Or was it something more subtle? Certainly what he'd seen had been a wonder, even when viewed at electronic remove. How much more vivid would that experience have been live? Was silence too much to pay for that kind of rush? And the Twins had money in buckets. Could potential traitors not be bought? Or did magic work its own coercion? If one could summon ancestors, could not one set a bond of silence on a few hundred predisposed souls? The Celtic druids could. Their bards could. A trick of the mind was all it took. A desire. A wish. And if someone wished louder than someone else and had power to back that wish . . . which wish took precedent?

And then he recalled those whispered final words: "Of what you have seen tonight you will not speak—nor remember beyond these walls."

Casual admonition? Or massive show of power?

All at once he was shaking uncontrollably.

He was also thirsty. And—dreadful thought—had to pee. Shoot, if he could find a bathroom, he could wash

his face too; a slap of cold water would work wonders just now.

Carefully, he rose. It didn't hurt *too* much—if he didn't let things dangle. Clutching his crotch to minimize that eventuality, he surveyed the room, finding his clothes neatly folded at the foot of the futon, with a can of Spraskin on top: evidence of greater concern than he'd supposed from his . . . hosts? Torturers? Comrades-in-mystery? Whatever their intentions, a lavish application from the can cooled his member back to normality. He let it air dry, then donned his clothes.

And tried the door.

Locked—of course. But his captors hadn't reckoned on the resourcefulness of Thalo Gordon, nosiree! Fumbling through his wallet, he located the ignition card to a car he no longer owned and inserted it between the bolt and the striker plate. Fortunately, the builders of this pile hadn't gone completely over the top for tech, and for many functions old ways were still best. It was thus no trouble at all to flex the card so that the bolt was forced back into the mechanism. A soft click sounded. Twisting the handle with one hand, he felt it give. Carefully, he eased the door toward him.

No footsteps sounded beyond, no noise at all, in fact—which he hoped meant that this part of the house was deserted. Taking a deep breath, he peered out. White walls greeted him, dimly lit by indirects and relieved only by a meter wide bas-relief frieze at eye level. Maya motif—of course. Another breath, and he stepped out, relieved to find carpeting underfoot. Now where was the loo? Bedrooms tended to be clumped together in places like this (as evidenced by a number of regularly spaced doors set in the same wall as his); and if, like his, they had no private baths, there ought to be a common one close by. He located one at the end of the opposite wall where it kinked around a corner, completed his mission (cold water really did help: he was thinking fairly clearly now—except that he was trying hard *not* to think about a number of things), and was halfway back to his room

when he caught a loom of shadows from the corridor this one teed into.

And since he'd obviously been locked in for a reason, if only to prevent unsanctioned prowling; and since the loo was on a corner with nowhere to hide between there and his room, and he'd surely be seen before he could get there and maybe be asked awkward questions, he whisked back to the corner and turned right. That corridor was empty, featureless save the frieze, and bore no apertures until a bend to the right at the far end marked another corridor—which should make the third wall of a square leading back to his room. He went that way, turned the corner without incident (he-of-the-shadow had apparently gone to the loo), and was trying to choose between retreat and continuation, when he heard voices.

That would've sent him scurrying in a wink, had there not been something so disconcertingly odd about them he had no choice but to investigate. Trying very hard to be utterly silent, he flattened against the wall and crept toward the source of those sounds: an arcade occupying the central third of the forty-meter hall. Firelight flickered there, and he caught the soft, tinkly pattering of falling water. Cursing his curiosity, he crept closer yet and finally peered around the ornamental frieze that edged the opening.

—Another courtyard (how big was this place, anyway, to encompass so many?), its center occupied by an opulent swimming pool complete with fountain, and fed by a two-meter channel set in the pavement of the eastern perimeter. Assorted statues and planters were artfully strewn about its wide margin, but more to the point, a number of men lolled there in beanbag chairs: big men— those weird-ass roadies, in fact. Only then did Thalo realize that he'd never heard them speak.

Well, they were certainly speaking now, and he quickly determined that a lot of the weirdness came from the way parts of both high and low registers seemed to be edited out of their voices so that he only caught part of some words. It was English, but the sounds didn't always match the images that formed in his mind. It made

his head hurt, too: as though his skull was vibrating in response to some inaudible noise.

And then he saw what occupied those men's attention: another big TV, projecting what was now a full-blown orgy in the temple quad. They were pointing at it and laughing.

"Fools, all of them," one chortled. "Stupid suggestible fools."

"Of course they are," another agreed. "They see what we summon for them to see."

"And they have agreed to the Earth Hour!" a third added. The ensuing laugh was shrill as a woman's.

"Earth Hour?" the first inquired. "I have not heard of this."

"It was in Blackmer's will—a very complex document, so I understand, that anticipated many things, including his funeral. Among them, he asked that for one hour a year—not necessarily at his death; he had not that much ego, though they have chosen to arrange it so—all technology on the planet would be turned off."

"All?"

"Save that necessary to sustain life, data bases, and security systems. It was to prove that humans can survive without such things. I understand that the Pope has requested voluntary curtailment for the entire day."

"Blackmer proposed it in his Peace Prize speech, fool," the second grumbled. "Or have you forgotten?"

"It is difficult to manage all these memories. Many are the same yet . . . different."

"Just remember that it is at the funeral we will strike."

"And that chord will be sufficient?" From a fourth.

"With us to augment it," the second snickered, "the very stone will run like water."

"I still do not understand."

"It is simple. First we—"

Thalo heard the rest—with his ears. Yet his mind simply would not accept the preposterous plan revealed. Chills marched over him, and more chills; but worse was the way all that information *entered* his brain only to drain off into some lost corner before he could assimilate

it. It was rather like hearing a foreign language. It was also awful. Indeed, it made him sick to his stomach.

Eventually that stomach revolted. He fought it down—still had sense enough for that; no way he dared betray his presence now, for all he only knew that he'd heard something appalling—long enough to regain the bless-edly-empty loo.

And then he was back in the corridor that contained his room. He slipped inside, breathing hard. The lights were out, as was the TV wall. "Lights: soft," he muttered automatically. But these weren't voice-ops. He fumbled for a switch, only then wondering why the road-ies had used the word "humans" so strangely.

"Don't bother with that," a soft voice called. He started. By the dim hall light behind him he could barely make out a figure—it had sounded like Verde—sitting with knees drawn up on the futon.

"Verde," he began, "something weird's—" He broke off abruptly, wondering if he dared trust her. And with . . . what?

"Yes?" she asked innocently, rising to meet him.

"Uh . . ."

She reached out to him, tipped his face down toward hers. "What color are your eyes?" she murmured.

"Huh?" he gulped, confused. But then he was looking into her eyes—and all those questions and doubts and fears and memories and theories that had plagued him since he'd awakened went spiraling away into some se-cret dark.

He grinned, forgetting everything save that he'd passed his initiation, been left here to recuperate, and was about to enjoy his reward.

"I . . . can't," he gasped, as Verde's fingers tugged at the hem of his tunic.

"Yes you can. I'll show you. And then you'll go home with me and I'll show you again."

"No!" a small voice shouted, locked away in the depths of his mind. He ignored it. Or perhaps it had never been there.

Chapter XXII:
Kamikaze

(West of Aztlan)
(Saturday, September 10—dawn)

"C'mon old gal, you can make it!" 'Bird pleaded, as the loudest clanking yet issued from beneath the battered Jeep. He was on the steepest slope—the last upward one—before the final run to Lox's compound. He'd glimpsed the gap already: the saddle between two taller rises that weren't big enough to call peaks. The rockslide that had blocked access the previous week had been cleared away—by him and Stormy, in part payment for their Ways. A level space beyond slanted gradually down, narrowing into the trail that led to the valley proper.

And payback time.

It was almost dawn, the eastern sky pinkening into gold, while a few stars still glimmered in the west—behind him, courtesy of a route that twined about like the skitterings of a drunk iguana. The rocks to either side were red as blood—crimson fresh and dull brown old alike—disconcerting, even if it was only sunlight. Worse was the noise the Jeep made, which effectively precluded the stealthy approach he'd intended. He needed stealth, too, since the presence of too-familiar tire tracks proved that not only had the battered Eagle that had forced him off the road passed this way, but two other vehicles as well: a four-wheel-drive and something small that leaked the same dark fluid he'd found at Rudy's place.

And of course he'd spent the last quarter hour squint-

ing straight into the rising sun, thanks to a windshield that, along with the rest of the Jeep's glazing save one curved triangle between the main roll bar and the support for the missing hatch, was now so many blue-gold shards strewn along the side of a dry riverbed two hours and too many kloms back.

He supposed he should be grateful it ran at all. Impulse alone had made him check it after his escape from the toasted werka. Wedged between the bank and the tree that had staved in the front, it hadn't looked good—yet it had cranked with perfect aplomb, the little V–6 as silky smooth as ever. That had led him to try backing out, which hadn't worked. The winch had. Half an hour later (complicated by a body that protested every act save total immobility), he'd lurched the Jeep out of the gully: a ruin of shattered glass, torn plastic, and shredded Kevlar that might once have been iridescent copper-gold. The running gear had been better—save that at least three axles were bent, to judge by the way the thing bucked and hopped; and the diagnostic computer had told him that no traction at all was reaching the left front. The upshot was that it absolutely would not go above thirty, and that with the steering kicking like mad. What Stormy would say when he saw it . . . well, he might've been better off with the werka. Being nibbled to a nub a morsel at a time could well be more merciful than the vengeance of Stormcloud Nez.

And naturally the phone had bought it—though who he could've called, he had no idea. Triple A? Yeah sure; he could just hear himself: "Uh, I've had a wreck and I need someone to come dig me out, only you can't report it and you *sure* can't tell the cops, and I need another Jeep right now, preferably well armed, 'cause I've gotta save my best friend from a bunch of megalomaniacal lycanthropic cetaceans!"

Cetaceans that were surely wise to his approach by now, given that the Jeep had just chosen to add a high-pitched screech to the ongoing clanking-in-earnest. Scowling, he switched off the forward drive, which reduced the racket but didn't stop it. At least the muffler

was still hanging in there, though the temperature gauge was on the rise and wisps of steam were emerging from beneath the crumpled hood. Or maybe that was dust kicked up by tires no longer wrapped by fenders.

Stormy was gonna be *so* pissed.

Assuming, of course, that the illustrious Mr. Nez didn't already have more important things on his mind—like survival. As best 'Bird could tell, he wasn't far behind his quarry. The Jeep was in sad shape, granted, but two of the three vehicles ahead weren't cut out for bad-road duty at all and had obviously crept along, hindered, no doubt, by drivers equally inept at maneuvering cars and the bodies that helmed them. Shoot, he'd even glimpsed one of 'em: had crested a gap and seen what he supposed, by its sorry lights, was the Eagle cresting another. Hopefully they hadn't been as observant.

Maybe he should park right here and reconnoiter. Only he wasn't sure his bod (especially his well-bruised thigh and hip) was up for even a short uphill trek on terrain as steep and uneven as he'd need to navigate. Besides, what the Jeep cost in conspicuousness, it made up in protection—sort of. It was a hard call, and he was simply too tired to sort options. *Besides*, the Jeep contained that part of Stormy's live-in arsenal he'd been able to recover after it had spilled during the roll. And that was a good thing to keep close by.

If only he had a plan. Unfortunately, that depended on what lay beyond the saddle. There were (presumably) three cars full of the things, for Chrissake; Stormy and Lox were two men. Not good odds, for all that the bad guys were unused to being human. Too, if they held to that peculiar ethos of theirs, and would not kill humans directly, they'd have had to lug a whole horde of flunkies to do their dirty work, and orchestrating that might require concentration. He'd never actually seen them "ride" someone when he knew that was transpiring, and wasn't sure if they could function independently under those conditions or not. Probably not—he hoped—since whatever troops they commanded would in effect be

functioning by remote control—the world's best remote control, granted—but still remote.

Which didn't tell him the first thing about what to do, save that it was probably gonna involve shooting.

Certainly was, he amended an instant later, as he neared the gap. Forget being heard; the crunching and clanking had been drowned by staccato bursts of gunfire. His heart leapt into his throat at that, for though he was nowhere near the gun nut Stormy was, he still recognized big-bore assault weapons when he heard them. They were distant, though: comforting—because, just possibly, it meant they wouldn't be aimed at him should he have been anticipated—and bad—because it implied that whoever was pulling the triggers was already in the valley. And Stormy was supposed to be inside.

As if in confirmation, a thin trail of smoke trickled into the sky beyond the saddle. Swallowing hard, he found a fairly level turn-off just shy of the right-hand peak and backed the Jeep in, nose pointing downhill in case it wouldn't restart. It was the hardest thing he'd ever done: trying to remain calm and rational when crazy amoral were-beasts were taking high-caliber potshots at his best buddy. On the other hand, he was the only cavalry that chum could expect to come riding over the literal hill, and if he got himself decommissioned, it would help no one at all. And though he knew that each report might be *the* report that sent Stormcloud Nez to the kachinas, he couldn't allow himself to dwell on that.

"Stay cool, man!" he muttered aloud, as he steeled himself with one final breath. "Oh Jesus man, stay cool, stay cool!" Wincing at the pain in his leg—which had just stabbed upward into his lower back—he gritted his teeth and climbed out. The .38 he'd already chosen (because he'd actually found ammo for it), and tucked into his right front pocket, but he hesitated at the array of larger artillery spilling out of the security locker under the jumpseats, finally settling on a heavy Glock automatic, with a half dozen extra clips. His jeans threatened to bag off his hips as he stuffed them in, but there was no other choice, in a hurry. Hopefully these would suf-

fice, if all he had to do was snuff a dozen-odd werkas—
as he was resigned to do.

At which point the longest volley yet ripped the air,
and before he knew it, reflex had him running.

Staggering, more properly, because that hip joint really
was acting up something fierce and wouldn't support
weight from certain angles or for long. Fortunately, his
route, which he'd chosen to maximize cover, was relatively level, and there were plenty of scruffy bushes to
grab hold of. Thus, he was still undetected, so far as he
knew, when he eased around one final stone and peered
into the gap.

He'd been right. Beyond the pass was an area of
maybe two acres, mostly level but sloping to a ten-meter
cliff, below which, bracketed by a series of shelves and
ledges that became gradually more overgrown the lower
one got, lay John Lox's valley. The only access was by
what might once have been an actual road over to the far
left, but that way was blocked by the troublesome Eagle.
Steam was roiling from under its hood, he noted with
satisfaction, but that was certainly not steam rising from
precisely the quadrant where Lox's hogan lay. Either
someone had torched it, or one of those rounds had shattered something inside that had set it alight—not that it
mattered. What mattered was whether the suddenly ominous silence that pervaded the area meant that the werkas had succeeded; whether he was too late and could
now write off two more friends courtesy of his own
ineptness.

Unfortunately, all that was clear at the moment was
that the region rimming the steepest part of the cliff was
occupied by an ancient tan Chevy Suburban 4WD and a
new white Dodge Whisper with rental plates. As for the
werkas, there seemed to be nine of them (it was hard to
tell, the way they were situated), all clumped up beyond
the Whisper, and intent on something in the valley. Even
in his hole, a good fifty meters away, 'Bird could feel
the mumbling buzz of their thoughts in his head: another
good reason to hang back. A more troubling one was the
real possibility they could've picked up *his* thoughts and

were even now waiting on him. Shoot, someone could be drawing a bead on him this very second. God, but it was hard not to think too . . . loudly or intensely when your emotions kept jumping between your heart, your head, and your gut, and you probably had more adrenaline in your veins than blood. Abruptly, he was shaking. A breath calmed him, and logic told him that the werkas were indeed controlling those unseen troops in the valley. *Letting winos and retards do their shit work*, he thought with a scowl. *Really great human beings!*

Setting his jaw against the pain in his leg, he eased closer, hunkering down behind another rock. A bit of quick mental arithmetic gave him a rough body count. There'd been six werkas in the Eagle, including the one he'd toasted. Five remained. The Whisper would hold five. The Suburban . . . eight comfortably, a dozen in a pinch. That made twenty-two, max. He saw nine. If each werka controlled one human (which made sense; he couldn't imagine trying to sort two sets of impressions, much less coordinate them), that made nine in the valley. Which jibed with the available facts.

Assuming they hadn't posted guards. Only why would they? Nobody lived near enough to hear gunshots; almost nobody knew this place existed anyway. (*But how had the* werkas *known? Lifted it straight out of his mind? Probably—dammit!*) And the person most likely to attempt a rescue (namely, him) was supposedly tied up in a riverbed halfway back to Aztlan. And—

A single shot, followed rapidly by two others, shattered his reverie. His heart leapt: the second pair were small caliber!—like Stormy surely had with him. And Stormy, representing Dinetah, the Dineh nation, had won the bronze medal in small arms back at the '20 Olympics. . . .

All *he* had to do, then, was find a higher vantage point so that more of the werkas would show beyond the Whisper, aim this nice little Glock, and fire. Of course there was the small fact that he'd never shot anyone before, and certainly not nine in the back in cold blood. (That he *had* participated in the death of far more orcas in their

own skins didn't trouble him, it being almost impossible not to equate shape with substance when determining what was human.)

Fortunately, they really did seem to be preoccupied, with two sitting right at the rim and the rest propped against the Whisper in a sloppy row. At which point it occurred to him that they might not all *be* werkas, and if he shot someone who was not, it was simple murder in lieu of the quasi-genocide he was about to perpetrate. On the other hand, these guys were sniping at Stormy and Lox, and one of them had likely taken control of an innocent Rudy Ramirez and splattered his lively, creative, and well-educated young brain all over a sandcrete wall for no more reason than the information that gray matter contained.

And that was enough: Rudy dead, awash with blood, and Stormy about to be. Taking a deep breath, 'Bird crouched behind his boulder, steadied his arm across a tree branch that had fallen there, and took aim. Not being particularly well-versed in either assassination, mass-murder, or instruments of mayhem, he hesitated. Left to right? Right to left? Or start in the middle and fan each way? The first were simpler, the last more likely to achieve maximum effect with minimum effort. Scowling, he thumbed the safety off and decided against the laser targeter since recoil would render that useless anyway. O-kay . . .

He put the middle one in his sights: the tallest, whom he recognized as the ringleader at the riverbed.

A final breath—he held this one—then a brief "God help me," and he braced his wrist with his free hand and squeezed the trigger—over and over. In spite of his efforts, the kick startled him more than the noise, which didn't last nearly as long as anticipated. But then he saw why, even as another part of his mind coldly tallied the results of his attack.

The clip had jammed with five slugs to go—what he got for not checking before stuffing it in; the thing *had* been jogged and jangled about in a rolling Jeep, after all. More to the point, though, some damage had been done.

The centermost werka was definitely wounded, and splashes of red marked at least two others. The eerie thing, however, was that there was no shouting—humans would've done that. But a heightened . . . pressure in his head told him that communication was still taking place.

He'd also lost the element of surprise. Already the werkas were diving for cover behind the car, their movements an awkward flurry of overcloaks and hoods, with the wounded ones completely out of sight. Meanwhile, 'Bird alternately poked and jerked at the clip to no avail. He had just started to swap Glock for .38 when the first bullet stung his left earlobe, the hiss of its passage louder than the report.

Someone was firing at him!

A careful glance showed a hooded shape crouched low beyond the front of the car, dark eyes glittering, with something long and metallic pointed his way.

So much for not killing people directly! Or maybe it didn't apply when they were themselves attacked. Nor did it matter in the grand cold scheme of things. No, what mattered now was dispatching as many of them as possible without getting offed himself. Which he tried— from the other side of the rock, aiming at the shape most visible through the Whisper's windows. He fired; glass shattered—twice—and the figure slumped. Unfortunately, the follow-up ricocheted off a roof pillar. He heard the telltale whistle-zing, but didn't stay to watch, since two more shots had come closer than he liked; one neatly severing a branch on the bush behind him.

Swapping sides of the boulder again, he got off another two rounds, one of which tore through the grill and *maybe* into the body crouched behind it, the other of which went completely wild. He was already fumbling out more ammo while he considered his final target. It would be good if this one counted. If this were thirty years back—and a movie—he'd have aimed at a gas tank and blown them all to kingdom come. But most cars had fuel cells now, and even the Whisper's battery pack was under the back seat and basically untouchable by anything at hand.

But there might be something better back at the Jeep—
if he could get there.

At least the werkas weren't *all* firing at him. Probably
they only had a couple of weapons between them, since
shootouts with hot-wired humans likely didn't suit their
grand scheme all that well. Or his either, dammit—as
another three shots zipped by.

Still, if not quite pinned down, he was clearly outnumbered, and the main plus was that he'd taken some of the
heat off Stormy and Lox—maybe. Even with a couple
of their number down and some of the rest unarmed, the
werkas still had better odds and, evidently, a greater
sense of the expendability of self. Which meant that he
had to get the hell out of there before they realized he
was soloing and came after him.

Desperately, and as scared as he'd ever been, 'Bird
reloaded the .38, fired a pair of shots at the first things
that looked even vaguely like werkas in hopes of keeping
them pinned for a crucial second, and moved. Fortunately, he was only exposed for an instant before reaching more underbrush, and it wasn't much further through
thicker cover to the gap.

Somehow he made it, and couldn't believe he was both
unharmed (saving the near-miss with the ear and further
abuse to his previous abrasions), and—apparently—not
pursued.

That wouldn't last, though, and he had to keep them
distracted long enough for Stormy and Nez to act on their
end—if either of them was in a position *to* act.

Which brought him back to the Jeep. There was still
a fair arsenal inside, but—as a quick search proved—
almost no ammo to go with it. Which made sense, given
that Stormy had snared most of it on the fly when he'd
sprung Kevin from that half-assed dissection lab where
they were torturing the secret of repeat-shape-shifting-
with-one-skin from a captive selkie. Stormy'd had eyes
for the big stuff, figuring (as he'd said) he'd get ammo,
which was more accessible—and legal—later. He hadn't,
and a half-day's indulgence at 'Wounds's private shooting range had depleted what he had.

"Water, water everywhere, nor any drop to drink,"
'Bird grumbled, as another ammo box came up empty.
It just wasn't possible that, saving the clips for the hopelessly jammed Glock and a handful of shells for the .38,
he was actually out of ammo. But he was.

He equally obviously had to do something. The werkas
were presently off-balance, caught between him and their
raid on Lox. And, as best he could tell, they weren't
particularly flexible on their feet. The key, therefore, was
to stay a step ahead of them. But if he didn't return,
they'd certainly come after him. And at the moment
(hopefully) they were fairly vulnerable: pinned down between the car and the cliff, with other vehicles blocking
access from left and right.

Abruptly, he had an idea. Stormy wouldn't like it, and
he wasn't that keen on it himself, but desperation made
for strange bedfellows. He'd blown it with small arms,
huh? Well he'd bring out the biggest weapon those guys
had ever seen!

Grunting softly, 'Bird climbed into the Jeep's cockpit.
Disabling the belt interlock, he inserted the ignition card
and held his breath until it cranked. The transmission
worked too, though not the forward differential, but that
didn't matter now.

Gritting his teeth, he eased the Jeep out of the turnoff
and pointed it toward the gap, expecting any minute to
find the place swarming with werkas with overcloaks flying and guns abaze.

Instead, there was more of that disconcerting silence.
Nature, it seemed, really was willing to fill the spaces
between sapients' altercations with activities of her own.
Even the crunch of the tires and the burble of the exhaust
seemed muted—or perhaps he was experiencing those
things at remove, as happened to people whose time had
come, and knew it.

Swallowing hard, he stomped the gas. Rocks flew—
which betrayed his position, if not his intent—but by
then he'd crested the gap.

Nothing had changed, or at least there were still three
vehicles and a number of shapes fumbling around beyond

them—if they were even vaguely like real folks, seeing to their wounded.

Fine.

Steering—barely—with one hand while continuing to press onward, he fired. Though the Jeep's constant jerks and jiggles made choosing any particular target impossible, he succeeded in part, because another figure grabbed a suddenly bloody arm and collapsed. He was fully through the gap now, and even without his foot on the gas, the Jeep was accelerating. And—beyond hope— the werkas still hadn't dispersed.

A pause for two more shots, and he stabbed a pair of buttons on the steering wheel: ON and ACCEL; gave the Jeep one final heading; consigned himself to the gods of the Ani-Yunwiya, and flung himself out of the cockpit.

He hit hard enough to wind himself, and added a third set of insults to a batch of his bruises as he rolled, finally fetching up against a desiccated stump. He grabbed it for balance—and barely got his bearings before the Jeep, now under full electronic command, gathered speed down the slope, bounced twice on hidden ruts, and once, to his horror, threatened to roll, then slammed full into the smaller Whisper. Trapped in the narrow strip between it and the precipice, the werkas had nowhere to go—nor time to go anywhere. Metal screeched, engine revs increased threefold, and then every single werka behind the Whisper was pushed first to the brink, then over the edge. 'Bird heard one scream—and felt angst like a whiplash across his mind—but any further sounds were masked by the slow rumble of the Whisper following the werkas. The Jeep nearly went too, but the impact had finally put paid to the little engine that could, and that, along with a burst front tire, was sufficient to stop the faithful vehicle with its front half teetering over empty space.

"Thank you, Ancient Red and Ancient White!" 'Bird muttered, as he carefully rose to take stock. No one moved. His head was clear of mental static. From where he stood, he could see more than one wet red puddle merging with the darker sheen of leaked oil. Still, he kept the gun poised as he crept closer, wishing for even the

tiniest bit of cover between him and the Suburban—or, though it was further away and at an awkward angle, the Eagle.

There wasn't, and his heart was pounding like the drums of a dozen powwows when he finally assured himself that he really wasn't going to be ambushed and eased around the Suburban's hood to peer into the valley.

He saw fire; the light drew him: Lox's hogan, as he'd expected, aflame. There was a lot of smoke down there too, which he'd check out as soon as he'd tended to more immediate concerns. Squinting against the smoke, which had found his eyes just then, he was gratified to see the Whisper folded into a W by a pair of boulders it had fallen athwart, with at least six bodies around it and maybe two more. Four weren't moving at all. Another was twitching vigorously but to no avail, its lower half thoroughly lodged between the rock and the car's front bumper. The other moved feebly, but its skin was already starting to split, as it reverted to its natural shape.

·Which would be a hell of a disposal problem for him and Lox and Stormy.

Stormy!

In the excitement of his triumph, he'd forgotten about his buddy! So where was Mr. Cloud anyway? Lox's compound was a fair way off, but he should still be able to make out something. By shading his eyes, he could just discern a number of figures moving around, but none he could clearly identify. Seeking a better line of sight, he shifted right—and kicked something that produced a plasticky clatter. A glance down (gun at alert: God, he was jumpy!) showed a pair of high-powered binoculars. He retrieved them and brought them to his eyes. The focus was screwed up, but once he'd sorted that out, he nearly dropped them again. "Oh, God, no!" he breathed. "Oh no!"

For there, between John Lox's burning hogan and a likewise flaming sweat lodge, was Stormcloud Nez propped stark naked against a tree, with a gun clutched limply in each hand—and his entire face and body washed with blood. Even as 'Bird watched, with his gorge threatening to erupt from his throat, Stormy toppled.

Chapter XXIII:
Dawn of a New Day

(Cumberland Island, Seminole/
Creek Coastal Protectorate)
(Saturday, September 10—the wee hours)

Perhaps, Carolyn reflected, as her mother's plain pine coffin thumped against the antique rowboat's seats, haste was keeping her sane. She *had* to hurry too, for the tide was near to turning, and the sooner they finished the funeral, the sooner they could deal with Crises Two and Three, namely what to do about Kevin (who, Sean assured her, still lived), and how to deal with the were-orca plot they'd uncovered. The latter required they contact someone in authority down in Aztlan, preferably someone like Red Wounds who wouldn't dismiss them as crazy cranks. But with no way off the island (they'd found the orcas' boat—scuttled), no communication on it, and no time since locating Liam in which to make the (presently) ten-klom trek back to the locked Gulfstream (the little ATV that came with the cabin had no functioning lights), that was at best a remote possibility. Liam was too traumed-out to work the com anyway, though he was fine at mindless tasks like helping her and Sean shift the coffin from the table on the porch to the beach, where the boat waited that, after one final rite, they would consign to the waves with the turning of the tide shortly after sunrise.

It said much about Nuala Griffith, Carolyn concluded, as she straightened and wiped cramped fingers on the

hem of her damp black tunic, that she'd not only had the
flare to plan a funeral such as this, but the connections
to pull it off.

Now if they could just lure Floyd—Dad—here for the
send-off, they could focus on contriving some way to get
Kev to the mainland without killing him. After that . . .
Actually, she hadn't considered what came after.

For now, she was caught between: between life and
death, land and water . . . human and selkie. Between a
thousand-thousand changes in her life.

So . . . one problem at a time. The boat was loaded.
Soon enough the tide would sweep in and spirit it away.
"Sean," she called, peering across the low hump of the
coffin to where the selkie was gazing dreamily out at the
Atlantic as though burying human women at sea while
under implicit siege by shape-shifting orcas was as common as rain. "Sean!" she repeated, louder. "Go tell . . .
Dad we're ready. Tell him I'd like to have him here, but
that if he doesn't come I'll understand and . . . manage.
Tell him you've agreed to sit for him, and that we'll
hurry. Tell him—"

"I will tell him," Sean said bluntly. "There are many
things in your world I do not understand, but death is the
same regardless, and the ways of death I know!"

Carolyn could only scowl while the selkie danced
down to the shore to wash his hands in the sliding surf,
then dashed back up the strand, passed the cabin, and
turned south, leaving her alone with a boat, a casket, and
what might be a crazy man. Certainly Liam would take
some watching. At least she had him where she could
keep an eye on him, and knew to be alert for sudden
changes in demeanor.

None appeared. And since most of an hour still remained until the tide changed, she moved grimly on to
the next piece of "have-to-do." That was how she was
coping: listing what had to be done, then puzzling out
how to accomplish those things, so that *doing* kept her
mind safe from *thinking* and the many dark roads that
led down.

Sighing, she motioned Liam to join her and trudged

back up the beach. Much work yet remained, to cover their tracks even minimally. And there would still be God's plenty of explaining after all this was over—and that without factoring Kev into the mix.

In the meantime, there was a threefold disposal problem.

The dead orcas (which had reverted to their natural shapes), were the biggest. Though adolescents, their corpses were still too heavy for her and Liam to move; they therefore hitched them to the ATV and dragged them to the ocean that way. The tide would take them there, and anything it refused would be disposed of by scavengers—mostly gulls and crabs.

Still, it took over half an hour to conclude the requisite trips, and by the end, she was exhausted. She was getting lightheaded, too; then again, hunger, stress, emotional shock, and sleep deprivation did that to a body.

Which wasn't necessarily bad—as she turned to the next task at hand: dispensing with the sewn-together human skins that had sloughed off the were-orcas when they died. She dealt with them the same way she'd dealt with dissecting a cadaver during a human anatomy class in college: by not thinking of them as specific wholes, but as piles of amorphous parts. And since the damp fragments of red, white, tan, and pink were already crumpled on the floor, it was easy to consider them simply as skins—as long as none of them unfolded and she did most of the work by feel. Fortunately, a lavish supply of black plastic garbage bags lurked under the sink, and one would hold a skin neatly. Liam lugged them down to the boat and arranged them around the coffin in a distressing modern parody of how it had been done of old: human slaves sacrificed and riding the Swan Road with their Viking masters. Except that these sad servitors had been slaves to their own misfortunes, that had in turn made them thrall to others. Carolyn wondered whether she too might not, in some way, be a slave. Certainly her life was not presently her own.

Nor had been those of the last things which must be elim-

inated: the poor humans who, with their minds clouded
by drink or else not fully formed, had found themselves
were-orca puppets.

That one was a damned hard call. They could neither
leave them on the beach like the orcas, bury them—because the bodies would eventually be found—or abandon
them where they'd fallen, for reasons too obvious to
voice.

The solution was more plastic and more trips down the
sand, this time with Liam helping tote make-do body
bags. It wasn't foolproof, and it certainly wasn't legal—
by Georgia law. Fortunately, were-orcas tended to work
their mischief on folks from society's fringe: folks no one
knew, cared about, or would miss. And equally fortunate,
Cumberland was now under Seminole/Creek jurisdiction,
which was more flexible than Georgia's, and with which
Red Wounds had some clout. Thus, while mainland cops
might eventually come poking about in search of a missing wino and a pair of foreign sailors, the Creeks
wouldn't suffer them for long. And while Cumberland's
new masters might note signs of violence around the
cabin, they would also accept Red Wounds's word when
he told them it was a high-security matter, and, bluntly,
that there were things the rank-and-file simply weren't
meant to know.

So it was then, that Nuala Griffith's burial barge was
much fuller than anyone had expected when they laid the
last plastic bag at her feet to balance those that flanked
her to left and right, and the smaller ones full of skins
that occupied the corners.

In spite of the extra weight, the tide was nipping at the
prow when they finished; Carolyn could see it rise and
fall as water sucked sand from beneath it. All that remained now was for Dad to light the ceremonial
torches—one on the prow, two on the stern—give the
boat a good solid shove, and it would all be over. The
torches would burn quickly, and in roughly ten minutes
would reach the layer of powdered magnesium with
which the coffin was both dusted and partially filled. That
would ignite with a flare like a small new sun, and in

turn kindle the paste of jellied alcohol mixed with more magnesium with which the boat had been smeared.

Hopefully, there'd be fire aplenty and nearly complete combustion. Hopefully, too, whatever survived would be dispersed in the usual way. If bones washed up on shore, scavengers would have at them. And if anyone bothered to question, there'd be sparse incentive to trace.

At which point Carolyn found herself stifling a nervous giggle. Mom had spent her whole life bending rules she said were stupid and defying laws which were absurd. How fitting that her daughter was savaging rules right and left to set her on her final adventure.

One last time, she bent to rinse her hands in the surf that, without her being aware of it, had crept closer in just the last minute and now slid around her feet. She skipped up the beach in reflex, steadying herself against one of the stern torches. It bent but did not break.

She hoped she was as sturdy.

But what was keeping Dad? Or Sean? Surely it couldn't take this long to reach a consensus regarding half-an-hour's custody of Kevin—and it couldn't take much longer than that to manage the sendoff: ten minutes in transit, ten—fifteen, something like that—to light the torches, push the boat away, and watch until the flames erupted, then ten minutes' transit again.

Abruptly a chill she hoped wasn't premonitory wracked her. To her surprise, Liam reached over to hug her. She relaxed into his numb warmth, grateful, however briefly, not to feel alone.

Time passed, and she simply waited while the tide dug trenches around the boat. It was riding up and down a lot now, and was more than half surrounded. Soon she'd have no choice but to take matters into her own hands. For the thousandth time that hour, she fingered the Zippo in her pocket.

A fish—she hoped—nipped at her ankle, where she now stood calf-deep in the surf. She kicked at it, even as she glanced down automatically. When she looked up again, it was to see two figures emerging from the woods.

More were-orcas?—for an instant. But it was only
Sean—in front. And Dad.

Sean clutched a bundle to his chest, wrapped in something green that looked like palmetto fronds. He seemed
both reserved and unconcerned—an odd mix in anyone,
much less a quirky quasi-human half-boy.

And Dad—Sean veered aside so that Floyd was revealed in the soft morning light. Her heart double
thumped as she saw what he carried: what slumped
across his two arms, with feet and head nervelessly a-
dangle.

"Kevin!" she shrieked—and was slogging through the
suddenly capricious surf onto sand that offered wet resistance, and then running up the beach. And all the while
that grim procession neared, growing clearer, but never
varying one iota from its pace or trajectory. Sean she
ignored, her gaze fixed firmly on her father and that shape
lolling between his arms, bathed in the red light of dawn
that at once masked those naked muscles and transfigured
them, so that for a moment they were clothed in skin
again.

Skin . . . !

Where was the skin that had hung in tatters around
Kevin? Surely it should show by now, flopping about like
a beggar's rags or jester's motley.

It didn't. And as she grew closer a thought struck her
so dreadful she banished it before it could fully register.
Surely . . . surely they wouldn't have cut Kev's skin
away! No way they'd do something so awful, were he
living or, as now seemed likely, dead. No way! No way!
No way!

But then she was close enough to see that there was
no break between his arms and the hands that thumped
limply against his father's legs as he trudged along. And
where was Kev's hair? That ridiculous medley of carrot
orange and fading blue? Surely that would be visible
now!

Abruptly, she froze, eyes huge, mouth dry as dust,
even as sweat sprang out upon her body. Not them too!
Not Sean and Dad! No way orcas could've co-opted

them—well, Dad maybe, hovering on shock as he had to
have been. But never Sean!

In response to those thoughts, which she had to have
broadcast far and wide in her confusion, dread, disgust,
and anger, another thought came to her: cool and clear
as mountain water. It was Sean—she could recognize
him now—and it was not so much words as reassurance
that he was indeed himself. And by the time that had
registered, he was close enough to speak.

"It is only us, sister. Myself and your father in our
own right minds—and Kevin, as you see, no longer in
any mind at all, nor any pain."

With all hope evaporated and finality made real, Carolyn sank to her knees in the sand. Her eyes were streaming, and she threw back her head and vented a long
anguished wail. "No! No! No!" she screamed, and then
her cries became inarticulate. She bent over and pounded
the earth. Grit splattered to grime Sean's bare feet. His
shadow stretched long across the sand.

Setting his parcel aside, he knelt beside her. A hand
touched her shoulder: warmer than human, but full of
life. She shuddered. How dare he be so alive when her
brother, whom she'd abandoned for years, only in the
last few weeks rediscovered, and was even now still
growing to appreciate, lay dead: a bloody ruin between
his father's arms!

Sean didn't speak, yet comfort flowed into her . . .
self—along with, she realized, love: a thing hard won in
the time they'd had together. She slumped against him,
let him hold her, gaze fixed on the beach and the ominous
bundle. And as she stared, a frond slipped free of that
awkward weaving, then another, opening the parcel just
far enough to reveal something pink, white, and—un-
mistakably—carrot orange and faded blue.

All she heard before darkness claimed her was Sean's
stricken voice (or maybe that was simply his thoughts)
whispering (as though there were any comfort in gentle-
ness now!) words she would never have expected to hear:

"He told us to do it. He told us why. And we agreed."

Chapter XXIV:
New Daze

(Aztlan)
(Saturday, September 10—early morning)

Thalo slumped back against the seat of the AFZoRTA bus, closed his eyes, and rubbed his temples with the fingers of both hands. *God, he had a headache!* A world-class hangover-clone that wasn't improved by the early morning sun shafting in on his side, which made him squint, which twisted already tense muscles even tighter. *Teach him to stay up all night carousing!*—even if it was to celebrate joining Outer Earth. And that wasn't counting a certain other something that also hurt—under certain circumstances. As for the *others*—well, there was supposed to be a fine line between pleasure and pain, and Verde knew exactly where that interface lay. In spite of himself—and its impact on his throbbing skull—he grinned. He definitely needed more nights like the last one.

And fewer mornings like this! Verde had to rise early to catch the breakfast crowd at the cafe where she worked, and since he'd spent what remained of the night at her place (he didn't recall leaving the Twins' compound at all, save that there'd been a cab), he'd asked to tag along on his way to the Embassy. Not that he was thrilled with the notion of showing up unkempt and fried; on the other hand, 'Bird didn't seem like the type who got anal about such things. Maybe if he apologized and kept a low profile, the guy would cut him some slack. Besides, today was Green Francis's funeral, and everyone

would be too distracted to mark him anyway.

He hoped. And rubbed his temples harder.

"Head still blasting?" Verde asked beside him. Unlike him, she wore shades (his were still at the motel with the rest of his gear—which reminded him that he absolutely had to connect with the realtor today regarding the condo his folks were renting). Much like him, she was tired and yawny-voiced.

"You could say that," he mumbled pitifully, laying it on thick in quest of sympathy. "I took every pill that looked safe back at your place and nothing's changed."

"Sorry," she murmured, twisting around. "I should've got you something before we left the Twins; they've got some stuff that'll cure a rainy day." She inserted a hand behind him and massaged the back of his neck, working upward to his scalp then down into his shoulders. He could actually feel the taut muscles there loosen, the pain begin to ease.

"God, that feels good," he sighed. "Wonder if they've got anything for amnesia."

An eyebrow lifted dubiously. "Amnesia?"

A shrug. "Or something! I sure don't remember much about last night, not after the piercing thing—I had to have been drunk to have done that. But after that, no . . ."

"Nothing?"

He tried to grin. "Well, I sure haven't forgotten what *we* did—several times, as I recall, if you count variations—though maybe I ought to so you could show me all over again. But seriously: no. I remember passing out. I remember . . . waking up someplace they'd put me to sleep it off. I remember being pissed at the Twins about something I *don't* remember. I remember getting up *to* piss. That's it. And a lot of that's veils and shadows."

Verde started to reply, but her face went suddenly blank, as though she'd briefly turned off. Two blinks later, she was back, shaking her head as though nothing had occurred. "You had a good time," she announced.

"So they tell me."

"What about the vision rite?"

Another shrug. "I know that I saw something really

weird—or thought I did. It was about the time all the
booze and stuff kicked in—when I was farthest gone. But
that memory's really vague now. Too bad—'cause it
seems like it was really neat. Actually, most of what I
recall are feelings.''

"Like what?''

"Like how great it was to belong, and then pain, and
fear, and anger—at the Twins, like I said. I *think* I found
out something important, but what it is . . .''

"It'll come back. Something'll press your buttons, and
there it'll be when you least expect it.''

Thalo shook his head—which was feeling remarkably
better in just that short time. "It better. I don't like
having holes in my life.''

"Now you know how I feel,'' she replied, lowering
her hand to stroke his leg absently. "I told you about my
stress spells. That's what they are, I'm sure: one of the
guys in 'Earth's a doctor and he told me. Only they're
actually more like mini-blackouts. For a minute I'm just
. . . gone.''

"Like just now?''

Verde looked startled. "I just *had* one? Oh jeeze!''

Thalo patted her hand. "Looks like between us we
make one whole person. We'll have to keep hanging out,
so we can keep the other posted on what they've been
up to.''

Verde chuckled and squeezed his hand back. "Next
stop's mine. See you at the funeral.''

"Funeral?''

"Don't tell me you forgot!''

"Evidently!''

"The Twins are doing the music for the Mass. 'Earth's
working concessions and backup crowd control. We get
badges and everything.''

Thalo took a deep breath. He really must've been out
of it, to have let something like that slip. And now that
he *tried* to recall it, he sort-of could. It was one of the
things they'd discussed at the meeting before the initiation, before . . . the Big Blank. "If you say so, I've *gotta*
believe you.''

Verde smiled and rose. "Check your wallet, you'll find your mem card and security pass." A pause. "You don't remember getting them either . . . ?"

"N-no."

She rolled her eyes, then bent down and gave him a healthy smooch. "Well, that oughta keep you from forgetting me!" And with that, the bus glided to a halt, Verde joined the file in the aisle, and a moment later was gone.

Thalo closed his eyes again. There *was* something he was supposed to remember, but he was damned if he knew what.

Nor had he succeeded eight minutes later, when the bus let him off beside the Kituwah Embassy. A lot had changed since yesterday, he reflected, as he stepped onto the walk and waited for traffic to clear. Twenty-four hours ago he'd been the new kid. Now he knew that his boss liked to pad around barefoot and was a dedicated practical joker; that one of the receptionists was nice and one wasn't; that he mostly liked his job; that Outer Earth looked set to be a big part of his life but needed some kinks worked out; that he was never *ever* going to get as drunk again as he had the previous night; and that Verde was one fine lady. And it wasn't even eight-hundred yet!

Shoot, if he let himself, he might even make it through the day without going black-brained about Green Francis. In fact, much as he hated to admit it, the pain of that loss was already healing. *In fact*, if he let himself, he could easily become *full* of himself, which wouldn't do if 'Bird got wind of it. Best to play Mr. Subtle. Which wouldn't be hard, given how fried he felt.

At which point the light at the corner changed, and he was free to cross the street.

He dutifully presented his ID to the burly Choctaw guards at the gate (four of them instead of the usual two—everybody was beefing up security today), but he had to wait for clearance, since he'd arrived before official opening time. He ate the downtime swapping hangover tales with one of the guards he'd met yesterday when the guy was off duty. And he hadn't taken two

steps past the turnstile when a girl's childish voice shrieked "Johnny! Johnny! Johnny!" with unrestrained enthusiasm at the top of her lungs.

Still muddled, he stared stupidly over his shoulder, and it actually took him a second to recall that Johnny was *him*—to some folks—and that it was no nameless urchin hailing him, but his own kid sister, Sara.

By the time he'd retraced his route past the blatantly smirking guards, he'd cleared his circuits sufficiently to wonder what in the world Sara was doing here, when neither she nor the folks were due until next week, and to steel himself for an impromptu debriefing with those same folks he wasn't up for at all.

And by the time he'd reached the sidewalk, he'd determined that the shrieking (which had never stopped) issued from the taxi stand across the street where his father was settling the fare while his mother stood stiffly by looking impatient and frazzled (as usual), and his sis tried vainly to drag her straight into Sequoya Avenue, oblivious to the fact that the light was now green and all four lanes full of traffic.

He waved. Mom waved back. Sara waved even more vigorously, which set her bright blue serape flapping. Thalo availed himself of a gap between cars to dash across and join them. "You're here!" he gasped breathlessly, hoping the sudden throbbing in the back of his skull was not the scarce-vanquished headache seeking a return engagement.

"Johnny! Johnny!" Sara yelled louder, abandoning their mother to tug on the tail of the green unisex tunic Verde had leant him in lieu of his too-formal vest.

Thalo squatted before her and gave her a brotherly hug, pausing to straighten her serape. She beamed as only a six-year-old could. Unfortunately, she was twelve—nearly thirteen—though one couldn't tell from her size (small, even for one of his clan, which tended to run scrawny), nor, regrettably, her IQ.

Illegal quantities of a US-banned pesticide in a shipment of imported fruit that Mom had, ironically, bought at a health-food store, had attacked Sara's pituitary in the

womb, thus the stunted growth; then lingered to dissolve the connections in her short-term memory—an unwelcomed aftereffect that had kicked in around six, thus the inability to retain anything she hadn't already learned by that age. Alton's Syndrome, it was called, for the physician who'd described it. There were ten known cases in the US, ninety-three worldwide. Sara was the eighth identified and the oldest. The Aytchaycee Center was the only place doing significant research on the problem and three related conditions. It was funded not by the Chinese company that had actually made and distributed the pesticide, however, but by the German mega that had sold the components. Thalo hated them anyway. Sara was one reason he'd gone Green.

"So what're you doin' here, kid?" he asked through a forced smile, even as his gaze queried his mother. She was a slim, tense-faced woman, with short hair blonding into a grey that almost matched her eyes. To her credit, she eschewed makeup entirely, but tended to dress young for her age, in which she was Thalo's opposite. Too much sun in her Arizona youth had dried her skin. She looked every year of forty-nine. She also looked like she was mad as hell and trying not to show it.

Thalo smiled dutifully and rose to bestow the obligatory embrace. She responded without conviction. "We tried to call," she said. "But you weren't at the motel like you were supposed to be, and the embassy couldn't find you."

"Sorry," he replied through a calculated yawn. "I, uh, met some folks and wound up stayin' there."

"You could've told us!"

"Jesus, Mom! Do we have to get into this now? You just got here, for Chrissakes, and already you're going at me! I'm a grown-up—as you're fond of reminding me when it suits you. Last I heard, you folks were comin' next week. Shoot, yesterday *morning* you were comin' next week! I didn't think I had to account for every minute, nor did I say I'd check in—nor did you!"

Having finally dispatched the cab, his father joined them, looking determinedly relaxed, which was typical.

He also looked younger than his wife (he wasn't, but wide blue eyes, good skin, and working out did that for you), and appeared, by his expression, aligned with neither side. Also typical. He hated confrontation, and if given the chance would always let others fight his battles—which freed him to be the nice guy. Thalo gave him the usual perfunctory hug, and suddenly they were all staring at each other. "Well," said his dad, patting his back pocket where his wallet was, "since we're a family again, how 'bout breakfast?"

Thalo breathed a sigh of relief. Since he'd planned to report to work early, eating wouldn't make him late. Since he was also hungry, it *would* make him full. And one more cup of coffee might help clear his head—and that was not to be ignored. "There's a McDonald's two blocks over," he volunteered, knowing his sister's fondness for the ubiquitous chain.

" 'Donalds!" Sara crowed, "Yeah! Yum!"

By his third cup of coffee (making five, counting those he'd had at Verde's, who'd apologized for not feeding him by saying that morning shift in a cafe meant never keeping breakfast on hand), Thalo had been able to calm his mother sufficiently to determine that the Aytchaycee Center had called yesterday afternoon to inform them that they'd had a number of cancellations and if they could get Sara there by 09:30 they could begin assessment early. Already wired out of her mind with anticipation, Mom had insisted they accept—anything to hasten the process that might one day free her from thralldom to a disadvantaged daughter—and Dad, of course, had acquiesced. Changing the reservations had cost the earth, since everybody and his Siamese twin cousins wanted to get to Aztlan just now, but a few strings had been pulled, and they'd managed. Fine. Thalo could deal with that. And, as Mom had insisted twice more, they *had* tried to call.

Trouble was, both parents had to return to the States absolutely as soon as possible, a number of important ends having been left untied. They'd arrived assuming

that Thalo (1) could be found where expected, (2) would
be cooling his heels until his job officially began on Mon-
day, and (3) would not, in the meantime, have made major commitments.

"I didn't do it *deliberately*!" he told his mother. "I
thought I was being, like, really responsible. But in case
you haven't noticed, things are really crazy 'round here,
what with the funeral and all; and they actually need me
at the embassy, 'cause they've gotta have an official response—only the Ambassador's gone, and the deputy's
a first-class bitch, and— See, I'm doing research—did
most of it yesterday, actually—and have to show some
high-ups the results this morning, and—"

"—You also have a responsibility to your family."
Which was his mother's second favorite line after "I'd
really like to have a life too."

"Yeah, but they need me at the embassy. And as soon
as I finish there—*if* I finish—I've gotta work the funeral.
Folks are, like, counting on me. I . . . promised."

"Then take your sister with you," his mother snapped
icily.

Sara sat bolt upright. "Yes . . . take me with you!" she
piped up unexpectedly. "I *love* funerals."

"Hush dear," her mother hissed, "you don't know
what you're saying."

"Do too!" Sara insisted, pushing out her lip. "*They*
told me."

"Who's they?" From Dad.

Sara wiggled in her seat. "You know . . . *Them*!"

His father's face blanked for a moment—which gave
Thalo a start, until he recalled what a stickler for time
his old man was. He'd been checking his watch, or Thalo
was a newt. "Sure, honey," he mumbled absently, as he
started to rise. Then, to Thalo: "We'll drop her off at the
embassy when we're done. You be there! Our return
doesn't leave till six, 'cause of the dratted funeral, but
we'll have to head for the airport way early, on account
of traffic, which is hell already. She's yours till we get
back."

Thalo rolled his eyes, having just encountered his fath-

er's *yang* side. No decisions or too many; that was Stan Gordon's style.

"I *love* funerals," Sara repeated, as she flounced out of her plastic seat. And something about the way she said that gave Thalo chills. Goosebumps rose on his arm. His sister was staring at him too, an odd expression in her eyes that seemed familiar from somewhere else, and not that long ago. He stared back, wondering what strange feral thing hid in there, then could stand it no longer and looked away.

A nondescript tan sedan sat directly outside—with the windows down, which, in Aztlan, was odd. And through the opening he saw what looked disturbingly like one of the Hero Twins' oversized taciturn roadies, gaze fixed squarely on the very window behind which the Gordon clan had feasted. And as Thalo's brow bent into a frown and he tried to puzzle out why that man's presence should bug him, the fellow smiled, powered up the glass, and drove away.

The smile had not been friendly.

Chapter XXV:
Shadows in the Dawn

(John Lox's Compound)
(Thursday, September 10—early morning)

'Bird didn't remember much about the halting, painful jog down the pig-trail that snaked down the western side of the valley to Hosteen John Lox's compound save that he hurt a lot, fell often—and, for the first time since coming south, forgot about tarantulas.

One moment he was stumbling along the final rocky slope, with the mountains piled up to the left in fractured shelves and ever more greenery showing below him to the right; the next, his feet trod the sparse turf that passed for a path between the cliffs and the burning hogan.

"Stormy!" he yelled. "*Stormy!*" A third shout died amid a coughing fit that left him panting. Somehow he was on all-fours, grass—withered, but still grass—the first softness beneath his hands in what felt like centuries.

Breathless, he rose: stiff, sore, and shaking; distantly aware that his arms showed an even mix of dust and blood, and that he probably looked little better than Stormy had when he'd glimpsed him from the gap.

Stormy!

Naked, covered with blood, but double-weaponed; slumped against a tree.

Collapsing.

That had set 'Bird running. He hadn't stopped—until now. Nor had he seen his friend.

Stormy!

With his last wind, he staggered on.

"Here, boy!" someone—Lox?—shouted. 'Bird was too tired to be suspicious as he limped toward that voice. "Lox?" he called back hoarsely. "That you?"

He didn't see the hulking shape that shambled from behind a clump of man-high bushes to his right until it was almost upon him. Clumsy, he stumbled to a halt, fumbling for his gun, questing, through sweat-blurred eyes, for cover. None being obvious, he raised the weapon.

"*¿Pistola?*" that one gaped, astonished; blinking at him with quizzical brown eyes. 'Bird gaped back, finally realizing that he confronted a fat, middle-aged Mexican woman wearing a shapeless cotton print dress beneath a dingy serape. She had a sweet face, and the most innocently dazed expression he'd ever seen. Blood oozed from a long scrape along her right arm as she stared at him blankly—hopefully. "*¿Pistola?*" Then: "*¡Pistola! ¡Pistola! ¡Pistola!*" whereupon she charged past him. Having no energy to follow, 'Bird watched her disappear into the willows by the stream.

"Let 'er go, boy," that voice called again. "Kind of help she needs, you can't give 'er."

'Bird shook his head and trudged on. An instant later, he nearly tripped over a body sprawled half on the path, half in the undergrowth: a dried-up old man—likely a wino—with his elbow shattered. Though unconscious, he breathed steadily and there was little bleeding, so 'Bird let him lie. The path curved around a car-sized boulder.

The third person he saw was John Lox.

The *hataalii* was hunched over a familiar long lean shape, busily engaged in tearing a worn white towel into strips. A pot steamed nearby into which he dipped those rags. His faded blue shirt was splattered with blood and he'd lost his headband. The hogan still burned merrily, but he ignored it.

'Bird sagged down beside him. "Stormy . . ." he mumbled. "How—" His hair fell into his eyes. He slapped it away and finally got a clear look at his buddy.

Stormy was breathing. That was good. He was also unconscious, which wasn't. In spite of the blood, he had

no obvious body wounds. The gore—most of it—had issued from a long gash at his hairline, now bandaged. 'Bird exhaled his relief. Scalp wounds bled a lot. They looked bad, but weren't, in fact, that serious.

"He . . . okay?"

"Brained himself runnin' out of the hogan when the shootin' started," Lox snorted. "Split his head wide open. Prob'ly saved him too: made him fall just as they fired. Bullet tore into the door frame there; I shot the son-of-a-bitch. Killed 'im, I reckon. Didn't want to."

'Bird nodded. "*You* okay?"

Lox patted his right side, where blood bloomed on the blue cambric. "Caught one in the love-handle. Went right through. Hurts, but I can live with it."

"You sure?"

"Have to be." A pause, while Lox wiped blood from Stormy's face. "Your buddy here's fine too; just wore out. No food, no sleep, and then havin' to fight. He did—like a fuckin' bear, once he came to—but he was runnin' on automatic. Soon as it quit, he did."

Another nod. 'Bird found a strip of towel and commenced swabbing Stormy's arm.

Lox motioned toward the gap. "You do all that?"

'Bird blinked. "Reckon so. Trashed the Jeep, though. Storm's gonna be mad as hell."

"He'll live. Might not have if you hadn't."

Movement from the corner of his eye made 'Bird flinch, all senses on max alert. It was only a small girl: ten or eleven, if that. She too had a sweet face—an Indian face—though a dirty one. She also clutched an assault rifle almost as big as she was. A calm, frank gaze met 'Bird's, then shifted down. Her eyes widened, as though she'd only then realized what she held. 'Bird was already thumbing the safety off the .38 when she dropped it. "*¡Odio!*" she spat. *Hate it.* "*¡Las voces me hicieron!*" *The voices made me.* All at once she was crying. Before he thought to question his action,'Bird folded her into his arms. Trickling tears turned to uncontrolled sobs. 'Bird cried too—from relief. From the fact that Stormy was still alive.

"How many . . . ?" he managed, to Lox, as he eased the girl away. She edged back a meter and plopped down, utterly silent.

"Never had time to count. Enough, I reckon: that 'un, two you saw alive, one I killed. Stormy shot to wound; so would I, 'cept I didn't think. He told me they weren't responsible, that they were being controlled. 'Least I didn't kill any women or kids." He paused, suddenly tense. "Godalmighty, 'Bird," he continued, his voice shaking, as 'Bird had never heard it before, "what're we dealin' with here? No, don't answer! I hadn't realized. Now I do, and it's awful and it's gotta be stopped." He peered at the girl. 'Bird followed his gaze. Sweet face or no, there wasn't much going on behind those eyes. A normal kid—he suddenly hated that phrase—would be fidgeting or asking questions; even in shock, more would be happening. This one was running on ROM.

'Bird patted Lox on the shoulder. "Yeah, man; it does."

"What does?" came a slurred voice from the ground. The arm 'Bird had been dabbing flinched away. Stormy's eyes fluttered open, squinting into the morning light. "Christ! I'm alive!"

"Thanks to your buddy here," Lox told him, rocking back on his haunches as Stormy sat up, fingers probing at the bandage around his head. He blinked and rubbed his eyes. " 'Bird . . . ? What the hell are *you* doin' here?"

'Bird grinned. "Savin' your skinny ass. Makin' up for last week, I reckon."

"Same bad guys?"

'Bird nodded.

"You get 'em all?"

A shrug. 'Bird started to speak.

Lox interrupted. "Seems to me there's two stories here. And—" he added, pointing toward the hogan, which had collapsed to its adobe walls, "the house may not be much to look at, but I'll bet it's kept the coffee warm!"

'Bird could only roll his eyes.

*   *   *

While Stormy finished a preliminary cleanup before wrapping himself with a towel and sampling Lox's virulent brew along with a round of cornbread that had survived the fire, a can of tuna, and an entire jug of wellwater, 'Bird told his half of the tale. "... and if they're not all dead," he concluded, "they soon will be—'cause we outnumber 'em now."

"What about the ... slaves?" Stormy wondered, sparing a glance at the girl: the only one who'd lingered. They'd fed her. She'd eaten. And not said a word.

'Bird shrugged again. "Who knows? Obviously some of 'em need a hospital. For the rest ... well, I'm glad we both know lots of diplomats."

"They're mostly poor Mexicans, I reckon," Lox observed. "Doubt there's any record of most of 'em. That's the only way something like this could happen. I hate to say it, but the best thing's probably to round 'em up, then patch up the hurt ones, take 'em to where there's people, and let 'em go. 'Couple of 'em are basically normal, just winos and stuff. Let them take charge."

"If they don't talk too much," Stormy cautioned.

"Our risk," Lox gave back. "For now, we gotta get 'em out of here. Basic ethics."

'Bird grimaced. "Might be room in the Suburban. Don't think I hit it."

Stormy's face darkened. 'Bird had told him about the Jeep—he'd had to, to complete the tale. Stormy had muttered a dull " 'S okay; it's insured." He hadn't sounded happy. "Sounds like a plan," he conceded at last.

"Good," 'Bird replied. "Now, what happened here?"

"Not much to tell," Lox began. "Started right at dawn. I was singin', drummin', and mindin' the fire. One sand painting to go, and I'd be done with that stage. Next thing I know, the air's full of bullets—*big* bullets—and I'm flat on my face in the hogan. I grabbed Stormy's guns—couldn't find mine—and started shootin' back, figured I'd ask questions later. I could tell that something was wrong with the folks—but not so much I was gonna talk first and act later. One of 'em ran up—teenage kid: microcephalic—and grabbed a stick from the fire with

his bare hands and threw it on the roof. Stray bullet got him—friendly fire: took one hand right off—but he kept on runnin'. Think he fell in the creek. Probably dead by now.''

"We'll check," 'Bird groaned.

Lox took a long swig of coffee. "Anyway, by then I figured there was no way to save the hogan, so I snatched a couple things and got back outside—just in time to see your buddy come runnin' out and brain himself. He came to quick, I gave him the guns, and he started shootin'. And then all of a sudden it stopped, and there were all these folks wanderin' out of the bushes lookin' lost. I looked around for more, didn't see any, and that's when I found my binocs and figured out your little trick with the Jeep.''

"Good thing *I* didn't," Stormy grumbled through a forced grin. "Might've shot the wrong guy."

"It'd help if I could've told shit about your fuckin' guns!" 'Bird snapped. "No ammo for half of 'em and the rest all jumbled up."

Stormy tensed, but Lox grabbed his arm as he started to rise. " 'Bird's not your enemy, boy! There's other cars; only one of him.''

"Thank God," 'Bird sniffed, as he rose. "So what d' we do now?"

"Get these folks back to Aztlan," Lox said. "Shouldn't be hard to find 'em. We take the Suburban, if it'll run. And then . . ."

"I try to get hold of 'Wounds," 'Bird finished. "—And if that fails, we try your guys," he added, to Stormy. Then: "Oh, shit! You don't know about Green Francis!"

Stormy started. "Won't like it when I do, either, to judge by how you're lookin'."

'Bird told that tale too, yawning every other word. "*Gotta* get some sleep," he apologized.

"I'll drive," Lox volunteered. "You can flat on the way back."

'Bird nodded. It was easier than arguing. Stormy simply grunted. "I'm better off than you are," he told 'Bird, when 'Bird made to rise. "You go jump in the creek and

wash the crud off, then take a nap. Me and Hosteen Lox'll round up the rest.''

'Bird didn't reply—because he was snoring.

It took nearly an hour to locate the remnants of the werkas' force. Two were dead: the man Lox had shot and the boy who'd torched the roof and fallen to friendly fire. He'd made it as far as the bathing pool, where, as predicted, he'd drowned. 'Bird found him when he went to clean up. Of the surviving seven, they bound the wino's arm, entrusted the little girl to the fat woman, and, as gently as possible, tied all the others' wrists and ankles. One woman was ancient—in her dotage, probably due to Alzheimer's. And one man actually proved not only competent, but helpful enough to be spared confinement. He'd apparently suffered post-traumatic-stress syndrome in one of the Haitian set-tos and withdrawn into the decades-long alcohol haze in which the werkas had found him. The attack seemed to have loosened something enough to activate his medical training, though not to bring him fully back to the world. As far as he—Sgt. Archer, so he proclaimed, with his serial number—was concerned, this was merely the cleanup after another guerrilla raid. He was crazy as a loon, but hell on wheels at first aid.

Both Stormy and Lox were filthy in the aftermath and treated themselves to quick dips while the revived 'Bird guarded the captives. Then, dressed in what clothing Lox had been able to salvage (most of Stormy's having been lost in the fire), they collected their charges and headed for the gap.

They were in sight of the top, with no more than a quarter klom to go, when Lox, who was in the lead, uttered a strangled "Shit!" and jumped back about two meters. The trail was steep there, and kinked around an outcrop, masking a section until one turned the corner; the cliffs were near vertical, both up to the right and down to the left, where a fuzz of manzanitas showed. Thus, they couldn't see what blocked the trail until they were upon it. 'Bird was beside Lox in an instant. The

clump of lost souls behind keened and mumbled but didn't bolt—possibly because Stormy, in the rear, wouldn't let them.

'Bird nearly did, having found himself facing four meters of black-and-white death sprawled across a two-meter-wide trail. The orca was gasping—dying; no way it could keep its weight from crushing its lungs. But its eyes were furious, and its jaws—big enough even in this adolescent to decapitate a man—were full of very sharp teeth. As soon as it saw them, it lunged forward awkwardly, using its last strength in one final effort to wreak some vengeance.

"Fuck!" 'Bird yipped, backing up as quickly as Lox had—almost too late, as the slashing jaws flashed toward him. He caught the stench of fish and raw meat from the creature's maw.

Another surge made him backpedal again—straight into the prisoners. Someone swore. He stumbled and fell. Unable to scramble out of the way, a third lunge brought the orca atop him, jaw resting on his belly, pinning his left leg with its bulk. He kicked at it frantically with the right. And finally remembered his gun.

He fired point blank down the throat, forgetting for the nonce that important bits of him were close beneath it and the bullet wouldn't discriminate. The beast reared up—its front third did—and 'Bird rolled aside before it crashed down again with sufficient force to shatter his pelvis had it connected.

Bullets barked. Blood erupted from three spots around the beast's right eye. It uttered a high-pitched squeal, writhed briefly, then collapsed, its final breath a long bubbly hiss from its blowhole.

Lox helped 'Bird up. As best 'Bird could tell, he now had five layers of bruises on his legs. Maybe he should call Guinness. Or drink one. "Thanks," he panted, dusting himself off.

"My job," Stormy grinned, blowing across his .44's smoking barrel. "Looks like you didn't get 'em all."

"I thought you were more important," 'Bird growled

through a shudder. "Damn, but those sons-of-bitches have a will to live!"

"Not to live," Lox corrected, "to accomplish their goal. Fanatics, is what they are. And a fanatic's hard to fight—or kill."

"Think we oughta check the others?" Stormy wondered. "Put 'em out of their misery if they're still alive?"

'Bird scowled. "I don't like killing these things, even if they are . . . well, not evil: kinda amoral, or something—but I guess we oughta. 'Sides, if any of 'em really are suffering, it'd be the humane thing to do."

"I was afraid you'd say that."

"I'll do it," 'Bird sighed. "You just got purified, and already you've got another ghost after you—but I've got a bunch. What's one more sin on my conscience? Or one more *chindi* hangin' 'round?"

"Can you get down there to do it?" Lox asked dubiously.

"That one got up here," 'Bird replied, "probably as an injured human. I'm beat up and bruised, but I don't have any holes in me."

Lox regarded him levelly. "Do what you gotta."

Five minutes later, 'Bird had finished. It hadn't been as bad as expected. Four werkas were dead already, crushed by the Whisper itself or victims of impact. Another had evidently killed a fellow—possibly for mercy, which they clearly understood, whether or not they practiced it. The remainder, all of which were pinned or otherwise incapacitated, he dispatched with bullets to the brain. Only one had retained human shape, and 'Bird considered taking it prisoner; a lot might be learned that way if one were careful. Before he could act on that assumption, however, he felt a buzzing in his head, raised his borrowed pistol—and shot the creature dead.

He blinked at it dazedly. That was the second time one had controlled him! He'd have to see if Stormy and Lox had any notions about that troubling new complication. Only when he'd climbed up to the gap, where Stormy was inspecting the remains of his Jeep, did it occur to him that the werka could well have ordered him to kill

himself. Why hadn't it? To escape pain? From honor? Or simply to keep 'Bird and his friends from learning too much? As it was, there was going to be a hell of a disposal problem. How would future archaeologists explain a batch of orca skeletons here, kloms from shore? Best to burn everything, he decided. And mix the ashes into sandcrete.

Stormy's face was grim when 'Bird made to return the co-opted .38. Stormy shook his head. "Keep it. Given what's happened lately, we can't count on stickin' together. We gotta be prepared for anything."

"Anything?"

Stormy nodded. "Suburban'll run. Eagle won't." He fished in a pocket, face even grimmer than before, then passed 'Bird a twice-folded sheet of beige paper. "Found this in the Eagle."

'Bird unfolded it. The paper seemed familiar; he'd certainly seen some just like it, and recently. But then he saw what was printed on the page. Names: a dozen or so. Some 'Bird didn't know, but many he did. His was there, and Stormy's and Lox's. So were Carolyn's and Kevin's, and Red Wounds's and Mary Hasegawa's. Rudy's was there too—lined through in red. And among the names he didn't know was one that caught his eye: Nuala Griffith—who had to be Carolyn's mom. Her name was also lined through.

Finally, at the bottom, as though placed there as an afterthought, were two more.

Blowgunner. Jaguar Deer.

The Hero Twins.

"Hit list," Stormy opined. "And if those lines mean what I think they do . . ."

'Bird swallowed hard. "They have to. I mean, I told you about Rudy . . ."

"Fuck!" Stormy said softly. "Fuck! Fuck! Fuck!"

"Poor Cary," 'Bird added. "Her mom's lined through too."

"What's that logo?" Lox asked, pointing to the other side of the sheet.

'Bird flipped it over and had to squint to see the design

printed in green ink on paper only slightly paler—not a good choice, if contrast was the goal. "Outer Earth!" he hissed. "Goddamned Outer Earth!"

Stormy scowled. "So what? Their flyers are all over."

"Yeah," 'Bird countered. "But this isn't a flyer, it's a piece of their stationery!"

The scowl deepened. "So you're sayin' there's a connection?"

"I'm sayin' we'd be smart to take down these tag numbers and see who they're registered to!"

Stormy whistled through his teeth. "Oh shit, man, it actually makes sense: Outer Earth as a front for werkas. It'd be ideal. Same agenda and everything—on the surface."

'Bird nodded, then cocked his head. The Jeep's radio was still on, and he'd caught something potentially important. He turned up the volume. Almost he turned it off again, before he caught the crucial phrase. They were discussing the Archbishop's funeral, in which he was supposed to be involved. Mostly the announcer was listing the dignitaries already in town versus those still anticipated, but one item made 'Bird shudder: *"The requiem mass will be in St. Tekawitha's. His Holiness, Pope Michael, is expected to officiate, and music, per Vatican request, will be provided by the Hero Twins."*

"God!" Stormy gasped. "*Wow!*"

"Yeah," 'Bird growled stonily. "And guess who bankrolls Outer Earth."

Stormy's eyes went huge. "Oh Jesus, 'Bird, you're right! Oh Jesus—"

"I'll drive," Lox said bluntly. "You boys get the folks in and belted. Looks like we're in a hurry."

Chapter XXVI:
Normality's Last Stand

(Sequoya Avenue, Aztlan)
(Saturday, September 10—early morning)

Haile Selassie II, Emperor of Ethiopia, Nubia, and the Upper Nile, was taking his time motorcading down Sequoya; waving at everyone in his trademark eager fashion through the bulletproof bubble top of a blood red, six-wheeled Bugatti limousine. The matched set of cheetahs flanking him did *not* wave, preferring to remain disdainfully aloof. The procession seemed endless. Could there be that many motorcycles in all of Africa? Thalo wondered, from where, full of coffee, breakfast biscuits, and admonitions from his folks, he'd been becalmed in the canopied bus stop across the street from the Native Southeastern Confederacy Compound's north gate.

He wasn't pondering ruling monarchs, however, or showmanship diplomacy. Rather, he was trying to convince himself he hadn't inadvertently fallen down a certain famous rabbit hole.

How else explain the fact that every time he got a chance to subvert the accelerating chaos around him— mostly via half-assed naps grabbed on the fly (he could scarcely remember the last time he'd flatted in his own space, save that it was nearly a week ago)—he emerged into something utterly different from when he'd gone in? He'd hopped a plane in Minneapolis, snoozed in transit, and stepped out in Disneyland South, otherwise known as Aztlan. He'd forsaken the chaos of Customs for the calm of *La Casa de Castro*, then discovered Green Fran-

cis was dead—followed by meeting Verde. Then had come city versus desert, from which he'd returned knowing his supposedly neat Indian dye job would only make him look foolish; and then the rally, which he'd entered as his own shade of Greenie and a moderate Hero Twins fan and exited as one of the Chosen.

Never mind last night's meeting. He'd flatted after what resembled a fraternity cookout, and awakened into a seventh century Maya . . . orgy. Another nap, and his perceptions had been skewed yet again by something he couldn't recall, but which involved the reality of magic; and then he'd concluded the evening with Verde back in the Real World—minus a hunk of his memory. And just now, he'd got off the bus expecting Embassy business-as-usual and wound up dealing with his folks—who'd scrambled his plans *again*. Would this jerking around never cease?

He sighed and slumped back against the warm sandcrete, pillowing his head with his hands. Some of it was okay. Shoot, some of it was downright neat. Only there was a lot he didn't understand. A lot that troubled him. A lot that, to put it bluntly, he flat out didn't like.

Take Outer Earth. On the surface they had a spotless rep. They raised lots of money, spent it responsibly, and were careful to examine all sides of their causes. They didn't resort to hysterical accusations, civil disobedience, or sensationalism—*on the surface*. At the inner level, though . . . well, he wondered. There'd sure been a shitload of excess last night! A ton too much food cooked (the surplus supposedly distributed to the poor in the border slums), an ocean of liquor gone down toilets, reprocessed or not. And booze was made from grain that could've fed any number of folks. Never mind that damned incense burning by the shovelful everywhere, which was probably made of tree resin, which couldn't do the trees any good; or the fact that the Twins' borrowed mansion was itself built of actual hacked-from-the-Earth stone in lieu of good old enviro-sweet sandcrete, which was made of beach sand, salt, and hydro-plastic foam. In retrospect (saner retrospect, rather),

the whole show reeked of Saladin's ploy, whereby the
fabled Lord of the Assassins during the Crusades had
lured guileless young Moslems into his service by drug-
ging them in familiar surroundings, to reawaken in his
own carefully contrived simulacrum of Paradise, with the
process then reversed. Having, so they supposed,
glimpsed heaven, they'd thereafter do anything he asked,
including leaping off cliffs—sans bungee cords.

Thalo had no such inclination. Oh, he'd stick around
'Earth a while—give it a second, and probably third and
fourth, chance—but he'd be wary, and at the first sign
of foolishness, he was out of there. He'd be polite to the
Twins—and give those asshole guards the finger.

Or roadies . . . or whatever.

They bugged the hell out of him: the way they were
all over the place yet didn't actually do much save stand
around and look ominous. Shoot, the Twins had been out
there in front of several hundred people last night—but
where were their bully boys? Not close enough to shield
'em from a bullet or thrown knife, that's for sure! Yet
damned close aplenty when it looked like one of their
anointed minions might possibly prefer to keep his dick
intact! Never mind that they also seemed to keep tabs on
other 'Earthers—witness yesterday, when Verde was putting up flyers, or just minutes ago, when he'd glimpsed
one watching him from outside McDonald's. Was that an
accident? Insiders acknowledging each other's presence?
Or was it deliberate, and if so, why? Guards didn't do
that kind of thing—did they? Nor roadies.

Nope, it flat out didn't make sense. He'd been too
trusting. Too anxious to please. Too eager to believe what
he wanted to believe. Too quick to embrace causes without examining their methods and agendas.

But be that as it might, he still had to switch realities—
again—and get his tired young butt to work.

Personnel having rotated since his breakfast break, he
had to deal with gate security all over again, so that instead of arriving early, Thalo wound up being late—not
that anyone noticed. He smiled wanly at Holly, ignored

her surly companion, and turned left along the balcony, aiming for 'Bird's office.

"Hey, 'Bird-man!" he called cheerily to the black-clad hindquarters protruding from beneath the desk, where his boss was evidently reassembling the report Thalo had left atop it the previous afternoon. Clumsy twit!

The figure stopped shuffling printouts, backed out, and straightened—and Thalo felt expectations shift yet again (unpleasantly) when the floor-feeler proved not to be Thunderbird O'Connor, but a taller, bulkier, older man in an expensive Brazilian silk suit. The man regarded him curiously from beneath grey-streaked black hair bound back in a tail. His eyes looked tired, and likely would have even had he not been scowling.

"You're not 'Bird!" Thalo blurted.

"You're not either," the big man rumbled, rather like a distant thunderstorm.

Thalo hopped back reflexively. "No . . . I'm Thalo— his assistant."

"Any notion where he might be?"

Thalo shook his head, wondering who this was, to make such brusque demands, and how he should reply— not that he knew anything. "Haven't seen him since yesterday," he continued politely. "He left before I did."

The man sat back against 'Bird's desk and folded his arms. "You're sure?"

Again Thalo nodded; then, suddenly distrustful, added, "I don't think I should say anything else until I know who you are."

"Ah, then there *is* more!"

"Not necessarily. But . . . there's the security thing."

An eyebrow lifted. Almost the big man smiled. "Yes . . . there . . . is."

Thalo edged toward the nearest phone, which was also, not-so-coincidentally, toward the door. "I'll . . . call the receptionist and see if she knows—"

"She didn't when I came in."

Thalo took a deep breath. "Look, I hate to be rude, but . . . exactly who are you?"

" 'Wounds," the man replied. "Red Wounds."

It took a moment for the name to sink in. At which point Thalo sat down on a chair arm with a thud. "Oh, sh— Gee."

The man cocked his head. "Shi-gee? Don't know that word. That Lakota?"

Thalo blushed to the roots of his dyed hair. "It was a stupid mistake, is what it was . . . *sir*. Really, I'm sorry, but I honestly didn't know who you were. I mean—"

"You don't expect to meet the star of the show ass-first? It's actually my handsomer half, so I've been told. 'Sides, you've surely heard me called an asshole at least twenty times by now, if I'm any judge of the folks 'round here. More, if Mary Jane was in all day."

Thalo relaxed a tad. "Twenty-two," he volunteered carefully. "Or was it twenty-three?"

Red Wounds laughed: a hearty laugh, and sincere, but Thalo sensed the man had little more patience for non-sense. He rose, squared his shoulders, and walked forward, hand extended. "Glad to meet you, sir."

"You too," as the hand was engulfed and returned. "And now that's settled, you have any idea what's up with 'Bird? I really need to know, both professionally— all this funeral stuff everybody else is havin' to handle should really be his show—and as a friend."

Thalo's eyes narrowed. Something about that last had tweaked a nerve, as though the Ambassador knew files more than he was saying. "I met him in the desert— couple of days ago. I was going out, he was coming in. He—"

"From where? Where was he coming *from*?"

"Someplace up in the mountains. He wouldn't say— actually, I didn't ask. See, I didn't know it was him."

"Ah! And was he on foot?"

"Driving. Nice little Jeep. Gold."

"That would be Stormy's."

"Who?"

"Stormcloud Nez. Deputy Security Honcho over at Dineh-land. Him and 'Bird are buddies."

Thalo nodded.

"And he didn't say what he'd been doing out there?"

" 'Fraid not. Mostly we talked about me. Leading me on, I guess, or getting to know me. Feeling me out when I was off guard—which I didn't appreciate when I found out, by the way. And then he gave me the grand tour: short version, and then we kinda had a falling out. I felt like an idiot when I came in yesterday and found out who he was.''

Red Wounds laughed again, but with a note of sympathy. "That's our 'Bird! But really, he didn't say anything about what he was doin' last night? Nothing about not being here today?''

Again Thalo shook his head. "He spent the night— night-before-last—with somebody; that much I do know. But when he left yesterday, I figured he was going home. Actually, I don't know where he was going. He kinda snuck off—actually.''

"I need," Red Wounds intoned archly, "to speak to him about that—again. But go on.''

"That's it. I finished the report I was doing—that's it there—and left.''

"Damn!" Red Wounds spat. "*God* damn!''

Thalo tried to look alert and attentive. "Sir?''

Red Wounds grimaced sourly. "Oh, it's just that I need to get hold of him, and I know he's a responsible lad for all his wildness, so he's probably got a good reason for whatever bullshit he's up to, but I need him *now*. Actually, several folks need him now.''

"If you told me, I could tell him," Thalo offered. "I'll be here if he calls . . .''

"As though that's likely, given how he feels about tech! Shoot, the Earth Hour's gonna be right up his alley, but . . . yeah, I reckon the more folks are lookin' for him, the more likely somebody is to find him. So if he calls, tell him to get his ass down here ten minutes ago. Then tell him that a . . . friend of his has died, and it's a probable suicide, and the Mounties need to ask him some questions, but *not* to worry, 'cause I'm on it, and that I thought he might want to go to the funeral, so I wanted to get word to him as soon as possible—as a friend. And *then* tell him—'' The Ambassador paused, cocked his

head, and studied Thalo intently. "That's not your *real* skin color, is it?"

Thalo rolled his eyes. "No sir."

"Well, it's the thought that counts. How tall are you?"

Thalo started. "One-point-seven-six, sir."

"Weight?"

"Seventy-one."

The Ambassador gnawed his lip for a moment. "And 'Bird's one-point-seven-eight and seventy-four . . ." Another thoughtful pause, then: "You'll do."

"Sir . . . ?"

Red Wounds levered himself off the desk decisively. "Well, Thalo Gordon, whatever happens, Kituwah's gotta put in an appearance at the funeral: that's Priority One. We'll figure out what to do about the Mounties and 'Bird's friend later. Basically, what *you* need to do is to sub for 'Bird in the Mourners' March. We'll be in native garb—Blackmer hated it that everybody's given up their cultural identities—'Mountains aren't valleys, and Chinese aren't Bushmen,' and all that stuff. The Pope's asked everyone to go native if they can."

Thalo nodded. "Then I guess I'm your man."

Red Wounds chuckled wearily. "Guess you'll have to be, though it's not in your job description. Check with Cathy Bigwitch in half an hour, she'll get you duded up. And if 'Bird shows, we'll use him. And now that that's settled, I've actually got work to do. Oh, and nice to meet you by the way. I promise it won't always be like this."

"I . . . hope not!"

"No," Red Wounds grinned from the door. "Usually it's much, much worse."

Thalo didn't reply, having suddenly recalled that his sister was to be delivered to the Embassy at noon. He chased the Ambassador down to tell him. The explanation took forever.

"Don't worry about it," Red Wounds sighed, once more on the fly. "We'll bring her along. Cathy *loves* kids."

"She can't stay here? With . . . Holly, say?"

Red Wounds shook his head. "Come noon, we're

shuttin' this puppy down. Soon as the Earth Hour chimes, there'll be guards around this place every ten meters. *We're* taking no chances!'' Whereupon he spun on his elegant Italian-made heel and was gone.

Holly favored Thalo with a wary smile. "Don't worry, kid,'' she chuckled, "you'll look great in feathers."

Thalo merely rolled his eyes again and returned to 'Bird's office. He raided the tiny pantry for more coffee, which he fortified with what smelled like white lightning. Just like him, too: trying not to get wired on the one hand, and trying to assure alertness on the other.

Having no official duties until the rendezvous with Cathy Bigwitch, he removed his shoes and socks, slid behind 'Bird's desk, and propped his feet atop it. "TV. On,'' he commanded. A small monitor promptly rose from the desk's right front corner and swiveled toward him. It was tuned to CNN—no surprise; they'd watched that all of yesterday. It was also coverage of the funeral; no shock there, either. At present, a pair of clerical types were debating whether or not Pope Michael would accede to the Archbishop's last request (as reconstructed from the notes to an unfinished address) and put Zaire, Zimbabwe, Malaysia, Australia, New Guinea, Indonesia, Brazil, Venezuela, Colombia, and most of Central America under interdict if they didn't stop cutting rain forests *now*. Already Those-in-the-Know were predicting revolution and war—between nations, religions, and megas alike. Blackmer could've kept them together—maybe; played them like a organ and made them like the song. Without him . . . no one knew.

Thalo sure didn't. He changed the channel. Sumatra TV was blithering about whether the Princess of Tonga would show up at the funeral wearing only her famous tattoos.

Televisión España was covering Their Boring Majesties of Spain.

BBC was *not* covering Prince William, who was to be His Ailing Majesty's rep.

CNN III was recounting the order of precedence, starting with Haile II—evidently emperors outranked *every-*

one, including kings. It was, someone noted tactlessly, the biggest gathering of wealth and power since the Shah of Iran had celebrated Persia's fourth millennium back in the Seventies, and everyone knew what had come of that. The big ongoing debate was whether the head of a mega outranked a president, during which it was noted that the Chairman of Ford Motor Company Limited, AG, Spa. controlled more people's livelihoods and far more money than all three Scandinavian monarchs together, with Finland, Iceland, Estonia, Latvia, and Lithuania thrown in.

Thalo changed the channel in disgust.

MTV was covering the Hero Twins, who were leaving their compound now, looking remarkably fresh, given what they'd been up to the previous night—which now seemed more a dream than a memory. Thalo wondered, though, why he had a chill when he saw them climb into their limo accompanied by nearly a dozen burly, cloak-clad guards.

Chapter XXVII:
The Soul Takes Flight . . .

(Over the Gulf of Mexico)
(Saturday, September 10—late morning)

The first things Carolyn saw when she dragged herself up from a deep well of senselessness indeed, were the sun, the sky, and appallingly blue water. She blinked groggily and shut her eyes again, seeking that cool, quiet, timeless place where there was no thought, no concern, no worries, nothing awful to react to—and nothing ever changed. Almost she succeeded. Yet something nagged her, told her she still had work to do and had best be about it.

Perhaps it was anger, for she felt a little jolt as though she'd been injected with adrenaline. Or maybe it was simply pain so all-encompassing that once awakened, it would never leave. That pain had a name, too—three of them: Finn the Far-sighted, Nuala Griffith, and Kevin Mauney. Finn—Nuala—Kevin; Finn—Nuala—Kevin: it made a dreadful litany in her head: the naming of her dead.

And with them, subtly, came the foci of her anger: Sean. Floyd. Her brother and her . . . dad.

Abruptly she sat bolt upright. "*Goddamn you!*" she spat, and made to rise. Something restrained her, tugged against her waist and held her down. Another blink, and finally she saw true. The sun, the sky, the sea; viewed through a square of glass. A porthole. No, the window of a plane: a small jet, luxuriously fitted with thick carpet,

expensive wood, and rich leather. Ambassador O'Neal's Gulfstream.

In spite of her anger, in spite of that welter of conflicted emotions that instants earlier had threatened to effect mental lockdown, she began to analyze.

The plane . . . flying. She was no longer on Cumberland. Therefore a fair bit of time had passed since . . . since she'd seen *that* and heard *that* and passed out on the sand. Shock, she supposed. Fatigue. Or cop-out.

Only . . . who was flying the plane? Surely not Liam; last she'd seen of him he'd been more zombie than human being: shell-shocked, walking-wounded, traumed-out; whatever term you wanted to describe someone who'd been forced to commit an act he would never in his right mind have done, then been made to recall it.

She knew how he felt.

But if Liam wasn't flying, who was? Floyd was no pilot, and Sean sure as hell wasn't! Someone from the mainland, maybe?

Muffled clinkings sounded aft. She twisted around to see Floyd padding toward her, and realized that her entire burst of analysis had occupied maybe two seconds, and all anyone had heard was a curse.

And then Floyd—*Dad*, she conceded sourly—was kneeling on the thick green carpet beside her, offering a heavy crystal glass that vented fumes she recognized. Irish Whiskey. Jameson's, unless she was mistaken; the same with which they'd toasted Mom on the flight over. She accepted it, drank greedily, coughed, and drank again. It exploded into her sinuses like cold fire, poured like lava down her throat, numbed her tongue, then set it alight. It was wonderful. She finished it.

And only then recalled that she was beyond angry at her dad. Shoot, anger wasn't near a strong enough word, yet hate was too dispassionate. There had to be another that meant ultimate disappointment, ultimate betrayal, and ultimate . . . *evil* rolled into one.

"Welcome back," Floyd murmured, as he gently pried the glass from her shaking fingers and poured another shot. "Go easy on this one. Oh, and by the way, it's a

waste of time to consign me to hell; I've already done it for you.''

She glared at him. ''Kev—''

''It was the hardest thing I've ever done—and it was what he wanted.''

''You can't want something like that!''

''Can't you?''

''It's awful!''

''It's a chance where there wasn't one.''

Carolyn claimed the glass, drank half, and swallowed hard. Already it seemed to be having some effect: making her drifty . . . muzzy. Maybe they'd put something in it to dull the pain, to make her forget about Kev and what her own father and half-brother had done to him—

No! She couldn't deal with that now. But her dad was still beside her, looking distressed, hurt, and imploring. His eyes were red too; likely from weeping. He'd also changed clothes. She had to speak or go mad, yet one thing alone filled her mind. Or maybe not. ''Who's flying the plane?'' she rasped: her only important concern that wasn't about Kev.

''Sean.''

''*Sean*?'' she almost shouted. ''*Sean* can't fly!''

''Liam can. And Sean can read minds.''

''You people really are crazy!''

''Probably. But with Liam already half in a trance, Sean could go into one and link with him. And since flying's mostly reflex, like driving . . . Well, as long as he stays under, we're fine. It's when he wakes—or Liam starts coming out of it—that we're in trouble.''

''Crazy,'' Carolyn sniffed, and rolled her eyes.

Floyd smiled wanly and rose to claim the seat across the aisle. He swiveled it around to face her and poured another drink, this one for himself. ''Necessity breeds madness.''

Carolyn took a deep breath—and a small sip—wondering suddenly if there was anything to eat about. ''I think the straight scoop's in order,'' she said. ''Since I obviously can't escape just now, I suppose I ought to

examine the facts before I press charges—or just go
ahead and have you all committed.''

Another smile. ''The short form is that we hit you with
... *it* all wrong, and you passed out. We couldn't bring
you around, and time was of the essence, so we went
ahead and did the funeral without you. No hitches there;
and you did exactly the right thing—or the same thing I
would've done, anyway—with the evidence. We torched
the cabin just in case, loaded you on the ATV, hopped
on the plane . . . and here we are.''

Carolyn regarded him grimly. ''That's hardly all.''

''How much of the rest are you willing to tolerate?''

Carolyn took a sip and gnawed her lip. Was she up to
... *that*? Then: ''How 'bout why you were in such a
hurry all of a sudden?''

''Because I found out some things that made us—me,
I guess, since I was the only one with decision power at
the time—need to hurry. See, number one, there were
gonna be other people on the island pretty soon. The
ferry'd be over by sunset, max; and we'd have a lot of
explaining to do. It's also possible that the power and
phone glitches registered on some kind of mainland
grid—I'm not enough of a technophile to know what
they can and can't tell—so that meant a chance of work
crews showing up even earlier. But the main thing's the
plot.''

''You know about it?''

''I know *something*. I'm not sure if I know what you
know. Sean was . . . shaky about that.''

''So what *do* you know?''

Floyd stirred his drink with his finger and absently
watched the ice swirl. He wouldn't meet her eye. ''To
talk about that . . . we'll have to talk about Kev.''

''I have to hear it eventually.''

A nod. ''So. Well, it's like this. Obviously one of those
were-orca things took over Liam, had him capture Kev,
then did . . . *that* to him, to the possible destruction of
Liam's sanity. But evidently it sensed our approach and
had to stop before it was finished. And—''

''I know all that!'' Carolyn snapped.

"Laying the groundwork," Floyd sighed. "But you also know that Kev survived. No way he could've lived, of course, unless we could've got him to a hospital immediately, but Liam was careful, and there wasn't much blood loss. It was a slow drain—and Kev was a fighter. Had more fight in him than I'd ever suspected—more than anybody should've had—unless they had a reason. He had one. More than once he came to and tried to talk, but then—I guess the pain'd get too strong and he'd faint. Every time, I thought he was dead, but then he'd start breathing again. I was proud of him."

"Me too," Carolyn whispered. And meant it.

Another nod. "Anyway, Sean showed up eventually—just about dawn—and told me you were ready, but we'd have to hurry. I asked him why, and he told me about the plot—as much as he knew—how there was something afoot down in Aztlan involving mass assassination. So I—"

"Christ!" Carolyn broke in. "Has . . . has anyone tried to get hold of them to warn them?"

"Sean can't 'cause it's taking all he has to fly—he can't fly in a trance and think independently too. I tried, but didn't know the procedure, 'cept that I did get through to somebody in Jacksonville—don't know if it was the police or the tower; I was—ah—in not much better shape than you just then. They thought I was a crank and broke contact. Miami thought something worse and tried to get us to land. Somewhere in there I found a radio broadcast and heard that the Archbishop's funeral is this afternoon. More to the point, the Pope's asked that, in his honor, the world, as much as possible, abandon tech for half a day in mourning. A lot of small stuff's already been cut off. Even Aztlan's observing a so-called Earth Hour bracketing the funeral. No one's supposed to make phone calls, answer the phone, or anything like that. No driving. No planes to land. Nice idea, but hard to implement, never mind dangerous."

"Sounds like Blackmer, though," Carolyn said. "He's proposed that before. The Pope was giving him his dream."

"Whatever," Floyd replied. "But to get back to our situation: somewhere in all that stuff Sean was telling me—he was pretty frantic about it, and I could tell it was important to him—Kev came to again. Maybe he heard Sean, I dunno. Maybe he picked up all that mental angst and *it* dragged him back. The point is, he revived."

"God!"

"Yeah, well, he did. And he obviously knew he was dying, and tried to talk, but couldn't really; but then Sean stepped in and made some kind of link between my mind and his, and Kev . . . *thought* us everything he knew about what had happened to him. Basically, it was like we figured: he went for a walk down the beach, heard shots, and started to return. But then he saw Liam walking toward him, and Liam said not to worry, and Kev said, 'Why the hell not? That's my sister and my dad, and they're both drunk!' And Liam grabbed him, did some kind of military thing, and knocked him out—and the next thing he knew, his hands are tied behind him, and he's bouncing along on Liam's back. He struggled; Liam put him down, but when he tried to run, Liam caught him and hobbled his legs with a rope—with the orca in control all the time."

He paused to wipe his eyes and take another swallow before continuing. "They wound up at Dungeness, and the orca put some kinda sleep-whammy on 'em and left 'em there for a spell, while it cased out what we were doing, and then it woke up Liam again and two of 'em . . . staked Kev down. Liam did the rest. Kev passed out after the first cut, but before he did . . . Well, he cursed them. Said he was half Eirish and the son of kings, warriors, and bards, and that if anything survived after death he'd find a way to haunt 'em—not Liam; he knew what was up with him; he was talking to the orca."

Carolyn stopped him with a frown. "And all this was feeding straight from his mind to you, via Sean?"

Floyd bit his lip, then nodded. "A lot of pain came with it too; no way he could shield it. It was . . . unbelievable."

"Okay . . . so what then?"

A deep breath. "Then's when the shit hit the fan. See, while they were doing all that to Kev, the orca was talking to him, or Kev was picking stuff out of its mind, or something—I think they have a thing about gloating. Whatever it was, it was about the overall plot of which the attack on us was just part. Number one, and the big thing: you're right, there *is* gonna be some kinda *coup* down in Aztlan. The were-orcas orchestrated Blackmer's assassination knowing that everyone on earth who thought they were anybody, or who needed to improve their image, would show up for the funeral. Once there . . . *poof*: instant 'accident' ops. Unfortunately, Kev couldn't find out more, except that it involves music."

"*Music*?" Carolyn exclaimed with a scowl. Then: "Shit, that's in line with the way they work, too; the way they sing up storms and all. And if they tried something on land, there'd be no way dolphins could defeat 'em . . ."

Floyd shrugged. "Like I said, Kev went under just as he was about to get the specifics. But he did find out something else disturbing, that really shouldn't surprise us if we think about it."

"What?"

"Basically, that the orcas had a hit list. They apparently have really organized memories, and stuff like that just plays through 'em like background music, and if they're thinking really strongly about any of it, it's easy to pick up. Sean says Kev was fairly psychic and just didn't know it, but that some of that stuff you guys did last week made him stronger. But anyway, he 'heard' this list, and there were a lot of names on it. Some I didn't know, but a bunch I've heard you mention."

"Who?" Carolyn demanded, even as she wondered at some remoter level when, exactly, she had forgiven her father.

"You were on it, so was Kev. *Nuala* was on it. Both ambassadors were on it, and that woman you work for— what's her name?"

"Hasegawa—Mary Hasegawa."

"Right. And that guy I heard you liked—Rudy some-

thing. And somebody named Thunderbird, and somebody
named Stormcloud, and . . . Keys—no, Locks.''

"Lox?"

"Yeah." He paused. "And Twins—"

Carolyn's scowl deepened. "Twins? Like *Hero* Twins,
maybe? They're certainly musicians."

A shrug. "Maybe. Anyway, that's all I can remember."

"God knows it's enough!"

"Which brings us to . . . *that*."

"Which brings us to that."

Another deep breath. "You remember what Kev was
talking about on the steps, right before everything happened? All those questions he was asking? Well, he figured this was the time to get some answers. See, he knew
your name was on that list, and wanted to protect you.
He knew he was gonna die anyway, so he wanted his
death to accomplish something—at least knowledge
would be served. And he . . ." Floyd paused, eyes
streaming. "This is hard, Cary. He thought there might
be a chance some aspect of him might persist past death
if . . . if we were to remove his skin *with his permission*,
like Sean said needed to be done, and—oh, Jesus, this is
hard!—you put it on. He said some of him might survive
that way, and if it made you change—it might keep you
alive, 'cause the orcas wouldn't be able to recognize
you."

Carolyn slumped back into her seat and closed her
eyes. No way this was happening! No way she'd heard
what she just had, rendered calmly and clinically by
someone she truly did, in some odd way, love. "No
way!" she whispered—aloud.

Floyd seemed to collapse where he sat, face unread-
able. Clearly, he'd been dreading this—nor could it have
been easy for him. Shoot, he'd been there! Shared it,
even! She'd only caught the aftermath. And Sean—dispassionate little Sean—was this what he'd stayed on the
dock to ponder? Was this what he'd all along been
scheming?

"It's your choice," Floyd choked finally. "And what-

ever you do . . . daughter, I'll know there was thought behind it and that you're trying to do the right thing. I'll only say this: I've just lost one child; I'd hate to lose another.''

Carolyn steeled herself for one last question, but a single word was all that escaped her lips. ''Where . . . ?''

''In the 'fridge,'' Floyd told her softly. ''The rest . . . We loaded it on the boat. He's one with the sky and the sea—and she who bore him—now.''

Carolyn's reply was to swivel her seat back toward the window and stare at that sky—that sea—and the sun.

Chapter XXVIII:
Locked Out

(West of Aztlan)
(Saturday, September 10—noonish)

"*Damn!*" Stormy spat, voice tight with genuine awe as the Suburban lurched around yet another pothole among the scores that pocked the quarry's rim: no different from any other—save that this sideways skip granted their first clear view of the eight-lane into Aztlan. "Oh shit, guys; we're fucked!"

'Bird gave up trying to stop the senile old woman wedged into the near corner of the cargo bay from unbinding the heavily-tranqued wino's shattered elbow, and twisted around, wishing the illustrious Mr. Nez had found enough Num-Joose in the Jeep's first-aid kit to send their whole payload of werka-workers off to La-La Land— with maybe something extra for his own multiply traumatized bod. And then he saw what had prompted his buddy's exclamation. "Double shit," he agreed.

Hunched over the wheel, Hosteen Lox held silent, but his scowl spoke eloquently.

They'd finally escaped the mountains that sheltered the *hataalii's* compound, and threaded the network of back roads that let, via the quarry, onto one of the three main thoroughfares into Aztlan; and they'd done it with ne'er a glitch, unless one counted the captives' endless queries, moans, and complaints. Blessedly, there'd been no traffic—no nothing but radio coverage of Green Archie's requiem. And, thanks to Lox's spirited but careful chauffeuring, they'd made good time.

But all that efficiency was rendered useless now.

Oh, the nearside lanes were clear all right—*they* led out of the Zone. But the eastbound ones were clogged with idling vehicles from horizon to horizon: worldclass gridlock if he'd ever seen it. Even more amazing, though, were the folks afoot: a slowly ambling crusade of them, all crowding toward the Zone, most in their Sunday best. Five kloms from the border and already it was like this? What must the city be like? No, scratch that; he didn't want to know.

"So what do we do?" Lox inquired, as he stopped just shy of the pavement.

'Bird peered out the window to his left, squinting along the loose-graveled shoulder. "Go cross-country, I reckon"—he glanced at Stormy—"unless you've got other ideas . . ."

Stormy shook his head. " 'Fraid not. I've biked out here a couple times on this side, so I know it's passable— if too many folks haven't had the same idea and blocked access closer in."

"Wanta try your phone again?"

"Wouldn't hurt," Stormy sighed, pressing three fingers to the hollow beneath his right clavicle. "Stormcloud Nez to Dineh Embassy," he continued, frowning as he listened. Then: "Stormcloud Nez to Kituwah Embassy." A long pause, and he tapped his chest again and shook his head. "No go. We're still too far out, and there's probably a zillion other folks doin' the same right now." He nodded toward the motionless traffic. "I mean, look at that. 'Least a quarter of those cars have phones, and probably half of *them* are in use right now: folks trying to find out what's goin' on, or looking for alternate routing, or explaining to folks expecting 'em that they're not gonna get . . . wherever on time."

"Tech!" Lox spat—and turned left down the shoulder.

Two kloms downcountry Stormy tried his phone again. At first he got nothing, but redial produced a recording that informed him that the Dineh Embassy was closed for the day. A mumbled code word 'Bird chose not to

hear overrode him to the Chief of Security, who offered
a few choice words concerning Stormy's absence, approved or no. Stormy brusquely requested the Ambassador herself, only to be told that she was already en
route to the funeral and that, from respect, she'd turned
off both her body phone and the one in her limo, as the
Pope had asked *everyone* to do for three hours either side
of the Mass—that in addition to the Earth Hour. At that
time, only the Mounties would have access to telecom.
A second call, placed a half klom closer, put him barely
in range of the Kituwah Embassy, which was further
away than Dinetah's. The tale was identical there, save
that he had trouble finding *anyone* to talk to, as the place
was apparently manned entirely by junior flunkies who
didn't know him. And unfortunately, one of the down-
sides of body phones was that you couldn't pass them
around, not with sensors in your gums and ears; never
mind that 'Bird's own phone, which would've done marginally more good, was still a mass of scar tissue.

"Best I can tell, 'Wounds has left too," Stormy grumbled. "Looks like we're on our own."

Lox merely shifted into all-wheel-drive to assail a dry
gulch, uttering not so much as a grunt until they were
out again, and then only a terse "Were-orcas connect
with Outer Earth, which is supported by the Hero Twins,
who're doing the music for the Mass. Surely there is a
pattern."

At which point the wino, for no obvious reason, began
screaming.

'Bird slammed the public phone's receiver down in
disgust and glared across the parking lot of Wal-Mart
number eight-thousand-five, which occupied a substantial
part of the horizon on the western fringe of Eggtown, the
first bastion of conventional civilization one reached before entering Aztlan proper. It also had the first working
pay phone they'd found in nearly an hour. Alas, all he'd
got at Kituwah was another low-level flunky who confirmed that Red Wounds had left some time back. He
then tried the Chief's limo and failed. He tried the Am-

bassador direct and failed. He tried patching through the
embassy and failed as well—because no one would believe he had an emergency, or else wanted explanations
he couldn't provide. Aztlan, it seemed, was in the hands
of paranoid incompetents afraid to trust anyone they
weren't actually looking at, or to take risks without concrete proof. Unfortunately, a truckload of mental aber-
rants didn't constitute that. Trouble was, if his contacts
so far were any indication, the city was already a werka
supermarket ripe for the picking.

But at least they'd solved one problem. One of the
more coherent captives had spotted a familiar logo and
screamed ''Burger King! Burger King! Burger King!''
for over a minute without stopping. Though he felt bad
about the crassness—it was a damned shitty thing to do
to folks on either side of the situation—he'd made Lox
stop on the fringe of the restaurant's parking lot; off-
loaded the entire batch of werka-workers; handed Sgt.
Archer, the traumed-out medic, all the cash he had; and
told him this was a forage mission but he ought to barter
for food if possible. The man had smiled broadly. Lox
had whisked away.

There'd be repercussions, of course, but he'd deal with
them when they came knocking. There were more pressing matters at hand.

More time passed—too much of it. They reached the
border, then *El País*, then the beltway. They were inside
the city now, and back on pavement. Traffic was for all
intents frozen solid. So would they likewise have been,
had they had any respect at all for curbs, yards, fences,
or—occasionally—flimsy sandcrete walls.

'Bird wanted to hit something. More specifically, he
wanted to draw back his right fist absolutely as far as
possible and launch it in one smooth jab straight into the
blandly handsome face of the young Canadian in full
formal kit who'd just spent a nervewrackingly long time
peering dubiously at his visa, then become the fifth person in as many minutes to inform him that diplomat or

no, he could *not* remove the roadblock at the juncture of Beltway Exit Four and the southbound lanes of Bolivar. The kid's words still chimed in his ears, there on the pavement eight vehicles up from the becalmed Suburban: "I'm sorry sir, but Her Majesty of Denmark is due to pass . . . soon, and we have to keep this route clear. Perhaps if you had authorization from your Ambassador, we could—"

"That's what I've been tryin' to tell you!" 'Bird yelled. "I can't get *hold* of him right now! I don't have a body phone, my car doesn't have a phone at all—and Red Wounds has turned off both of *his*—thanks to the damned *Earth Hour*!"

"It was the Vatican's request," the Mountie replied— as though that explained everything. "The Archbishop supported nature over tech, and the Pope thinks body phones are unnatural. He—"

The rest of his remark was drowned out by a blare of horns, as a phalanx of motorcycles glided from beneath the overpass to the left, followed quickly by two standard-length silver Mercedes, a stretched one in gold, and two more standards. Danish flags—white cross on red field—waved from staves on the limo's bumpers; the arms of Denmark glittered on the doors. In spite of his haste, 'Bird wished Her Majesty would clear the privacy glass. He'd never seen a queen.

"What's the holdup?" Stormy asked when a disgusted 'Bird had threaded his way back to where the Suburban idled behind a battered GMC pickup, whose cab and stake-bed alike were crammed with grim-faced rural Indians, every one of whom sported a black-and-green armband.

"Never mind," 'Bird spat, as he paused with a hand on the door in lieu of climbing back in. "At this point, I think we'd be better off ditching our wheels and heading overland. It's what?—five kloms to the Cathedral? Surely we can hoof that before things get goin'."

"Be tight timing," Stormy replied, gnawing his lip. "What d'you think, Hosteen Lox?"

Lox stared through the windshield. "I think progress-

ing toward a goal is preferable to standing still. If we continue, we might accomplish something. If we wait, we achieve nothing at all.''

Stormy nodded decisively. "Gimme a sec to armor up, and we can pound pavement.'' He grinned at 'Bird. "You need any heat?''

"Small, loaded, and *not* jammed," 'Bird snorted. "Mounties are bound to be nervous as hell, so we don't want anything they'd notice—nor to attract attention anyway, for that matter. Shoot, I can't believe *my* name didn't set off alarms with that kid in connection to Rudy.''

"I should've gone," Stormy muttered, from where he was rummaging under the front seat. "Guess luck was with us—for a change.'' A moment later, he straightened and passed something to Lox that 'Bird couldn't see from outside, then climbed out the passenger door and eased close to 'Bird. Slick metal brushed 'Bird's hand: the .38 he'd carried earlier. He slipped it into his jeans pocket and tugged his tunic down over it, with his serape over that.

Lox switched off the Suburban and joined them, squinting in the bright sunlight. He alone was not wearing shades, though he sported a wide black felt hat banded with silver conchas. "Which way?" he wondered, sounding suddenly shy and indecisive. 'Bird suspected he now knew why the old man hated cities.

Stormy indicated the barricade—which showed no signs of being removed, probably because Someone Else was expected anon. "We follow that, turn left, and . . . basically, just aim for the Cathedral towers. That's them beyond that clump of trees.''

'Bird shaded his eyes and peered eastward, past a mini-park and the long arcade of a mall. Australia's pyramid rose beyond the park, the sunlight sparking off its red-gold facets (it was meant to evoke a fire opal) so brightly it hurt to look at. The cathedral towers wavered in the heat-haze to the right, looking even more insubstantial than (as holos) they were.

Lox slammed the door and started walking.

The barricade was still up when they reached it, the eager-faced young Mountie talking animatedly on an actual walkie-talkie as they passed. 'Bird saluted him absently and continued on, bearing right into a bank's forecourt to avoid the crush of pilgrims on the sidewalk. His hip protested the effort—as, in varying degrees, did the rest of his body. He winced at the pain, but kept on, limping as he fought to keep pace with his companions. A moment later, a lesser street intersected the one they'd been flanking—blockaded, naturally. A pedestrian bridge arched over the main one there, guarded by Mounties on either side. Still, they'd have to cross at some point, and this was as good as any. The crowd was thin there, too; mostly content to dawdle along looking dazed.

Stormy indicated the bridge. "I've got my security ID if anybody gives us grief about what we're packing."

"Let's just hope nobody does," 'Bird sighed.

The Mountie tensed as they approached, and swung his rifle from vertical to horizontal, frowning as he did. Stormy moved into the lead. "We just need to cross," he told the man.

The Mountie's eyes blanked, likely checking the time. He gnawed his lip, then nodded. "Make it fast. The Twins' motorcade's due in two minutes and the bridge has to be clear by then. If I see anything funny going on, you get one warning and then—"

"What?" From Stormy.

"I shoot you."

"No problem," Stormy assured him, and started up the stairs.

Fortunately it was a simple passage: up, across, and down. The second guard regarded them keenly as they disembarked, motioning them to hurry with his rifle. They needed little urging. 'Bird couldn't help noting how hard it was not to look suspicious when you really were.

At which point a siren sounded behind them. Mounties again; that particular tone was reserved for them alone.

"Twins," Stormy hissed, slowing. "If they're mixed up in this, we oughta watch. God knows we won't be the only ones."

'Bird scowled, but followed his companions as they angled toward the street. The crowd there was turning too, craning their necks in quest of yet another celebrity fix. Fortunately, 'Bird and Stormy were taller than most and had no trouble seeing the red-and-gold Mercury Mountie-cruiser that had just emerged from beneath the bridge and was cruising at a purposeful clip down the center of Bolivar, lights flashing on its roof, sirens wailing intermittently. Another followed, then an emerald-green Lincoln limousine, trailed by a matching Humvee. The limo's privacy glass was clear, and—true to their avowed desire to be as accessible as possible—the Hero Twins were clearly visible in the back seat, one to a side, and clad in full ceremonial regalia.

'Bird spared the rock stars barely a blink, his gaze drawn as by a magnet to the two men who accompanied them as chauffeur—and guard, presumably—and the eight more in the Humvee.

Big, heavy-faced men in loose hooded over-cloaks.

"Werkas!" 'Bird hissed, elbowing Stormy in the side. "Look."

"Damn!" Stormy gritted. "What the fuck is goin' *on*?"

'Bird stared him square in the eye. "I dunno, buddy-o, but it occurs to me that the place those guys are staying is only 'bout four blocks from here. And if we were to zip by there while they're gone, we might learn a lot."

Stormy puffed his cheeks. "Assuming it's not occupied."

"Right," 'Bird agreed. "But we can probably handle any of our kind we meet, and as for others, we've got . . . contingencies."

"It's a hard call," Stormy mused. "If we go, we may be too late to do any good at the Cathedral, but if we don't, we could miss important info." He glanced at their companion. "What d'you say, Hosteen Lox?"

In reply, Lox turned square toward the street, left side facing the Twins's motorcade—now disappearing behind a stand of palms—right toward the more wooded area from whence they'd come. Wordlessly, he extended both

hands before him, palms down. He closed his eyes and inhaled slowly—twice. For a moment nothing happened; then, very clearly, his right hand began to shake.

'Bird gaped stupidly. He'd forgotten that the old *ha-taalii* had powers of his own to command, and that one of them was that arcane finding skill known as hand-trembling.

"Okay," Stormy said, when Lox opened his eyes again. "We go right."

Chapter XXIX:
Road Trip

(Aztlan)
(Saturday, September 10—early afternoon)

"Stop pulling my feathers!" Thalo growled at his sister from the cream leather jumpseat they shared in one of Kituwah's three "official" limos. He resisted the urge to smack her hand—she was, after all, female, a child, retarded, and scrunched up next to someone in full formal Cherokee drag ca. 1820 (when the first nation had dissolved): too much temptation for anyone shy of their teens. Never mind that the ornaments in question were fixed to a tooled deerskin armband bound around one sleeve of a wraparound thigh-length coat, worn beneath a turban—which, alas, she'd just discovered. He took the roving hand firmly in his own and returned it to her lap. She stuck out her lower lip. He rolled his eyes helplessly at his fellow passengers and wondered what in several alternate hells he'd got himself into: first, by agreeing to impersonate 'Bird in the procession (a specified number of warm bodies being required, and 'Bird, who was handsome anyway, looking especially good in period garb); and second, by letting his folks stick him with his sister, whom he'd had no choice but to bring along, the Embassy being closed save for skeleton staff, none of whom he knew well enough to trust with a child like Sara.

Facing him in the back seat proper were a rugged, tight-lipped man named Eric Bauchenbaugh, who was Kituwah's Resources Officer (the Eastern Band derived most of the income that assured its independence from

endangered species research and breeding programs); a tiny, nervous woman named Louise Awiatka, who was Kituwah's Corporate Liaison; and (occupying rather more than the requisite third of the Lincoln's spacious rear lounge), the aptly named Cathy Bigwitch, who was officially Information Liaison, but had also, until Thalo's arrival, doubled as Under-Assistant Cultural Attaché. Which basically meant she spoke some Cherokee, knew half a dozen myths, could sing a couple of songs, do three dances, and had her own regalia.

Still, she'd known enough to fit Thalo up proper—aided by the host of holos of 'Bird in costume strewn about his office. She'd been chatty and motherly in the vaguely listless way of obese women who'd resigned themselves to spinsterhood long before middle age. Unfortunately, she was silent now. They all were, except Sara—and Thalo, when he shushed her. The solemnity of the occasion had descended with a vengeance.

Thalo wished he could twist around to see what lay ahead—besides two other limos, the first bearing Ambassador-Chief William Red Wounds and his wife, Alexandra Arneach; the second transporting the deputy Ambassador, Mary Jane Mankiller (who, though presently single, apparently lived up to her name, having been wed five times), and three officials he didn't know.

Instead, he was doomed to what little view survived the limo's slit-like rear window when three feathered turbans were factored out—basically, a dozen security guards on blood-red Harleys—or what he could manage surreptitiously out the side.

Mostly it was crowds. As of noon, all private traffic was banned inside the Beltway, so that the remaining diplomatic motorcades could reach St. Tekkie's on time. Which meant that (by reliable radio estimates) ninety percent of the remaining population of the city was converging on Cathedral Square. They wouldn't get in, of course (the three thousand plus VIPs, of which Thalo, apparently, was one, would themselves be jammed in like sardines), but a number of huge TV screens had been set

up around the square (Earth Hour be damned), and the Mass itself would be beamed everywhere.

Thalo hoped it was worth it. And wondered when, exactly, he'd become so jaded. Expensive new cars, pristine buildings; wide, clean streets; bright, well-educated, overachieving people. Free food, free liquor. Parties in palaces. It all sounded great on paper, but in reality it was just too much! He'd give a lot to get off someplace small, worn, and . . . comfortable—with dirty dishes in the sink. Suddenly he knew why 'Bird went barefoot so often. Maybe he would too.

At which point Sara abandoned his feathers for the fringe of his woven belt.

They were passing the World Pool now: the reflective basin between the Big Four Pyramids in the center of Aztlan, that was supposed to remind folks that man was born of water and all great civilizations had risen around it. A network of canals radiated from it in the cardinal directions to form moats around the Big Four, before branching into an ever-more-intricate pattern that laced the city together with threads of blue and silver. Sometimes those canals widened into reflecting pools, sometimes they narrowed to mark the medians of major thoroughfares. Certainly, one never went far in the city without being aware of them. It was like the Alhambra, Thalo concluded: the Moorish palace in Granada, Spain, that had used moving water to instill an air of tranquility.

Trouble was, it made him anything but tranquil. Indeed, it reminded him of something unpleasant, though he couldn't quite recall what. What had Verde said about his amnesia? Something would push the right button, and down the block would go? Well a button was definitely being pushed by all that water, but the wrecking ball wasn't connecting!

He was still trying to puzzle out what was so damned disconcerting about common H_2O, when the limo began to slow. *Screw decorum*, he decided, and looked out the window (Red Wounds refused to allow privacy glass, so folks could see in too)—and gasped. Never had he seen so many people. Thousands and thousands of them, most

in their Sunday best, shuffling grimly down the sidewalks
and the two outer lanes. Most wore serious expressions.
Many had obviously been crying. And far more than
Thalo expected sported crucifixes and fingered rosary
beads. Not one in a thousand eschewed the requisite
green-and-black armband.

Roughly a minute later, they stopped.

Everyone sighed in unison.

"This is it, folks," small Eva piped, her eyes very
bright—and not with excitement. Thalo wished he'd
thought to bring a hanky. Before this was over, he might
need one too.

By prior reluctant agreement (Thalo's reticence, not
hers) Cathy had agreed *not* to form part of the official
procession, but to wait with Sara, the chauffeurs, and a
cadre of embassy guards in the VIP parking lot. Thus,
he tarried with them inside while Eric and Eva (who outranked the rest of them anyway) disembarked. Hot air
hissed in, overwhelming the AC, and Thalo was instantly
sweating. Nerves, probably, but anxiety wasn't van-
quished by waiting. Taking a deep breath, he told Sara
she'd better mind Cathy 'cause her name was *Bigwitch*,
and that he'd be back as soon as he could, hugged her
as well as the awkward seating allowed, plucked one of
the feathers from his turban, and presented it to her. She
regarded him with wide-eyed solemnity. And for a moment he forgot that she was not—quite—all there.

Farewell accomplished, he scooted left through the
open door. No sooner had he reached the pavement, however, than Cathy uttered a startled "No, Sara, don't!"
Whereupon a small blond blur zipped out of the car behind him and darted into the crowd, which absorbed her
with vexatious ease. Having no choice, Thalo gave
chase—difficult, since every square meter of space in the
plaza not actually cordoned off for vehicular traffic was
crammed with milling, sweating people. Doggedly, he
waded after her, wondering what in the world had set her
off like that—until he saw the giant TV screen that
masked the facade of the three-tiered step pyramid fronting the square's north side. Sara loved TV. More to the

point, she loved to sit with her face inches from the tube. Having been deprived of that familiar comfort for at least a day, she was merely doing what her brother wished he could: seeking a security fix.

"Sara!" Thalo yelled desperately, as he twisted, shoved, and apologized his way through the mob. "Sara, no!"

And then he burst into a clear space—apparently a cordoned-off staging area for media (who, though exempt from the Earth Hour, were hedging their bets with their own generators). More specifically, he'd blundered into the MTV enclave, where someone had actually managed to lay hold of a Hero Twin for an interview. And of course, where the Twins were, the bulky roadies couldn't be far behind. Indeed, one hovered beside the grim-faced megastar while another paced nervously along a nearby stretch of canal. Two more lurked in the shadows of a large shiny van that bore Chinese ideograms. All wore their hoods up—odd in this heat, given that Thalo wore less than they and was sweating.

And there was Sara, standing stock still, not four meters from the nearest, staring with innocent wonder at rank on rank of monitors that showed that Twin's face from every possible angle.

He dashed forward and scooped her up. "Sorry," he mumbled to a phalanx of scowling techs. The Twin glanced at him languidly, with no sign of recognition—which pissed him—until he recalled how he was dressed. Unfortunately, one of those damned roadies did recognize him—as a potential threat, if nothing else—and strode toward him.

He felt a sudden buzz in his brain, as though it had been stuffed with static, followed by a mental jolt. He blinked, stumbled, then regained his equilibrium—to find himself face to face with that selfsame roadie. Face to sternum, more precisely; the man was that tall, and his features—oddly smooth and . . . unfinished-looking— were shadowed by his hood. Thalo suddenly wanted to get as far away as possible.

The roadie, however, had other plans; and, ignoring

the protesting Sara, proceeded to lay both beefy hands atop Thalo's shoulders. They felt like railroad ties, and Thalo's knees actually started to buckle—that without any downward pressure. And before he could say a word, the man thrust that strange bland face close to his own and grinned the widest, most evil grin Thalo had ever seen.

Sara promptly stopped struggling, became so tense he feared she might shatter if she moved. And then, in a queerly cadenced voice that was totally at odds with her normal tones, she uttered one very disturbing phrase. Almost Thalo blanked it as soon as it was spoken, for it was one of those things so removed from his primary reality it almost had no meaning. But then, by its very alienness, it *did* connect, and something told him that, though delivered by his sister's tongue in a version of her voice, those words carried another's intent. But what she said, what fell like cold stone from her lips was simply this: *"Red Wounds must remain in the Cathedral. If he does not, I will kill you when you sleep."*

Abruptly, she relaxed, became so flaccid Thalo nearly dropped her. Something swished nearby, the weird buzzing clogged his head again, and when he blinked back to conventional cognizance, the hooded man was gone.

Thalo had no desire to search for him, though something awful—and unbelievable—had just occurred. Instead, he clutched Sara tightly and plunged back into the crowd, cutting through it like a laser through ice.

Cathy met him at the limo, along with a glowering Ambassador Red Wounds. And, short of spouting what would surely be construed as nonsense right there in the middle of Cathedral Square, Thalo had no choice but to relinquish the child. She seemed perfectly normal now, and he knelt down, hugged her very tightly indeed, and kissed her one more time, whispering (though his words seemed appallingly superficial and hollow), "The limo's got TV too. Cathy'll let you watch whatever you want. Why, I bet they've even got cartoons."

"Sure I do, honey," Cathy laughed, and drew the child away. Thalo bit his lip, and rose. With six-plus adults,

two of whom were Embassy security, nearby, she was as safe as she reasonably could be, certainly as safe as with him. Still, his eyes misted and he shivered, even as he squared his shoulders, muttered hurried apologies to every Cherokee in sight, and took the place Red Wounds indicated in the line that was forming nearby.

A moment later, they were moving: pacing slowly toward St. Tekawitha's, with Thalo bearing the Kituwah standard. Before he knew it, the facade was looming over them: a symphony of nouveau-Gothic stone. The towers rose above, wavering in the midday glare but casting no shadows, for they were as insubstantial as sunlight.

Thalo shuddered, so that he feared he would drop the heavy bronze pole. That approaching arch of tympanum above the massive central door reminded him far too much of a certain looming grey hood; and the tenuous towers beyond, of shifting reality. He chose not to consider the antique gargoyles. He already had his own demons.

And then fate swept him forward into history.

Chapter XXX:
Aerial View

(North of Aztlan)
(Saturday, September 10—early afternoon)

"Liam's back!" Floyd called from the Gulfstream's cockpit. "You'd better get up here!"

Carolyn couldn't tell if he was frightened or elated, but that one comment plopped a whole new batch of anxieties atop the mountain she'd, for the last hour, been sorting. Scowling, she swiveled her seat around toward the aisle and rose, hands braced against chrome rails at either side of the bulkhead between the passenger lounge and the control deck. As if acknowledging her attention, the plane promptly lurched, then angled down. A glance out the ports showed the same view as earlier: water, water everywhere, with an occasional sprinkle of islands. But now, to the right, a larger smudge might be the mainland: the horn of Mexico proper, or the Yucatan Peninsula; she couldn't tell. Aztlan lay on the curve between.

Which meant they'd crash into something dry instead of wet if things went awry, as Floyd had hinted they might, should Liam rouse too soon. As already might be happening.

But then the plane leveled again and continued on: smooth as a marble on glass. False security, maybe. But there was only one way to lay that demon. And with that in mind, she slipped into the cockpit proper.

Floyd rose from where he'd been wedged into the steward's jumpseat. His eyes were tired; his face wore the same tight frown it had assumed when the wilder part

of the current madness began. His posture was cautiously relaxed, though: guarded, but not on red-alert. He was, in short, impossible to read.

''What—?'' she began.

He pointed to the control board, where both steering wheels were presently unmanned, though each moved subtly, in synch. ''Autopilot,'' he whispered. ''Sean shifted to that as soon as Liam started mumbling and moving his hands. Best I can tell, kid's trying to maintain his trance *and* keep Liam under control at the same time. I thought you might be able to help.''

Carolyn started to protest, then steeled herself and nodded. Claiming the other jumpseat, she closed her eyes and willed her consciousness toward her brother and the pilot.

And found confusion. Instead of the crystal clarity that would normally have been the men's *selves*, she sensed a tangled mass of muddle. No, more a net stretched thin between two torches, one of which shone bright and clear, though with a hint of flicker, while the other was dimmer and prone to flares and sparking. As best she could tell, the stronger—Sean—was drawing information from Liam, while simultaneously feeding him raw will-power and editing out certain memories and responses: a delicate balance for certain.

Before she knew it, she had become a third pole in that web. Sean felt her there immediately, and she could almost hear his sigh of relief. *Follow me*, he told her. *I will keep the link to the flying skills; you take over the other. Find the . . . good things and build on them, and if the bad would join them, wall it off, as I am doing. Simply turn off your thinking and copy. Like . . . a word in a foreign language. Forget the meaning, but try to repeat the sound perfectly. That is all you need to do. It is a reflex, not a conscious act.*

And since that message was delivered as much via feelings and images as actual words, Carolyn responded. Thread by thread she traced Sean's thoughts to Liam's and made her own connections, freeing her brother for other endeavors. Over and over she did that, instinctively

balancing the strengthening and the shielding. And then the effort lessened abruptly—because Liam was taking control himself. Delicately—carefully, lest she have responded too soon—she eased her thoughts free of his, aware when she reached the surface level that Sean and Liam were engaged in a rapid exchange of information. And when she blinked back to primary reality, it was to Floyd looking vastly relieved and Sean venting an enormous sigh when Liam mumbled, "I'll take it from here, lad. I seem to have . . . dreamed the big picture about the plot; you can pass on the details later. Now, where're we goin'?"

"Aztlan," father and daughter chorused as one. "We've gotta hurry," Carolyn added.

Liam nodded dazedly and tweaked his headphones. Carolyn watched intently while he conversed with someone in Aztlan Tower. As best she could tell from half a conversation, there was strong resistance to them landing. The International Airport was apparently closed until two hours after the funeral. The Jetport, which served the business and diplomatic communities, was theoretically still functioning, but there seemed to be a problem with Liam not having filed a flight plan. He was rising to the occasion, however, and bullshitting like mad, claiming the Eirish Ambassador was aboard, running late, and would appreciate his limo be waiting on the runway— and counting on bureaucracy and backlogged communications to prevent anyone knowing that O'Neal had actually arrived by commercial carrier half a day before. The Ambassador had been unavoidably detained, he added, but still hoped to make the Mass on time, so they'd prefer there be no trouble at customs. A series of numbers followed, verifying Liam's identity and the plane's serial number. A moment later, he relaxed, removed the phones, and twisted around to face them, grinning like a fool. "We're cleared to land," he chuckled. "We're in a holdin' pattern 'tween the President of Latvia and the Chairman of Royal Dutch Shell."

"What does that mean in real time?" Floyd wondered.

"Should be on the ground in less than fifteen minutes."

"And then?" From Carolyn.

A shrug. "I think, lass, that's your call."

Carolyn grimaced sourly. "I was afraid you'd say that." A pause, then: "Any chance you could raise either the Kituwah, Dineh, or Eirish Embassies? Or the Mounties? Say it's an emergency."

Liam shrugged. "I'll give it a shot."

The shot, alas, went wide. All three embassies were closed. The Mounties routed them through a dozen levels of bureaucracy to a tired-sounding woman who seemed more interested in getting names, addresses, and numbers than the problem at hand. Likely she'd feed them into some database of cranks. No way anyone could mount a reasonable investigation in two hours, especially as Carolyn was Nobody, Liam only worked for Somebody, Sean didn't exist anywhere on the planet—in print or on the Net—and Floyd was just another North American. Their "emergency report" was thus on hold as well: lost in a slowly-narrowing spiral of potential crazies, each with his own private concept of hell. Trouble was, *her* version was true.

Everyone else . . . well, as much emotion as had filtered through Aztlan lately, death threats and conspiracy theories were probably packed twenty deep in the Mounties' files.

With nothing left to do forward, she returned to her seat in the cabin. The dark line of mainland had grown clearer. She wished her own battle plan was as obvious.

If impatience were a fatal disease, Carolyn figured she'd be dead by now. And the worst thing was that there was nothing to look forward to: no goal after which she could relax and know it was all over. Instead, there was a looming dark blankness vaguely labeled "plot," with a plethora of lesser nebulosities bouncing around it like cartoon cannibals around a pot of stewing missionaries she thought of as "threats." As to specifics—there just

wasn't much to go on. For the millionth time she reviewed the facts.

The orcas were planning a mass assassination; that was a given. The best place for one was the Archbishop's funeral: another fact. What it entailed, she had no idea. Though the range of the creatures' talents was impressive, she had little sense of their limitations, and Sean, for all his selective flashes of brilliance, was scarcely more helpful. The most useful thing she'd gleaned from him was last night's comment about the way orcas thought: that because they lived a long time in what she considered a slow-paced environment, they therefore tended to *think* slowly. Their plot, then, would likely have been in place long before the hurricane she, 'Bird, and Kevin had aborted. Shoot, this could easily be a fall-back: more complex and wide-ranging, but equally long in the planning. The hit-list, on the other hand, could only have been compiled recently, because only in the last week had the orcas known any of the people—save perhaps Red Wounds and the Hero Twins (if that's who "twins" meant)—who were on it. But even for slow thinkers a week was plenty of time to construct such a list.

Yet a possible weakness showed in the clumsiness of their various . . . executions. Given time, they could surely have concocted less obvious ways of effecting the same results than, for instance, an awkwardly rendered and very blatant attack on five people on an island. Those were not good odds, and the haste with which it had been attempted hinted of a perceived *need* for haste—a deadline, even—which led her to suspect that they regarded herself and her cohorts as threats to the plot itself.

Which gave her hope that there were weaknesses in their adversaries' plans, yet filled her with massive frustration because she couldn't figure out what those flaws might be. Were-orcas, though overtly human, were too suspicious-looking to allow themselves to be seen en masse in public, and with the added security bound to be in effect around a state funeral, no way they'd simply attack. They therefore had to be working through an in-

termediary—like mentally deficient people. But even then, the controlled parties would be fairly obvious. Something more subtle was called for: some sort of inside job—but what? That was where the glitch lay.

There was also something to do with music, but again, what? The Mass would be in the cathedral. The cathedral had an organ. The Hero Twins were accomplished musicians. What did all that imply?

Well, the orcas she'd battled before had worked weather magic via a collective mental bonding that supported the "psychic singing" that had manipulated the latent forces of the earth. But that had been at sea, with them in their own bodies. What could they do on land? Or would it even *be* on land?

Taking a sip from the whiskey she'd been nursing since returning aft, she gazed out the window again. True to Liam's announcement, they were descending toward Aztlan, describing a tightening spiral that had first taken them around the city's southern end, then north over the foothills of the Sierras, and then east toward the ocean. They were on their third pass now, and very low indeed, paralleling the nearly perfect crescent of *El País*. One more pass ought to do it.

"Landing in three," Liam called on the com. At which point she heard a scuffling and saw her dad scrambling to take the seat across from her. She reached out and took his hand. "I wish I knew what to do," she groaned.

"You'll figure something out," he assured her. "Or I will—or Sean. Or Liam. There's too much brainpower here not to."

She smiled wanly and looked out the window again.

And got a shock, for in just that brief while their altitude—and speed—had decreased noticeably. Landmarks were absurdly easy to spot now, not only major buildings and streets, but minor routes and access roads, and smaller structures. Cars were no longer vague rectangles, but individual shapes; sedans discrete from vans, and vans from pickups or convertibles. Someone keen on such things could probably distinguish specific makes—especially as every one of those vehicles seemed to be

either parked or caught in a sea of gridlock that grew
denser the closer to Cathedral Square one got. A few
major streets were clear, however, and she could see the
occasional motorcade sweeping along them, generally attended by flashing lights. Some vehicles even sported
recognizable flags: Saudi Arabia, India, and Mitsubishi,
to name three. And crowding around that mass of becalmed tech were people: thousands and thousands of
them, all making for St. Tekawitha's, the majority clad
in black.

And then the plane banked suddenly, and they were
buzzing the northern residential area, where the estates
of Aztlan's elite snuggled between the beltway and *El
País*, on the fringe of the hills that bracketed the city on
that side. The Jetport lay beyond, right at the rim of the
Zone. Once they arrived . . . well, it'd be damned tough
to get anywhere, what with all that gridlock.

Lower and lower, and she couldn't help but enjoy the
view, as one palatial estate after another was revealed,
most in parklike enclosures behind high walls. One in
particular drew her gaze because of the publicity that had
attended its construction: a quasi-Maya palace-cum-
temple complex that, though nominally the property of a
reclusive entertainment mogul so secretive no one even
knew his name, was in fact known by anyone in the know
to be the retreat of the Hero Twins. Everyone had seen
it from outside. Far fewer knew what lay within.

It looked like she'd be doing a bit of surreptitious spying, though, because their route was taking them right
over it. It was damned impressive, too, with all that stone,
and those myriad courtyards and colonnades, yet still
with plenty of greenery about. Water too: far more than
was actually Maya, in fact.

Not that Aztlan lacked water—salt water, anyway. A
veritable maze of canals, some decorative some not,
threaded the city. And one of the larger traversed the
Twins' compound as well. She could see the grill through
which it breached the western wall, then the quadrangle
of what was effectively a man-wide moat parallelling the
wall fifty meters in, occasionally crossed by bridges.

Even more interestingly, those canals continued on to form a second moat around the house proper, from which two arms vanished beneath the structure, to reappear in the rearmost courtyard, where they widened into an enormous pool.

And by then they were low enough to make out the statues, friezes, and frescoes that decorated the walls there. Abruptly, Carolyn's heart turned over; chills raced across her skin.

That pool was occupied! Dark shapes swam and swerved around each other there—easily half a dozen.

Not *human* shapes, however. Nosiree!

What she was seeing, and had degrees enough to render close inspection unnecessary, were orcas.

—In a pool on the edge of Aztlan, yet connected with the sea via the omnipresent canals.

—Apparently untroubled by being on the premises of a pair of famous eco-rockers.

Musicians . . .

The plot involved musicians . . .

But . . . the Twins were solid corporate citizens! They were clean; they hobnobbed with the world's elite. They influenced policy.

But what had wrought the orcas' enmity toward mankind?

The environment. Specifically, the damage her kind had wrought on land and sea. The orcas' agenda, as far as she knew, had always been to stop pollution by walloping land-based civilization with enough natural disasters to hurl mankind back to the stone age, from whence, presumably, it would never again rise to technization.

It was a bold plan—and wildly optimistic. It was also a threat from a quarter no one would expect, using means—magic—that didn't officially exist.

So were the Twins in cahoots with the orcas or not? *That* was a damned hard call.

But then something occurred to her, and her heart twitched all over again. The Twins were clean—now—but that hadn't always been the case. They'd once been

famous dope-heads; had in fact made a big deal about their reformation.

But perhaps they weren't reformed at all! Or maybe during that shadowy period something had stepped in while they were tripping and strapped down the controls, leaving them on autopilot. If Liam were any indication, it would've only taken once: one drug-induced stupor; one alcohol-born haze.

Of course that was only theory, but it jibed nicely with the data at hand. Her mouth popped open with a start, even as the plane jolted as the landing gear went down.

"Landing in two," Liam informed them.

Carolyn barely heard. "Dad—Sean," she cried. "Soon as we land, be ready to hit the ground running."

"Good," Sean called back brightly. "I'll bring Kevin."

Chapter XXXI:
Confluence

(Aztlan)
(Saturday, September 10—early afternoon)

"First thing that's gone right today," 'Bird sighed, as lock bolts withdrew with a whir in the wall beside the eastern postern gate of the Hero Twins' compound. He didn't like this place: the alley between two estates in the ritzy northwest quarter of town; it was too closed in, too confining. What with walls towering at least two meters above his head, it reminded him far too much of the alley in which he'd been attacked and almost skinned alive by werkas. Then again, all alleys would probably remind him of that for a good long time to come. That this one was traversed further on by a canal didn't help; there'd been water in *that* alley too.

At least their break-in wasn't as blatant as it would've been had they assailed the main gate that fronted the boulevard behind them. Shoot, he shouldn't complain at all, given that it was Aztlan's fire codes alone that required these corridors between estates whose primary structures were more than a quarter klom from a highway. Things could've been much harder.

A final flourish of something Stormy pocketed before 'Bird could note it, and his friend was motioning him and Hosteen Lox toward the carved stone panel that had just separated itself from the rest of the wall and was silently swinging inward. "How'd you *do* that?" 'Bird wondered, as he edged through the opening.

"Fire department has a master code that opens all

these things," Stormy grinned. "I was surfing the security nets one time and found it by accident. Figured it'd come in useful."

"You get the luck I don't," 'Bird grumbled from what proved to be a narrow side garden. "But I reckon this is no time to bitch."

"I'll consider it *lucky* if we don't set off a zillion alarms," Stormy snorted as he joined him. Behind them, Lox was silent, but 'Bird could tell by his eyes that he missed nothing.

"Suggestions?" 'Bird wondered edgily. "This is a mondo big place."

Stormy shrugged. "I saw this setup from the air one time—it's hard to miss, with the bogus pyramid and all—and if memory serves, there's a big pool in the rear courtyard—which is where I'd hang out if I was an orca fakin' it on land and might go fish again any time I hurt myself too bad. Plus, if they're posing as live-in security, they'd want to keep a low profile, so they'd probably stay in the servants' quarters, and those're usually in the back, if there are any."

"Sounds like a plan," 'Bird sighed. "Let's do it."

Fortunately, the garden was fringed on three sides by shoulder-high privet that didn't quite butt up against the walls, so that they had decent cover as they skirted its perimeter en route to the square-pillared portico that comprised the fourth side, pausing every few steps to watch and listen.

"No noise," Stormy noted. "No residual hums or anything. It's like everything's . . . turned off."

"Earth Hour, maybe?" 'Bird ventured.

"Could be. Seems more like the place has just been . . . abandoned."

'Bird regarded him skeptically. "You can tell that already?"

Another shrug. "Maybe I'm still flyin' from the Way."

Hosteen Lox joined them. "Maybe," he mused, "but you're right. A place this big, there'd be people talking, sprinklers going, somebody mowing grass—music—and

there isn't. Doesn't mean we oughta drop our guard, though.''

"Wouldn't dream of it," Stormy grunted, skulking toward the arcade—which evidently doubled as a garage for a squadron of expensive-looking bicycles. 'Bird eyed them appreciatively, even as Stormy urged him on.

Three large rooms, two small courtyards, and four halls later, 'Bird began to trust his friends' hunches and relax. They'd found no sign of present occupancy, though evidence of *people* was everywhere, once they'd left the more formal areas up front. It was subtle at first: a cigarette butt here, a bottle cap there, a scrap of paper somewhere else. And there'd been braziers all over the place, in which incense had obviously been burned—none emptied, much less cleaned. Indeed, a few were still warm, and one actually smoked. Lox inhaled the fumes and wrinkled his nose, then frowned at his companions meaningfully. "Copal, cedar—and something else: some kinda underscent." He sniffed again. "Don't like it. Makes my head cloudy—just one snort. Sneaky, though.''

'Bird's gaze locked with Stormy's, matching his scowl of alarm. "You mean, cloudy like . . . high?"

Lox took another whiff. "Enough of it . . . yeah, I'd say so.''

'Bird inhaled in turn. "Damn!" he spat. "This smells like the stuff Rudy was burnin' the night I stayed over!"

Stormy's eyes went huge. "And if you were drunk on top of it, would you say it might put you in an . . . altered state of consciousness? One where you'd be suggestible—by werkas, say?"

'Bird bit his lip. "Could be. It was still damned strong when I found Rudy; maybe that's how that one made me run in front of that car.''

"Oh, jeeze!" Stormy breathed. "This is bad! 'Cause if the Twins are snorting this all the time, and they're holding Outer Earth meetings here, and werkas've wormed their way into being security for 'em . . . Well, the critters'd be in a perfect position to manipulate all kind of things.''

"One answer down," 'Bird muttered, "—maybe. Another thousand to go."

No one responded, so Stormy led the way into a suite of large, luxuriously decorated rooms, all of which opened onto a garden court—likely, so they speculated, the Twins' living quarters. Or so the number of personal effects strewn about indicated—along with the amount of half-consumed food and drink littering the low cedar tables and polished marble floor. The opposite side of the adjoining arcade ended in an arch that let onto a long hall from which another eventually branched left, revealing a number of doors spaced with the dull regularity of a motel. All were unlocked, and proved to be sparsely furnished bedrooms: basically a rumpled futon on the floor, a low chest, a wall-sized TV—and—far too often—a can of Spraskin atop a blood-spotted towel. Stormy eyed the last two with a muttered "I don't *wanta* know!"

'Bird backed into the hall and paced his companions to where it kinked around a corner onto a long doorless corridor. Another corner—and Stormy slowed, motioning his companions to silence. 'Bird caught the first real noise he'd heard in all that vast pile: the tinkling splash of water into water. "Bingo," Stormy mouthed, flattening against the wall, before checking around the bend. 'Bird mirrored him.

An arcade pierced that passage a third of the way down on the right, and 'Bird held his breath as he shadowed Stormy toward it, pistol poised, every sense alert. Half a meter shy of the opening, Stormy turned, raised an eyebrow, then hunkered down and peeked around at waist level. 'Bird saw him relax even as he rose and waved them through. "Bingo," Stormy repeated—aloud.

It was a pillared courtyard like all the others, only larger and centered by an enormous swimming pool, at one end of which a fountain played, the whole bordered by stone pavement easily six meters wide. The eastern edge, 'Bird noted, was breached by a shallow trough through which water flowed beneath a grating. "Bet that ties into the canals," he observed. Stormy indicated the

opposing side, where a much wider and deeper equivalent was spanned by a picturesque bridge.

"Bad things here," Hosteen Lox rasped abruptly.

'Bird swung around to look at him—and got a shock. The old *hataalii*'s hands were trembling uncontrollably. Lox stared at them—glared at them, rather—and they stopped, but only after he'd clamped them hard together.

Stormy strode closer to the pool, kicking at a crumpled pink-and-tan towel someone had abandoned at the foot of one of the lounge chairs ranged around the pool. And jumped back instantly. "Oh shit!" he gasped. "Oh fucking shit!"

'Bird crept up beside him, looked down—and felt a chill of horrible recognition. "Skin," he hissed. "One of 'em's sloughed off right here."

Stormy looked him straight in the eye. "And what does *that* tell you?"

'Bird blanked momentarily—he was that burnt out—but then a number of things occurred to him at once. "They don't usually do that unless they're under duress. Only there's no sign of that—nothing obvious, anyway."

"Which means," Stormy grinned, "that whoever left that didn't plan to return."

"Nor," Lox noted, "did anyone clean up after him."

'Bird had been surveying the area carefully. "There's more," he observed, pointing to the far corner. "Looks like a bunch of 'em over there."

Stormy raised an eyebrow. "Guess we just missed the exodus; I bet they all split when the motorcade did."

"So maybe," 'Bird whispered, "those guys don't plan to come back either."

"But why leave the skins, when they need 'em to pass as human—and, more to the point, when they're so hard to come by? I mean, everybody they have to skin is one more risk. They're not stupid; they'd have to know that!"

Lox scratched his head. "Suppose you're right, though; suppose they *didn't* intend to return; that whatever they were doing here was finished. Then suppose that whatever they're planning at the Cathedral will kill

a lot of people, including the Hero Twins—their name *was* on that list you found, wasn't it?''

'Bird fished it out of his pocket and checked, though he knew already. "Yep."

"So whatever hits at the funeral involves the Twins, then *kills* the Twins. An investigation follows. They check out this place and find—''

"—Skins!" Stormy finished. "Of course! It's perfect: They leave the skins as evidence! The Twins are rock stars, so they're automatically suspect if anything weird goes down. And then the Mounties find skins at their compound, and the Twins get blamed for all those flay-ings. And there's the bogus temple, so that ties into the Xipetotec stuff: the revival of the old Aztec religion!''

'Bird scowled. "But Xipe's not Aztec, and neither are the Twins. And the Mounties know who's actually skinned those folks—a lot of 'em, anyway—and this doesn't fit with that!''

"Yeah, but even a lot of smart folks don't bother to distinguish between the two—like most Mounties. And there *is* evidence of mind-control goin' on with the in-cense. It wouldn't be *that* big a leap to thinking the Twins were controlling those folks instead of things nobody knows exist.''

"I dunno," 'Bird muttered. Then froze. Stormy did too. And Lox.

Footsteps sounded in the corridor by which they'd en-tered. And breathing: heavy—someone in a hurry.

"Shit!" Stormy growled, motioning them to cover be-hind the assorted lounge chairs, planters, and statuary.

'Bird crouched into the scanty obscurity of a potted saguaro and waited nervously, holding his breath as he thumbed the pistol's safety off and aimed it at the en-trance. One lounger up, Stormy mirrored his action. Lox was behind him. The moment stretched endlessly.

And . . . movement: a shadow-shape behind the en-trance columns. He released his breath slowly; drew a second. His hand shook. He steadied it with the other. A spot of crimson light blossomed on the pillar nearest the shadow. Stormy was taking no chances.

More steps, further back. A figure moved forward. Another, smaller one lurked behind. Awfully small for a werka, but 'Bird slid his finger to the trigger anyway. A second only it would take. A second . . .

A too-familiar buzzing clogged his head: that disconcerting sensation of werkas fooling around with his mind. He tried to shut it out—and succeeded; but that only confirmed his fears. His finger twitched.

The figure stepped into the light. His finger tightened. Another millimeter and—

The point of ruby light skipped sideways—

—and *up*, as Stormy rose abruptly. "Clear, guys," he called—by which time 'Bird had yelled "Cary!"—and realized that such enthusiasm was stupid, given that they merely assumed that the compound was deserted. Not that it mattered—now.

Carolyn started as though she'd actually been shot, and might've fallen, had that smaller figure not rushed up to steady her. A boy, it was: slim, good-looking, shirtless, and with a preposterous flag of blue-black hair. "Is that what I think it is?" 'Bird muttered as he and Stormy strode forward.

"Probably," Stormy replied on the fly, by which time a third figure had joined Carolyn and the boy: older man—fifties to early sixties, but fit; with bright, intelligent eyes that also looked a trifle dazed. He was, incongruously, lugging a pair of medium-sized coolers. A fourth man brought up the rear: young, stubbly red hair, fatigue-clad, and erect. Soldier type. He did not, however, sport any obvious weapon; and there was an odd hesitancy about his movements, as though he had to concentrate on them. On the point of relaxing, 'Bird tensed all over again.

Carolyn, who was in the lead, followed his gaze while continuing to approach. "He's cool," she said without preamble. "He's got a problem, but he's . . . safe."

They were within easy speaking distance now, but 'Bird couldn't stop being wary. It was as though each side distrusted the other. Abruptly, he felt that mental clogging again, and slowed. Cary laughed. It was a real

laugh, but 'Bird sensed a taut edge to it: one not far from hysteria. And she looked awful. She was also regarding him curiously—and rather sympathetically. She laughed again. "Sorry," she sighed, letting her shoulders slump, "someone's obviously been prowling around in your mind and got you all jumpy."

'Bird shook his head. "Not some*one*: some*thing*."

"The somethings we're lookin' for," Stormy added. "Which raises the question—"

"—what're we doing here?" Carolyn finished for him. "Same thing you are, I suspect; and fine timing it is, I must say."

"Not luck, though," Lox said, and fell silent.

Throughout their interchange, the boy's eyes had flitted about like a laser beam in a maze of mirrors, while the older man hung back looking pensive. All at once the lad's eyes fixed on what had been hidden behind 'Bird, Lox, and Stormy. "Skins!" he snarled. "They've left their skins."

The older man immediately pushed forward. There was something familiar about him, but 'Bird couldn't place what. "Seems like we've jumped into the middle without bothering with the start," the man said, extending a hand to 'Bird, who stood closest. "I'm Floyd Mauney: Cary's dad."

Cary jerked as though she'd been shot, then relaxed. *God, she's jumpy*, 'Bird thought. Then again, she had a right to be, given where she was. She vented another nervous laugh. Then: "Sorry, guys. It's been a tough pair of days, and looks like it's gonna get tougher, so I've kinda got sloppy about manners. We're in a hurry, see; and—"

"So're we," Stormy interrupted. "And much as I'd like to stand here playin' the leisurely intro game, we'd best get 'em over, and find out what the hell we're all doin' here."

Carolyn nodded. "You've met my . . . dad. And this is Sean. He's a—"

"Selkie," Sean and Stormy chorused as one. Then, from Stormy: "I know."

"*I* know we've gotta hurry," 'Bird snapped edgily, much of his impatience due to the fact that he was running on pure adrenaline. If he relaxed for long . . . Well, he wasn't sure what would happen, but it wouldn't improve either his reflexes or alertness, both of which he expected to need at full strength soon.

Carolyn flopped down on the edge of the nearest planter. "Okay, guys; we have to start someplace, and where it started for us was when I . . ."

Ten minutes later, the short form of both sets of adventures had been sketched, ending with Floyd pretending to be Ambassador O'Neal and commandeering the limo he'd left at the airport—Liam had a diplomatic ID and had claimed to be O'Neal's driver, and indeed often served in that capacity. "Whew!" 'Bird whistled, when the older man had finished. "So what do we have to go on here?"

Stormy counted on his fingers. "One: we both know there's a werka hit list that includes everybody here and a bunch of our friends"—he'd tactfully omitted mentioning Rudy, likely because Carolyn's tale had already included the deaths of two people she was close to—maybe three, depending on how one counted Kevin, who might be dead or might not.

"Two: we've both figured out that there's some kind of werka plot to do *something* unpleasant at the funeral, probably involving that hit list.

"Three: what me, 'Bird, and Hosteen Lox knew but you either didn't know or only suspected, is that it most likely involves Outer Earth and the Hero Twins."

"And what *we* knew and you didn't," Carolyn concluded, "is that it also, apparently, involves music."

"Which means we need to get there fast."

"Wherever there is."

"The Cathedral, I'd assume."

"And what do we do there?" Carolyn wondered. "Since none of us seem to have any luck getting hold of anyone useful, or being believed if we do."

'Bird shrugged helplessly and looked at Stormy, who

looked at Lox, who shrugged in turn. "Trouble is," Stormy said finally, "we don't know how the assassinations are supposed to occur."

'Bird, who'd consumed the dregs of his patience hearing things he already knew recapitulated, started to say something harsh, rash, and stupid, but just then Sean, who'd been prowling the courtyard like an animal confined too long, pranced up with a grin on his face that could've lit a small city.

"What?" Carolyn demanded.

The grin widened—which 'Bird had thought impossible. "When I was riding in Liam's head, I learned some things I didn't know I learned. One of them is what a terminal looks like. I have found one here. It is still on—"

Before he could finish, Floyd was pushing past him, with Stormy close behind. The rest followed. By the time 'Bird arrived—an alcove set in a corner, with a carved stone seat occupying one side and the usual screen and keyboard opposite—Stormy and Floyd were already debating who would have first go.

"What's the deal?" 'Bird grumbled. "Do we have time for this?"

Stormy grimaced, even as he conceded the seat to the older man, whose fingers proceeded to dance across the keys. "No reason to have a setup this complex in a place like this; voice-op's enough for housekeeping. But this is a lot more than that; in fact, it looks like a data base."

'Bird frowned. "Don't werkas have photographic memories? Why would they need to keep anything on disc?"

"Not for themselves," Stormy replied. "I bet it's more of the plot. Their plan succeeds—they hope. Everybody dies—including the Twins. The Mounties check this place. They find the skins. They find a computer 'accidentally' left on. In it they find a database, but not one that's so secure they can't get into it—which they're intended to. In that, they find plans for the plot."

"Sounds like a stretch," 'Bird snorted.

"Maybe," Stormy conceded. "But we'd be crazy not to check."

"I'm in," Floyd announced. "Now where should I look?"

"Try Outer Earth," Stormy suggested. And Floyd set to work.

'Bird couldn't take it anymore: all this inaction. They were burning daylight, dammit, and typical of computer jocks, the moment Stormy and Floyd saw a terminal, all need for haste evaporated, as hacking became its own end. Venting a gritted "Fuck this!" he strode down the arcade. Maybe *he* could find something useful—and unencumbered with tech.

A door stood open to the right and he sauntered reck-lessly in—even a fistfight would help right now, though it would be pain on top of pain on top of pain. The semi-gloom made him blink, but he'd already made out what might've been military barracks—the place was that aus-tere. Two beds to either side. Plain mattresses, no cover. No pillows either, no comforts at all. The only items of note were a TV built into the far wall, a sofa facing it, and a control pad dropped carelessly atop the latter. A storage cubby showed below the screen. 'Bird opened it curiously. It was full of video discs, and he nearly slammed it again in disgust until he noticed one lying atop the others, which, atypically, bore a scrawled nota-tion in longhand so poorly rendered it looked like a child's script. He fished it out, squinting to decipher it. *Bloodletting*, it read, along with the date: the previous night. Scowling, he told the TV "On" and inserted the disc, then stepped back against the wall, so as to keep tabs on the entrance. The screen promptly resolved into a long view of what proved to be the courtyard with the bogus temple. It was night, and the place was lit by torches. Scores of young people thronged there, many in Outer Earth T-shirts. Braziers full of incense smoked everywhere, which seemed to confirm their suspicions about the stuff. He perked up at that, eyes narrowed in-tently.

Abruptly, the view shifted to an interior—probably the

temple at the top of the stairs, which they hadn't had time to check earlier. The view was from high-up, likely via a hidden camera, and showed some sort of altar and two werkas—dressed in something besides hooded over-cloaks, though these robes too were hooded. As he watched, two men entered wearing elaborate costumes he recognized from countless magazine covers and TV appearances as Blowgunner and Jaguar Deer, the Hero Twins. A third figure stood between them, slighter but nearly as tall, and clad only in a skimpy breechclout. There was something familiar about him too. 'Bird peered closer, wishing there were some way to get a better view, but then the guy turned to sit on a low platform before the altar, and 'Bird's mouth dropped open in amazement.

It was Thalo! Poor, well-intentioned, naive little Thalo! Well, *he'd* certainly wasted no time pursuing his goals—though what he was doing *here* . . .

'Bird found out soon enough—and had to avert his gaze from the worst part: *nobody* should have to undergo that! Never mind that such a private act of self-humiliation had also, apparently, provided vicarious entertainment for . . . probably werkas.

Another muttered curse, and he ejected the disc in disgust—just as Sean poked his head in. " 'Bird?" he called. "We've got something."

"So do I," 'Bird growled. He pocketed the disc and returned to his friends.

Stormy looked up wide-eyed. "Got a list here you might wanta look at."

'Bird's mind was still on his own discovery. "Sure," he agreed absently. He flopped against the wall, eyeing the terminal where Floyd was conjuring screen after screen of data.

"It's a list of new members of Outer Earth," Stormy supplied. "Evidently they held some kind of initiation last night."

'Bird stared at the glowing print. Under the general heading *OUTER EARTH: NEW MEMBERS* was the subhead *NEW GOVERNING COUNCIL* and beneath that, one entitled

NEW INITIATES: CONDITIONED. A list of names followed, and 'Bird found himself scanning for one in particular. He found it all too quickly: fifth from the top. "I know that guy," he said, pointing.

Stormy frowned. "John Gordon? Where do you know him from?"

"Thalo," 'Bird corrected. "He's my intern. He started at the Embassy while you were at Lox's."

"That makes sense," Stormy gave back. "Check the next screen."

Floyd tapped a key. Pixels danced. A new heading appeared: *VIP PAIRINGS: TENTATIVE.* 'Bird found Thalo's name again—and his breath caught. The name linked with the kid's in whatever chip of the plot they'd uncovered was Ambassador-Chief William Red Wounds. "If I had to guess," Stormy ventured, "I'd say he's responsible for spying on your boss."

"Or killing him," Lox countered. " 'Wounds's name was on that list."

'Bird slapped the wall behind him—hard. His hand tingled. "Goddamn!" he spat. "That . . . goddamn fool *kid!*"

Stormy stared at him. "You think he's part of this?"

'Bird puffed his cheeks. "Probably not intentionally, but . . . I'd have to say that he's really romantic and idealistic. He'd be a prime candidate for manipulation."

"And," Carolyn broke in excitedly, "if he had access to someone on the hit-list, they'd want to cultivate him."

Stormy raised a brow. "Like making him think he was important? Like by making him part of their governing council?"

"Telling him that," she corrected. "We already know who's really in control."

Floyd looked dubious. "But . . . how could they acquire so much control over someone so fast?"

'Bird told them about the incense. "And," he continued, flourishing the disc, "I've got more proof right here—if you've got the stomach for it. It's a real leg-crosser, guys."

Lox sighed. "We're running out of time. Still—"

"Now you're talkin'," 'Bird snapped. "TV's next room down."

Less than a minute later, every man in the place gasped as one. Stormy actually yipped, and Carolyn uttered a stunned "Oh gross" and looked away. 'Bird ejected the disc. "Proof that Thalo was here," he announced. "Proof they did something to him."

"I'll say!" Stormy muttered, looking pale. "Talk about being shafted!"

'Bird glared at him. "What puzzles me is why go to so much trouble?"

"Proving loyalty?"

"Yeah, but you'd think that'd scare people off—"

"Unless they had no choice," Stormy gave back. "Or unless they were under the influence of . . . something."

Lox cleared his throat. Everyone fell silent. "One other thing," he said quietly, his accent shifting to a subtly more urbane mode: "Many rituals use blood, including the one we've just seen enacted, which is quite legitimate, historically. Now consider this: we've seen that in some cases at least, the part is equal to the whole—like with shape-shifters, under certain conditions. Our adversaries know this. Suppose, then, that blood, which is part of a whole, also has some power that those versed in certain . . . manipulations can access. Suppose that they acquired your young friend's blood as an additional link to him. Magic worked on one might work on the other."

" 'The blood is the life,' " Floyd quoted.

"So it's their hold on Thalo?" From 'Bird.

Lox shrugged. "One of 'em."

"So what do we do?" Floyd sighed.

Carolyn glared at him. "We try to stop it, of course. Or them."

"Which it?" Floyd gave back. "And which them? And, more to the point, is that really our job? Shouldn't we call the police, or the CIA, or somebody?"

Carolyn rounded on him. "You do that . . . *Dad.* You sit here and get busy signals and hold messages and run-arounds and put-offs until the world goes to hell! I can't.

I—'' She broke off, looked away. Ran her fingers through her hair. "No, I'm sorry; that wasn't fair. It's just that . . . Well, we've dealt with this before, and you can't *handle* it through channels. They take too long, for one thing. And while there're people in power who'd give us a listen, we can't get hold of any of 'em right now—thanks to the damned Earth Hour.''

"So . . .'' Floyd began.

"So,'' Stormy took over, "you stay here—you and Hosteen Lox, since—no offense, but you're older than the rest of us, and this could get physical. Plus,'' he added, to the *hataalii*, "*you've* got a matched pair of holes in your love-handles.''

Floyd started to protest, but Stormy stopped him with a glare. "No, sir: you're right—in part. Someone should try to go through channels, and since you're good at hacking, and since Hosteen Lox knows the lowdown on most of the big stuff, you guys should try to work the system.'' He glanced sideways at the silent Liam. "Somebody needs to keep an eye on him too, looks like; and I'd as soon it wasn't anybody who's got to make fast decisions. As for the rest of us''—he grinned at 'Bird wearily—"we're used to working together, so what we've gotta do is get ourselves to the Cathedral and do what we can on that end. At least we can get more of a grip on what's actually going on. Shoot, maybe we can find somebody with enough clout to delay the whole thing—which would play hell with trying to pin all this on the Twins. And maybe 'Bird can connect with Thalo and find out what *he* knows.''

'Bird nodded. "Sounds good.''

Sean was dancing from foot to foot, looking by turns eager, anxious, worried, and impatient. "What about me?''

Carolyn started to reply, then stopped, gnawing her lip. "I oughta tell you to stay here,'' she growled finally, "'cause you're just a kid—and 'cause you're all the blood kin I've got left. But . . . Dammit, something tells me we might need you.'' She eyed the pool speculatively. "In fact,'' she went on suddenly, "why don't you do the

seal-thing and hop in right here? The canals all connect, and there's a big one behind the Cathedral, so you might even get there ahead of us. They follow a regular grid, so you'd just need to go east and south. Surface when you can and check for landmarks—it's that twin-towered building I showed you from the plane.''

Sean nodded, already en route for the door, then paused with a hand on the jamb and twisted around to look Carolyn straight in the eyes. ''This might be a good time,'' he said softly, but with deadly seriousness in his voice, ''for you to try on Kevin.''

Chapter XXXII:
In the Triforium

(Aztlan)
(Saturday, September 10—early afternoon)

Any other time, Thalo reckoned, attending Green Francis's Requiem would've been the high point of his life. No way it could've failed a romantic like him. Shoot, eschewing the circumstances entirely, it was a display of pomp and ceremony not seen this century, rendered all the more impressive for having been orchestrated in less than two days.

He had a good seat for it too! A good stand, anyway, since Kituwah, as a small, new, and poor (though monetarily self-sufficient) nation merely ranked a place between two rearward piers in the triforium, and he, as drafted banner-bearer, wasn't granted an actual pew like the rest of the delegation. He was, he reflected, window dressing.

But that wasn't necessarily bad. The place he'd been assigned (wedged into the flutes of a pier) offered a fine view of the main door, through which, for the last hour, the world's elite had been processing in the same slow paces the Kituwah crew had automatically assumed—what was it?—forty minutes ago.

That he'd never forget, no matter what else bedeviled him: that long stately march up a quarter klom of shining marble, with gleaming white vaults rising to dizzy heights above, like a forest of frozen sequoias; and stained glass glowing like dreams to either side, their

images enhanced by holo-projectors, so that the Archangel Michael's spear stabbed endlessly into a writhing
dragon, and Adam and Eve strode eternally from the Garden like joggers on a treadmill.

As banner-bearer, he'd come third in line behind two
guards: that place designated by Aztlan's Chief of Protocol, who'd arranged folks at the door as they entered
for maximum TV impact. As such, he'd been reduced to
staring at the head of the woman before him to keep from
gawking. Somehow, he'd avoided tripping as they
mounted the low steps up to the crossing, where he got
a fine view of the north and south transepts thundering
off into distances that in any other place would've been
cathedrals in their own right. Then the inlaid map of the
world was passing beneath his feet, and he'd recalled that
those seas were made of slabs of lapis lazuli and mala-
chite dusted with powdered emeralds and aquamarine;
and that each nation was wrought of some native semi-
precious stone imported from that place, with the capital
marked by a faceted jewel. Nor was the seamless transparent disc that protected it mere lucite; it was actual
glass: a rejected blank from an aborted telescope mirror,
with the strengthening honeycomb laborously ground
down. The whole thing took ten paces to traverse, not
counting the marble compass rose that framed it.

The apse came next, where, just below the high altar,
the rough pine coffin lay. That location had been contro-
versial too. Normally Important Personages lay in state
in the crossing, but His Holiness had pointed out that
since Archbishop Blackmer had transcended the world,
his coffin should likewise transcend it, and that he would
never have allowed his own poor clay to obscure the
earth at large.

There'd been no viewing of the body—not burned as
it was—but their party had circled the bier once, each
person (under the watchful eye of the Vatican's stoic
Swiss guards) allowed to run a hand along the unpainted
wood. He'd dared as much himself—risking disaster by
bracing the heavy banner pole in the crook of his arm—
yet even that brief touch had brought a thrill. The wood

had been smooth, worn nearly to a gloss by a steady stream of pilgrims since being placed there the night before.

And then it was over. From the altar, they'd been pointed up a turnpike stair in one of the crossing piers, from which they'd emerged in the triforium for seating—near the entrance.

And since delegations were paying homage in reverse order of precedence (roughly—it officially dated from the ratification dates of their current constitutions, but also factored in such elements as power, prestige, titles, and who'd arrived when and was impatient) he'd got to see most of the world's elite file by below, no more than fifty meters away. A certain amount of egalitarianism was achieved by limiting all parties to an equal number of constituents, namely ten; otherwise *he'd* not have been there. The banner-bearer for Fiat just passing by was the eleventh son of a Persian Gulf potentate, and New Ukraine's had been a lately authenticated Romanov prince. They'd get to stand too; just like common-born Thalo Gordon.

It was hard not to grin, though—as the sturdy Inuit one set of pews back was doing. Kituwah at least outranked the Arctic Federation, along with the rest of its section, namely the remaining members of the Native Southeastern Confederacy: the Choctaw, Chickasaw, Seminole/Creek, Tunica/Biloxi, and Yuchi in that order; each accorded full autonomous status here, since they were all independent nations who only functioned in concert for convenience—like sharing an embassy block none of them could've afforded otherwise.

At which point the clash of halberds on the floor by the door signaled the arrival of yet another Important Party. Thalo craned his neck, hoping to identify the newcomers by iconography before they were announced.

Green livery on the guards . . . Green flag bearing a golden harp . . . *Eireland*—as the Official Herald (on leave from the Lord Lyon's office in Scotland) proclaimed something incomprehensible in Gaelic, followed by ''The Sovereign Republic of United Eireland; Am-

bassador James Patrick O'Neal representing President
Marjorie MacNamee.'' And a third time, in Spanish.

And another procession began. Halfway down the
aisle, a new group appeared at the door. Once more halberds rang on marble.

Furs and skins: another polar nation. He strained to see
the banner: blue field, two narwhals curving around to
form a circle: the configuration called by heralds *in an-
nulo*.

''Thule,'' the Herald announced, somewhat perplexedly.

Thalo felt a shudder race through him: one of those
capricious chills his grandmother called ''someone walking on your grave.'' He coughed and shifted his feet, then
glanced back at the procession. Something about the flag
troubled him—possibly the narwhals, though that made
no sense. He shifted again.

Red Wounds caught his eye, winked, and grinned. He
grinned back and tried to stand straighter, wondering why
narwhals should affect him so negatively. Probably it'd
simply been the cumulation of excitement that had been
building in him since they'd arrived.

Only . . . that wasn't right either. He closed his eyes,
trying to concentrate; and with that, all the lesser demons
that the overwhelming spectacle around him had thrust
into abeyance came flocking back: those annoying little
mental mumbles that kept this from being the perfect
high it would otherwise have been.

And yet, like vultures, they circled:

Outer Earth: Was it what it claimed to be?

The Hero Twins: genuine nice guys or manipulative
phonies?

Those screwy roadies, who really did have some kind
of mojo working—if nothing else, via raw intimidation
born of their impressive size.

His sister . . .

What in the world was up with Sara? She'd been prone
to weird pronouncements for a while, but that bit about
loving funerals had come right out of left field—since
she'd never been to one save perhaps on TV, to which

she was addicted. More to the point, what was that about killing him while he slept? And why hadn't that put the wind up him more? Shoot, had he even heard it, or was it merely another function of the sensory overload to which he'd been subjected the last few days?

Trouble was, the memory was cloudy, like something glimpsed from the corner of the eye that vanished when viewed directly. God, but this was screwy! He felt like two people, one of whom existed superficially and observed primary reality as it occurred—which was certainly worth observing right now; the other the little guy who sat back and analyzed. Thalo's little guy seemed very busy indeed—clamoring, almost, to make himself heard, like a movie in which someone pounded vainly on a glass wall mouthing words that, while obviously shouted, nevertheless fell on deaf ears. Thalo—surface Thalo—wondered what his deep self wanted.

He closed his eyes, trying to hear—to read those phantom lips—*anything* to shake off this sense that beneath all this panoply something sinister was afoot that he—perhaps—could prevent had he all his functions. Something he should tell Red Wounds. Something he dared *not* tell Red Wounds—or anyone—lest his sister be endangered.

Unbidden, words entered his head: soft persuasive voices from . . . outside. *Yes*, they whispered, *if you do not do as instructed, she will be ours forever. There is no limit to what we might ask her to do.*

"Fuck!" Thalo gasped under his breath, gaze once more seeking Red Wounds, even as he wondered where such a blast of mental bullshit could've come from—beyond his imagination. But at that moment a trio of priests entered the triforium from the far end and marched along the gallery behind them. Softly—clearly in the perfect, computer-tuned acoustics—came the words of an *a capella* anthem: "*Kyrie eleison; Christe eleison. . . .* " They carried thuribles too: incense burners. The Cathedral's efficient air conditioning wafted the fumes toward him as quickly as the voices, and—as by some long-established reflex—he inhaled deeply. With

his second long appreciative whiff, the little man behind the glass fell silent. A check showed Red Wounds slouching sleepily in his pew. *He must stay here*, something told Thalo. *He must!*

Chapter XXXIII:
Skin Tight

(The Hero Twins' Compound)
(Saturday, September 10—early afternoon)

"*Kevin*?" 'Bird puzzled aloud. Then: "Oh, Christ, Cary; you're not gonna—"

A glare silenced him. She wondered when she'd acquired so much power, so much . . . authority. Or maybe it was simply the crazy stress-push she'd been on for what seemed like weeks now, that had made her brook no more patience with delay. Maybe she'd simply run out of energy for explanations or arguments. Maybe, she admitted finally, it was purely desire for revenge. "I seem to recall," she growled, more coldly than intended, "that a week ago tonight you and Mr. Cloud here were trying to talk me—a total stranger you'd rousted out of her warm bed—into putting on a dolphin skin. 'You don't want its death to have been in vain,' as I recall. Well, I don't want Kev's to be in vain either. Besides," she added nervously. "It might not work."

No one replied, not even Floyd, who, as Kevin's sire, had most right to protest. He wouldn't, though. The flaying had been his decision as much as Kev's, the responsibility his as well. Yet what father would not, if pressed, prefer any existence for a beloved child to none?

Finally, Hosteen Lox took a deep breath. "Whatever you do, you need to hurry."

Sean, who'd seemed ready to explode from sheer impatience, promptly dashed off to retrieve the coolers, returning far too quickly for Carolyn's tastes. She stared at

him for a long moment, then at the innocuous hunks of red-and-white plastic. "I'd prefer to do this in private," she announced at last. "No, on second thought, Sean, you know more about this than anyone, you'd best stick around."

"Sure," the selkie agreed. "It would be an honor."

She studied the room—barracks, or whatever—then caught 'Bird's eye. "Guys . . ."

'Bird motioned the others out. "We'll guard. But if anything goes wrong, for God's sake *yell*."

An instant later, Carolyn stood alone in an austere room with her newfound brother.

For his part, Sean seemed relieved to have something to do. He wasted no time removing the lid from the nearer cooler, but balked at withdrawing the contents—packed in ice from the plane's refrigerator. "If you don't wish to see this, look away and I will hand it to you. It can be no worse for me."

Carolyn gnawed her lip, then nodded. "I'd appreciate it." And with that, she turned and began to strip. It didn't take long to shed the baggy black tunic and jeans she'd swapped into during the flight down from Cumberland, and by the time she finished, the rattle of ice against plastic had ceased. She tried not to hear the slightly raspy hiss that had to be . . . *that* being shaken out. She shivered as she waited, hugging herself, then heard Sean pad up behind her. His heat warmed her. He really was a first-rate guy. No: a first-rate *brother*.

"Hold your arms back and I will do the rest," he urged. "It was not well done around the nails, but it should make no difference. Think of the hands as gloves, and the feet—"

"I understand!" she snapped. "Sorry, but I'm not ready to hear this. I think I need to run on reflex now."

Sean's breath caressed the back of her neck in a way that was far too sensual. She inhaled deeply in turn—and thrust her arms behind her. Her finger brushed something ice-cold and sticky-damp. Her flesh recoiled, but she steeled herself, expecting nothing, even as she extended her arms again. For a moment there was no reaction, but

then she felt Sean's thoughts joining hers ever so gently, and a resistance she didn't know she'd been exerting dissolved—and with it came the first tiny lightning-bolt tingle, as some nameless power buried deep within her—and Kevin too, perhaps—forged a bond between the surface of her skin and the lining of her brother's.

She gasped as prickles raced up her fingers into her wrist, and again as they lapped across her palms, even as they flowed up her forearms. And then it was like an infinitesimal thunderstorm sweeping across her flesh—from her shoulders too, now, where the skin was resting; and the crests of her hips; and her scalp, where Sean had thrown the worst part like a hood.

And then her whole body became an explosion of tingles that were not—quite—pain. It was strange, too, she reflected in that part that sat back and analyzed: like becoming both dolphin and seal—yet different. There was less contortion, for one thing—none, really: likely a function of the fact that she wasn't shifting to something with an utterly alien stance—or none. There *was* an odd stretching, however: mostly in her spine and limbs. And as the storm raged over her face, the effect was akin to the skin-too-tight feel of being badly sunburned.

But the Change was still more than surface, and perhaps *that* was the difference. Or the fact that during those other Changes so much had been happening she'd had no attention left for specifics. Here, it was more superficial—but even as she considered that, the Change worked further inward. Previously, her senses had realigned, while new instincts patterned across her brain. This time her senses stayed nearly the same, and instinct altered less than . . . *memory*. Memory not her own. Feelings, emotions . . . a sense of another self suffocating her. No, not suffocating; expanding. She was everything she'd ever been and more. She was—

A tension in her gut distracted her, and she discovered that certain parts of her had reached an impasse. A twisting-burning-wrenching wracked her groin, as female structure and male surface each sought ascendancy. It was awful—as unpleasant as any aspect of shape-shifting

had ever been—and she found herself resisting the Change. More tingles ensued, and a tearing, followed by a sharp eruption of pain, then a brush of cool air. She promptly relaxed.

No! came Sean's thought sharply. *You are rejecting him. You are starting to change back, and if that occurs, you may fail . . . and lose Kevin in the bargain.*

But I don't want to lose Kevin! But I don't want to lose myself either!

You will not! But you and your brother must choose.

Kev . . . ? she asked automatically.

It doesn't matter. I won't fight you.

It took her a moment to realize that those hadn't been Sean's thoughts, but a third consciousness sharing her mind with herself and her selkie-brother. It was also her first concrete proof that *everything* was working.

Sean broke in again, forcefully; overriding both herself and Kevin. *Be what you will . . . or end this now!*

Her eyes were already closed, so she couldn't shut them further, yet she performed some mental equivalent and slid deeper into whatever state suffered the Change. As she did, the grinding tension in her groin subsided, while a pressure—an external pressure—that had lingered there likewise abated. And in that moment, she could choose. Male or female—or both. On one level a new sex might be fun: an exercise in academic curiosity, if nothing else. But with Kev already haunting the fringe of her consciousness, she needed nothing more to adapt to. And so . . .

A final warping, and the familiar pattern resumed. One last storm of tingles washed her flesh as isolated segments concluded the transformation, and she finally dared open her eyes.

She saw Sean—before her now, and at a higher angle—and met his eyes, which were smiling. He was sweating, though—playing intercessor clearly hadn't been as easy as it seemed.

"Well," he breathed, "that was interesting."

A rush of . . . something caught her unaware; she

sagged against the boy for support. *Careful*, came that other voice. *This is new to me too!*

Kev . . . ?

Who else?

One of us has *to be crazy.*

Or both.

Good to have you back, though.

Good to be back.

Uh, what—?

I share your senses unless I choose not to. My thoughts are my own unless yours are too loud—like having noisy neighbors. Otherwise . . . it's like riding a horse. I have to prod you to make you go where I want, which tires me. It's easier just to let you drive.

Thanks—I guess. And—sorry, but I have to ask— where are you when you're not with me?

A pause. It's like sleeping, like dreaming, except that you can control the dream. It's not bad. It's nothing you have to worry about.

Sorry, but like I said: I had to know. I didn't want to feel like I was killing you every time—

You won't.

That's a relief. But we can . . . discuss it as much as we want to later. For now—

—we have a problem. I know. With what you know that I did not, we now know more than either of us did before. Word and Way we were, once—and separate. But to defeat our foes, we may have to be both together.

The plot?

I know what Sean read in my mind and told you. I know about the hit-list and the assassinations and that it involves music.

There's more, though: things we've only learned in the last little while.

Think them to me, and I'll tell you if you've missed anything important. Together we should know quite a lot.

Carolyn did, and for the briefest instant it was as though her thoughts went on fast-forward. She was aware of a sorting too, with some segments given cursory attention and other minute consideration. A rearranging

seemed also to be in effect, likely Kevin's ascendent artistic right brain trying to make sense of her own, more ordered, left.

Tech, Kevin announced finally: the word settling out of the chaos of her thoughts. *If they're going to use music, and if it's at the Cathedral, it'll almost have to involve tech.*

And?

Well, if we're going to fight them, we should attack where they're not looking—

You mean . . . ?

Probably. We know they're hidebound in their thinking—don't forget I've shared head-space with one. And we know they think of us as working a certain way. So we hit them somewhere else: we hit them with magic.

"Magic!" she cried aloud.

"What?" came Sean's startled reply.

She blinked, shocked to recall that there was still an external world and that a good-looking selkie boy was gazing at her perplexedly. "We fight them with magic," she said.

"Then we have to hurry," he replied, flipping the lid off the remaining cooler with one hand while fumbling with the drawstring on his shorts with the other. An instant later, he was bare. She didn't stare, though he was certainly easy on the eye; rather, she fished through her own clothes, realizing as she found her jeans that she'd been avoiding looking at herself. Well, she couldn't see her face, but the rest . . . She forced herself to look down. Not much different, really, save that she was taller: an even split between herself and Kevin, it appeared, which was borne out by the different angle from which she'd seen Sean. Not quite so round, a bit sparer of fat and leaner of muscle, which was also reasonable, given Kev's wiriness. Her breasts were the same, but looked smaller against her longer torso; and the nipples—her whole skin—had changed color and texture and were now rosier, fairer, and rougher respectively. She had more body hair. The rest of her hair— Well, something brushed her shoulders where her old style had cleared them. The dead

TV was as much mirror as she could find, and confirmed that her face, too, was not her own. Nor was it Kev's. He'd been all angles; she all curves. The new one was pleasantly androgynous, with enough chin, jaw, and cheekbone to give it character, and sufficient darkness in brows and eyes to define them. Her hair, as best she could tell, was auburn.

"You look good," Sean told her tersely. "And you do not look like yourself. But we have to hurry."

She tore her gaze away from that strange new self, found her tunic, and shrugged it on. Sean had his back to her, his seal-skin fully unfurled. "My sister is finished," he called toward the door. "You can enter, if you are curious."

Stormy was first to venture in, followed by 'Bird, then Hosteen Lox, who looked both keenly observant and nonplussed. Floyd arrived last, with the plodding Liam, who, in the absence of Sean's constant mental tweaks, seemed to be lapsing into shock again.

"Wow!" 'Bird yipped, wide-eyed. "It worked, huh?"

Carolyn nodded. "Evidently."

"And . . . Kevin?"

"He's here too. He thinks the orcas will use tech. He thinks *we* should use magic, since they won't be expecting it, and it'll catch 'em off guard."

'Bird scowled. "What kind of magic?"

"Perhaps we will find out when we get there," Sean snapped, showing actual anger for the first time. "*If* we get there," he added sullenly. And with that, he wrapped his seal-skin around his shoulders like a coat, flipped the head-skin over his own dark hair, and knelt.

Carolyn watched peripherally, and saw the skin mold to the contours of Sean's lithe body, then that body stretch, twist, and contract as the seal-shape reasserted. "He's going to swim," she told them wearily. "But how do the rest of us get there, what with gridlock and all?"

'Bird's wide grin surprised her. "We passed a whole rack of bikes comin' in. What say we give those nice, long legs a workout?"

Chapter XXXIV:
Squaring Things

(Aztlan)
(Saturday, September 10—early afternoon)

Five kloms, Stormy had claimed with conviction: five kloms from the Twins's Compound to Cathedral Square—as the crow flew. It was, however, much further than that as the Thunderbird rode a ten-speed. And that wasn't counting a body that was now, after an eternity without sleep and half a day's undermaintenance and overexertion, on the verge of simply quitting. He could no longer tally the parts that hurt; easier to list those that didn't. Maybe his eyelashes—no, scratch that: they were clogged with dust.

Only a little longer, 'Bird promised himself, as he launched the expensive Merlin touring bike down yet another flight of steps—these leading from the parking deck of the German Embassy to the sidewalk below. The impacts—a dozen-plus—rattled his teeth and made him think his spine was coming unstrung, never mind what they did to his legs and tailbone. Still, he hung grimly on, gaze fixed alternately on Stormy's back, where he guided their little posse expertly through the cross-country maze of Aztlan, and on the towers of St. Teka-witha's, which rose ever-nearer straight ahead.

Behind him, Cary was holding her own—after an excruciatingly slow start courtesy of her new height screwing up her balance. She'd fallen twice, but her shadow—how he'd kept track of her—still angled forward and to the left the same distance behind his it had

since the press of people on the streets and sidewalks had forced them overland—through parks, lawns, parking lots, and (once) the center of a shopping mall. Any other time it would've made grand comic theater.

Any time the fate of the world didn't depend on reaching the Cathedral in time. What they'd *do* there, he had no idea. Cary—make that Kevin—had suggested they use mojo, but beyond that, he hadn't a clue. He only hoped they didn't depend on him, because, frankly, he wasn't up to it. Shoot, all that kept him going now was the knowledge that two hours hence it'd all be over. He might be *dead*, but it'd be over.

And then they had to slow again, for the mass of pilgrims on the sidewalk and spilling into the stationary sea of vehicles that was Hudson Avenue was too thick for even Stormy's reckless riding. (He'd have said intense, but it was harrowing all the same, to participant and witness alike.) They were really close though: the Cathedral less than a quarter klom away.

A quarter klom packed solid with people and gridlocked cars.

Yet Stormy found a path. It involved a fair bit of intimidation, and the last minute was touch-and-go as the crowd (mostly rural types) threatened to turn surly. Eventually Stormy braked to a stop, passed the bike to a startled teenage boy, snapped "take this with my compliments," and leapt off. 'Bird did likewise, and never saw who was attached to the well-tanned hands that snatched his handlebars, because by then Stormy was moving on: making his way through the mob by main force toward the portable sandcrete barricade that, with the Mountie-mobiles and limos beyond, blocked the nearest entrance to the square. 'Bird followed doggedly, with Cary sometimes ahead, sometimes behind. His knowledge of this part of town was sketchy, but they'd approached from the northwest and were presently navigating the neutral zone between the Vatican Embassy and the HQ of the Central Bank of Aztlan. Both buildings used all available space on their blocks, and the street between wasn't a major thoroughfare, so 'Bird found

himself plunged into gloom. Light glimmered beyond, however, and suddenly they were there.

—Facing a waist-high portawall, beyond which lurked a Mountie Mercury, the gaps at either end manned by three RCMPs apiece.

Stormy slowed when he saw them, and 'Bird finally got close enough to catch his ear. "I'd as soon not try to pull rank," he gasped, steering Stormy toward the nearest wall, with Carolyn becalmed a dozen meters back. "I'll give you even odds my name's on file with them by now, in connection with Rudy's murder."

Stormy grimaced, glancing toward Carolyn, who was approaching quickly. "And we still haven't told her."

"Not unless she grabbed it out of our heads, so . . . let's just be cool."

Which was as much as he dared before Carolyn joined them. Her odd new face was flushed from the exertion, and she was panting, but a grim determination hardened her features that was almost frightening in its intensity. He had to keep reminding himself that she'd lost far more than he in all this, and had a shitload more coup to count.

She nodded toward the barricade and the empty square beyond. "They're not letting anyone through?"

'Bird strained on tiptoes—he was still taller than she— and shook his head. "Doesn't look like. Lots of guys with guns; lots of sharp eyes and itchy trigger fingers."

Stormy slapped the wall behind him. "So what do we do?"

Carolyn's face went blank, as though checking the time, but 'Bird suspected she was up to something far less trivial. "Kev says to remember magic."

'Bird glared at her. "Like what kind? I mean, I'm not a wizard or anything. I don't have a magic wand or a grimoire or—"

"No," Stormy agreed, "but you do seem to have easiest access to the . . . Otherworld of anyone here. And you said yourself that you made fire reach out and torch that werka."

"Yeah," 'Bird snapped back, wondering even as he spoke what their fellow "pilgrims," pressed close as sar-

dines around, thought of such conversation. "Yeah," he repeated, "but I had no choice."

"And now?" From Carolyn.

'Bird looked doubtfully at Stormy. "I don't suppose you know any of these guys and could bullshit us through . . . ?"

Stormy shook his head. "I've been checking, believe me, and it's a no-go. Looks like they've imported a bunch of lads from the Great Cold Place, and they're not likely to deal with someone like me. Plus, I've got a gun, which I'm sure they'd find and confiscate—and without weapons, what good are we?"

'Bird slammed the wall in turn—hard. "Great. Just great."

Stormy lifted a brow. "I'm open to suggestions."

'Bird scowled at him. "Sounds more like you're limiting my options."

Stormy regarded him levelly. "Well it *is* the unexpected thing. That's our ace in the hole."

'Bird grimaced. "Thanks a lot!"

Carolyn rounded on him. "If you're not gonna try, I am! But it seems to me you'd be better. Kev and I— Well, it seems like the Word and Way part has to work . . . differently. I can't say how I know that, but I know!"

'Bird closed his eyes and tried to focus on the hard wall behind him—anything to shut out the press of people, of decisions, of all this . . . *stuff* that threatened to overwhelm him. It was too much, dammit! It was simply too much, with him burned out like he was. He'd give anything to get away for even a minute. Desperately, he focused on his breathing, trying to shut out the world as he hovered on the ragged edge of trance. It was relaxing, so relaxing . . . He'd just hide there for a minute—only one—then get back to the matter at hand . . .

A deep breath. Another . . .

Pain in his ankle yanked him back to himself. He gasped, blinked, opened his eyes. *He was in that other place!* The forest glade where he'd met the Ancient of Raccoons! The pain was courtesy of the Ancient Himself

(smaller than 'Bird remembered, but clearly Himself), who'd just bit the crap out of him.

"Could be rabies," the Ancient said. "I will let you puzzle *that* out. For now, I will tell you three things. First, you are the predator, because you are free to move as your foes are not. They have wrapped themselves in a shell of stone, and that may be their undoing. Second, your kind see what they expect. And last, Ancient Red and Ancient White are pleased that you honored them, and more pleased with the sacrifice you made—and might possibly grant you one more favor."

"But what?"

The 'Coon did not reply. Rather, It growled at him and sauntered off through the woods, looking very well-fed—and ordinary.

'Bird remained where he was, on the edge of two Worlds. But though mind and body alike cried for sleep, he was thinking hard.

Fire owed him a favor, huh? That had struck him most forcefully. And fire had served him once before, and maybe more than that, depending on how you reckoned internal combustion engines and gunpowder. But what good would Fire do now? How could it accomplish his most immediate goal: getting him, Stormy, and Carolyn across fifty meters of open pavement and into St. Teka-witha's?

How indeed?

Something warmed his forehead, and he blinked reflexively: opening his eyes onto Stormy's concerned face and Carolyn's. Something had changed: something simple yet fundamental. And then he knew: they'd been shadowed; now they were in light. That was the only difference.

Light . . .

He shut his eyes again. What was light but energy? And what was energy but Fire? And Fire had promised him a favor. So perhaps he could convince Light, which was an aspect of Fire, to do him one in turn. Abruptly, he was slapping the wall to a certain cadence, while

words shaped themselves in his mind, as they once before had done, back in the riverbed:

Sge! Hark to me, oh Ancient White, oh Ancient Red! Hark to me in my hour of need! I know the joy with which you consume things: the glee with which you turn wood into charcoal and then to ash; the skill with which you turn dull stone to bright metal; the strength with which you battle cold and dark with warmth and light. And it is your bright and accomplished child, Light, that I summon now: Light that goes everywhere, that runs as fast as anything can, that holds color yet is colorless. That paints the rainbow and shows us the blue sky and the green earth and the red of our blood. But I know that my brother Light likes to play, and it is a trick I now ask of Light. A simple trick, but one that will earn my everlasting devotion. The trick I ask is to shine on myself and my companions as we enter yonder square. But I ask Light to veil us as we move, and show those who would watch us— who would keep us from saving a thousand bright human lives, who likewise praise the Light—reflections of ourselves where we are not. Give us shadows with colors. Make us ghosts in the air. For the honor I have given Ancient Red and Ancient White, I ask this: I am Thunderbird Devlin O'Connor.

And with that, he opened his eyes. And suspected that the sun had briefly pulsed warmer on his face.

Stormy was staring at him, squinting, blinking, and rubbing his eyes. 'Bird stared back, but even as he did, a shadow swallowed his friend, and suddenly, unless he looked very hard, Stormy wasn't there. It was the same with Carolyn. The rest of the crowd seemed to share his problem, too, for those who'd stood nearest were glancing about perplexedly, while others not so attentive moved automatically to fill what they now—apparently—considered a void.

"We're invisible—I think," 'Bird hissed. "And I'd as

soon not hang around, 'cause if I think too hard . . . Well, who knows . . .''

The shadow that was Stormy seemed to nod and eased toward the nearer trio of guards. People blocked their path—unintentionally—and they had to nudge unsuspecting pilgrims aside, but that only confirmed his suspicion: they really were invisible. And then they reached the barricade, and the guards were squinting in their directions, frowning, but not—by the way their eyes were directed—at them.

''Stop!'' one shouted, and 'Bird froze before he realized it had come from the other end of the barrier. The Mounties there were moving to block something, which had caught the attention of the nearer ones as well.

''Now,'' 'Bird growled, and wasted no more time. Seizing Carolyn's hand and shoving Stormy ahead, he twisted past the befuddled guards into the hot emptiness of Cathedral Square. One of them yipped but there was no other impediment. 'Bird released the breath he'd been holding and angled right, toward the massive edifice. He couldn't resist a sideways glance, though—and saw, sure enough, three shapes the size of himself and his companions matching their pace in the opposite direction. They glanced his way too, and then he could contain himself no longer—and ran.

A hundred meters later, they halted in the shadows of the massive white stone buttresses that braced the near corner of the North Tower. ''God,'' 'Bird panted, gazing back into the square, where two of the six guards they'd hoodwinked were staring about stupidly and scratching their heads.

''A good choice—here—I think,'' Stormy breathed, likewise surveying the square. ''Best I can tell, our . . . reflections ran straight into a blank wall.''

''Good for them,'' 'Bird gasped. ''Jeeze, but this is weird: begging favors from elementals.''

''I won't ask,'' Carolyn snorted. ''Kev says it was neat, a clever bit of thinking, and the poetry wasn't bad— for free verse.''

'Bird stared at her. Her shape was like thin smoke. "You *heard* that?"

She shook her head. "Kev. He's in here, but he seems also to be . . . out there. It's weird. It's probably gonna drive me crazy before long. But for now—"

"—we've got a job to do," Stormy finished. "We're practically atop Ground Zero and still have no sign of a plan."

"Winging it seems to work," 'Bird countered.

Stormy nodded reluctantly. "Wing and a . . . prayer."

"Don't count on it again," 'Bird advised. "I may've blown my wad."

Carolyn was gazing around speculatively. "So what now?"

"You ever been here?" From 'Bird.

"Once—because I'd heard it wasn't to be missed. I've never done a service."

"Mr. Cloud?"

"Took the nickel tour a couple times, and read some stuff—mostly 'bout how it faithfully follows the traditional Gothic plan—which I did study back when I was an Art History major for about five minutes."

"Good," 'Bird chuckled, " 'cause I don't know shit. I was just hopin' one of you might have a clearer idea about the inside layout than I do—besides the tourist thing; even I know that!"

Carolyn puffed her cheeks. "Two things—and I don't know if this is me or Kev, not that it matters—but we probably ought to check the back in case Sean's arrived; that's where the nearest canal runs. We're on a hill here—one of the few in town—and the canal fronts the crypt level. Plus," she continued, "since the Twins are doing the music and Kev thinks they'll do their thing via tech— Well, we'd be better off getting as close to them as possible."

Stormy grinned. "Like via a side door?"

She nodded. "Magic or no, marching in the front might be stretching our luck *too* far. I mean, there's security out the wazoo on the steps. And once in, there'd

be cameras and a zillion people to sneak past to get any-where useful.''

'Bird shut his eyes against the glare, trying at once to think, plan, and listen. To his surprise, he heard music—from inside. Baroque. Bach, maybe—but set to some weird beat, something Latin—no . . . *native*. Music by the Hero Twins. *Organ* music.

"Organs," he observed slowly, "are *very* high tech."

Stormy's eyes went wide. "And inside's the biggest pipe organ in the world. I—"

He broke off, head cocked, listening. 'Bird caught it too: footsteps approaching from the east front around the corner. Hard, purposeful shoes moving quickly. "Oops," he whispered. "Guess my deal didn't include sound."

Stormy didn't reply; silent on rubber soles, he was already running—left, skirting the outer wall of the nave. 'Bird followed doggedly. Windows flashed above their heads like flames frozen in white stone, the pointed arches at their summits a hundred meters nearer Heaven. Fortunately, as Stormy had noted, the architects had been slavish in their devotion to Gothic forms, and the nave's entire vast length was bracketed by flying buttresses like the spiky white ribcage of some unimaginably huge le-viathan. It was in the shadow of the next one down that 'Bird joined his friends—not a minute too soon. Just as they ducked behind it, a uniformed figure eased around the corner of the tower, gun poised. He remained there a long moment, then shrugged, said something into a walkie-talkie, and turned away.

'Bird heaved a sigh of relief.

Stormy, who'd already scooted down to the next but-tress, was surveying their route critically. "There's a stair turret in the corner between the nave and the transept," he pointed out. "It's even got a door. If we can get there before 'Bird's mojo wears off . . ."

"Big *if* there, kid," 'Bird snorted. "Plus, we'd have to break in."

The shadow that was Stormy shook his head. Teeth—possibly—flashed in what 'Bird supposed was a grin. "Wrong! It's closed but not locked, 'cause you can see

power cables snaking out the corner to that generator complex over by the bank.''

'Bird squinted into the afternoon glare, but could only make out a dark blur. Either Stormy's eyes were much better than his, the mojo was stronger on him, or he was just too fried to focus.

"Go for it," Carolyn urged. "We don't have time to play 'What If.' ''

"What about Sean?" From 'Bird.

"It's out of the way to check canalside just now," Stormy replied. "Once we get in and figure out how the land lays, then we can decide what to do."

'Bird exhaled wearily and wondered if he was up for the dozen-plus between-buttress sprints needed to reach their goal. Stormy slapped him on the back—an odd sensation from someone with less discernable mass than thick fog or dense shadow. "Now or never, kid," he chided. "As you're fond of saying: we're burning daylight."

"Go," Carolyn snapped. "Now!"

Stormy did. She followed. 'Bird came last, uncomfortably aware of how sore his legs were, how his right hip joint felt like it was lined with sandpaper, and how, in spite of his efforts at silence, his breath was coming fast and thick, and his footsteps sounded loud as thunder.

Somehow they made it, and without pause for discussion—wise, given what might lie beyond the door—slipped through the thick bronze portal, with Stormy in the lead.

They entered darkness, which surprised 'Bird; it was a sunny day, and he'd expected the turret to butt against one of the side aisles, which should've been brightly illuminated. Instead, they stood in a grey-green gloom lit only by narrow, widely-spaced windows following the tight spiral of the stair up into obscurity. As expected, there was another door: a small, pointed affair opposite that by which they'd entered. Stormy—more tangible now—was already trying it, but shaking his head. "Locked," he grunted. "And we don't dare hit the lights."

"What about those cables?" From Carolyn.

"They go up *and* down. Up gets us to the triforium," Stormy continued, "but that's bound to be crammed full of vips, never mind whoever's doing video."

"I'll check," Carolyn volunteered. Then: "You're right. It's like a solid mass of thinking up there, too many to tell if there're any orcas or not. Down, though— That seems clear."

"So we go down?" 'Bird wondered dubiously.

Stormy nodded. "At least one level, since we'd have more freedom of choice down there. There's a stair in each of the crossing piers, for instance. If we could access them below, we could come back up right in the middle of things."

"Also," Carolyn added, "it'd put us closer to where Sean's likely to be."

"If he makes it," Stormy cautioned. "Frankly, I'm not sure how much good he'll be. Not much, if he stays a seal, and—uh—easy to spot if he goes human, given that he'd be in a restricted area stark naked."

"Trust him," Carolyn said tersely. "Let's travel."

Stormy edged past her toward the head of the stair. Half a turn lower, they'd have been in total darkness had it not been for faint glimmerings from above. And the light got worse.

Reduced to fumbling along at the end of the file, 'Bird hated it, and hated it more when the stair showed no sign of ending. "Damn," came Stormy's frustrated whisper, "I forgot there's a whole other chapel down here as big as some churches. Twenty-meter vaults, if I recall."

"And we've come . . . maybe ten?"

"This is a crock," Carolyn grumbled in the dark. Then, softly, but with a desperate edge in her voice that gave 'Bird chills merely to hear: "Oh no! Oh, dear God, *no*!"

"What?" 'Bird hissed.

A frantic "Shhhh!" brought silence—but only for an instant, as 'Bird heard, far too clearly, the sound of heavy footsteps clumping down the stone steps above. He swallowed hard, not daring to breathe, and felt for the safety

on the pistol clutched to his chest beneath the serape, wishing he wasn't last in line because he'd be first to encounter whoever it was, and therefore first to act. Fighting in a space this confined—and effectively in the dark—was not a notion he relished.

Only . . . why hadn't whoever approached switched on the lights? Surely cameramen—

Abruptly, a too-familiar sensation clogged his brain, and he knew who—what, rather—approached less than two turns above.

Something used to navigating the depths of the sea when there was little light.

The "click" as he released the safety was masked by more footsteps, the pounding of his heart—and laughter.

Chapter XXXV:
Smoked Out

...He must stay. Red Wounds must stay inside... That command had been playing with such dull monotony through Thalo's thoughts it had worn a mental groove there, so that he was no longer even aware it existed. It was like his hair or nails: an inert part of the whole until something plucked at it. Nothing did. The thrill of the day had caught up with him, along with too little sleep the previous night, and the mix was making him muddleheaded: exactly the right state in which to forget a number of things that had been deviling him (of which he could recall none just now), and focus on the music alone.

Indeed, all he could actually think about was the music of the spheres. He'd known the Twins were world-class serious musicians, in spite of their equally deserved rep as rock 'n' rollers. But when he'd heard they were performing at Green Francis's Requiem— Well, that had seemed a bit of a push even to him.

It had clearly been the right decision.

And while the Twins could crank out decibels with the best of them, and wail on guitar or synthesizer alike, what they were *doing* was a superbly subtle piece rendered on the massive Bosch organ whose myriad enormous pipes were so well integrated into the flutes and filigree of the four huge crossing piers they were nearly invisible. But though he suspected those pipes could thunder like the very trumps of doom, at present they were scarcely sighing, because whichever Twin manned the console presently commanded a keyboard connected to a hundred

crystal spheres, each of which sounded a different tone when struck with a silver mallet. A secondary keyboard produced the breathy tones of a wooden Andean flute, and the effect was like wind wafting through the gates of Heaven.

It was apparently some sort of prelude: a favorite of the Archbishop, so the program said. No wonder! As soon as this was over, he was going to run to the nearest music store and retrieve a copy for himself.

And then the music whispered away into a still silence, broken only by one final perfectly timed "ping."

Then silence indeed.

—Followed by a rustle from the entrance nearly straight below, which was followed in turn by a mumbling hiss of anticipation, as, with no more fanfare than the Twins had claimed—which would still have been enough for most people—a pair of the fantastically garbed Swiss guards paced to either side of the monstrous front door, pulled each half of that portal wide—and admitted His Holiness, Pope Michael I.

Everyone gasped again.

Michael I had grown up in a poor suburb of London, and while not quite so young, popular, or accomplished as the late Archbishop, was still the youngest pontiff since one of the Borgias had risen to the Throne of St. Peter while still in his teens. Though often at odds with the liberal fringe of the Church, he had nevertheless wrought reform after reform, and had sealed his fame with a sense of showmanship not seen since the early days of John-Paul II. Why else claim the right to officiate at his rival's Requiem? Why march into the heart of the enemy's citadel?

Because it was good theater—and theater begat popularity, which got you heard, where sermons, scholarship, and good works did not.

Pope Michael I had obviously concluded it was excellent theater indeed to perform this most sacred of offices clad only in a plain green stole over a white gauze robe identical to that in which Francis Blackmer had been immolated. No cope, no tiara. No shoes, even; his bare feet

moved silently on the marble floor as, flanked by no more attendants than the two Swiss guards, he strode the whole length of St. Tekawitha's nave. No one coughed. No one whispered. It was a moment thick with portent, and Michael, who was tall and powerfully built, with long golden hair only slightly greyed—and a face that more than one languishing devotee had said would do an archangel proud—played it to the hilt. Not once did he shift the rhythm of his steps; not once did he look to either side. This was *his* moment. *His* entrance. *His* time of penance and homage.

The trek took most of a minute, and described the same route as the other dignitaries, save that instead of claiming a seat after he had walked around the coffin, stroking it with both hands, he turned his back on that vast elite multitude, ascended the wide steps of the high altar, knelt there briefly, then strode to a small platform behind the bier raised barely high enough for those in front to see. Only then did he turn to face the congregation, hands raised in benediction.

Thalo was enthralled. Indeed, he had to keep reminding himself this wasn't a dream. That all this splendor and panoply was actually occurring in his presence, and wasn't some media-morphed fake. And then he was enchanted all over.

With the raising of the Pontiff's hands, the music recommenced—softly, like waves sliding up long white sands. This time, however, a choir accompanied it, and as their voices rose and mingled, more priests moved about, swinging thuribles from which wafted that sweet, potent incense.

Thalo was amazed at how quickly the stuff tainted the air—the scent was already *everywhere* from the three censings the building had endured since his arrival. And now, as His Holiness waited for the Processional to conclude (it had just gone *a capella*), the Twins left their organ consoles and moved to flank him, their full Maya court regalia contrasting less with the Pontiff's simple robe than might've been expected—purely from the power of Michael's presence.

"*Kyrie eleison . . .*" Michael began, voice carrying perfectly. "*Christe eleison . . .*"

A prayer followed: a reminder of humanity's sins.

In the reflective pause that ensued, each Twin took a candle from the countless number that flared and flickered around the crossing piers, and paced to matching wide braziers set up at the junctures of transepts and choir. As one they touched those flames to those bowl-topped slabs of stone. As one flames flared up high, quickly subsiding into swirling clouds of white smoke that stank even more strongly of pungent resin.

Someone did cough then, and Thalo wondered why more folks weren't having trouble with the stuff. That is, he wondered at some deep level; surface was simply riding along with the rite: observing but not reacting. More coughing *was* occurring, though. Even Red Wounds, two meters to the right of where Thalo leaned against his pier, fumbled inside his ceremonial coat for a handkerchief, then buried his face in it.

Thalo coughed too.

The movement startled him. He blinked, and coughed again. The motion made his stomach flutter, which drew his attention to something he couldn't believe he hadn't noted sooner.

He needed—badly—to pee!

He glanced around frantically, attention abruptly centered on his bladder, which now he was attending it, had become very strident indeed. *What was the etiquette of this kind of thing*? Did you stand and grit your teeth, ease off quietly—or hold it as long as possible, then wet your pants?

Definitely not the latter—if for no other reason than because they weren't his pants. Besides, with so many people packed into a structure this huge for this long, somebody had to be in similar straits. Of course he didn't know where the nearest loo was, but given that this was a new building (for all its antique style) one couldn't be far away. Probably off the gallery behind the triforium pews.

Ah-ha! One of the Twins' bulky roadies (something

about them bugged him, though he couldn't remember what), who'd been haunting their end of the triforium ever since they'd been seated, had suddenly flinched as if stricken and hurried down the passage. And if that guy was free to roam around during Important State Occasions, Thalo could too—especially when he had a perfectly reasonable excuse.

Without further ado, he propped his banner-pole between two white marble flutes on the pier beside him, mouthed a silent "pit stop" to his glassy-eyed Inuit counterpart, and padded up to the access gallery down which the roadie had fled.

The silence there caught him off guard, and the relative freshness of the air, though it took a moment to recall that air was *supposed* to be fresh, not clogged with incense, and that the "pause for reflection" had to be nearly over. According to the program, another prayer would follow; and while he wasn't much more than a virtual Christian, it was probably not cool in any cosmic sense to be flitting about the triforium of the New World's shiny new Holy-of-Holies while *His* Holiness invoked the Deity. It was with that in mind that he doubled his pace in the wake of the roadie, who was now turning right (away from the heart of the building) through a small door at the juncture of nave and crossing—close to where the outside wall ought to be.

Which, though there was no sign to that effect, was as good a place as any for a loo.

He followed quickly—and had just sense enough to realize that the space he entered was not a restroom but the landing of a tight spiral stair, when the door clicked shut behind, thrusting him into gloom.

Not what he wanted at all! Reflexively, he tried the knob, and discovered to his horror that it had locked. He didn't dare knock—no telling who'd hear, who'd open it, or what they'd say when they did.

Which left up or down.

"*Up*" was even more stupid than most things he'd done lately, which left "*down*"—from which level he

might possibly find some way to complete his business and work on getting *"up"* again.

It was while he stood debating that he heard the laughter.

Though no more than a surprised chuckle, it was disturbing, almost maniacal, and his first impulse was to cut and run—if not back into the triforium, then simply higher, away from that sound. Somebody was bound to be up top, after all, to judge by the heavy power cables snaking up the spiral. But then he heard the muffled rasps of what were surely more than one set of feet, which seemed to carry an urgent note, and in their wake came heavier tread that was probably the vanished roadie, and then an edgy voice groaning, "Oh shit, folks, we're fucked!"

At which point the lights came on. Thalo gasped, and instinct suggested two things immediately. One was to seek the rush of fresh air from a narrow window in the outer wall half a turn lower. The other was to realize that the voice hadn't been just anyone's, but someone he knew, namely 'Bird O'Connor.

Which raised dozens of possibilities, one of which was that since he was impersonating 'Bird, and the real one had arrived, they ought to connect and swap off, which would spare him the angst of returning to the delegation. Another was to wonder what in the world 'Bird was doing *here*. And a third was whether that exclamation carried as much raw fear as it seemed.

Somehow he found himself that half-turn lower, with the window on his left and more fresh air feeding in than he'd tasted in ages. And as he drank deep of those sun-warmed breezes, the clouds of muddle began to melt from his memories, and he recalled that something awful was going on involving blackmail through his sister, which was mixed up with the Hero Twins' troublesome roadies (whom he didn't like at all), all mingled with something bad he was supposed to do and didn't want to.

More laughter sounded, then a panicked "Fuck!" from 'Bird—and yet more laughter.

He moved: chasing the dizzily twisting spiral down the turret, window slits passing sporadically, each admitting more clean air and sanity. At some point, he reached a landing with actual doors to either side, ignored them, and continued on.

Abruptly, he found himself facing the wide, beefy back of one of the roadies (Christ, the guy filled half the stair!), just as the fellow snapped something from the depths of his cloak and flourished it before him.

It glittered in the light. *Glass.* No, not just glass: *flaked obsidian*, such as he'd observed more than once at the Twins' compound the night of his initiation—which pushed yet another button. That—and the despair on 'Bird's face, where he appeared below, as though rising from a cloud of dark fog—was enough.

"Lookout!" Thalo yelled—and lunged forward and down, shoving the roadie as hard as he could.

The man staggered, caught himself, then staggered again. 'Bird grabbed an outflung arm, yanked, and the man toppled for sure and good. Thalo added a kick to the knees for good measure, but that might've been over-kill, because the next thing he knew, a whole mess of folks ('Bird was apparently not alone) were tumbling down the stairs. Thalo felt a twinge of sick horror when he realized that a fall like that was unlikely to benefit anyone and, dislike of the roadies or no, he might well have just committed murder, but then the jumble of sound ceased abruptly, and a clearly female voice said "Damn!"

An instant later, he'd caught up with whoever it was, and found himself gaping at another landing, this one writhing with arms and legs that required serious puzzling to reconcile into two—no, three—people, with the roadie (why didn't he regard him as "people" anymore?) sprawled atop. It was hard to look at them, too—they seemed made of dense smoke—but even as he tried, they slowly solidified, and 'Bird was worming his way from beneath the heavy cloaked figure. Another guy accompanied him—could've been his brother—and a slim, an-

drogynous person with auburn hair he decided was she who'd said "Damn!"

"He out of it?" the woman panted, twisting a foot free to slump against the wall. She looked more solid by the second—and more female.

The unfamiliar man prodded the roadie with a toe, the dark barrel of a small pistol protruding from his fist, aimed at the fellow's head. "Not dead, but soon will be. We can't take any chances."

'Bird opened his mouth as though to protest, then blinked and peered up the stairway. "*Thalo*?" he burst out. "Jesus, kid, what the fuck are *you* doin' here?"

"Looking for a loo," he responded truthfully, surprised to note that his urge to "go" had abated. "Saving your butt, evidently."

'Bird regarded him narrowly, and raised the small gun he'd been clutching to his chest beneath his serape. "You're not . . . workin' for them?"

Thalo felt a moment's panic, wondering what 'Bird knew, what 'Bird thought *he* knew, and what he was *supposed* to know and didn't. But then the woman's face blanked, he felt an odd clogging in his brain, and she relaxed, looking relieved. "He's not one of theirs," she announced. "In fact, he hates 'em as much as we do. But"—she scowled—"he also knows about the plot—I think. I mean, his memories are full of stuff, but they're . . . veiled. It's weird. And it's like I can still smell that damned incense!"

"It's a drug," 'Bird reminded them. "It makes it so they can fuck with your mind."

Thalo was trying to download all that and failing. "Look," he sighed, "what the hell's going on?"

He got no answer, for the roadie had begun to twist and groan. "Kill him!" the woman rasped. "Just kill the son-of-a-bitch."

"And have him Change right here?" 'Bird's friend challenged. "That'd be dumb—especially now, when we need info more than revenge."

"Speak for yourself!"

"Actually," the man said, "I was hoping *you* could

dig into this lad's mind and find out what's going on.''

The woman glared at him. "I've *been* in their heads. It's not fun.''

Thalo cleared his throat. "You said something about a plot . . . and that I knew something. And that I was . . . a good guy? How'd you know that?''

"I read your mind,'' the woman snapped. "It's a trick I've picked up.'' Her expression softened. "I'm Cary,'' she added with a tired smile, ''—mostly; but never mind that. This is Stormy and . . . it seems you know 'Bird.''

Thalo nodded. "And why're you here?''

'Bird grinned. "We saw the video your pecker starred in, and had to get your autograph. No, seriously: these guys here aren't human, which *you* must suspect by now, if you've been around 'em as much as I suspect. They're shape-shifted orcas trying to bring down our civilization—technization, more specifically. At the moment, they're planning to off the vips upstairs. We know it involves music, but not how.''

Thalo gnawed his lip. "I think I do.''

The roadie groaned again and twitched. 'Bird eyed Cary grimly. "We have to do something—''

"Knock 'im out again,'' Thalo urged.

'Bird shook his head. "I'd like to *kill* 'im, but I—we—can't. If nothing else, we can use him as a hostage.''

Stormy shook his head in turn. "No go. We've already seen that individuals don't matter with them. Hostages require loyalty.''

"We've still got to—'' 'Bird broke off, eyes wide and wary, on full alert again. He glared at the door across the landing, against which Stormy was lounging. "Someone's—''

Cary's face blanked instantly, but before she could speak, the door opened.

Thalo's heart leapt to his throat as anticipation ambushed him—until he got a good view of the latest arrival. A boy! A *naked* boy. Teenager, actually, with more black hair than he'd ever seen. He also looked, there was no other term for it, feral. Intense—and feral.

"Not dead," the boy spat without preamble, in an odd lilting accent Thalo couldn't place. He was staring at the twitching roadie as though it were more loathsome than any slug.

"We were just discussing that." Cary sighed. "We need to know what he knows."

"And Cary's not keen on checking," 'Bird finished.

The boy didn't respond; rather, he stared fixedly at Thalo. Once again, Thalo felt his thoughts clog and wondered if that was what it felt like to have one's mind read. To his surprise, the boy grinned. "*He* knows!"

"I tried to tell you!" Thalo shot back. "I . . . don't know *what* I know, but something tells me I do."

"I can look," the boy volunteered, then paused. "Or I can use the evil-water-one, which would be less pleasant. It is your choice. Since you are a person of good will, I would rather have permission."

Thalo exhaled wearily. "Whatever."

"We have to hurry," Cary hissed. "And don't forget *that*." She pointed at the roadie.

"Only take a moment," the boy retorted. "I'm Sean, by the way. I'm also a selkie, and Cary's brother."

Little of that registered on Thalo before he felt that clogging again—this time more gently, like a sparkling stream trickling into his mind in lieu of the raging flood that had been Cary—or Sean initially.

Abruptly it was gone, almost before Thalo could register.

"I have it!" Sean crowed. "It is as you said: music. There is a certain chord which, when sounded and amplified by These Ones' minds, will shake the stones of this place and make it fall. Panic will follow, and people will try to escape, but when they do, certain ones—our friend here is one—have been . . . made to keep certain others seated, so that their deaths will be assured."

Thalo's mouth dropped open. "Is that *all*? Christ, what've I got myself into?"

"Doesn't matter," 'Bird snorted. "Not your fault. If it weren't for you, we wouldn't know what we do."

"Which still isn't enough," Stormy grumbled. "We

don't know what the chord is, or when it's supposed to happen.''

''I could find out,'' Sean countered, looking at Cary. ''Or we could. I would rather not enter this one's mind alone.''

Cary frowned, puffed her cheeks, then nodded. ''Do it. Now. I'll follow.''

Thalo saw nothing, the selkie's face being turned away, but Cary's went blank again. The roadie stiffened abruptly. An instant later they were back.

''More would have killed him,'' Sean panted. ''He fled, but we caught him before he crossed the Barrier.''

''And?'' 'Bird prompted impatiently.

''It will be after the . . . the—''

''Response,'' Cary supplied. ''There's an anthem then that ends with a powerful organ chord, but before it comes in, the Twins are supposed to sing—Psalm 104, I think—and the lyrics include the phrase 'Let the sinners be consumed out of the earth, and let the wicked be no more.' It's one of the most environmental Psalms, one of my favorites, in fact—only this time it carries a subliminal suggestion. There's something in the incense, see, and—''

''How well I know!'' Thalo groaned. Then: ''Wait a minute! I may have something useful.'' He fished in his coat for the program he'd stuffed there. ''Ah-ha!'' Then: ''Oh shit!''

''What?'' From Cary.

Thalo felt sick. ''According to this, the singing starts any minute.''

''We move *now!*'' Cary was already rising.

Sean blinked at her, and Thalo realized the boy had blanked again. His eyes were wide. ''I have just scanned this structure, and it is as Thalo said. I sense numbness from countless human minds. I sense musicians full of genius who are running on—''

''Automatic?'' 'Bird supplied. ''That figures.''

Sean nodded. ''And . . . I sense the evil-water-ones leaving. There are perhaps a dozen of them. By ones and

twos they abandon their positions and seek the level by which I arrived.''

"Escaping," Stormy growled. "Those sons-of-bitches! They've wound up the Twins like robots and are leavin' them to do the dirty work.''

"They'll take the canals," 'Bird added. "Like Sean did.''

"Unless," Stormy mused, "we kill them.''

"Big *if*, man," 'Bird snorted.

Stormy grinned and patted his pistol meaningfully. "And if we catch 'em at the canal, we push 'em in before they Change. End of disposal problem.''

"Except this one," Cary noted.

Sean grinned in turn. "I can control him. It will not be pleasant riding in his head, but I can do it. I will march him to the crypt and out at the water gate. There, I will cut his throat with his own blade, and while his life pours out, I will push him into the water.''

"There'll be questions," Cary cautioned.

Stormy shrugged. "There'll have to be.''

"Anything I can do?" Thalo wondered.

"You've been up there," Cary replied. "You know the lay of the land. You can show us where everything is. Now—let's travel.''

'Bird's brow wrinkled in consternation. "One thing—Stormy's our best man with a gun. Won't *we* need him?''

Cary shook her head. "Kev says no. He says the only way to stop all that screwed-up tech is with magic.''

Thalo blinked in surprise. "Who the hell is Kevin?''

"My brother. Actually, I'm him too, only he's also a . . . spirit. We'll explain later, if there is one.''

"But—magic?''

Cary had already vanished up the stairs. 'Bird followed. Thalo hesitated, twisting around to see Sean stare at the roadie—who twitched briefly, then, moving like a groggy automaton, slowly got to his feet. Stormy helped him up, holding him at gunpoint while the boy urged him toward the single door.

"Coming?" 'Bird called from the next twist up.

"Right now!" Thalo had just discovered that for the

first time in two days his mind felt truly his own.

Less than a minute later, they reached the triforium landing. 'Bird hesitated, staring at the still-locked door. Scowling like fury, he aimed his pistol at the latch. Fortunately, the gun was silenced. Close as he was, even Thalo heard no more than a sharp cough-click. What he did hear, much more loudly, was the harsh tinkle of metal exploding to flinders. And louder yet, the tones of the world's largest organ, as 'Bird eased the door back and peered through.

"Try not to breathe," Thalo cautioned. Cary patted his hand. "I can shield my mind," she whispered. "And Kev and I together can keep track of you and 'Bird. If anything goes wrong, we'll step in."

Thalo rolled his eyes, but skipped aside as Cary squeezed through. 'Bird followed, then him—and the whole world turned to song and music.

Not the music of the spheres, however; rather the Heavenly Choir. Actually, it was merely the Hero Twins singing in absolute harmony the words to that portentous song, the Cathedral's perfect acoustics carrying them along like angelic messengers riding some divine wind. It really was a transcendent moment, and Thalo immediately lost himself again—until he realized that they were coming up on *those* words. His blood promptly froze. He literally *could not move* as imminent death loomed before him. A minute from now he might not exist, and everyone here along with him. Yet even as that thought twisted his gut like a crazy thing, he heard those fateful words, sung by Blowgunner and Jaguar Deer, the Hero Twins, where they flanked St. Tekawitha's high altar, with Pope Michael I about to perform his most important oration at the Requiem for Archbishop Francis Blackmer.

"... *let the wicked be no more!*"

The world disappeared.

For a second Thalo simply *wasn't*. And then he was himself again, but a different self. It was as if in that moment of not being his conscious mind and unconscious mind swapped places, so that his rational, analytical, eth-

ical aspect was once more imprisoned behind soundproof glass, while that other, darker self, who'd been exiled in disgrace, went ascendent.

"*. . . let the wicked be no more . . .*" the song repeated, and those lyrics were like a command, like a whiplash of compulsion across his mind. What was he doing here, anyway? His job—his *duty*—was to be part of Kituwah's delegation, and more to the point, to ensure that the Honorable Ambassador-Chief William Red Wounds remained in his seat, so that he could fully appreciate the message the Esteemed Archbishop of Aztlan had bequeathed to the world via his messengers, the Hero Twins.

"*Let the wicked be no more!*"

Man *was* wicked, wasn't he? Man couldn't continue as he had. But to understand that, one had to hear the entire message—and if he didn't see to it that Red Wounds heard, a crucial cornerstone of Green Francis's dream would go unset.

All at once, he was running. Dimly, distantly, he heard voices calling out to him, then feet dashing down the gallery in pursuit. He didn't care; the music would give him strength and carry him on. He ran harder. Arches flashed by to the right, every three strides, and he was aware of people stirring restlessly in their pews, some seeking to rise, scuffles breaking out among others. Once he saw a tall man gain his feet, only to be dragged down by two companions; another time a woman straight-armed a child to keep her in place. People were moving toward the exits, too—all in Outer Earth T-shirts.

And then he was skidding to a halt at the archway in which Red Wounds was seated. He almost slipped as moccasined feet fought for traction on the polished floor, then was pounding down the shallow steps, with pews full of murmuring people to either side and straight ahead the banner he'd abandoned.

He paused there, breathless, eyes combing the ranks for the Ambassador's bulky figure. Not there, no—but—*there!* Still in his assigned place, as was the rest of the delegation, though some were shifting restlessly. But

wait—the Ambassador, with a look of grim determination on his face, was rising . . .

Thalo leapt toward him, oblivious to the feet he trampled, the bodies he forced aside. "Stay!" he yelled desperately. "You have to *stay*! You have to *hear*!"

His hands went around Red Wounds's throat. "*Let the wicked be no more!*" He had no idea who actually said that, but suddenly "no more" took on a cold new meaning. The Chief had to die. Everyone in power had to die.

His grip tightened.

Hands yanked at him, but their efforts seemed distant and dreamy, the muscles that drove them weak and ineffectual.

"*. . . no more . . .*"

No, Thalo! The command slashed his mind like lightning, overriding that other, so that once again he was *not*. He paused, relaxed the pressure on the man's throat. Vented a startled "What?"

Lightning again, and a stronger command: *NO!*

This time the lightning struck true: white fire and ultimate agony—but behind it lay genuine concern and appalling anger—not at him—and fear beyond any he'd ever felt. And as it passed, it caught those other compulsions that lay like a net across his own desires and with speed beyond thought seared them to nothing.

A third instant of *not*—and his mind flip-flopped again. Two names—faces—who knew?—flashed through his awareness. Cary. Kevin. Man and woman. Brother and sister. One.

He stared down at his hands, still clamped around Red Wound's throat, and screamed in terror, then flinched—or was hauled—away. He blinked into the older man's eyes. "That w-wasn't me!" he stammered. "I—I . . ."

"I know," Red Wounds rumbled. "I felt—"

His words were drowned by one final perfectly harmonized chorus: "*Let the sinners be consumed out of the earth, and let the wicked . . . dieeeee!*"

And fast on those words, like a wind from the apocalypse, came one vast, deep chord from the organ.

Chapter XXXVI:
How Firm a Foundation

". . . dieeeeee!"

Carolyn never knew whose eyes she looked through when those words sounded, Thalo's or her own. All she saw for a fractioned second was Ambassador Red Wounds's face framed by scores of shocked Native others, and beyond, like a wall of splendor, the whole sparkling length of St. Tekawitha's nave: pointed arches, fiery windows, and brilliant banners wreathed in drifts of smoke, with far at the other end, the white-clad form of Pope Michael I behind the Archbishop's bier, flanked a few steps lower to his left, by a Hero Twin in quetzal plumes and jade, standing still as a stela behind one of those enormous braziers.

And then the other Twin laid down an organ chord that would've made the opening bars of the fourth movement of Saint-Saens's "Organ Symphony" seem brief random discord—and the world changed.

She had never thought of sound as having physical form, yet that note was almost visible: a vast velvet denseness that welled from a hundred huge pipes at once and spilled onto the floor, whence it soaked into the very fabric of the building itself. The air thrummed; felt suddenly thin and insubstantial, as though it were wrought of glass that would shatter any second into shrieking vacuum. And the incense—the shifting pillars of white that, suddenly much denser, billowed from the braziers— seemed even as she watched to thicken even more, and writhe, as they twisted toward the vaults, into something more substantial than mere smoke.

She didn't move, nor 'Bird behind her, nor anyone in sight to either side. Breathless, aflame with awe that anything earthbound could produce such cosmic sound, yet filled with dread at what it portended, she waited for that chord to cease.

It didn't.

A hundred meters away, the Pope fell to his knees, hands clamped over his ears, anguished voice rising to merge with that chord, that was growing louder yet. "Nooooooo!" he screamed, and fell senseless. The standing Twin looked on with absent interest but didn't move, though something red gushed from his ears.

The building began to shake.

At first she assumed it was simply an earthquake, for the Zone had suffered several even in the brief time she'd lived there. But this was more: much more. The floor hummed, and that hum rose up into her body and rode through her bones to her brain, where it conjured bright stars and terror. Her ears stopped, then cleared, then clogged again. Across the nave, a meter-wide banner detached from its hanger and fell, heavy brass pole and all, onto the seething throng below. Another followed. Something snapped in the distance; an irregular white shape dropped from the smoky vaults thirty stories up. People screamed, scrambled to their feet, and pressed toward the exits. They were blocked—likely locked. Outer Earthers stood there, eyes blank, faces grim as death. Some wielded brass stanchions as clubs.

And still the organ roared. Carolyn couldn't stand, could barely think, and the part that *could* think knew she'd soon be dead; the small victory she and Kev had won, for control of Thalo's mind, having been in vain. Shoot, the entire building was moving. The pillars that sustained the vaults vibrated, their edges gone to blur. Cracks appeared everywhere, like black lightning awakened in white marble. And then, commencing with those nearest the organ, the stained glass windows began to explode. Air rushed in; smoke went everywhere—except out.

Dimly, she felt 'Bird's hand clamp onto hers, dragging

her toward the gallery behind the pews. It was marginally quieter there—barely tolerable. She lay there panting, even as he tugged her on—toward the altar, which was not where she wanted to go. "We have to stop 'em," he shouted. "We have to stop the organ!"

"How?" she yelled back—and, for all that her vocal cords nearly tore in twain, could barely hear her own voice.

"Hell if I know!"

Magic! Kevin countered. *This is not mere sound. Other forces work within, seeking the stresses in the building and*— He broke off, as, with a crash that out-decibeled even the howling organ, the arch supporting the section of triforium nearest the crossing cracked all along its curve and collapsed, taking seating with it. People spilled atop people, and the screaming redoubled, but Carolyn's emotions had gone numb. A banner drifted down atop that new chaos: *Republic of Quebec.*

Somehow 'Bird got her on her feet, and was dragging her on—closer, though that was insane, to the crossing.

"*Cary!*" someone shouted behind her, outpacing the rising chaos in the gallery. A backward glance showed a wide-eyed Thalo, one ear streaming blood, elbowing through a group of panicked Tongans. Behind him loomed a larger, bulkier man she identified, in spite of his outlandish dress, as Red Wounds. And though she had no idea what to do with them, she welcomed them with the grim resignation of someone who knew she was doomed, but did not want to die alone.

Another snap, and a section of vaulting slammed to the floor, crushing an Arab delegation who'd sought shelter in the choir. In the side aisles, people clambered over each other to gain the windows, while sparkling glass rained atop them like knife-edged ice. Those sills were three meters above the floor; she doubted many would make it.

And through it all, the organ screamed.

Carolyn screamed too, and clutched her head, fearing any second that her brain would shake to mush. Instead—so suddenly it was like falling from fire into cold,

clear water—came silence, and she was somewhere else.

Not really, Kevin assured her with a silent chuckle. *You're just more with me now.*

Why? she retorted bitterly. *It's too late. Nothing in the world can stop this!*

Silence can.

And how do we get silence?

Destroy the organ, of course!

As if challenging his remark, the loudest crash yet thundered through the Cathedral, as a full set of arches—those nearest the entrance, unfortunately—unspanned and dropped splintered stone onto the mob struggling with dazed-faced 'Earthers there.

But with that, the chord altered slightly; became one small degree less potent. Carolyn gasped her surprise, and noted that one of the pipes that carried all that noise had torn loose from its pier and listed at a crazy angle above the compass rose. Steam poured from it—smoke—who cared?

The building shook harder. She fell, regained her feet, lost 'Bird's hand, and fell again. Ahead, she was vaguely aware of 'Bird fighting through the tide of humanity flee-ing the triforium. He vanished in the press, only to reap-pear, leaning far across a railing with something dark and metallic in his hand. The crack of gunfire was lost in the roar of wooden pipes and brazen, and his shot went wide. Somehow she was beside him, with Thalo and Red Wounds. 'Bird aimed again, forcing his hand to still, though the building quaked around him. He was firing at the organist Twin—or the console itself, as if it mattered. But though he pumped off round after round, nothing changed.

He exhausted the clip. As he fumbled to reload, Car-olyn's gaze followed that motion—and she had just sense enough to mark aberrant movement before a massive shape hurled itself upon them.

A roadie! No, a *werka!* Even brain-numbed, she could sense its awful singlemindedness, as it gathered them into its arms, striving with main force to thrust her and 'Bird

over the rail, even as it ground them to pulp against that hard-carved marble.

She fought back frantically, alternately pummeling the thing and seeking any stable grip that might forestall a fall, while 'Bird kicked and bit and swore. Yet she knew in her heart they would fail, first one, and then the other.

Abruptly, the werka's strength dissolved. She caught only its startled gape, as, with a terrified shriek, it arched above her head and vanished. "Fucking *thing!*" came Thalo's shout. She barely had time to determine that he and Red Wounds had actually hurled the creature over the rail, before a scream—too high to be human—made her jerk back around to see the thing sprawled squarely atop the nearer brazier. It lolled there a moment as if winded, then began to writhe, as flames exploded from its billowing clothing. The smoke went black—and for a second time, the organ faltered.

But some crucial threshold had obviously been crossed, for the collapse was proceeding on its own momentum, with another archway folding every few seconds. Most of the nave was clear of people now, those who'd sat there having claimed what shelter they could in the side aisles, from which more and more were achieving the windows. Some would live, but bodies littered the floor. Too many bodies, though one would have been too many.

Carolyn reached for emotions and found none save resignation. She felt nothing at all as she stared at the flame-wrapped shape splattered across the brazier, blood pouring from rents in its clothing, while skin split like a sausage too long in an oven. The Twin behind it was staring too, standing as though frozen, moving only to maintain his balance. Even at this distance, she could tell his eyes were glassy.

The numbness continued. The deadness in her brain.

Fight it, Kevin commanded, from somewhere deep within. *So much emotion struck so fast you had to hide, and it left you hollow. I almost had to hide too—almost went . . . beyond, where you dare not follow. But we have to fight, we* have *to! Close out all that fear and pain and*

*let's be what we are: Word and Way. The Singer's here
too, and . . . two others who've been through a lot and
know what'll happen if this ends like it may!*

But—

Now, Cary—or everything is lost!

And with that, Kevin fled. She followed, unable to bear
the thought of being alone. Of failing. Of all those dreadful things she dared not consider.

But Kev was further away, then further yet again. She
reached for him. Missed, then touched him and reeled
him in.

And as she reveled in the proud essential fire of her
brother's passion and creativity and intellect, she also
brushed other presences. Not focused; and not truly
aware they were functioning on that level, but presences
nonetheless. *'Bird*, she identified. *Thalo. Red Wounds.*
And with Kevin to aid her—though when or how they'd
linked, she neither knew nor cared—she shattered the
wall of their fear and found something stronger beneath:
anger that this was happening, and under even that—
down where the lizard brain guarded its nest of instincts—the simple desire that all this should cease so
they could live.

That was a strength she could use. Without asking permission, she seized it and wrapped it around her desire
for success. She grasped Thalo's thought as well, amazed
at the wonders there. But as she sought to bind him into
the weapon she was forging—to what end, she didn't yet
know—Kevin simply vanished. Before she could gasp
out her dismay, he returned, that part of him that was not
her aflame with some smug new confidence.

Give me all you can, he demanded. *Give it now, and
trust me!*

No, she challenged back. *Show me your plan and trust*
me!

As if from instinct, he resisted, yet she was stronger.
His will surrendered to hers, and with it came everything
else. All at once she *knew*.

Bypassing countless levels of awareness, she gazed at
the real world again.

Smoke—

The world had turned to smoke.

The flames that embraced the werka had subsided, but in their wake had come thick oily vapors that twined with the clean white incense to seek freedom in the heavens glimmering like blue hope through countless rents in the shattered vaulting.

She *knew* . . .

She watched—but yet she *knew*. . . .

The fumes began to weave together, forming a grey-silver coil two meters thick that rose higher by the second, while a darker core took shape within. Carolyn could barely breathe, could barely function; indeed, could barely *watch*, as within that roiling greyness a darker heart took form. Though she'd seen its like before, she dared not name it, even as she called it in her soul, aware on some level that the deepest part of her was in control and *summoned*.

The smoke was impenetrable now; the column, at maybe three meters, far too wide to issue solely from the fumes that begot it. Yet still it rose, past the triforium to the clerestory. And there, where fresh breezes blew, rather than dissipate onto the wind, it split asunder. *I'm doing this?* she marveled, as the cleft widened and that dark core oozed its way outward—then erupted in a violent rush of emerald scales and feathers.

"*Quetzalcoatl!*" someone yelled from the floor—the first focused voice she'd heard in what seemed like ages.

"Vision serpent!" another countered, with an awe-struck sob.

And so it was: were-orca blood and pain had fed 'Bird's friend Fire, which had opened the gate for the snake that connects the Worlds. And from the vast scaly jade-toned maw that was now more real than the building around it, fingers appeared.

Fingers gave way to hands—pale slender hands. Those hands tapered into slim white arms, and in due time, a head thrust from behind the fangs, then half a white-clad torso. Carolyn held her breath, as amazed as anyone at what her own deep-self had conjured.

This was no Maya king or pre-Columbian deity; this was a white man—caucasian, she amended. Young, stern-faced, angry. Clad in a plain white robe around which tiny flames flashed and flickered.

"¡*San Francisco*!" a distant voice shrilled.

"Saint Francis-of-Aztlan!" a second echoed.

"¡*Es un milagro*!" from a third.

"A miracle!"

"¡*El Arcobispo verde*!"

"Bishop Green-Jeans!"

Whatever—*whoever*—was manifesting, his upper limbs were free now, and he stared out across the shattered nave, then reached to either side, expanding all the while, so that his flesh was as tenuous as the column that sustained him when his hands finally grasped the trembling piers of the crossing. He held them firm; stilled them, though cracks raced through them, and Carolyn knew they'd been on the verge of crumbling, which would've been the catalyst that brought down the rest of the edifice.

A final beatific smile, and the man dissolved.

The serpent didn't, though the column that contained it had thinned dramatically at the base, as though sucked away by that denser shape. The organ was still thundering, too; howling out that dreadful, protracted wail that, even with half the pipes that released it torn from their moorings, was still only slightly discordant.

But the walls no longer shook; the piers and arches no longer blurred; the floor no longer quivered.

'Bird was gaping at her wide-eyed, but she tore her gaze away as the serpent-head slowly withdrew into the pillar of smoke—withdrew, but did not vanish, though the pillar itself scarce existed below the monster's throat.

Abruptly, moving with the whipcrack precision of a living rattlesnake, it dived past the altar into the choir, mouth agape like the gates of a very different hell than the Maya Xibalba. The organ felt its bite and disintegrated with a roar like forests splintering. The pipes shrieked into sour discord, then fell silent.

The hush that followed was like the pause between the lightning and the thunder.

One breath . . .

Another . . .

An anguished cry shattered the fragile calm. A cloaked and hooded figure ran from the shadows of the south transept straight toward the prostrate body of the Pope—who was dazedly finding his way to his feet. Something dark and glassy glittered in that one's hand, but before it could cross those last crucial meters, the serpent's head snapped around—maw stretched wider yet, fangs sparkling—and those jaws closed around it. And vanished. Carolyn felt a pulse of utter despair and agony as the victim—certainly a werka, for only their emotions burned with such intensity—died.

Silence—again.

Then, from Pope Michael I, "Lord, have mercy!"

"Where've I . . . been?" from a haggard-looking Hero Twin.

"In hell, my brother," from the other, who was making his way from the ruined organ.

"*¡Es un milagro!*"

"*¡Viva San Francisco de Aztlan!*"

"God Almighty," from Thunderbird O'Connor and Carolyn Mauney-Griffith together.

Then silence indeed.

Epilogue I:
Encryption

Cool air tickling his nose brought 'Bird back to senses he didn't recall abandoning, and for a long blessed moment he was content to sprawl across hard stone ridges and simply relish not moving, not being, not even thinking. But then that breeze brought, faint but pungent, the fading scent of incense—*that* incense—and also noise: cries of hysteria, wails of despair, the distant clamor of emergency vehicles and the sharp slap of purposeful boots against cold marble.

"I fainted," he announced numbly, surprised to hear his own voice: how strangely muffled it was. He wondered if—

Something warm dripping on his nearer hand distracted him, and he looked down, scowling.

Wet . . .

Red . . .

Blood!

He was bleeding from the ears. There was also a ringing, an endless dull-toned thrum, like being underwater: legacy of too many decibels heard far too long and close by. "I fainted," he repeated, and this time he sounded marginally more sure of his own existence. He felt stronger too, and finally raised his head—to gaze on brightness that made his eyes hurt so much he flinched. Sunlight on white stone, tattered banners, and colored glass.

"You fainted," someone affirmed. Female. Familiar, yet not quite. "Cary?" he ventured.

"Among others," she chuckled wryly, and this time

he got his eyes to focus long enough to see that tough new friend sitting beside him, clutching his unsullied hand. She looked tired enough to have sat there a century, but a glow he could only identify as triumph flushed that strangely pale new face. "We win?"

She nodded through a weary shrug, during which he became aware of two other men slumped in nearby pews, both in torn and disheveled Cherokee ceremonial garb. Otherwise, the environs—a section of triforium seating—were empty. The glare was ordinary sunlight lancing through rents in the roof where vast sections of vaulting had collapsed. They were like wounds, he decided. "Wounds," he echoed aloud.

The older man frowned theatrically and stuck out his lower lip. "You talkin' to *me*, boy?"

" 'Wounds . . . ?" he dared again. "Red Wounds?"

"You got it!"

He tried to grin. "I'm gonna need more time off."

Red Wounds grinned back. "I'll let you fight that out with Thalo—soon as either of you are *up* for fightin'."

'Bird sat bolt upright—which made his head spin horribly. "Fighting," he mumbled. "Fighting . . . Oh my God—Stormy!"

Carolyn closed her eyes for an instant, then went very still. "He's fine," she whispered. "He and Sean were lucky: the rest of the orcas sneaked downstairs one at a time. Interestingly enough, the stink worked on them too, at least enough that they couldn't warn each other something was up until it was too late. Otherwise— Basically, young Sean caught them as they emerged, nicked their throats *just enough*, thumped them on the skull, and shoved 'em in the canal to Change."

'Bird shuddered, unable to choose between relief and despair. "So they got away?"

Carolyn shrugged. "Sean and Stormy are on their way, and seem to be in good spirits; that oughta tell you something. I'm surprised you can't feel them, given how much time you just spent in my head."

'Bird regarded her perplexedly. "Me—? In your head—? I thought you were in mine!"

"Me too," Thalo broke in. "It was really strange. I was . . . here, then all at once Cary was in me, and I was in her, and you were there too, and Red Wounds and . . . some guy I didn't know."

"That would be Kevin," Carolyn supplied. "Looks like he's gonna be living with me a while."

Thalo frowned. "But there was someone else too. And what happened there at the last?"

"Tell you in a sec," Carolyn sighed. She stood and surveyed the arched gallery behind the ranks of deserted pews—mostly intact here. Beyond her, 'Bird could see figures bustling about, but no longer hysterical. Someone was singing: a hymn, it sounded like, though it wasn't English. And far away on the distant floor a distinctive Oxfordian voice that could only be Pope Michael I was barking orders in French, Spanish, and Portuguese. Red Wounds evidently saw 'Bird cock his head and grinned again. "Hell of a guy, that one. And those musicians too—now that they're drivin' their own selves again."

"Wish *I* was," 'Bird muttered, and finally found strength enough to try to stand—whereupon he discovered exactly how many parts of him hurt. Still, he'd managed, with Thalo's help, to affect an unsteady slump in a pew when he heard more voices approaching, one of which sounded irate and angry, the other like an excited boy speaking quickly with a very thick brogue.

"I told you he was okay," the boy—Sean—protested. "I told you I could feel him in my head. He was only tired. He has pushed harder than any of us the last few days."

"Serves him right," Stormy—for so it was—snorted. "Goddamn martyr!"

At which point the smug young Navajo lurched into view at the top of the shallow steps leading down to the seating section. Save for a coating of marble dust over his entire body, he looked little the worse for wear. Behind him, Sean the selkie was grinning like a fool—or a very pleased animal. He was also, 'Bird was relieved to note, dressed—in what looked suspiciously like an em-

broidered altar cloth wrapped around his hips and secured with an ecclesiastical stole.

"I don't think martyr would be a good term to use frivolously right now, Mr. Nez," Red Wounds rumbled.

"No," Carolyn agreed smartly, "I think you're right."

'Bird gazed at her intently. "So what happened here? Was that magic, or what? Kev said we'd need magic, but it . . . wasn't like before. It was . . . strange."

She shrugged, then closed her eyes, face pensive—as though listening—then vented a little chuckle. "Kev says that when you're half a ghost yourself, it's easy to talk to others."

The implications of that statement struck 'Bird like a blow—and Thalo and Stormy as well, to judge by the way they gasped. "Oh, Jesus!" Stormy groaned. "More *chindi!*"

"Not *chindi*," 'Bird corrected quickly. "If *chindi* are the bad parts that hang around, can't the good stick around too?"

"And," Carolyn added, "if they die before their time—and in great pain—with work unfinished . . ."

'Bird stared at her. "You talkin' 'bout Kevin or Green Francis?"

Another shrug. "Who knows? Both, maybe—for a while. Kev made the initial contact, and we all gave him—it—me—whoever—strength as it was needed."

"I don't understand," Stormy grumbled. "What're you guys talking about?"

"Death and . . . resurrection, maybe?" Carolyn replied. Then: "One of you better tell him. I don't know what was real and what was wishful thinking."

Red Wounds did: short form. When he finished, Stormy merely whistled. "Me and Hosteen Lox have *got* to do some talking."

Red Wounds grunted and rose. Marble dust flew as he slapped his thighs. "Well, boys and girls," he declared, "it'd be nice to stay here jawing, but the fact is, I'm a man with responsibilities, and I've got a job to do. Gotta see to the rest of my folks—I reckon *that* part of this place is still intact—then see what else I can do to help."

He paused at the top of the steps and turned. ''You folks seem okay, 'cept for what you'd expect, but not everybody's so well off. So I hate to sound cold-blooded, but see if you can get out on your own. Help whoever you can *if* you can, and if you can find my limos, have 'em take you home. I'll be along . . . someday.''

''See that you are,'' 'Bird called, as, with Stormy's aid and Sean's, he finally made it to his feet and began the long trek . . . away.

He fainted again before they got him outside—''Exhaustion,'' the paramedic who gave him a once-over, said. And only when he was finally lolling in the air-conditioned comfort of Red Wounds's Continental, with Thalo's sister watching him with large untroubled eyes, did he recall that the person who'd caught him when he stumbled and helped him the last few meters to the waiting EMTs had been one of the Hero Twins.

He slept for twenty-one hours.

Epilogue II:
Waters of Babylon

(Cumberland Island, Seminole/
Creek Coastal Protectorate)
(Tuesday, September 13—dawn)

Even without those strange new abilities she was still
assimilating (yet feared she never would), Carolyn Mauney-Griffith could've sensed the other nine people standing barefoot in a crescent on the damp beach sand behind
her. Waves lapped ankles old and young; island breezes
teased hair black and fair and tawny. The air smelled of
pines, salt marsh, and live oaks: incense enough for any
ceremony. Closing her eyes, she took a deep breath, and
named them in her soul in the order she had met them,
there where the tenth of their number resided.

Floyd Christopher Mauney. James Patrick O'Neal.
Thunderbird Devlin O'Connor. Stormcloud Nez. John
Lox. William Red Wounds. Sean Griffith-O'Finn. Liam
Kelly. John "Thalo" Gordon. Friends, all of them—and
family, some, as well—whom two weeks ago, excluding
Dad and one ambassador, she hadn't known even
slightly; and even Dad she might as well not have, so
skewed had perception become from reality.

For now, their presence was sufficient. For now, she
had eyes for the sea alone: a sheet of grey-silver across
which the rising sun laid lines of fire.

Fire of a more tangible sort blazed in one hand. Steadied by the other, a rowboat dipped and bobbed in the
rising tide. It was empty, save for ninety-five sheets of

tan recycled paper bearing the seal of Outer Earth in green. Each sheet bore a name: one of those who hadn't survived the disaster at St. Tekawitha's. Mass hallucination, that had been dubbed. Mass hysteria brought on by shock, by mourning, by too much media hype, by too much spectacle and too much power assembled in one place. And by a serendipitous earthquake. For the rest— the vision serpent and the manifestation of the Archbishop himself—alas, no confirmatory footage survived. Personal cameras had been banned from the premises because they were tech, and the lone TV crew permitted had lost *everything* during the quake. There was therefore no proof of what should not—or could not—*be* proven.

Except that proof *did* exist, in a way: in the names of those ninety-five, who numbered among them kings and presidents, captains of industry and princes of the church. And a girl named Marci Alvarez whom Thalo had known by a greener name entirely.

But to that ninety-five, Carolyn had insisted they add four more, and no one had said her nay. She'd written their names herself, on white paper in lieu of brown. Nuala Mauney-Griffith. Finn the Far-sighted. Kevin Mauney (he'd protested, but she'd remained adamant). And—not without tears and a promise of a long quiet walk with 'Bird—Rudy Ramirez.

The World's dead, and her own.

And as the boat lurched again, Carolyn took the torch flaring in her right hand and flung it into that heap of names, and the tide stole the boat from her fingers and dragged it out to sea. She and nine others watched until the last flicker vanished, then turned and walked back up the strand.

Leading them—prancing unhurriedly into the coastal dawn—Sean the Selkie, who was also her brother, was whistling. It was a tune by the Hero Twins.

AVONOVA PRESENTS
MASTERS OF FANTASY AND ADVENTURE